2 - 12
H

Dining with Joy

**Center Point
Large Print**

Also by Rachel Hauck
and available from Center Point Large Print:

Lowcountry Series
Love Starts with Elle
Sweet Caroline

**This Large Print Book carries the
Seal of Approval of N.A.V.H.**

Dining with Joy

A Lowcountry Romance

Rachel Hauck

CENTER POINT PUBLISHING
THORNDIKE, MAINE

This Center Point Large Print edition
is published in the year 2011 by arrangement with
Thomas Nelson Publishers.

The text of this Large Print edition is unabridged.
In other aspects, this book may vary
from the original edition.
Printed in the United States of America
on permanent paper.
Set in 16-point Times New Roman type.

ISBN: 978-1-61173-031-9

Library of Congress Cataloging-in-Publication Data

Hauck, Rachel, 1960–
  Dining with joy : a lowcountry romance / Rachel Hauck.
    p. cm.
  ISBN 978-1-61173-031-9 (library binding : alk. paper)
  1. Television cooking shows—Fiction. 2. South Carolina—Fiction.
    3. Large type books. I. Title.
  PS3608.A866D56 2011
  813'.6—dc22
                                                    2010052182

For my mom

 # One

Driving the Sea Island Parkway with her windows down, the nose of her Dodge Ram cutting through the swaths of shadow and light cast through the limbs of shading live oaks, Joy surfed her hand through the textured, saline lowcountry breeze.

Yesterday she'd been at peace, finally home from three months on the road, guesting on radio and morning talk shows, hosting food fairs, judging cooking competitions, riding in convertibles as a parade marshal, waving at the crowds standing on the curb, acting the part. Always acting the part.

Joy Ballard, host of *Dining with Joy*.

But when she returned home to Beaufort from the spring promotional tour, she ached to sink back into being plain ol' Joy Ballard: lowcountry girl, softball player, aunt, daughter, friend.

This morning she'd planned to sleep until the noon sun spilled through her window with a golden heat. Then she'd tug on a pair of baggy shorts and a tank top, wrap her hair in a ponytail, mosey outside with a lawn chair, and sit under the ancient live oak with her feet pressed into thick blades of green grass, wiggling her toes down to the red South Carolina dirt.

After a few hours in the shade, Joy would move to the backyard dock, catch rays from the afternoon sun while dangling her legs over the side, breaking Factory Creek's velvet surface with her red-stained toes.

What she hadn't considered was a predawn call from her executive producer, Duncan Tate.

"I'm driving down from Atlanta. I'll see you around four."

"Duncan, it's my first Monday home."

"We need to talk."

"If this is about Omaha—"

"See you at the studio."

"No, McDonald's."

"Joy—"

"I need a Big Mac."

And that's how she found herself driving the parkway toward the Boundary Street McDonald's. Served old Duncan right. Disturb her vacation with business. She'd disturb his diet with McDonald's.

Her cell chimed from where she'd propped it in the cup holder, displaying Mama's smiling face—tanned and lined—on the phone's rectangle screen.

"Joy, I know you won't forget the girls' softball game this afternoon."

"Duncan called, said we needed to talk. I'm on my way to meet him. I'll try to get there."

"Doesn't he know it's your vacation?"

"I think this is about Omaha." Over the drawbridge, Joy peered right toward the Atlantic, catching a glint of sun off the mast of a drifting schooner.

"Serves him right. He should've watched your back."

"Maybe he didn't know."

"As your producer, it's his job to know. It's his show, Joy. You'd think the man would know the fine details."

"All right, thank you, Mama. I'll see you at the game." Mama wasn't a big fan of Duncan Tate since he finagled the show away from Joy's father.

"Four o'clock. They only play five innings, so don't think you got gobs of time."

"I know how many innings they play, Mama."

"Bring Duncan, let him see you have a life outside his show."

"Mama, *his* show affords us some of the nicer things. In case you forgot, my income made up the difference last year when Ballard Paint & Body ran into trouble." Joy braked for the traffic light, switching to red just as she exited the bridge. Her irritation over Duncan's surprise visit eased up as she gripped the steering wheel of her own truck, inhaled the scent off the Beaufort River, and gazed over the familiar landmarks of home.

"Yes, and I'm grateful, but it don't give him no right to own your time off."

"I'll tell Duncan to talk fast. See you in a bit."

Joy ended the call, set her phone back in the cup holder, and tapped the gas when the light turned green.

Mama. The woman had definite ideas. Like the notion Duncan stole *Dining with Charles* from Daddy. But during Joy's brief stint as an associate producer on the show, watching Daddy from the studio shadows, she suspected Daddy didn't care much for the business and production side of television. The man merely wanted to share his cooking creations with America, or his segment of it. How and when, why and where didn't matter much to him.

Then he died. Joy resituated in her seat, hands tight around the wheel, taking the bend of Carteret to Boundary, the aroma of sunbaked pine and steaming palmetto leaves saturating the air blowing through the cab. And *Dining with Charles* became *Dining with Joy*.

A sliver of light glanced off the edge of the Bible verse Joy had clipped to the truck's dashboard. Old Miss Jeanne had passed the verse to her one Sunday after Daddy's funeral, the week she'd agreed to take over the show.

"God's got your back," Miss Jeanne had said, handing her the slip of paper, her lively blue eyes sparkling from their high perch above her round, crinkled cheeks.

Three years later the square ends were bent and

cracked from years of sitting under the windshield, the words on the old, lined notebook paper dim and sun-faded.

"MY FOOD IS TO DO THE WILL OF HIM WHO SENT ME." JOHN 4:34

 # Two

In the McDonald's parking lot, Joy eased into the spot next to Duncan's Lexus. Cutting the engine, she angled down for her Alabama ball cap tucked inside the door's side pocket.

"Sure you want to eat here?" Duncan asked, watching her, propped against the polished hood, dressed in crisp khakis and a stiff, blue button-down, the wind tousling his silver hair.

His blue eyes communicated nothing but disdain for fast food.

"I've been hankering for a Big Mac." Joy peered over her shoulder as she tugged open the restaurant's door, Duncan stepping up behind her. She scanned the horizon for a glint of light off a camera lens or a shadowy movement among the trees. "No cameras?"

"Not today."

Duncan liked to send the show's cameraman, Garth, into Joy's everyday life sometimes to film spontaneous clips for the show. It'd become part of their unique brand.

But Garth had been with her on the road gathering footage for a new opening segment, and he'd probably had enough of her. In fact, he was probably enjoying his first day of vacation. Unlike the show's host . . .

"What's with the hat?" Duncan followed Joy to the front counter, a bit of sarcasm lacing his voice. "Hiding?"

"Yes, my dirty hair." But if the hat obscured her identity too, then so be it. When she first became the host of *Dining with Joy*, someone snapped a picture of her eating Cheetos in front of a 7-Eleven and a headline ran the next day: THIS IS HOW WE'RE DINING WITH JOY?

The shiny-faced teen behind the counter eyed her as she ordered a Big Mac Extra Value Meal, tipping his head to peer beneath the cap's bill. "Hey, aren't you—"

"The hungriest woman in Beaufort County? You bet."

"Yes, she's Joy Ballard, the cooking show host." Duncan tossed a twenty onto the metal counter. "I'll have a grilled chicken salad and a water."

The teen grinned as he punched in their order. "My mom can't stand your show."

Joy's sigh slipped through her puckered lips. She'd heard similar comments dozens of times, if not hundreds, but the words stung fresh every single time.

"Tell you what." She tugged a napkin from the dispenser and signed it with the Sharpie she kept in her handbag. "Tell your mom I'd love for her to come by the studio next month when we start filming our fourth season. We can give her a behind-the-scenes tour, show her around."

He laughed as he took the napkin, jamming it into his pocket. "She won't go, but I bet my dad will." The counter jockey handed Duncan change from his twenty. "Mom says she feels like a bloated tick when she watches you on TV."

"Just give her the napkin."

"How come the host of a cooking show eats at McDonald's?" The teen set Joy's Big Mac on a tray next to Duncan's salad.

"Because a foodie loves all kinds of food." Joy tugged her cap low and snatched up her drink cup. "But let this be our little secret, okay?" She aimed two fingers at her eyes, then swung her hand around to his face. "You and me, eye to eye, our secret." She nodded once, giving him a good, stiff stare.

Duncan mumbled, "Good grief" and picked up the food tray, leading Joy to a booth by the front window, the teen's voice billowing through the dining room. "The cooking show lady—Joy Ballard—is eating a Big Mac."

"You'll be on the front of the *Beaufort Gazette* tomorrow." Duncan drizzled low-fat dressing over his chicken and lettuce.

"I haven't been on the front of the *Gazette* since Daddy died and I took over the show." Joy peeled the paper from her straw and wiggled it through the top slit of the cup lid. "People around here don't really care about my claim to fame. Just another hometown girl trying to make good."

Popping open the Big Mac box, Joy took a large first bite, eyes closed, savoring the scent and taste of the special sauce and warm beef. When she swallowed, exhaling, she glanced at Duncan.

"My friends and I used to ride our bikes over the bridge to this McDonald's on Saturday afternoons."

"How old is this salad?" Duncan frowned at the cherry tomato speared on the end of his fork.

"We'd go to the beach in the morning, bake in the sun, then ride our bikes across the bridge, our money tucked into our bathing suits."

"Hmm, nice." Duncan leaned over his salad and sniffed, making a face. "So, you want to tell me about Omaha?"

Joy reached for her napkin to wipe sauce from her fingers. *Right, Omaha.* "Wenda Divine blindsided me. We were watching two young chefs demonstrate Culinare's latest cookware, and all of a sudden, I have an apron over my head and I'm being challenged with a secret ingredient." Joy eyed her Big Mac, her appetite waning. "I panicked."

"Panicked?" Duncan nibbled at his chicken, the lines of his face accented in the light falling through the window. "Panic is burning the food. Panic is undercooking. Panic is forgetting an ingredient. You, my dear Joy, fell off the stage." Duncan twisted the cap from his water. "Garth showed me clips."

15

"I didn't *fall* off the stage, I swooned." Joy shoved her food forward and folded her arms on the table. "After the initial shock of crashing onto concrete, it was pretty funny." She smiled. "You should've seen Wenda's face as she bent over me, her bow lips tight with fake concern while her fat eyes fired daggers."

"You could've broken your neck, Joy." Duncan slapped the plastic lid onto his uneaten salad.

"What would you have me do? Try to cook with the secret ingredient?"

"Yes, if you must know. I'm sure you could burn food with the best of them." Duncan tipped up his water bottle for a long, hard swig.

"Burn the food? I'd have to *graduate* to burning food. Got to know how to cook before I can burn." Joy closed the lid on her Big Mac box. "Did you know, Duncan? That I'd end up on stage with Wenda Divine? I have a rider on my contract. No cook-offs."

"No, I didn't know." Duncan sipped his water again, his gaze drifting out the window. "Who were the men who picked you up from your swoon?"

"The men of Delta Tau Delta, University of Nebraska." Joy sipped her soda. Part of her success was her male following, especially on college campuses. Whole fraternities TiVoed her show and watched at night.

When Joy came up with the idea of Stupid

16

Cooking Tricks, college men across America were the first to submit videos.

Duncan picked at the wrapper on the water bottle. "Your mom . . . how's she doing? Your nieces still living with you?"

"Mama's fine. Lyric and Annie-Rae are fine. In fact, they're playing softball right now." Joy leaned toward Duncan. "As we speak."

Duncan nodded. "Your brother and his wife—"

"Sawyer and Mindy."

"Still in Vegas?"

"Still in Vegas. Trying to find themselves." Joy regarded Duncan, trying to determine how his demeanor started a swirl of dread in her chest. "So, what's new with you, Boss? Ready for season four of *Dining with Joy*?"

The man leaned forward, cupping his hands around his water. "Remember how you felt when you stood on the pitcher's mound, bottom of the seventh, your team was up by one and the opponent's next batter was their best hitter? And if she hit off you, the NCAA championship would be lost?"

Joy narrowed her eyes at her producer. "Is there a reason you're talking softball to me?" She didn't like the way the conversation settled over her soul.

"You're going to need the same courage this season."

"Courage? What are you talking about?" Why

did he hesitate? A no-nonsense producer and businessman, Duncan hardly wasted time with small talk or cushioning hard news.

"We've had fun, haven't we?" Duncan smiled, slow and steady, more cushioning of the conversation.

"We've had fun, yes. Despite the fact your show's host can't cook, we've had some success. But you didn't drive down from Atlanta to remind me of the good times, did you? What's going on? Did we lose a big advertiser?"

Duncan lifted his eyes to Joy's. "I sold the show."

The declaration pressed against her. "Excuse me?" She slid her soda cup to the edge of the table. "You sold the show?"

"Closed the deal two weeks ago." Duncan started stacking their uneaten food onto the tray.

"Why? To who?"

"Allison Wild at Wild Woman Productions. She needed a show to pitch to a network and contacted me about *Dining with Joy*. She thinks you're fabulous, by the way. She's on her way to Beaufort. We're meeting her at the studio tomorrow morning, nine o'clock."

"This is incredible . . . Duncan, you can't just sell the show. What happened to all the *fun?*" A thin tremble started beneath Joy's skin, creeping through her middle. She gripped her hands in her lap. "This makes no sense."

"Out of the blue like this, yeah, it doesn't. I should've said something, but toward the end of last season, I realized I'd taken the show as far as I could. I was bored—"

"Bored? How can you be bored? The show is coming into its own. Stupid Cooking Tricks alone is putting us on the map. We're defining our brand, creating a cooking show that's about the viewer, the fans. There's no cooking show out there like ours."

"I agree, all true, all true, but I'm tired of cooking shows." Duncan's flat monotone conveyed his boredom. "This would've been my eleventh season. Seven with your dad, three with you. I'm out of ideas. Out of zeal. To be honest, Joy, if I didn't get out of the way, I'd wind up killing the brand. So when Allison called, nearly salivating over the phone about you and the show, I knew it was my chance to do what I want to do. I'm forty-nine years old, and if I'm ever going to try movie production, I'd best start now. I have a friend in L.A. who's been asking me to merge DT Productions with his company."

"You should've talked to me." Joy shook her head, squinting beyond the window at the pale blue horizon.

"Look, I know this doesn't seem fair."

"No, it doesn't." Joy swept up the napkins from the table and wadded them onto the tray, slightly aware that the volume of her voice drew stares

19

from around McDonald's dining room. "Not even close to fair." She jerked to her feet, tray in hand, and started for the trash bins.

"Joy, listen." Duncan's grasp on her arm stopped her in the middle of the room, between tables. "You're still in business. Still host of the show. Your contract remained intact. Allison is very talented and creative. I don't know which network she pitched the show to, but you can bet your audience will double or triple this season. We'd gone as far as we could on the Premier Channel."

"I hosted the show because you were desperate." Joy freed her arm from his hold and leaned toward him. "Because Daddy asked me to help you as he lay in a hospital bed, dying."

"And we've done well. But I can't believe in three years this show hasn't woven into your DNA, become a part of you. You don't get a little bit of a thrill by hosting your own television show? Being a celebrity?" His grin mocked her.

"You think I enjoy lying to the viewers? That I get a kick out of pretending to be something I'm not? Do you think I like falling off stages and joking my way out of cooking questions?" The trembling in her middle intensified. "But I did it for you and because my dying father asked."

"Seems that new Dodge Ram out there was a nice pill for your pain."

"Duncan, I'm a cooking show host who can't cook. It's a miracle we've pulled off the charade this long. Now you want me to continue with a new producer, a woman I don't even know? Did you even tell her?"

"She knows what she needs to know. That you took over the show after your father died suddenly of a heart attack. She knows you did it to help me save my financial investment. She knows we changed the name from *Dining with Charles* to *Dining with Joy*. She knows you're funny, clever, and very popular with male viewers and the under-thirty crowd. She knows you're gorgeous and absolutely dynamite in front of the camera."

"You look like a caught teenager, Duncan. Why didn't you tell her?"

The man inhaled, his lips forming an answer, then he hesitated. "Because I wanted the sale, and frankly, I don't think she needs to know."

"Then I'll tell her." Joy spun toward the trash bins by the door. The dining room was beginning to fill up, and she wanted to leave before the teen behind the counter pointed her out. She was too tired, too on edge to play cooking show host tonight.

"Don't bite off your nose to spite your face, Joy. There's no reason for Allison to know. My guess is she'll oversee this first season with you, then back off to develop other projects. Ryan will move from director to producer. You'll take on more of a producer role, and this time next year Allison will never be the wiser. Until then, the crew will back you up. Sharon will continue to do all the recipe development, prep work, and cooking. I've filmed dozens of cooking shows with all kinds of folks and trust me, the prep chef can make a monkey look like Emeril Lagasse."

"Are you equating me with a monkey, Duncan?" Joy slapped the emptied tray on top of the bin, tugged her Bama cap down over her forehead, and pushed out the door. "I'm telling her."

"Then what, Joy?" Duncan's footsteps scraped along the pavement behind her. "Hmm? Try for a coaching job? Maybe take your liberal arts degree and what . . . write freelance articles? Wasn't this the year you planned on buying your own place?"

As a matter of fact, a pre–Civil War home on the corner of Federal and Pinckney. "It doesn't feel right, Duncan." Joy jerked open the driver's side door, climbed behind the wheel, thinking. "As much as I love the show, and yes, the money, and the fans and the travel, it's hard to pretend I'm a cook when I'm not. It's like finding out Mr. Rogers hated kids."

"Tell you what." Duncan moved close to peer into her eyes. "Give Allison a chance. If you don't like her, tell her the truth, break your contract, and walk. But I've been producing for a long time and you're a rare talent, Joy. No, you can't cook." His low laugh was laden with the familiarity of an inside joke. "But you're an entertainer. The camera loves you. Your fans love you. My guess is Allison will take you to the moon."

"And once I'm there? Then what?"

Duncan lightly kissed her cheek, a fatherly gesture. "Then on to the stars."

 # Three

Luke lowered the heat under the saucepan and tasted his saffron sauce. Beautiful. Just the way he liked it—rich and smooth. He'd been off his game a bit since losing Ami's and leaving Manhattan for the lowcountry.

"Luke, shug, are you going to serve that gravy or propose to it?" Mercy Bea peered between the heat lamps, the ends of her piled-high hair barely missing the bulbs. "I got hungry customers."

"Sauce, Mercy Bea, it's saffron sauce. Not gravy." Luke ladled a bit into a dipping bowl. "And it's good enough to take home to Mama."

"And my mama would also call it gravy. In the South, anything you slather over meat or fish is gravy."

"I'll have you thinking my way by the time Andy returns from his back surgery." Luke tipped his head toward her as he backed away from the service window.

"And I'll have you thinking mine." With an exaggerated tip of her head, Mercy Bea glared at Luke, picked up her *gravy,* and turned for the dining room.

Luke laughed. After six months he was starting to feel like a part of the Frogmore Café family. A strapping Emmitt Smith-like chef, Andy Castleton owned the place with Mercy Bea, a single mom of two.

Luke liked the routine of working nights, getting lost in the comfort of cooking, forgetting about the past year of bankruptcy, failure, and defeat.

When his cousin, Heath McCord, suggested time in the southern sun and surf as a way to recoup and get his bearings, Luke packed a bag and drove down the next day.

He found a job at the café working part-time until Andy announced he was going out for back surgery. He clapped his broad hand on Luke's shoulder and asked him to oversee the back of the house.

Luke glanced around the kitchen, at home among the old walls and creaking rafters. But he couldn't hide out here—or board in Miss Jeanne's third-floor apartment—forever. He was thirty-six years old.

Sooner or later, he'd have to face his peers, return to New York, and redeem his tarnished restaurateur reputation.

Across the room, Russell, the prep chef and dishwasher, stacked trays of clean Mason jars under the counter.

Luke collected the saucepan and emptied the contents into a warmer. Yeah, when Andy returned to the café, Luke would give his notice.

Until then, he'd enjoy the café, the lowcountry,

and life by the ocean. Beaufort was a great little town.

Grabbing a towel, Luke wiped down the prep table, then checked the lowboy for supplies. A church book club came in every Monday night around eight looking for comfort food—pies, cake, or chocolate.

Wandering into the dining room, he took a jar from the tray under the lunch counter, scooped it with ice, then filled it with sweet tea.

The dining room was quiet, peaceful, ethereal with end-of-day light slipping through the windows. The golden glow of a hurricane lamp gleamed off each of Andy's polished tables.

Sipping his tea, Luke leaned against the back of the counter and watched Mercy Bea cackle over a story being told by a couple of older gentlemen at table three. Paris drew a broom over the slick, smooth hardwood by the front door.

If he ever opened another restaurant, he wanted servers like Mercy Bea and Paris, characters who brought the café's essence to life. Luke raised his tea jar up to the light. And he'd have strong sweet tea on the menu.

The café's front bells rang out, clattering against the glass as the door opened. Luke glanced up just as *she* walked in. Athletic, confident, beautiful. In full stride, she made her way to the counter, perched on the middle stool, focused on her phone. He jerked his back straight and set his tea aside, checking the room for Paris. Mercy Bea was still engaged with her customers.

Luke, man, wait on the customer. "Welcome to the Frogmore Café." Grabbing a menu, a napkin roll, and a paper place mat, Luke set up Joy's place. "What can I get you?"

"I'll have a piece of apple pie and a Diet Coke." She tapped the phone's screen, her posture resolute.

"Diet Coke and apple pie coming up." Luke lifted a drink jar from the tray. Filling the jar with soda, he watched her, almost willing her to lift up her head. "Must have been a heck of a day." Ah! Soda spilled over the rim of the glass and covered his hand. With his free hand, he reached to the second shelf for the dish towel.

"To put it lightly." She turned her phone sideways and started typing. "It was supposed to be my first day of vacation, but instead my producer—"

She stopped when he set the Mason jar in front of her, his blue gaze meshed with hers. "I'm sorry, I'm sure you don't care about . . . Luke, right? Heath's cousin."

"One and the same." He handed her a straw. "And you are Joy Ballard, cooking host, friend of Heath's wife."

"Elle, yes, I'm impressed." She peeled the paper from her straw, then stirred her ice and soda. "You remembered me."

"Sure, why not?" How could he forget? They'd met in Heath's backyard under a twilight sky with the tangy scent of barbecue perfuming the breeze. "Apple pie, right?"

"I need it like I need a hole in the head, but yeah, apple pie." She regarded him for a moment as if she wanted to say something more, but she returned her attention to her phone.

He scrambled for something suave and witty to keep the conversation going, but the steely blue of her eyes stymied his thoughts. As Joy bent back to her phone, a silky sheen of burnished hair drawing a curtain over her face, Luke stepped toward the kitchen doors.

"Apple pie coming up."

Joy peeked up at him. "Make it a small piece, please."

Luke plated a warm, crusty slice of pie, dusting the crumbling crust with a cinnamon and brown sugar mix. Joy Ballard could sit at his counter anytime.

He'd heard his New York foodie friends talk about the *hot* cooking show host, Joy Ballard, but at the time, he'd been consumed with keeping his restaurant alive and well.

Then during his first month in Beaufort he attended a barbecue at Heath and Elle's. He'd just pulled an icy root beer from the cooler when a *vision* emerged through a gauzy veil of sunlight. Elle introduced him to her friend, Joy Ballard, and in his suave, debonair manner, Luke offered her the root beer in his right hand while tipping up his left for a nice cool drink of . . . air.

The rest of the night he watched her from afar, fascinated and curious, an odd sensation twisting in his chest. When she walked in tonight, the same fascination and odd sensation gripped him.

In the kitchen, Mercy Bea peeked around his arm as he trimmed the blue apple-pie plate with caramel and chocolate.

"What are you—Oh, great day in the morning." Mercy Bea fell against the prep table and shoved his arm so he had to look at her. "Right here, in my eyes . . . Luke, looky. Sakes alive, she got to you that fast? Vroom, gone in sixty seconds."

"She who?"

"She who? The redheaded bombshell out there. That's who." Mercy sighed with a faraway look in her eyes. "I should've been a redhead."

"Got to me? I'm serving a slice of pie." He wiped the edge of the plate with a damp towel. Presentation was as important as taste.

"Bubba, we don't swirl caramel on our plates 'round here. What'd you charge, ten, fifteen bucks for something like that in New York? That's two-fifty on the menu."

"You can read minds now? You know what I'm thinking and feeling? I'm a chef, Mercy. I make specialty items for our customers." He held up the cinnamon-salted plate and started for the door.

"Besides, she's the first customer all night who doesn't smell like coconut oil or fish bait."

Luke set Joy's plate on the counter, scooting it close to her hands as she tapped on the phone. He reached for her coke glass, but she'd barely sipped past the rim.

With one glance, Joy reared back. "Wow, fancy." She turned the plate, examining it from different sides. "Does Andy know you're doing this to his dishes?"

Luke's soul bristled. "I thought you'd appreciate a finer presentation."

"I guess you did." Joy picked at the cinnamon-topped crust, smiling, then sipped her soda and returned her focus to her phone.

Luke waited.

Joy shoved the plate aside as she tapped out a message.

Luke inched the plate back in place. "Can I get you anything else?"

With a weighted sigh, she glanced up at him. "How about the last few hours of my day? Got any of that kind of magic back in the kitchen?"

"Time travel? Nope. All out." Luke scooted her pie plate closer. *Eat, Joy.*

"Joy, hon, welcome home. Ain't seen you around in a while." Mercy Bea set a tub of dirty dishes on the counter, propped her elbow on the edge, and leaned toward Joy. "But I heard about Omaha."

"Did you, now?" Joy set her phone aside and unrolled her napkin from her silverware, her confidence burdened by something subtle and intangible.

"Falling off the stage?" Mercy swatted gently at Joy's arm. "You could've broken your neck."

"You sound like my producer." Joy speared the tip of her pie, cutting off a small bite.

"Well, shoot, girl, I sound like anyone with a sound mind." Mercy wrung a towel she pulled from a tub of clean water and started wiping down the counter. "I see you've met Luke. He's filling in for Andy until his back heals. Used to own a restaurant up in Manhattan. Ami's, right?"

"Yeah, Ami's." Luke split his gaze between Joy and Mercy Bea, holding his breath, bracing to act if Mercy brought up their kitchen conversation. *Vroom, gone in sixty seconds.*

"What happened?" Joy set her fork down, the bite of pie still on the prongs, and drew a short drink from her soda glass.

"A little bother called bills and debt." He nodded to Joy's plate. "I can make that pie à la mode if you want. The crust is extra fluffy tonight."

"À la mode? And ruin your caramel and chocolate swirl?" She surveyed the plate, tucking her hair behind her ears. Her phone pinged and she shoved the pie forward again, lost in the world of tiny e-mails.

"Okay, I'm off to run these through the dishwasher." Mercy Bea picked up the tub of dirty dishes. "The book club gals will be in soon. Don't you know they're more sugar than a quarter can buy?"

Joy laughed, shaking her head, tapping her phone's screen. "Any business is good business, Mercy."

"Says the girl who fell off the stage." Mercy disappeared through the kitchen doors.

Joy still smiled, snickering softly. Luke liked the melody of her voice. It made him wonder how long it'd been since he laughed. A good belly laugh. Turns out the bankruptcy, losing Ami's and the life he'd chosen for himself, was a real killjoy.

But lately, he'd been waking up whispering prayers, hope in his thoughts, the weight of despair off his chest.

And right now, if he had any idea what Mercy Bea was talking about, he'd laugh along with Joy.

"Not worth the effort."

Luke bent to see Joy's face. "Excuse me?"

"More sugar than a quarter can buy. It means it's not worth the effort."

Luke smiled. "Ah, good to know. The book club ladies can be demanding."

"You need a dictionary to understand Mercy Bea's sayings."

"Just when I thought I was catching on too." Luke shoved Joy's pie plate forward, under her hands, as she held her phone. "I can warm up the pie for you if you want."

"I've known Mercy my whole life and still get caught off guard." Joy shoved the pie out of the way. "The pie's warm enough."

Luke wondered if she even liked pie. For a second he watched her, then shuffled around the counter, checking the napkin rolls and stack of clean glass trays, thinking it rude to stare at a customer. No matter how beautiful she was. After another minute he backed away, brushing his hands down his apron. "Well, I—"

The café bells chimed and clattered, weighting the air with a brass ting. Luke expected to see the book club ladies filing in, mingling, chatting about the evening's selection of what they wanted off the Frogmore's menu.

But it wasn't the book club making a beeline for their spot in the back corner booth. It was Helen Woodward, a recent and annoying acquaintance of Luke's, striding for the counter.

"Luke, there you are, shug." Helen dropped down hard on the stool next to Joy, her apple-round cheeks flushed, her dark hair frizzing about her forehead. "This is my lucky night." Helen pulled aside Joy's hair. "Don't think you can hide behind your gorgeous red sheen, Joy Ballard. You never returned my calls."

Joy raised her chin to Helen. "I'm not emceeing the Water Festival Cook-Off, Helen."

"Heavens to Betsy, not this again. I get it. A thousand times over. You do not want to *compete*. I have your rider right here in my folder." Helen waved a black attaché above her head. "Well, you can *talk* like nobody's business, and since you're one of our most famous citizens, you are the emcee of this cook-off." Helen jerked some papers from her attaché and slapped them down on the counter. "So stop your bellyaching. Luke Redmond here is going to cook against Wenda Divine. So you can lower your hackles and stop baring your teeth. These are the release forms. One for Luke, one for you, Joy. Luke, be a sweetie and pack a jar with ice cubes and drown them in sweet tea."

"Release form?" Joy held her form up to the light as if examining for some secret code.

Luke reached for a jar and scooped it with ice. He'd done a few cook-offs in his day and a bit of television. The release form appeared to be the standard lingo—permission to use his likeness and name for the contest, for media and television.

"It's hotter than you-know-what tonight, I tell you." Helen knocked back her iced tea like it had a bit of extra kick besides sugar. "You got any questions, Luke?" Helen flipped her hand at the paper. "It's just a silly little thing that says we can use your name and image to promote the cook-off. And if you accidentally cut off your finger while preparing the food, or catch fire, you won't sue the pants off us."

"Helen, I'm not going anywhere near Wenda Divine. I'm thinking of leaving town that day." Joy dropped the form, floating and fluttering, in front of Helen.

"Oh, grow up, Joy Ballard. You're not leaving town. You're doing your civic duty and hosting your town's Water Festival Cook-Off. It's great publicity for all involved."

"I host a television show from this city. That's great publicity. This cook-off is all about Wenda."

"You should've finished her off in Omaha when you had the chance." Helen nodded at Joy, tipping up her tea jar for another long slurp.

"How does everyone know about Omaha?" Joy stabbed at her pie. "I'm not emceeing anything if Wenda Divine is involved."

Luke stared at his release form. "I don't know about Omaha."

Silence. Then, "What'dya live under a rock, Luke?"

"Nope." He lifted his gaze to Helen, then Joy. "Just haven't heard about Omaha."

"Well, see, Wenda Divine, you know who she is, right? Of course you do. She got our Joy up on a food convention stage and challenged her to a cook-off. So Joy can't stand to be in a contest, though she's twice the cook of Wenda, I'm sure, and what does she do? She falls—"

"Helen, just . . . stop." Joy dropped the fork to the plate. "I fell off a stage. No big deal."

"Shug, you can fall off the stage here if you want, I don't care, but you're my emcee. End of story." Helen blew a stream of hot breath toward her bangs and rolled her eyes at Luke, mouthing *diva*.

"Can I get you anything else, Helen?" Luke reached for his form, taking a pen from the jar on the counter. He'd signed forms for the other shows and events he'd participated in, including as a contestant on a season of *The Next Culinary Star*.

"Just get this girl here to do her duty." Helen thunked her glass down on the counter. "And I'll be happy as a tick on a bloodhound."

"Since you love this event so much, Helen, why don't you emcee?" Joy unzipped her purse, dug around, and dropped a ten-dollar bill onto the counter.

She was leaving? Without touching her pie? Luke stepped around the counter. "Come on, it'll be fun." His words bounced around the café.

"Fun?" Joy paused and leaned against the counter. "Have you met Wenda Divine, Luke?" She plopped her bag down on the counter. "Have you ever been in a cook-off?"

"I've not met her, but she seems like a nice woman. And yes, I've been in cook-offs. It's just cooking on speed." Luke passed his signed form to Helen. "An adrenaline rush."

"Looky there, Joy. Luke signed. And he's only

been in town six months. All the flyers and advertising have gone out. If our own *Dining with Joy* backs out, do you think other celebs and distinguished guests will want to come in the future? I think not, I think not."

"Oh my gosh, all right already." Joy snatched the form from Helen. "You beat all, Helen. Is this how you got George to marry you? Manipulation?"

"Mercy, no. All that took was a short skirt and a kiss." She snapped her fingers in the air.

"I must be out of my mind to do this, but—" Joy paused, her pen pressed into the paper, her eyes on Luke. "You're cooking, right?"

"I'm cooking." He'd all but forgotten about the event. Didn't care much one way or the other. He enjoyed a cook-off now and then, but if Joy was going to emcee, the event took on a whole new meaning.

"Cook-offs are a dime a dozen. Trust me. Anyone with a pot and a spoon can be in a cook-off." She checked Luke with a quick glance. "No offense."

"None taken."

"But *Dining with Joy* is different." She angled toward him, a passion infusing her voice. "We're a different kind of show, and I don't want our brand to be watered down with me jumping into a cook-off or chef challenge with all the other TV celebrities." Joy passed the signed form to Helen.

"Seriously, don't you just roll your eyes when you see another celebrity chef in a cooking challenge like it's some kind of rite of passage?"

"You're the emcee, baby, so I think your *brand* is still safe. Thank you very much." Helen snatched the form before Joy could take it back and tucked it into her case. "Iced tea is on the house, Luke?" Helen boogied toward the door. "Night, all. Thanks." The air in the dining room swirled in her wake, floating, drifting, trying to find a place to settle.

"She's like an emotional whiplash," Joy said as she slipped her bag up to her shoulder. "With her 'honey,' 'sugar,' and 'darling,' while she presses her steely knife into your back, 'Sign here or I'll kill you.'"

Luke regarded Joy. "Sure seems to be a lot of protesting for just an emcee gig."

"Yeah, well, I don't trust Helen or Wenda Divine." Joy's gaze mingled with his—blue touching blue. When she stepped back, the magic broke. "I need to go."

"Your pie?"

"Not hungry."

When she exited, the dining room settled with an odd quiet. For the first time, Luke heard the rhythm of rain drumming down. Tucking the ten-dollar bill by the register, he carried her plate back to the kitchen.

"I see Joy didn't eat her pie." Mercy Bea peered

at the plate in his hand as she carried a tub of dirty dishes to the dishwasher.

"Said she wasn't hungry."

"She never is, shug, she never is."

Luke took a clean fork from the dishwasher and leaned against the prep table, digging into the pie, musing over the counter exchange with Helen and Joy, trying to suppress the smile on his lips and reckon with the sensation that somehow tonight he'd glimpsed into his future.

 # Four

"Lyric, you've got ten minutes. All aboard for the train to Ballard Paint & Body Shop." Joy rapped on her niece's bedroom door. "Granny wants to leave on time this morning. She has a customer dropping off his car at eight o'clock. Lyric? Annie-Rae's out of the bathroom, so all your excuses are gone."

"I heard you the first eight hundred bazillion times you called me." The hard thump of Lyric's heels echoed against the floor.

"Really, then how did I miss the eight hundred bazillion times you answered me?" Joy rapped on the door to keep Lyric stirring and moving. "Is bazillion really a number or something David Letterman made up?"

"David Letterman?" Lyric's door flew open. "Oh my gosh, Aunt Joy, he's a dinosaur." Lyric— fourteen, beautiful, and angry—marched toward the bathroom, her long, sculpted legs shooting out beyond the hem of her nightshirt. "By the way, bazillion is slang. A combination of billion and gazillion. Beaufort High just called. They want their diploma back." She twisted on the faucet so the water blasted into the sink. Then she smeared toothpaste on her brush, and when she jammed it under the cascade, most of the toothpaste fell into the sink.

"I'm sure they do. See you downstairs in five minutes." Joy backed toward the stairs. In the year Lyric and Annie-Rae had been living with them, she learned to roll with the sarcasm instead of butt up against it. When she acquiesced, it soothed the fire in Lyric's belly.

"What? Five? What happened to ten?" Lyric rammed the toothbrush into her mouth.

"You burned it up spouting your classic wit."

"Aunt Joy, why do I have to go to Granny's shop?" Lyric's toothbrush rounded out her cheek. "Can't I just stay here? It's summer. All my friends are going to the beach, taking vacations, and what am I doing? Watching *Roseanne* reruns at Ballard Paint & Body with my kid sister."

Roseanne? That explained the sarcasm. "You had home privileges until you threw an unauthorized party."

"You wouldn't have known if Annie-Rae hadn't snitched." Lyric bent forward, flipping her hair, twisting it into a thick, wavy knot.

"Annie-Rae only shortened the investigation. We were on to you when we found Amos Watson's driver's license in the front bushes."

"How am I supposed to fit in when I'm treated like a baby? How will I get Parker Eaton to notice me?"

"If he doesn't notice you, Lyric, he's blind."

A soft sigh relaxed her shoulders. "You're just saying that to shut me up."

41

"Normally, yes. But not this morning, baby." Joy eased her way toward the bathroom. "You're more beautiful than you know. And with your wild attitude and anger, you're way more dangerous than you realize. Relax, Lyric. Let love come to you. You're not even fifteen yet."

Since the girls moved in with Mama while Sawyer and Mindy tried to find a life for themselves in Vegas, Joy postponed her plan of buying her own place in order to help out. She tried to marry wisdom with compassion, letting the girls heal. But she also refused to let their truth become grounded in their circumstances and their faith in their feelings. She still fought that battle herself.

"Is that what you're doing? Letting love come to you? You're almost thirty, Aunt Joy. How long do you have to wait?"

"Certainly past your fifteenth birthday. Now please, get in the shower. Today. Now. Two minutes . . ."

The bathroom door slammed. Next the shower water hit the porcelain tub. Joy paused at the top of the stairs, listening to the song of the shower, wrestling with Lyric's caustic observation. *Letting love come to you? You're almost thirty . . .*

She'd known love once. But for the past seven years she'd been busy running from her own broken heart and the hollow echo of her own tears. Then she joined *Dining with Charles* as an associate producer, which shockingly turned into *Dining with Joy.*

Love seemed like a million years away. The shower water cut off. Joy stirred and started downstairs. What she didn't have time to ponder today was romance. Not the morning Duncan Tate planned to introduce her to her new boss, Allison Wild.

At the bottom of the stairs, Joy slowed her step, sniffing the air, captured by a silky scent that brought to mind the image of Luke Redmond.

The *Dining with Joy* studios were in downtown Beaufort on the second floor of the Old Bay Marketplace building. Duncan Tate built it for Daddy after his first heart episode. He thought a hometown studio would relieve the stress of traveling to Atlanta to tape the show. Plus, it would give *Dining with Charles* a cozy, hometown feel. The brand caught on with viewers and Daddy's star started rising. But bad hearts don't care about hometown studios, rising stars, or the collateral based on the power of a man's name.

"Joy, good, you *are* here," Duncan greeted her, wearing a suit and tasseled loafers, his face pinched and his voice strained.

"Nine o'clock. Just like you said." She peered at the woman with Duncan, then crossed over to the conference table, smoothing her hand over her new jeans, curling her toes against her flip-flops. She'd dressed in preproduction casual.

"Joy, I'm Allison Wild and I've been looking forward to this meeting for a long time." Allison worked her way around the end of the mahogany table, her extended hand guiding her forward.

She wore a tailored blue suit and taupe heels. Her dark hair was shiny and smooth, the blunt ends brushing against her jawline. Creases fanned from the tips of her hazel eyes, and she carried the confidence of one who earned her way by work and wisdom.

"It's nice to meet you." Joy gripped Allison's hand. Her skin was dry and thick, a contrast to her crisp appearance and eager tone. "Though I was surprised by Duncan's news."

"Yes, yes, and I'm sorry about all the last-minute details." Allison motioned for Joy to take a seat. "Duncan brought me up to speed, but I want to assure you I am very excited about this show, and—" Allison's shoulders lifted with a long, slow inhale. Her smile showed in her eyes. "I have some great news. TruReality phoned last night. They have picked *Dining with Joy* for their fall lineup. Eight o'clock Thursday nights."

Joy froze, her hand on the back of a chair. "TruReality? *The* TruReality?" The third largest cable network. Five times, six times, a gazillion times the viewership of the Premier Channel.

"*The* TruReality. You won over the vice

president of programming with your wit and humor, Joy. The comedy and realness of the show is fantastic—exactly what the network is looking for in a show. Duncan, I'm surprised you didn't try to take the show there yourself."

"I did. Twice. Once with Charles and again when Joy took over, but I guess I just didn't have your magic touch, Allison." Duncan shook his head, burying his hands in his pockets. "Congratulations."

"TruReality believes Joy is going to revolutionize cooking shows."

"Revolutionize?" Her pulse clamored in her ears. There'd be no sitting down now.

"Revolutionize. Every other cooking show is about the host, the celebrity." Allison cut the air with her hands, emphasizing every word. "The sets are canned and flat, the show feels small and claustrophobic. But *Dining with Joy* is about the viewers, the fans, everyday people. I laughed until I couldn't breathe at the Stupid Cooking Tricks."

"Yeah, we tried to show the funniest ones." Joy let the news seep into her heart, soaking up her doubts, softening her fears. TruReality would mean more money, more opportunities not just for Joy but the crew. "What's your plan, Allison? Are we keeping the format?"

"Don't see any reason why not. TruReality might ask for a few changes, but why mess with

45

such a golden format." Allison walked back to her spot at the table and opened her laptop.

The morning light ricocheted off the adjacent building's windows, haloing the show's new owner and producer with a soft glow. "The network mocked up a new site." She turned the screen to face Joy. "We might consider a few tweaks to the show, but *you* are the star, Joy. Ryan will remain associate producer and director. The rest of the crew will stay with the show. We are going to need them to help train new crew members. Because if my gut feeling is right, and it usually is, we are going to be a very popular and busy show."

Joy bent beneath the sun's glare to read TruReality's website. *Joy Ballard, the face of Thursday night. Come Dine with Joy.* She jerked upright, squinting. "The face of Thursday night?"

"You are the face and the lead show for Thursday evenings, the network's biggest ratings night. They're all in. Publicity, advertising, wardrobe, personal appearances, whatever we need. Wild Woman and TruReality plan to make you a household name."

"H–household name?" Oh, now this was going too far. Wasn't it?

"You're more than a foodie or a cook. You're an entertainer, Joy. A star. We all see it. You're the girl next door meets glamour and fame. I'm surprised Duncan let me steal you away so easily."

"I've done all I can with the show." Duncan cleared his voice as he stared out the window. "Besides, we all have our dreams to chase, Allison."

His tone didn't soften, nor did his stance give a little. How could Joy not see how much he'd wanted out? After last season, with their growing fan base, stronger market share, and distinctive brand, Joy finally exhaled and believed the whole scheme of her posing as a cooking show host might be a good idea. Duncan had been full of ideas for the future. Never once did he hint of selling out. But gazing at him now, Joy saw the reflection of his heart in his eyes.

"Joy, are you with us?" Allison snapped the air. "I know this is a lot to grasp, but the best news is yet to come. Contract negotiations. The entire crew is getting a raise, and if we make our financial goal at the end of the season, bonuses all around."

"Raises and bonuses." She pressed her hand against her diaphragm. "That's really generous, Allison." The floor rumbled beneath her feet. "Duncan, can I see you for one second?" Joy barreled toward her office.

He treaded heavily behind her, entering her office and closing the door. "Don't blow this, Joy. It's a great deal. What's wrong? You look green."

"TruReality? Raises. Bonuses. I can't do this, Duncan." Joy walked around her desk. "She has to know."

"Is she asking to know?"

"Why would she ask, Duncan? How many cooking show hosts do you know who can't cook?"

"You for sure, but I have suspicions about a few others. Have you seen that woman from—"

"Duncan." Joy's plea hissed through the cool office air. "I care about *this* host. Me." She patted her hand against her chest.

"Then keep quiet. Why does Allison have to know?"

"Why do I have to keep quiet? If it's not a big deal, then let's tell her, get it on the table."

"She'll walk. She won't risk her reputation with TruReality on a fake cook."

"Then why do I want to do this? Risk *my* reputation, the good Ballard family name?"

Duncan's countenance darkened and he came around the corner of Joy's desk, bearing down on her. "I sold the show to Allison. Now you sell *you,* all your charm and star quality, to her. She's halfway there as it is. Then, have at it, confess. But you tell her now, it's over for everyone. You, me, the crew. Do you want to destroy everything we've all worked so hard to achieve?"

"You mean, what *you've* worked to achieve."

"No, Joy, all of us. You are on the verge of fame. People have done way more for way less than their fifteen minutes. Who knows, you might just learn to cook one day. Give this season a chance.

Once you win everyone over, then, well, you know, confess. By then, they'll be star-crossed in love with you and won't care you can't make toast."

"I can make toast, Duncan." Joy sank down into her chair. "You're awfully arrogant for a man no longer holding the keys."

He lowered his nose to hers. "I've worked with a lot of hungry artists and actors before, Joy. But I've never seen one as starving as you. You won't walk because it's not in you to quit. That ability made you a great ballplayer, an entertaining show host, and a determined aunt, but—"

"Not a great cook?" Joy glared at him.

"Joy, just do the show." Duncan stood back. "See what happens. Let the routine roll like it has for the past three years. By the time Allison finds out, *if* she finds out, you'll be such a big hit she won't care." Duncan perched on the edge of Joy's desk and reached for her hand. "She's right. You are definitely star quality. It's why your daddy asked you to take over the show. He saw it before I did." He squinted at her as if seeing Joy anew.

"Daddy saw star quality in me?" Joy withdrew her hand from his and moved her pencil tin from one side of her desk to the other. It was full of yellow number twos, sharpened to a fine point, erasers on the bottom, tips toward the ceiling. Daddy didn't want his legacy to die. That's why he asked her. And she answered because she had nothing else to do. Because for once in her life, she wanted to say yes to his request without an argument or stomping away to do her own thing. "What about the live competitions? I'm not doing them."

He winked as he reached for her hands. "I told her you had a phobia."

"A phobia? That's the best you could do?"

"She loved it. Thought it added to your nuance and character."

Duncan squeezed her hands. "I'm going to miss you. You are the one woman I can truly say never let me down."

He rounded the desk for the door. "It's going to be fine. I promise."

"I won't lie," Joy said. "Not outright. I may not confess, but if she asks—"

"Believe me, she won't. Allison is way beyond the question of whether or not her host can cook. She has a star in her pocket, and she's going to find every way possible to let you shine."

 # Five

The twilight of the June evening made the surface of Factory Creek look like melted gold. Joy positioned her porch chair to face the water. Next to her, a cold four-pack of Orangina sat on the cedar table.

Mama collapsed into her chair, stripping off her garden gloves and dropping them to the porch floor. "Today I painted one car, primed two, and repotted fifteen plants."

"Sounds like a successful day." Joy twisted the cap off the first bottle and passed it to Mama. "Where are the girls?"

"Swimming at the Lawfords'." With her fingers, Mama combed her wiry bangs away from her sunburned forehead, working the ends into the rest of her hair. "Orangina?" She surveyed Joy, a glint in her hazel eyes. "What's up?"

"Nothing." Joy slumped down in the chair, rested her head against the broad slats, and closed her eyes. The breeze off the creek carried the scent of potting soil and dew.

"Nothing? That'll be the day. You only break out the Orangina for special occasions."

"Yeah, like what?" Joy sipped her soda, holding the taste of citrus on her tongue.

"Oh, I don't know." Mama stretched out her

legs, pressed her toes against the heels of her sneakers, and slipped them off. A suntan line rimmed her ankles. "When you got your softball scholarship to Alabama. When you made the dean's list. When you broke up with Tim. Like your daddy with his banana bread. Any excuse, any occasion, good or bad, happy or sad, he'd say, 'Rosie, I'd better make banana bread.'"

"Did he?" Joy swigged more Orangina. "I don't remember him making banana bread for stuff like that."

"Joy Elaine, don't say such things now. Makes me feel like you didn't grow up in my house. Couldn't walk into the kitchen without running into a bunch of brown spotted bananas."

Joy peeled back the bottle's label. "I remember banana bread, but not for special occasions."

"I guess we remember what we want to remember." Mama set her bottle on the corner of the cedar table and a lone sweat bead snaked down the side. "Sure don't know how you could forget warm, cinnamon banana bread with chocolate and peanut butter chips. Makes my mouth buzz just talking about it."

"Why don't you make it, then?"

"I reckon I could, but I know me. I'll buy the banana and fixings, get busy, forget about it, and by the time I get back round to it, the bananas will be spoiled. Besides, I don't even know where Chick hid all his recipes. He was funny about letting people see them. Kept them close to the chest."

"He was an up-and-coming cooking-show chef, Mama. Most of the ones I know keep their best ideas to themselves."

The air shifted and the twilight glow moved behind the trees. A choir of crickets sang from the creek bank. Mama drank deep from her Orangina.

"He'd be proud of you. Taking over the show. I'm not sure he thought you'd do it. Growing up, you never listened to him much."

"I majored in English and Creative Writing like he told me."

Mama laughed. "All you did growing up was read, play softball, and write in your journals. Wasn't hard to figure out which direction to point you."

"Yeah, well, I sure didn't know what to do with myself after graduation."

"The Lord knew. He brought you right back here and plopped you on your daddy's show."

"Mama . . ." Joy lowered her empty Orangina bottle back into the carton and retrieved another. "Duncan sold the show . . . to a woman named Allison Wild of Wild Woman Productions."

Mama regarded her for a long moment, the way she used to when she wanted to see whether Joy was fibbing. "My, my, Duncan sold the show. Never imagined I hear those words. Did he give you a reason?"

"He said he'd taken the show as far as he could." Joy picked at the frayed hem of her old, baggy shorts and recounted the details from McDonald's last night and the studio this morning. Mama listened, sipping on her soda.

When Joy finished, Mama returned her drained Orangina to the carton and rubbed her hands together.

"Does she know? This Allison woman? Can you get out of your contract?"

"She doesn't know. Duncan and I talked it out and decided nothing needs to change about the way we do the show. He recommended giving our current way a chance, and by the time Allison finds out, if she finds out, we'll be such a hit she won't care."

What defined a lie anyway? The absence of truth? No, changing the truth. Or shading the truth. If Allison asked outright, Joy would confess. But so far, none of Allison's plans had anything to do with Joy's cooking prowess. Or lack thereof.

"Now would be a good time to break free, Joy. You don't have to fill in for your daddy anymore or do Duncan any favors. You could chase that writing dream of yours. Freelance, write for the *Gazette*. What about coaching? You were always helping your friends with their batting or pitching. You can't tell me you don't miss softball."

"I'm almost thirty, Mama." Joy stood in the last slant of sun falling through the porch screen, hunching her shoulders against the chill rising from her bones. "And all of that sounds like starting over. Duncan's right. I need to give Allison a chance. Besides, writing is a hard life. Pays next to nothing for more years than I've been a host. I'd never get out of here and into my own place. And yes, I love softball. And I miss it. But that part of my life is over, you know? In the closed-up past." Joy watched a spider work its way up the weave of the screen. "I suppose I could tug on a pair of overalls and work at Ballard Paint & Body with you."

Mama whistled, slapping her hands against her tanned thighs as she stood. "How long have you been waiting to let that zinger out?"

"Just thought of it."

"Felt marinated in sarcasm to me." Mama stepped into Joy's shadow. "Enough is enough, Joy. You can let this show thing go. Get on with *your* life. What do you want to do?"

"I don't know." Joy exhaled, reaching up, trailing her finger behind the spider. "There's this verse in my truck. Jesus says something about 'My food is to do the will of Him who sent Me.' That's what I want, Mama. To figure out God's will. And all I know right now is to do this show because Daddy and Duncan, and now Allison, are asking." Joy faced Mama. "Really, the show isn't

Daddy's anymore. More and more of it revolves around my personality. Shoot, in two years we may not even have cooking segments. Mama, Allison sold the show to TruReality. I am *the* face of their Thursday night lineup. They want me to become a household name."

"Well, that's something, isn't it?"

"I can't tell what you're thinking with a comment like that."

"I mean it's something. Household name. Not many can lay claim to such a tall title."

"The money will triple by this time next year. And that's just the start. Allison has more ideas than Carter has pills, Mama. We're going to revolutionize the way people think about cooking shows."

"Revolutionize cooking by a woman who cannot cook. Not even a little bit." Mama gripped Joy's arms. "Make sure you know what you're getting into, and I'll support you. But you think about this."

"I've thought about it all afternoon. Sharon will still develop the recipes. I'll present them. In that sense, I am being honest. Besides, every cook, chef, foodie has recipe developers and food preps."

"Yes, but at the end of the day, when all the lights are out and the cameras are dark, they can actually make what they sell. You burn popcorn." Mama reached for the last Orangina.

"If I quit, everyone loses their jobs. Allison loses her entire investment. If I stay, nothing changes. It makes sense to me." Joy nodded, more to herself than Mama. It did make sense to her. It did. "This feels right."

"I can't deny, the oddest doors seem to open to you."

"Then maybe that's God's way of leading me, Mama. Some people hack out their destiny through hard work. Maybe my destiny's in embracing the opportunities before me. I certainly wasn't aiming for a Thursday night slot on TruReality."

"No, you weren't."

"Aren't you a little bit suspicious that He's the one holding open all the doors?"

"Rosie, Rosie, quite contrary." Miss Jeanne's cherub face peeked through the screen door. "How does your garden grow?"

"Very well, thank you." Mama eased open the door, extending her hand to Miss Jeanne, a Beaufort matriarch and old friend of Grandmamma Ballard's, as she maneuvered up the steps.

"Shew." She collapsed in Mama's chair, fanning her face with her hand, her blue eyes lively. The sleeves of her dress arched above her thin shoulders, exposing white layers of under-garments. "It's a warm one today. Any more Oranginas, Joy?"

"They're all gone, but we've got iced tea in the fridge."

"Don't go to any bother. I just came by to see the sketches Rosie's dreaming up for my car's paint job."

Mama popped her hands together. "I've been waiting for you to come around. The sketches are upstairs." Mama darted inside like she might be afraid Miss Jeanne would change her mind.

"Joy, darling, what on God's green earth is going on with you?" Miss Jeanne tugged the hem of her dress down over her fleshy, white knees.

"Just life. You're letting Mama paint your car?" Joy angled sideways in her chair, drew up her knees, and hooked her heels over the edge of the seat. She loved Miss Jeanne. When she was little, Joy used to beg to sit with Miss Jeanne in church because she traveled with contraband—lemon drops, spearmint gum, and coloring pencils to decorate the bulletin.

"Yes, don't you know I finally caved. She's been after me for a month of Sundays to bring the old girl in for a fix-up. I'm just so sentimental about that car. First one I bought after I graduated from law school." Miss Jeanne peered at Joy, the light in her eyes intense. "How are you doing today?"

"Treading water, paddling to shore."

"Got a little cloud forming over your head?"

Joy laughed. "And I left my umbrella in Omaha."

Miss Jeanne sat forward. "Hold out your hands and close your eyes."

Joy made a face as she offered her palms. "You're not going to pull a ruler out of your purse, are you?"

"Heavens to Betsy, girl." Miss Jeanne scooted to the edge of her chair. "Close your eyes now."

Weariness took up residence in Joy's soul the moment she closed her eyes. Her shoulders rounded forward as her bravado about the show's change fell into the fallow soil of her soul. How could she do this? Really? Should she even try? Oh, Duncan . . .

"I have two gold nuggets for you." Miss Jeanne's fingers feathered softly over Joy's right palm. "God is good." Then her left. "God is love." The older woman closed Joy's fingers. "Hang on to them, Joy. The will of the Father is always good. Always love. And you can spend them anywhere, anytime."

Joy clutched her fists to her chest. "Thank you, Miss Jeanne." *God is good. God is love.* The declarations refreshed her dry soul.

"Here we go, Jeanne." Mama emerged from the house, but Joy kept her eyes closed. It was peaceful sitting in "the dark," holding her two gold coins.

"My, my, my, Rosie. A lightning bolt?"

Joy smiled. *God is good. God is love.*

Water Festival Food Fair

Meet the star of *Cook-Off!*, Wenda Divine,
at Waterfront Park
Saturday, July 10 at 3:00 p.m.
Water Festival Cook-Off starts at 4:00 p.m.
against the Frogmore Café's Luke Redmond
Hosted by Joy Ballard, star of *Dining with Joy*
See you there

Around three thirty on a balmy Saturday afternoon with sea foam clouds drifting across a lazy sky, Luke inspected his Waterfront Park kitchen station. Unrolling his knives, he lined them up by the stove. He liked the feel of the kitchen—the rustic colors and stainless steel—the atmosphere of a competition.

He checked the burners. Tested the oven. Losing to Wenda if she outcooked him would be one thing. Losing because of a malfunction would be humiliating.

The kitchen's drawers glided open and contained all the necessary utensils. Helen's staff had done their job.

Stationed between Luke and Wenda's stage, a digital clock the size of a refrigerator counted down the minutes to the cook-off.

Luke's adrenaline injected energy into his enthusiasm as he watched the seconds tick away.

Last night he'd sat down with a pad of paper in the loft apartment he rented from Miss Jeanne and brainstormed recipe options for various surprise secret ingredients. He figured he could handle just about anything but onions and octopus.

People were beginning to gather, choosing seats from the rows in front of the stage. Luke glimpsed Wenda's golden head moving through the crowd. At one point, she tossed her hair with a laugh and disturbed the gentle breeze.

"Luke Redmond, my competitor." Wenda greeted Luke with a phony tone and pretend applause. "Ladies and gentlemen, make him feel welcome at *Cook-Off!*" She kissed the air around his cheeks. "Are you ready, Luke? My crew is eager to film a great show."

"Then I must tell you, I plan to win." He'd spent the last few weeks researching Wenda during his short breaks from the café's kitchen. A classic competitor, Wenda hated to lose. But as far as he could tell, she was a sincere, true-blue foodie trained in New York and France. The woman was no Cat Cora, but she had mojo. Besides wanting to win, she had an affinity for exercise and plastic surgery.

"Luke, darlin'." Wenda patted his cheek. "I always win."

"There's always a first time." He was feeling a bit of his own mojo this morning.

"I'm sorry about your place in Manhattan. I heard the food was lovely."

"The restaurant business isn't for cowards."

"Neither is the food entertainment business." Wenda stepped into him, her arms still crossed, batting thick, black eyelashes. "My network, the All Food Network, likes to see me in fun, lively competitions."

"I can do fun and lively." Luke understood she was leading him, but where? If he was going to be roped and tied, he'd like to see it coming.

"Certainly, but every once in a while I like an all-out foodie war, you know? A little smashmouth cooking." Her tone lowered as a dark glint shadowed her gaze.

"For all the bragging rights?" If she wanted a battle, Luke could step up to the line. He'd welcome the chance to win back some self-respect he'd lost when he closed Ami's. Earn the right to keep the title *Food & Wine* declared over him when he started out: "The chef to watch."

"If it were only bragging rights, I'd not make this request. This is about a personal best, hon. The impossible." The wind lifted the ends of Wenda's stiff blonde hair as she strained to communicate her message to Luke. "I didn't come here to rumble with you, Luke."

Luke stepped back, the light dawning. "You want to battle Joy Ballard."

"So bad I could roll it in batter and deep-fry it. She's *the* trailblazing show host, Luke. Her show is fun, entertaining, and witty. She presents great food. And she's the only host I haven't competed against."

"She says it's not her thing. Doesn't fit her brand."

"Is she still saying that old line?" Wenda tossed her hair when she laughed. "We've joked about it for so long she's actually started to believe it. She knows it's coming sooner or later. What do you say?"

"What do I say?" Luke's adrenaline shifted energy from enthusiasm to caution. "Nothing. This isn't my competition to call, Wenda."

"I've cleared things with Helen, and she's game to let Joy substitute for you. My producers and crew will go nuts. And I'm sure *Dining with Joy*'s crew will have cameras rolling. But I won't leave you out, Luke. I'll work out some benefit, maybe a promotion for the Frogmore Café. What do you say?"

"Don't do it, Wenda. Joy doesn't want to be on this stage. I promise you."

"Oh, but I think she does." Wenda turned to go. "Just yield the stage, Luke. I'll make sure it's worth your while."

Watching Wenda go, he pondered her plan. If she manipulated Helen into letting Joy compete after all her protesting at the Frogmore that night a few weeks ago, then who was he to stand in the way? Maybe Wenda was right.

Who was he to fight for his right to compete? He was trying to gain *back* his good name, not destroy it.

 # Six

At five till four Joy nestled in the cab of a Carolina Carriage. Helen would come looking for her soon, but Joy was determined to stay out of sight until absolutely necessary.

Alfred agreed to let her sit in his ride until a paying customer came along. A few minutes later his bristled face peered down at her. "The big clock is ticking."

"I can hear it from here." She pushed out of the carriage, stepping down hard on the pavement. "Thanks, Alfred."

"One of these days, you ought to actually hire a ride."

"Yeah, one of these days." Joy pressed a twenty in his hand.

"Where have you been?" Helen scurried down the center aisle toward her. "We had show prep to do. You missed it." She jabbed Joy with her elbow.

"Just hand me the mike." Joy reached for the handheld and took to center stage. She'd done four weeks and twenty cities of hosting and emceeing. She could probably do this in her sleep by now. "Good afternoon, everyone, and welcome to the Water Festival's Food Fair and Cook-Off!"

A small applause swelled from the crowd.

"Come on, y'all, you can do better than that!" The applause was strengthened with cheers and whistles. "That's more like it. This is going to be on national television, and we need the viewers to hear and see our lowcountry pride." Joy walked the stage, pointing to the empty seats in the front row. "We have room up here. If I didn't know better, I'd say y'all were acting like this is Sunday morning church."

Waiting for a family to make their way up front, Joy jerked around at a movement just beyond her peripheral vision. She exhaled relief. It was Allison, dressed in khaki shorts and a white T-shirt, scooting across the stage with cameraman Garth and sound tech Reba in tow.

Since their Tuesday morning meeting in June, Allison had been in transition. This was her first week in Beaufort, and she was ready to go to work.

"Are you ready for a cook-off?" Joy's voice swept through the air and rousted the crowd to their feet with applause. "Let's meet our contestants."

Joy motioned to the kitchen station on her left. "Please welcome the lovely and talented Wenda Divine, star of the All Food Network's *Cook-Off!*"

Instead of greeting the crowd with her signature bow, Wenda exited her kitchen station, striding toward Joy with one of her cameramen tight behind her.

"Y'all want to see a real duke-'em-out competition?" Wenda bent toward the crowd and punched the air with her fist. "Then let's hear it for Joy Ballard, my *real* competitor for this year's Water Festival!"

"What?" Joy's hand tightened around the mike. "Wenda, what are you doing?" She snatched at the woman's long, thin arm. "You're cooking off with Luke, not me."

"No, you are my competitor today." Wenda's smile widened with bold confidence. "All cleared with Helen."

Joy whirled around, scanning the stage area. *Come out from hiding, Helen, you coward.*

"Y'all want our own host, the woman who is going to star on Thursday nights this fall on TruReality, to beat ol' Wenda Divine at her own game?" The crowd applauded in response, chanting, "Joy. Joy. Joy. Joy."

Wenda spurred on the chanting until Joy couldn't hear herself think.

"No, no." Joy waved off the cheering. "Luke Redmond is your competitor. A chef at our very own Frogmore Café. Don't diss the man, y'all."

"We want *you,* Joy." A passel of college-age men stood on the edge of the crowd, being good fans and cheering her on.

"Chefs, take your kitchens . . ." Now Helen appeared, jerking the mike from Joy. "You have fifteen seconds. Joy, best get going."

The low rumble of her name paralyzed her. *Joy, Joy, Joy* . . . A sound tech wired her with a mike pack.

When the buzzer sounded, Joy stood in her kitchen station, pure panic surging through her.

"And the secret ingredient is—" Helen unveiled the item with grand flair. "Peaches! And the Water Festival Cook-Off! is happening now."

Think, think, think. Joy raced to the grocery station. If she loaded up with peaches, all the peaches, then there'd be none left for Wenda. And what could she cook?

As Joy carried an armload of peaches back to her kitchen, she caught sight of Luke watching from the edge of the stage and fired him a thousand blazing daggers. *Traitor.*

Dropping the peaches into a ceramic bowl, Joy gave them a cold water rinse and then set them on the counter. *There you are, honorable judges, washed peaches. Believe me, it's way better than some of the dishes I've eaten for competitions. Did I tell you about the roadkill in Ohio?*

"Psst, Joy, what are you thinking of making?" Luke had moved closer to the front of the stage.

Joy turned off her mike. "Roasted Luke à la peach sauce."

"Don't get mad at me. This wasn't my idea."

"Why didn't you refuse?" Joy snatched up a couple of peaches and bent to Luke's ear as she walked around the kitchen station to the front of the stage, peach water dripping from her hands. "I think you could've taken her if she'd agreed to wrestle for it."

He laughed. "But it wasn't me she wanted to wrestle."

"Lucky me." Facing the crowd, Joy switched on her mike and began to juggle, water droplets arching in the air as the fruit sailed in a circle. "Hey did you hear the one about the peach, orange, and banana?" The peaches floated up and around faster and faster. "Anyone? The peach, orange, and banana."

"You would sure look good in my fruit salad," a man called from the crowd.

"What? Fruit salad? That's all you got?" Joy caught the peaches, making a face, searching the crowd for the one who delivered the line. "I was hoping one of you could tell me a good punch line."

No one laughed. She was dying here. In more ways than one. When would she learn? Never, never get within a gazillion miles of Wenda Divine. "All right, enough of this, back to work." Joy ran around to the other side of the set, peeking over at Wenda, who worked with intensity and precision-chop-chop, blend-blend, sear-sear.

The air intended for Joy's lungs hovered just beyond her nose, refusing to fill her chest. She gazed out at the crowd. Maybe she should call for volunteers.

"Joy, psst, what are you doing?" Luke knocked against the stage floor, calling for her to look at him. "Wenda's way ahead of you."

"Giving her a head start." Joy tossed the peaches to the bowl. Falling off the stage wasn't an option. She'd already done that stunt. A repeat would look unprofessional. Probably arouse Allison's suspicions and blast Wenda to the moon.

The briny breeze off the river warmed Joy's already hot skin and brushed the hem of her skirt against her shins. A narrow sliver of light cut through the crowd . . . She could run.

"Fifty minutes to go, chefs," Helen announced.

"Joy." Allison moved across the front of the stage with her little crew. "Love the juggling and bad comedy bit, but get cooking. The TruReality host should destroy the All Food Network's host."

"Since when were we at war?" Joy tried to grip the paring knife laid out on the countertop, but her fingers refused to hold on.

"Since she challenged you to a duel. Look, I know Duncan said you have a phobia about this sort of thing, but you're here, onstage, so get going." Allison backed away, giving Joy a thumbs-up and motioning for Garth to shoot some footage of Wenda.

Okay, Jesus, what should I do? Just, you know, confess? Blurt it out. "I'm a fraud." The idea paralyzed Joy. *I'm in Your hands here. You can have it all.*

Even you, Joy?

Joy snapped her head up as the wind dipped low and shook the tree limbs. She hesitated, pondering the echo moving across her heart, just as Luke swept past her, his shoulder brushing hers.

"Let's get a plan," he whispered. "Are you thinking of a peach sauce? How about with pork? We'll have to do chops since we don't have time to do a roast." He set a food processor on the counter.

Hello, my way out, where have you been?

"Sauce is good. I like pork." Her fingers tightened around the paring knife.

"For dessert, what about peach ice cream? If we can't get it cold enough, milkshakes."

"I like milkshakes."

"Joy, we need to move fast." Luke's hand covered hers and slipped the knife from her grasp. "Go to the grocery area and pick out four thick chops. Bring some potatoes and rosemary. I have a good idea for them."

"Why are you doing this?" The fragrance she'd encountered on the stairs the other morning wafted around her head—a textured, warm musk. "Helping me?"

"The first time I was in a competition, I panicked." He spoke low and melodic as he worked. "My blackened beef was raw on the inside, I cut my hand, and I caught the emcee on fire. And I'd *willingly* entered the competition.

Here you are, yanked out of the crowd more or less, all flustered and off-kilter." His knife slipped clean and smooth through the tender peaches. "Better get going." His eyes searched hers. "But walk slow, take a few seconds to pull your thoughts together. When you come back, have on your game face and we'll kick Wenda's dish clean out of the lowcountry. You do have a game face, right?"

"I have a game face, but I need blacking for the full effect."

"Save it for next time."

There won't be a next time. Joy stretched out her hand to touch his arm—*thank you, my way out*—but hesitated, folding her fingers to her palm. "Thick chops, you say?"

"About an inch. Less, if you can find them. Hurry, Joy, time is—" He paused all motion, all sound. "Hey, sorry, guess I'm taking over." Luke backed away from the counter, motioning to the food processor.

"Take over, Luke." She pressed her hand against his back, pushing him toward the counter. "I'm not such a big ego we can't share the stage. You do your thing . . . food process. And I'll do mine." Joy smiled at him. "Shop."

"Hey, hey, hey, what's going on over there?" Wenda's objection sounded over the kitchen station. "Are you cheating, Joy?"

"The only one cheating is you, Wenda," Joy

said, running down the ramp to the grocery station, snatching a waiting wicker basket.

"Helen, what is going on here? Joy is cheating. She can't have kitchen help."

"Oh, good grief, Wenda." Helen rose from the judges' table. "You wanted to compete against Joy and you're competing. Be quiet and cook."

By the time Joy returned to the kitchen with her basket loaded, Luke had the sauce reducing in a pot as he zoomed about the station in chef mode.

As she unwrapped the pork chops, Luke shoved a bowl of flour at her and pointed. "Salt, pepper, dunk in the chops and go. Oil's heating up in the large skillet."

Oh, sweet Jesus, I owe You. I owe You. Joy seasoned the flour with sea salt and ground pepper and covered the pork chops, pressing the flour into the meat like she'd done a dozen times on the show.

When the chops were ready, she flicked a few drops of water into the skillet to check the oil temperature. The hissing sizzle gave her the green light to start frying. Joy arranged the pork chops in the skillet, glanced at Luke fussing with the ice cream maker, then made her escape to the front of the stage.

"Don't you love a man who can cook? The aromas up here are delectable." Joy released her lavaliere mike and aimed it toward the saucepan. "Can y'all smell it?"

Luke watched her, scooping his cream mixture into the ice cream maker, his gaze piercing. Her heart surged with the passion behind his eyes. What was he seeing, so deep and intense? Surely he couldn't see through to her weak, trembling core.

"Want to check the chops?" He tipped his head toward the skillet.

"Checking on the chops." Joy hooked the mike back to the edge of her top, picked up a fork, and did a jig as she headed for the stove. The seasoned juice flowed over the side of the meat into the bubbling oil.

"How do they look?" Luke ran his knife through a pile of rosemary leaves.

"Scrumptious." Maybe a moment ago, with his acute stare, he saw her. But this time she saw him—kind, selfless, knight in a white chef coat.

The low murmur of conversation faded from her hearing. The grind of boat motors on the river silenced. Wenda disappeared. Allison and the crew were faraway specks on the horizon.

In Joy's universe, scented with sweet peaches, the only beating hearts belonged to Luke and her.

She pressed her hand against his arm and he straightened. "Are you okay?"

Without a word, she pressed her hand to his chest and touched her lips to his. At first, he didn't respond. He barely breathed. Joy gripped her hand around his collar, pulling him tighter, closer.

When she broke the kiss and stepped back, exhaling, the magic of the moment fading, the heat of realization crept up the side of her neck. She'd apologize the first moment her heart found a sane word.

But before she could back away, Luke captured her with the taut power of his arm, bringing her into him, his lips covering hers. He tasted like flour, vanilla, and cream, like the comforts of home at the end of a long, hard journey.

Allison snatched the collar of Garth's T-shirt. "Please tell me you're getting this. Every last delicious inch of it."

"I'm getting it. Trust me, I'm getting it." He might have been taping, but he wasn't watching the stage from behind the camera. Instead, Garth lifted his eyes above the lens, gaining an unobstructed view, his Adam's apple bobbing.

Allison felt downright giddy. Unbelievable. Twenty-five years in the biz, working like a mule, giving up vacations and holidays, letting romances slip through the thin cracks of her heart, leaping over obstacles, crashing through iron doors, lining up for every parade of opportunity television offered, and Allison had finally discovered her own pot of gold.

Right here in the steamy corridors of the lowcountry. In the heart and soul of delectable Joy Ballard.

Oh, God, if You're real, thank You. Even if You're not, thank You. Allison engaged the camera on her BlackBerry and lifted it over her head. "Garth, look at the screen. Do I have them framed?"

He leaned over, grabbed her wrist, and lifted her arms another inch. "Now you do."

Allison snapped the shutter just before Luke broke the kiss. It was a sign . . . a sign. Everything was going her way.

Not quite a month into her deal with TruReality, and the starry-eyed phase was already over and they were asking Allison for little changes and tweaks. Marketing had gotten involved, advertising and program development. "We need a bigger 'wow' factor for the show," they said. "A slightly better angle to fit within our network brand."

Allison peered at the image of Luke embracing Joy and smiled. She'd been sleepless the last few nights, her mind racing with ideas of how to "wow up" *Dining with Joy*, but on this blessed day, the "wow" factor came to her.

The kiss started out innocently enough, in Joy Ballard's grandstanding style. Allison enjoyed a small tingle of magic musing over the idea of having Luke as a guest on the show.

But then Joy's little peck grew into a bushel as Luke surrounded her, drawing her into him, firing sparks and *amore* into the atmosphere. Beside her,

75

Garth cleared his throat and ducked back behind the camera.

"Jealous?" Allison peeked up at him. Onstage, Joy and Luke were fumbling around.

"Three years I've been filming her show. One hour on the stage and he gets the kiss?"

Allison laughed. "This is my lucky day."

What motivated Joy to pull such a stunt, Allison didn't know or care. The girl was pure gold. She'd stolen the show right out from under Wenda Divine. It wasn't about food anymore.

Allison forwarded the picture she'd just taken to Dan Greene at TruReality with "Wow Factor" in the subject line. Then she motioned to Garth and the camera. "Upload this clip to YouTube. I'll get it up on Joy's website. Let's get the buzz going, start invoking the magic."

# Seven

Monday evening Luke carried the Frogmore's trash across the sand-and-broken-shell parking lot to the Dumpster.

The dinner rush ebbed a few hours ago and he'd spent the evening prepping the café for Andy Castleton's Tuesday morning return. Luke's tenure as executive chef was complete.

After tossing the Hefty bag into the open container, he walked to the edge of the yard and gazed toward Waterfront Park, his heart straining to see the ghost of his Saturday afternoon kiss with Joy.

For two days his lips had tingled with her phantom taste. She invaded his thoughts. Every time he heard the café's front bells ring out, he craned around the edge of the stove to see if she entered the dining room.

At first, Joy's spontaneous kiss robbed his breath, then morphed to a fun stunt, a dig at Wenda. Bravo, Joy. But then it became something deeper, and when she softened to break away, his heart panicked. *Don't let her go.*

He'd been kissed many times, but not wooed until he drowned in the sensation of being wanted.

Luke's eyes scanned the park one last time before turning back to the café and the waiting inventory. UPS would deliver an early morning shipment of supplies tomorrow, and he wanted the walk-in and stockroom organized and ready to go for his boss.

When Luke entered the kitchen, Mercy Bea eyed him from her propped position on the porch post, cleaning her teeth with a toothpick.

"You got a visitor." She bent back to toss the toothpick in the trash. "And no, it ain't Joy."

"Now why would I want it to be Joy?" Luke swung the screen door wide, letting it clap against the tabby wall and paused at the sink to wash his hands. When he reached for the towel, Mercy Bea held yesterday's *Sunday Gazette* under his nose.

"This is why you want it to be Joy." Mercy Bea flipped through the pages with exaggeration. "Let's see. Who won the Water Festival Cook-Off? Wenda Divine or Joy Ballard? Gee, I can't find news of it anywhere here in the front section." She snapped her knuckles against the front page. "But I sure know who Joy Ballard's kissing. What a humdinger. Felt it all the way to the second row."

Luke mashed down the paper and peered into Mercy's eyes. Enough. He didn't need a reminder. "Where'd you sit my visitor?"

"Back booth." Mercy tucked the folded newspaper under her arm. "Just so you know, I'm keeping this for posterity."

"You do that." Luke exited the kitchen into the

dining room, sweeping his gaze around the tables in case *she* happened in while Mercy Bea picked her teeth. Paris waited on a couple of tourists, and Russell bussed the tables left over from the dinner crowd.

And there was no Joy in the room.

But in the back booth, sitting in a wide swath of southern light, sat a petite dark-haired woman.

"Afternoon," Luke said as he approached. "What can I do for you?" Luke remained standing, his arms folded over his stained chef whites. It'd been a messy day in the kitchen.

"Luke Redmond, I'm Allison Wild." The woman motioned for him to slide into the booth across from her. "I hope this is not a bad time."

"No, not a bad time. We're in a bit of a lull. What can I do for you?" Had he seen her before? Maybe. In town? At the cook-off? In the café?

"I like a man who gets to the point. I'll do the same." Allison pulled a form from the attaché sitting next to her in the booth. Sharp angles outlined her features, and the glint behind her dark eyes inspired the word *intense*. "I'd like you to join the *Dining with Joy* show."

Luke tightened his jaw as he settled against the back of the booth, the leatherette seat cool to the touch. "Why would I want to join Joy's show? Better yet, why do you want me to join the show? Because I beat Wenda?"

"Beating Wenda is always a good thing, no

doubt about that. And you have a good presence and stellar culinary skills. But until that kiss, you were just another hunky man in a chef coat."

"Never imagined a kiss could become a part of my résumé."

"It's a bit unusual, yes."

And private. Luke shifted forward, unsure if he wanted the intimacy of a kiss to be on the bargaining table. He was a chef, not a Hollywood actor. "I'm not sure what you're after, Allison."

"We posted a clip of you and Joy on YouTube Saturday night. Within twenty-four hours the clip was viewed a hundred thousand times. Unique hits. Not return viewers." Allison let the stat of a hundred thousand views hang in the air without further explanation. "But we weren't the only ones who posted a clip. Of those posted by fans, and I'm guessing most of those were uploaded by the frat boys, the kissing scene earned another twenty-five thousand hits. By the time I got in the car to come see you, those numbers tripled. And it's only Monday."

"What a sad, sad world."

"Sad? Luke, this is amazing. The magic between you two was palpable. Everyone in the audience Saturday was mesmerized. The men wanted to be you. The women wanted to be Joy. The comments on YouTube tell the same story. You're the new Brad and Angelina, a throwback to Bogie and Bacall, Hepburn and Tracy."

"Listen, I hate to burst your bubble, Allison, but I just met Joy a few weeks ago. The kiss was spontaneous, in the moment. We couldn't recreate it if you paid us a million dollars."

"I'm offering you a show and the chance to try. I'm betting the spark I saw on Saturday is the tip of a volcano."

Luke speared the table with his elbow and ran his hand over his head. A volcano? He hated relationship drama. Besides, this was nuts. A woman offering him a cooking show because of a kiss.

He glanced up as Mercy Bea set two jars of iced tea and a basket of Bubba's buttery biscuits on the table. "Listen, Allison, I'm a trained chef. Can you hire me because I'm technically qualified?" Luke lifted his tea for a small, cooling sip. Without breaking into full-on prayer, he tried to discern the moment, sense what God might be saying.

"If you weren't a skilled chef, Luke, I wouldn't be sitting here. If you were just a dynamic kisser, I wouldn't be sitting here. It's the combination of your skill and chemistry with Joy that brings me to the table." She raised her tea glass. "Luke, I don't need a chef for the show. I have Joy. She's my star. My talent. But what I need is spark, magic, the wow factor. That's where you come in."

"How do you know we won't go the other way? Hate each other. From a kiss to a punch in the nose."

"As long as it's passionate, I don't care. Wow me. Wow the viewers." Allison turned over the paper she held in her hand and set it on the table. "You're Luke Earl Redmond, named after your grandfather, Earl Redmond. Your parents are Earl 'Red' Redmond, Jr., and Ami Redmond. You call your dad Red, as a matter of fact."

"Where'd you get all of this?"

"I have people." Allison watered her words with a drink of tea. "You're a chef from Manhattan by way of an Oklahoma ranch. Midwest meets big city meets the South. Your mother died when you were sixteen and you ended up dropping out of high school your senior year. Got your start in Manhattan's Hell's Kitchen district. A few years later you enrolled in the Culinary Institute of America. While attending there, you passed your GED. You opened Ami's just before your thirtieth birthday but filed for bankruptcy last year. Moved to the lowcountry this past January. Lived with your cousin, author Heath McCord, for a few weeks but now live on the third floor in the downtown historic district." She sat back when she finished, a look of pomp on her face. She'd recited his bio from memory.

"Well now, I'm a bit embarrassed." Luke angled over the table. "I didn't have time to dig up any dirt on you."

"There's not much to dig up. A couple of ex-boyfriends, but you'll never find where they're buried. Been in show business for twenty-five years. I don't own any pets or plants because I don't have the time or the patience to care for them. This business is my life and this show, *Dining with Joy*, is my baby, the one that will take care of me when I'm old and gray, sitting by the river watching the sunset."

"Something tells me you're never going to be old or gray, or sitting by the river watching sunsets."

Allison exhaled a laugh. "Look, you know me already."

"What does Joy say about all of this?"

"I needed to talk to you first." Allison retrieved a manila envelope from the attaché. "First-year contract with an option for three more." She slid the envelope toward him. "If you don't like it after one season, you can walk. No strings."

"What makes you think I want to do television?"

"Two years ago you made it to the final round on *The Next Culinary Star*. You were let go after a particularly grueling competition. Want to keep challenging me?"

"Allison, Allison." It was Luke's turn to laugh. She was so intense and . . . in his face. "Then you know I got cut from the show because the judges didn't see 'star' in my future. I could cook but lacked the 'critical charisma' to hold an audience."

"But when you were on the Food Network, you

weren't paired with Joy Ballard." Allison arched over the table. "Joy's a fine cook, but her sweet spot is entertainment. You will be my foodie ace in the hole. *Dining with Joy* is moving to a major network, and I'm going to bring my A game. You'll placate the snobby purist. Joy will continue to woo the everyday cook, the kitchen noodler, the busy mom who doesn't have time to make"—she swirled her hand in the air, thinking—". . . jellied onions for a grilled-out peppercorn hamburger. You trained at the Culinary Institute of America, the perfect juxtaposition to Joy's down-home style cooking and church potluck recipes. And if she should kiss you again, or you kiss her—"

"The ratings go through the roof." Luke opened the envelope and removed a contract, flipping through the pages. Did he want to do television? It was more hazardous than opening a restaurant. He paused as he read the numbers on page three. "You're kidding."

"Salary plus bonus. Also, I'm talking to a publisher about a cookbook. I'd like you and Joy to write one together this year. Perhaps next year, your own cookbook."

Luke exhaled. The color of opportunity changed the way he saw things. He'd be able to repay Red and his friend Linus, who both tried to help him sustain Ami's with unsecured monies. When he filed for bankruptcy, they were left out.

Allison started to speak, then pinched her lips

together, smoothing her hand over the table, her eyes on Luke. "What do you say?"

"I'll think about it." He'd learned from Ami's that the "fire, ready, aim" process didn't really work all that well. And he didn't have anything discernable on what God wanted for him.

"In the meantime"—Allison slid out of the booth and flipped Luke her card—"go watch the YouTube clip. See if that doesn't entice you. If you're the man I think you are, you'll do the show. I'll be expecting your call."

"A cohost? Why? This is the *Dining with Joy* show, Allison. Not *Joy and Friends* or *Joy and Luke*." Joy paced the small space between her desk and the credenza. "What happened to *not* making any changes to the show?"

"I wasn't until you kissed Luke."

"A kiss? You're gambling our brand, our success, on this wild idea of a cohost based on a kiss?"

"Have you seen YouTube? We're at nearly half a million hits in three days. It's been picked up by *E!* and TruReality is already running it as a teaser for the show."

Joy folded herself into her chair. "So you want to marry me and the show to Luke." This didn't make sense.

"You sound more panicked than my ex when I told him I might like to get married someday." A mixture of amusement and determination threaded Allison's tone. "I offered Luke a one-year option. If it doesn't work, he's out." Allison rose from her chair and paced toward the window. "I didn't say anything, Joy, but TruReality demands I take a good concept and push it to greatness, then toward the spectacular, and finally to the sublime ridiculous. The formula is their hallmark. It worked for them and it will work for us."

"Fine. I love it. But we can do all of that without a cohost. Without Luke. What is he going to do? I do the comedy and cooking. Sharon develops the recipes, does the show prep. I won't let you replace her for Luke."

"Sharon will be more critical than ever because we'll have two very different cooks presenting food. Luke will work with Sharon to bring his culinary point of view. You'll work with her to enhance yours. It's a win-win."

Wait, wait, wait. A crazy notion nudged Joy's thoughts. *Hello, my way out, where have you been?* "You know, Allison, we could really play to my strengths and Luke's, if he joins the show. Let me do all the comedy and Luke do all the cooking."

"No. You're still the star, Joy." Allison pointed at Joy, jabbing the air with her finger. "You're our golden girl. I'm not replacing you with Luke, so don't worry."

"Worry? Me?" Sigh. Joy rocked back in her

chair. "Never." But really, she should just flat out tell Allison there wouldn't be any more kissing. In the quiet moments, Joy shuddered at the memory of kissing Luke, so brash and brazen. What must he think of her? "Listen, Allison—"

Allison's ringing phone broke up the conversation. "Hold that thought, Joy, it's Dan, vice president of programming." She raised the phone to her ear. "He's calling to see if we have Luke. Dan, good morning." Allison tipped her head to the side, her gaze drawing out Joy's assent.

"It's your show." From the moment Allison presented the plan of bringing on Luke, Joy understood the conversation was merely a courtesy. In the end, Allison would do what she wanted to do.

"Dan, we're good to go. Luke's agreed."

The door clicked behind Allison, and Joy stood by the window. Tourists strolled leisurely along Bay Street. One of Alfred's Carolina Carriages rolled past with the *clip-clop* of the horses' shoes against the pavement.

Joy deliberated most of the weekend on how she'd let her guard down so easy, in such a public fashion, exposing her heart, leaving herself vulnerable.

The passion between them surprised her, leaving her breathless and dazed. She didn't realize everyone else noticed.

Panic fired up her heart. Luke would find out. How could she hide her secret from him? His presence would change everything.

This morning she'd wondered if and when she might see him again. Debated if casually dropping by the café looked too obvious. Now she fretted over how to prevent Luke from discovering her secret: that the *Dining with Joy* host can't cook.

# Eight

A thick crowd lined the elongated brick sports bar of Luther's Rare and Well-Done. As Luke worked his way toward the back table, he could just see the crown of Heath's head.

In the front corner, hometown boy and country superstar Mitch O'Neal set up for a nine o'clock show. Luke tried to refuse tonight's invitation from cousin Heath to go out with him and Elle, and Mitch and his wife, Caroline.

Spending an evening with two happily married couples with Luke as the fifth wheel had "pitiful" written all over it.

But Mitch would pack the house, and Luke planned to blend in. Meanwhile, he'd sip a Coke, people watch, and try not to feel like a fish out of water. The kitchen was the only place he felt comfortable.

Being the new cohost of *Dining with Joy* hadn't settled in yet.

"Luke, how does it feel to be Beaufort's newest celebrity?" Elle's bracelets slid down her arm with a gentle ting. "Aren't you just, like, awed by the door God opened for you?"

"Awed. Surprised. Hoping it's a door He really opened." Luke motioned to the waitress for a Coke.

"How can you doubt, Luke?" Elle's question didn't inquire but challenged. "Allison came to you. You prayed for God's will."

Luke wished he had Elle's holy confidence. "All I can do is have faith, right?"

The house lights dimmed and Luke pressed against the wall beside Elle. Up front, a spotlight fell on Mitch.

"Hey, Luther's Rare and Well-Done." Mitch strummed softly. "It's good to be home."

The room stilled under the melody of Mitch's guitar. The only distinct sounds were the clinking of glasses. Luke set his empty glass on the table and was settling in to hear Mitch when a slender redhead sliced through the spotlight.

"Joy Ballard, it's about time you showed up." Mitch played a short, driving riff. "Give it up for the host of *Dining with Joy*. And a good friend of mine and my wife's. Joy's new cohost is also here tonight, Luke Redmond."

The Luther's crowd complied and cheered halfheartedly. Yeah, who the heck was Luke Redmond?

Joy breached their little group, breathless, flushed, her hair loose about her shoulders. She wore a pale blue sundress that danced with the color of her eyes. Luke watched her until she looked at him. Then his heart retreated inside.

"How're you?"

"Good. You?" Ah, so much for the smash-bang

chemistry Allison loved. Luke had seen Joy once since Allison paired them for the show. The meeting passed smoothly with little or no tension. Luke had gone in with a single game plan. Play it cool. The egomaniac chef part never served him well.

"Good. Keeping busy." She glanced over her shoulder when the waitress paused to take her order. "I write the bits for the show. Now that you're in the mix, I have a feeling Allison is going to run me ragged this season."

Still singular. Me. It'd take time. It'd take time. "Yeah, she seems like a tiger on the hunt."

"I have a lot of ideas for her too."

Luke laughed. "Am I going to regret this?"

"Maybe." Joy eyed Luke under the waitress's arm as she tried to meet him halfway with his drink. Her tray bobbled. Luke grabbed his glass and steadied the tray.

"If I spilled another one, I think they'd fire me." She smiled a sad smile.

"Hang in there. It takes time." Luke lightly touched her shoulder. "You'll get it."

Luke caught Joy's eye. She was watching him. And he felt his heart sink a little deeper. As he transitioned onto the show, the last thing Luke needed was the complication of falling for Joy.

From the small corner stage, Mitch started another song, the rhythm of his guitar and the smoky texture of his voice pushing Luke to a peaceful, melancholy place.

At the end of the day
it's about loving you
like the rain on the meadow
with sweet drops of dew

A group of marines pushed through the crowd toward the deck doors, shoving Joy against Luke. He peered at her, nodding his head toward the doors.

"Wanna go for a walk?"

She set her glass on the table and whispered something to Elle, then opened the double doors and stepped onto the deck.

Out on the deck, the air seemed so still. The river so quiet. The melody of Mitch's next song pressed through the glass.

"Seems like the whole riverwalk is listening to Mitch." Joy inhaled, lifting her face to the array of stars settled deep in the dark sky.

"Do you want to go back inside?" Luke jerked his thumb over his shoulder. "If you want to listen—"

"The night air feels good." Her focus remained on the stars, but after a moment, she looked at Luke. "I'm not thrilled about you joining the show. But I won't interfere, won't make it hard for you or any of the crew."

"If you were in my place, would you turn down such an offer?"

Her eyes narrowed a bit. "I was in your place,

kind of, and no, I didn't turn down the offer." The long strands of her hair sailed on the breeze. "The kiss . . . I'm not sure why . . ." She shrugged. "It just felt right, but I want you to know I'm not one who goes around kissing strange men. Onstage. For show."

If that kiss was for show, Luke didn't want to imagine a real one. "I'm not one who lets strange women kiss me. Onstage. For show."

"It was the moment . . . just the moment."

Luke tucked his fingers into his jeans pockets. *Sometimes the night, trimmed with city lights, became a friend, a guardian for hearts to speak freely.* "What *was* the moment, Joy? You turned over the pork chop, I whipped together a batch of runny peach ice cream?"

"I've been asking myself that all weekend." Joy started down Luther's walkway toward the river.

. . . and sometimes the night, trimmed with city lights, became a guardian for hearts to hide.

"Anything I should know about the show?" Luke moved the conversation to safer ground.

"No, but," she spun to face him, "it is my show. The crew depends on me. I depend on them."

"I used to watch *Dining with Charles*."

"He loved doing his show."

"I could tell. I actually modified one of his recipes for the restaurant I worked for at the time."

"And how do you like *Dining with Joy*?"

"I think I'm going to like *Dining with Joy*." The

93

double meaning of Luke's answer boomeranged in his ears. "The show. I mean, well, I haven't been able to watch because I was running a restaurant. But—"

"I'm not sure it matters, Luke. Everything's changing with Allison as producer now. You as cohost." Joy started down the riverwalk. "I never said thanks for helping me with Wenda. So, thank you."

Oh, she'd thanked him. Plenty. Over and over, every time the kiss crept across his mind. "It was good to see her stunned, without words."

"I think the entire universe noticed." Joy walked backward, facing Luke. "Are you a runner, Luke?"

"Once upon a time. Played some ball in high school." He quickened his step to keep up with her.

"Want to race?"

"Want to race?" He lifted his eyebrows. "To where?"

"There." She motioned behind her to the drawbridge, dropping her flip-flops with each consecutive step.

"I think I could race you—"

"Go!" Joy swooped up her shoes, dangling them from her fingers as she jetted down the pavement, her heels kicking high, the hem of her dress twisting around her legs.

Luke shook his head. Really, he should just let

her run . . . leave her hanging . . . but, yeah, he wasn't crazy. He fired off after her, the soles of his sneakers in rhythm with his racing heart as he lengthened his stride to close the gap between them.

"Joy? Luke? Are you ready? Let's make this run-through as painless as possible." Ryan directed from his booth in the far corner of the studio. "Rolling tape, cue music, Joy coming to you in . . . five, four, three, two—"

Joy crossed the set, smiling, and stopped on her mark by the counter.

"Welcome to the fourth season of *Dining with Joy*." The opening music played under her greeting. "I'm Joy Ballard, and we are thrilled to be airing this fall on TruReality. We have some great things in store for you, including more wild and zany Stupid Cooking Tricks. But first up, meet my cohost this season, Chef Luke Redmond."

Luke walked onto the set, stiff, wearing jeans and a plaid snap-button shirt. Allison asked him to come in his street clothes . . . Joy grinned. She'd had fun with him the other night, racing along the riverwalk, blistering the soles of her feet. But oh, it felt good to run.

Then she'd stumbled, and Luke swooped her up in his arms without missing stride and ran with her all the way back to Luther's. When he'd set her down on the back deck, her knees buckled.

Oh my . . .

Remembering it now made her face warm.

"Hey, everyone. It's good to be here." Luke gave a windshield wiper wave at the camera. Then he smiled at Joy. Stiff-lipped and lifeless.

Joy reared back. What the heck happened to Luke? She cut through the air with a wave of her hand. "Wait, hold on a second. Where's Luke Redmond?" Shielding her eyes, Joy peered off set. "Will the real Luke Redmond come onto the set? Luke? Oh, Luke . . ." She walked out of the kitchen into the bowels of the studio, Reba and camera two following. "Luke, where are you? Some robotic dude with a pompadour is impersonating you."

"Your stylist did this to me." Luke smashed his hair against the side of his head. But the gelled and sprayed ends bounced right back.

"Allison, really, are you going to let him tape my show looking like a Channel 9 anchor?" She waited for Allison to call cut. Or Ryan. But neither did, so Joy went on with the rehearsal. "We are *so* having a meeting with the stylist later today."

"So, Joy, how was your weekend?" Luke's cold monotone read from the teleprompter tempted her to laugh. The image of the cowboy sweeping her off her feet in the middle of the footrace the other night challenged her sense of reality. Had it been a dream? Did she really feel his muscled arms beneath her back? After he settled her on Luther's deck, he disappeared into the darkness in search of her flung-from-her-fingers flip-flops.

"How was my weekend?" *Lovely. Really lovely.* "Luke, don't ask." Joy tossed a couple of almonds from the prop dish into her mouth. One of *Dining with Joy*'s hallmarks was sampling food related to the recipe throughout the show. She directed Luke with her eyes to reach for some almonds. "I had a date." She recited from the script. "An unbelievable date."

"Good unbelievable or bad unbelievable?" Luke's line didn't sound as plastic this time.

"Bad, bad, bad." In past seasons, Joy bantered with a crew member off camera, but with Luke on set now, she'd written the script to include him. Allison loved it. Next show, Luke would have a whopping wild tale of how he learned to surf.

"How bad is bad?" Luke read, gathering a few almonds with his fingers.

Joy and the crew chorused. "Real bad."

A circus ditty played, and when it faded, Joy started her story.

"He was supposed to pick me up at seven, but by seven thirty I was getting worried. I called his cell." Joy popped another few almonds into her mouth. The routine forced her to slow down, breathe, think, and engage the viewer with her storytelling. "He didn't answer, so I left a message. At eight," she angled toward the camera, "he's an hour late and still no call. Ladies, do not put up with this nonsense. Eight-o-five, he calls."

She paused for Luke to read next. After another second of silence, she peered up to prompt him. "Luke?"

But his face beamed red and he grabbed at his throat. "Wa-*ter*."

"Cut!" Joy called. "Luke, are you okay?"

"Wa-*ter*."

Garth appeared on the scene, twisting open a bottle of water from the snack cart and passing it to Luke. He chugged, gulping and gasping. After a moment the red on his cheeks faded. But when he'd drained the water bottle, the color returned to his face.

"Sorry, y'all." He averted his gaze as faint snickers traced around the back of the studio. "Never choked on an almond before in my life."

"Are you all right?" Joy dipped low to peer into his eyes. He'd carried her when racing blistered her feet. She'd not chide him about this. Being on camera could be nerve-wracking. She'd had her throat close up more than once.

"Luke?" Allison slapped her clipboard on the edge of the kitchen set. "Avoid the almonds from now on. Just relax and read the script. Let us know when you're ready." She backed away with a shaky smile at TruReality's Dan Greene, who'd flown in from New York for the first week of taping.

"Luke, are you ready?" Ryan called.

Nodding, Luke stood on his mark.

"Five, four, three, two—"

"Women go for men like him all the time." Luke's voice remained weak from the almond dust. His line carried no spark or energy.

"Cut, cut," Allison interjected, waving her hands.

Joy exhaled. It was going to be a long day.

"Luke." Allison came around to the set. "Where's your intensity and charm? The Luke I loved at the cook-off?" She patted his back. "Relax. Be yourself. Go off script if you need to. Imagine the lights are the stars, the cameras are the sailboats off the South Carolina shore."

Luke's countenance stiffened, and he reached for a second bottle of water handed over by Garth. "I'm fine, Allison. I don't need to turn the lights into stars."

Allison regarded him for a moment, then backed away. "All right then. Ryan, whenever you're ready."

Joy bent toward Luke. "Want to pull it together before Dan Greene changes TruReality's mind about us?"

He twisted the cap onto his water bottle. "I am together. I'm the same man who saved you from Wenda Divine."

"Saved me? More like interfered. I was doing fine on my own."

"Fine on your own? Really? How'd that go

again?" Luke gathered three limes from a prep bowl. They were for the drink recipe coming up later. "Did you hear the one about the peach, banana, and pear?" His attempt to juggle started the crew laughing. "Look, I'm Joy Ballard. I can juggle." When one of the limes went wild, Joy scurried off her mark.

"You are *so* not me. And you *so* can't juggle." Joy elbowed him out of the way and snatched the floating limes from the air. "This is how Joy Ballard juggles." She arched the fruit in a fluid, circular motion.

Luke hip-butted her, trying to cut in and catch the limes. They fell to the floor with a dull thud. Joy glanced at Sharon, who stood by camera one, gaping. "We're going to need new limes."

"Perfect." Allison rushed the stage. "This is what I'm talking about. More of this kind of action." She smiled over her shoulder at Dan. "Didn't I tell you? Magic."

# Nine

When the heat faded from the evening, Joy settled on the back porch with her laptop and watched her mama stride across the lawn with their neighbor, Miss Dolly, trailing after her, wagging her finger.

When Mama stopped short, Miss Dolly crashed into her and their argument rose on the breeze.

Launching e-mail to the melody of Mama's rebuttal to Miss Dolly, Joy scanned her Inbox. In the week they'd been taping, Joy learned one solid truth about Allison. The woman *loved* e-mail.

Subject: Show Prep

Subject: My Beaufort Address

Subject: Recipe Ideas

Subject: Reality segments

Subject: Photo Shoot Food & Wine Cover Next Week. Monday!

Subject: Luke's hair

Joy laughed. *Luke's hair.* She was getting used to the pompadour. And more and more she honed the notion that Luke wasn't just her way out of Wenda's Water Festival cook-off trap but her way out of the web Duncan Tate had taught her to weave.

She had to convince Allison to assign Luke all of the show's cooking segments. It just made sense. While he simmered, chopped, and pureed, she'd ski down a mountain, munching on one of his recipes. While he taught the world how to spice up everyday macaroni, Joy could tape Joywalking segments, exploring the lives of singles, the dating scene, and cooking.

Luke could develop his own recipes with Sharon. Then, through the miracle of editing and Ryan's genius, Luke could actually appear lively and energetic on camera.

Luke was the *Tru* element of the show. Joy, the *Reality.* The notion had her wide-awake at three o'clock this morning. Even as the day faded, the idea stirred Joy with vigor.

She composed a new message to Allison.

Allison,

Great show this week. Seems we're working through the bumps okay, don't you think? I have several ideas for bits we might add, upping the "wow" factor TruReality is so into.

I'll do the development work with Ryan but just wanted to run these ideas past you.

Guest spots with home chefs, sticking with our brand of focusing on the viewers.

Duncan and I talked about a Letterman-like Top Ten list, for example Top Ten Things You Do with Meat After You Drop It on the Floor, Top Ten Things You Do to Your Mother-in-Law's Cooking When She's Not Looking, Top Ten Reasons to Own a Rolling Pin, Top Ten

Foods You Eat When Watching Football. How about a contest for the easiest meal to clean up; stupidest ingredient; shopping on a budget for frat guys and sorority girls, or any dorm rat; recycling appetizers into dinner; Pizza Tonight, Pizza Tomorrow, "How cold pizza saved my relationship."

Crazy, I know, but I have notes from our college fans who claim day-old pizza saved their love lives. Which leads to another idea: The Power of Italian. We focus on pasta, pizza, bread, cheese, tomato sauce, olive oil, garlic. My stomach is roaring as I type.

Let me know when you want to talk. I'll bring more details to the table when we meet.

Joy

The screen door swung open with a creak as Joy clicked Send. She glanced around to see a sullen Lyric crash into the Adirondack chair beside Joy. She flipped her hand in the direction of Mama and Miss Dolly.

"What's going on with those two?"

"Weeds and pesticides."

Lyric sighed as if she could no longer bear the burden of being fourteen *and* the grandchild of a woman who picked a fight over bug spray.

"I should pitch a show about them to TruReality. *Lawn Wars of Silly Southern Women*." Joy closed her laptop. "How was softball practice?"

"Boring." Lyric hugged her legs to her chest. Her shorts were too short, her top revealed too much tender flesh. Joy guessed it to be a size too small by the strain of the Disney World logo. "Aunt Joy, how do you know if a boy likes you?"

So the truth surfaced easily today. "If he's kind, nice, carries your books for you."

"No boy carries a girl's books, Aunt Joy. That's, like, from Granny's day." Lyric rested her chin on top of her knees.

"You know what I mean. Pick a boy who looks out for you, talks about something other than himself."

"What if I'm not pretty enough?"

"Is this about Parker?" Joy patted the arm of Lyric's chair to get her attention. "Want me to talk to him?"

"Don't you dare." The girl shot up straight.

"Then listen to me, Lyric. Don't let any boy ever convince you that you're not pretty enough."

Lyric bit her lower lip in contemplation.

Joy let her stew on the idea and then broke in with a question of her own. "Have you heard from your mama or daddy lately?" She braved the parent-waters because Lyric's emotional dams seemed open. For the moment. But probably not for long.

"Why would I hear from them?" Lyric's hazel eyes glistened, but her tone was flat. Cold. Wavy wisps of hair escaped her ponytail and curled around her neck. "Who needs them anyway? They can stay in Vegas. Die there."

"I'm not defending them, Lyric, but being mad at your parents won't change who they are or what they've done. It'll only plant bitter seeds in your heart. After a while you won't even recognize yourself because you're wrapped in anger and bitterness."

"Please don't lecture me on my parents." Lyric lowered her forehead onto her knees and hid her face with her arms. "You have no idea what it's like."

"You don't know everything, Lyric. My daddy and I didn't always get along. We had lots of fights."

"At least you had a daddy to fight with." Lyric's watery words exposed her heart.

"You're right, baby." Joy leaned to brush Lyric's flyaways from her cheek. "Never looked at it like that before."

"Can I go to Siri's?" Lyric stretched as she rose from the chair.

So, the heart-to-heart ended. The dam's gates closed. "You can go until dinner."

"I'm eating at her place. Her mother cooks real food."

"What? We cook real food here."

"I mean roast beef or meat loaf. Not Campbell's soup and grilled cheese." Lyric slid open the glass door. "I'll be home for bed."

"Change out of those shorts and shirt. They don't fit—" The door cut Joy off with a soft clap.

Joy sighed, reclining against her chair. What was it Lyric said? At least she had a father to fight with? Where was that great thought when Joy was sixteen? When she thought the man ensconced in the kitchen night after night was an evil overlord, she'd have welcomed his absence. Thrown a party.

Instead, Charles Ballard was home every night, developing recipes and filling the house with the aroma of meats and sauces, sweets and bread.

Every once in a while, when the house slept, Joy imagined she heard the clatter of Daddy's pans. And if she drew a deep breath, expanding her lungs to their limit, the phantom aromas of baking bananas and cinnamon swept past her nose.

Joy wandered off the porch in search of Mama, thinking of Daddy's banana bread recipe. Sharon might be able to recreate it. She'd worked with Daddy long enough before he died.

Around the side of the house, Joy met up with Mama.

"Where's Lyric going?" Mama motioned toward the driveway with a spray can. "She took off on my old bicycle."

"Siri's. What are you doing with that spray can? Where's Miss Dolly?"

"She's gone." Mama patted the side of her can. "I'm going to spray pesticide on her lawn."

"Mama—" Joy snatched at the can's handle, but Mama was too fast. "You can't go spraying her yard with pesticides."

"And why not? How does her organic method trump mine? Hmm?" Mama pushed around Joy, aiming for her shed, "The Lab," as Joy and Sawyer used to call it. "Dolly's treatment—or should I say lack of treatment—is turning her lawn into a bug maternity ward. The little varmints are getting fat on my shrubs. The leaves look like Swiss cheese."

Swinging open the shed door, Mama disappeared inside. Joy hung around by the opening, listening to the melody of clanking bottles and gurgling liquid. The last time she ventured in, she broke out in hives.

Mama emerged, testing the sprayer on the ground around Joy's feet. She scurried out of the way. "Careful, Mama."

"I'm going in." Mama hunched down and inched toward Miss Dolly's twin magnolia sentries. She peered back at Joy through the branches. "If I'm not back in twenty, send in the search party."

"If she calls the sheriff, I'm not bailing you out."

"Fine with me. The sheriff's antique Corvette is in my garage."

Joy laughed. Mama was loony but savvy. Making her way back to the porch, Joy gathered her laptop and phone to head inside. With a single glance, she noticed a phone message from Allison.

Joy, I have the most incredible news. I just got off the phone with The Bette Hudson Show. *You, my dear star, are going to be on this September.* A chill of dread shimmied through her. *More deets later, but congratulations.*

The Bette Hudson Show? The most popular syndicated talk-show host since Oprah wanted Joy? Sliding open the glass door, Joy took a deep gulp of cool, air-conditioned air. It was too soon to panic. Too soon to panic. Actually, being on with Bette could be fun. All Joy had to do was make sure Allison submitted her "no cook-off" rider, and she'd be golden.

Joy paused beside the kitchen. *The Bette Hudson Show.* A blip of excitement journeyed through her. Then she thought of Luke with his stubborn cowboy chin and watchful expression. He'd look fine on Bette's yellow leather couch, appealing to the women in the studio gallery.

Hello, my way out, where you been?

# Ten

When he downshifted to turn into the Ballard driveway, the gears of Luke's duct-taped Spit Fire complained and the engine backfired, blowing his planned stealth approach.

In the city, Luke didn't own a car. Didn't need one. But when Heath urged him to the lowcountry, he purchased the old Spit Fire, a rattletrap rust bucket, from his former sous chef.

Cutting the engine, Luke checked the time. Eight o'clock. Was it too late to stop by unannounced? In the city friends would just now be calling to see if he had plans for the evening.

Sitting in his lonely loft at Miss Jeanne's—the eighty-year-old had more of a social life than he did—with the heat rising, seeping through the cracks in his floorboards, Luke came to a conclusion. He wanted to be with Joy. Not as a cohost or colleague, but as a friend. As a . . . boyfriend. He'd prayed while he showered, heart wide-open to God talking him out of driving to see her, but here he sat.

He should've called on his way over. But forewarning a woman clearly communicated preparedness, I-was-thinking-of-you. Showing up out of the blue, however, said spontaneity, I-wasn't-thinking-of-you-at-all-but-here-I-am. For his ease of mind, the latter worked better.

Popping open his door, he took a quick peek in the rearview, finger-combed his hair, and brushed the stubble on his chin. Rough beard indicated I'm-not-planning-to-kiss-you.

He inhaled courage and slammed the car door shut. The car horn blasted. Luke jumped, wincing and shushing. The horn blast happened every time the door shut too hard. If Joy didn't know he was here before, she did now. Tomorrow, he'd get the dang horn fixed.

The front door swung open, revealing Joy. His heart beat a little faster. She regarded him as she stepped onto the porch. Luke stared up at her from the bottom of the steps.

"What brings you around?" she asked, her hand resting on the doorjamb, confident and casual. Her hair cascaded over her shoulders. Her baggy pants rode low on her hips, and her bare toes peeked out from under the hems.

Did it just go up ten degrees out here? What happened to the breeze? Tingles raced through Luke as he strained to focus on Joy's face, fighting to keep his gaze above her chin. Every molecule in his body ached for a slow visual scan down the curves of her frame to the tips of her toes, then up again, absorbing every nuance, right down to the golden highlights in her hair. While the kiss had been weeks ago, the fullness of her lips and the soft swell of her hips beneath his hand remained very vivid.

Alluring without seducing, Joy's beauty deserved to be admired.

"Thought we could grab a coffee or late supper?" Luke waited at the bottom of the steps, eyes locked on her face. *Steady, man.*

"With who?" She moved onto the porch and leaned against a porch post.

"The president. I heard he's in town."

"Oh, the president. Yeah, he called but I forgot to call him back." She snapped her fingers and smiled, crinkling her eyes.

"You're free then, to grab a bite with me." Luke motioned to his car, which in nanosecond hindsight was not a bright idea. Get her to say yes before pointing out the junkmobile.

"We just ate barbecue."

"Coffee then? Or a big Diet Coke?" He braved one step up, but he already knew he couldn't trust himself to be within arm's reach.

"Do we have company, Joy?" An older woman appeared in the door. "Are you going to leave him outside? Hey there, I'm guessing you're Luke. I'm Rosie Ballard, Joy's mama. Come on in, please, take a load off." She approached with her hand extended, but stopped, gazing toward the yard. "My, my, is that your car? I'll be, an '80 Spit Fire."

Luke laughed. "Very good. How'd you know?"

"Cars are my business. I can't tell nothing about iPhones or BlackBerrys or computers, but I can name a car's make and model, get it right ninety percent of the time."

"Mama runs Ballard Paint & Body here on Lady's Island."

"You ought to bring that thing around. I could fix her up for you."

"I'll do that when I wrangle up some spare change. In the meantime, can you help me talk your daughter into going out for a cup of coffee?"

"Absolutely." Rosie held open the screen door. "Twenty-nine years old and she's in her sleeping pants before eight o'clock. At this rate, I'll never get the house to myself."

"Mama!"

"Oh hush, he knows what time it is. Luke, come on in." Rosie waved him inside and patted the arm of an overstuffed chair with one hand while pressing Joy in the back with the other. "Joy will be right down."

He bet she would. Luke sank into the soft chair as the women jostled and struggled up the stairs amid their bass whispers.

Warm with lamplight and the lingering glow of the fading day, the room embraced him because *home* knew no strangers. The limp bag of Cheetos leaning against the sofa said the room tolerated everyone.

The air was scented with lavender and vanilla.

"Oh, *nooo*."

Luke rose to his feet at the small voice cry. He angled to see around the half wall.

"Stupid, stupid can. Aunt Joy?"

Making his way toward the plea, Luke peered into the kitchen. A stout, curly-haired little girl— maybe eight, nine years old—smashed the can opener against the granite counter.

"Bad can opener." Luke approached with caution but smiling.

The child whirled around, studying him with sparkling hazel eyes. "Can you open this?" She offered up a can of SpaghettiOs. "I try and try, but I can't get it. Stupid thing."

"Yes, they are stupid. But necessary." Luke smiled down at her as he reached for the can and opener, twisting until the top popped free.

The girl watched with her hand against her cheek. "I like you."

Luke dropped the lid in the sink. "And you must like SpaghettiOs?"

"If I didn't, I'd starve." She dumped the can contents into a microwaveable bowl.

"I'm Luke."

"I'm Annie-Rae." She stretched to punch open the microwave and shove the bowl inside.

"Joy's your aunt?"

"Yep." She set her chin on the counter to watch the noodles spin around.

"Ah, very cool." Luke leaned against the counter.

"What else do you like besides SpaghettiOs?"

"Pizza. Pop-Tarts. Smokey's barbecue takeout."

Pop-Tarts? SpaghettiOs? Pizza and takeout? Luke bent forward to peer through the pantry door opening. The light was dim and his angle awkward, but from his vantage point, cereal boxes, Pop-Tarts, cans, and jars occupied the shelves. And a taco kit. Did he see boxed macaroni and cheese?

"I see you've met my niece, Annie-Rae." Joy pushed the pantry doors closed with a short glance at Luke. "We need to go shopping."

"Shopping . . . Hard to get it done on a busy schedule." Luke stepped back, reckoning with the feeling Joy didn't want him examining her pantry shelves. Around him, Joy's floral fragrance cast its scent against the aroma of SpaghettiOs. "Annie, what are you doing? We just ate barbecue."

She gazed down at the girl with one hand on her hip, her frown unconvincing. Her simple top exposed the curves of her arms. Her jeans hugged the contours of her hips. She was assured, more than he'd seen on the set. Comfortable. If the doorway image of Joy greeting him in her pajamas got to him, this scene sent him to the precipice.

"I was still hungry," the girl said, without hesitation or trepidation.

"Hungry? Well, we can't have that, can we?" Joy smoothed Annie's hair before bending to kiss her forehead. "When Lyric comes home, tell her I said—"

"Joy." Rosie's voice carried from the living room to the kitchen. "I'll deal with Lyric. You get along now, stop fretting, stop keeping Luke waiting."

"That's what he gets for showing up unannounced." Joy pressed her palm to the pantry door, picking her purse off the counter. "Next time he'll call."

"Next time? You think there will be a next time?" Luke tugged his keys from his pocket, turning down the hall for the door.

"Oh yeah, there'll be a next time." Joy jerked open the front door, glancing back at him, a glint in her eye. "Bye, Mama."

"Have fun. Stay out late. Make me worry."

Five minutes later the Spit Fire shimmied and rumbled down the Sea Island Parkway.

"So?" Joy captured her flying hair and worked the ends into a loose braid. Under the fluttering, ragged top, the wind collected, filling the space between Joy and Luke. From the radio sitting askew in the dash, Josh Turner sang about the South Carolina lowcountry.

"So?" he echoed, shifting gears, precise and smooth. His cuffed, three-quarter sleeve exposed the strength of his arm. "I'm not getting the hang of the show very fast, am I?"

A clear, honest question deserved a clear, honest response. "Not really. But to be fair, this is my fourth season with the same crew and I'm used to hitting the set on the run, going through the script and the recipe while constantly looking for ways to be spontaneous, have fun, add humor."

"I feel like a talking brick."

She laughed. "I was thinking cardboard, but brick is good."

"I've done cooking shows before but not where the director sets up ten different angles of you washing your hands or stirring chocolate." He shifted again, the scent of pine and palmetto collecting between them. "I've definitely not had the privilege of working with a show host who suddenly decides we can't say the word *sauce* or *pan* for an entire show."

Joy laughed. "But what a fun show."

"Yeah, if you like the host yelling 'Gotcha!' every two seconds while you sweat through your clothes."

A sensation, almost intangible, seeped through her as she listened to him, as she inhaled his clean, soapy fragrance. In the blink of a firefly's light, Luke Redmond geared up from chef, from annoying cohost, to being a *man*.

Joy jerked around, angling away from him toward the door, wishing for cold air-conditioning to blow over her. Jutting her hand out the window, she gathered clumps of moist air to ease her hot skin.

"Sorry about the car . . . It was born in New York and delivered without air-conditioning."

"The night air is cool enough, thick and moist." Luke slowed as the drawbridge light flashed from yellow to red. Beneath them, the Beaufort River cut through the darkness, flowing with the force of the tide toward the amber lights of the city. "Must have been difficult stepping into your dad's show shoes."

"It was, at first." For a lot of reasons. "But I've worked hard to make it my own. Enjoy the journey."

"Didn't you have something you wanted to do before the show? Coach? What'd you study in college?"

"Coaching is too consuming. At one time I wanted a fam—Well, anyway, ideally I wanted to be paid to read and write. Majored in English at Alabama and thought I'd make it as an editor or writer."

Luke whistled. "Speaking of torture."

"Torture? Please." She laughed in her chest. "There's nothing like curling up with a good book, or that moment when an idea sparks and I sit down to write and it all flows." Cooking? Now that was pure torture.

And living with the fear of failing, of being exposed by a nosy reporter digging too deep. Or of Wenda Divine finally trapping her beyond escape. If one reporter found the right college roommate, the whole world would know about her infamous fiascos with microwave dinners.

"Naw, naw, there's nothing like curling up for a good, old movie with a plate of steaming tomato-and-garlic-drenched pasta, hot buttery bread, with chocolate cake waiting in the wings. It all comes together when I'm cooking, creating. I know what I'm doing in the kitchen, but not on set, not in front of cameras."

"Just forget the cameras are there, Luke. Be yourself. The viewers will love you."

"Yeah?"

"Yeah." She smiled, his humble *yeah?* slipping through her soul, a pearl casting an incandescent glow over her heart.

The bridge light flashed green and the Spit Fire motored forward, Sara Evans's smoky vocals coming over the radio, cocooning Joy in bright, bold melody.

"Who knows, maybe Allison's instincts are right. We're a good team, the tortoise and the hare. The stoic chef and the effervescent entertainer." Luke urged the car forward the second the light turned green. "Not saying you're not a great cook too, Joy. More like maybe one day I'll make a good entertainer."

"No offense taken." She glanced at him, the dash lights accenting the high plains of his face.

"You taking on the role of chef works for me." *Hear what I'm whispering to you, Luke.*

At eight thirty on a weeknight downtown parking slots weren't hard to find. Luke slipped the Spit Fire into a parallel spot by the coffee shop.

"Downtown Beaufort is hot with activity tonight." Joy motioned to the quiet sidewalk.

"Fits my plan. No waiting. But you?" He held up his hand to Joy. "Wait."

"Wait? For what?"

His door dropped on its rusty hinges as he shoved it open. "Just let me . . . now wait, Joy." Luke hitched up the door as he worked the door closed.

Joy watched through the windshield as he walked around the front of the car, his American-flag print shirt swaying loose over his boot-cut jeans. His boot heels resounded on the pavement until he stopped at her door and tugged it open. The hinge popped and squeaked.

Joy stepped out. "It's been a long time since someone opened my door for me."

"Feminism aside, it's an honorable gesture toward women, don't you think?"

Joy's gaze lingered on his face. The streetlights dimmed. The city music faded. The only two people in the universe—she broke the moment by stepping back.

"Yes, I do think." Her words sounded thick in

119

her cloudy throat. She was going to do it again. Kiss him. What was wrong with her? There was no show, no audience, no Wenda Divine.

Clutching her handbag, she followed Luke to a corner table, away from Common Ground's counter and foot traffic. He drew a chair out for her. "What can I get you?"

"A latte and . . ." She tugged her wallet from her handbag as she sat. "And a cinnamon roll. They make the best in the city."

"One latte and cinnamon roll coming up." Luke walked away before she could fish a ten out of her wallet.

"You don't have to buy, Luke."

He turned, walking backward. "After I dragged you out so late? Made you get dressed? Yeah, I do."

She dropped to her chair. What was Luke up to with his sweep-a-girl-off-her-feet, cowboy charm? Had she let her guard down too soon? If she wasn't careful, he'd discover her secret before she had a chance to charm Allison into letting Luke man the kitchen while Joy went on the road, worked up comedy bits, provided the spontaneity and laughs.

Luke was the perfect straight man, and he might be struggling in front of the camera right now, but once he became comfortable, once the fans related to him, Joy's pretense could fade away.

When she glanced up, Luke was watching her

from the counter. Joy shifted her gaze to her purse and fished inside for her phone. How did he make her feel so exposed, so vulnerable, as if he knew what she was feeling?

She tried to focus on her e-mail, but she couldn't seem to get past the distraction of just being out with him, the light in his blue eyes, or the cute way his brown bangs lobbed over his forehead.

When he returned to the table, Joy had gathered herself, shoving aside her imagination. Luke was a colleague, a professional chef. Her way out of this mess. But oh, the narrow pathway between success and disaster.

"Never could get into the smart phones," he said, setting down her latte and cinnamon roll. "I just have a little flip. It rings, I answer, all is right with the world." He tossed sweeteners and stir sticks onto the table.

"You're an alien, then." Joy slipped her phone back into her bag. "From the twentieth century."

"Growing up on a ranch, you learn to live simple and work hard."

"You grew up on a ranch?" She smiled. "That explains the boots and plaid shirts. I just thought it was all you could afford after losing . . . I mean . . . Gee, Joy, open mouth insert foot."

"After losing my restaurant. No shame in talking about it, Joy. I did go bankrupt. And yes, these are not only the clothes I can afford but also the clothes I like to wear. You can take the cowboy out of Oklahoma, but you can't take Oklahoma out of the cowboy."

"So, how'd a Manhattan cowboy end up in the lowcountry?"

"The idea of sun and water and hanging out with Heath appealed to me way more than dust and tumbleweeds, manure scented breezes, living at home, bunking in my first 'big boy bed,' listening to my dad grouse about the weather."

Smiling, nodding, Joy sipped her latte. "And here I sit with you, pushed out the door by *my* mother."

"It's different for women."

"Thank you for that kind answer." Joy pinched a bite from her roll, unwilling to shove the two-inch mound of dough, cinnamon, and icing into her mouth in front of Luke. "I'd planned to buy my own place this year until my brother and his wife decided to take off to Las Vegas without their girls."

"That's how Annie-Rae ended up in your kitchen opening a can of SpaghettiOs?" He blew gently over the surface of his steaming, black coffee.

"Yep. I'm so used to them being around now, I'd be lost without them." Joy took another small bite of her cinnamon roll. She ordered it, but now she wasn't hungry for it. "So, how'd you get to New York?"

"Long story." Luke folded his arms on the table

and leaned toward her. "But for your listening pleasure, I'll give you the short version. Went to visit Heath upstate one summer, we went down to the city and I found a job in Hell's Kitchen as a line chef. The executive worked me to the bone, but I'd found my passion."

"Passion is good." Joy swirled the foam into her latte before taking a sip.

"I'm a fan."

The tone of his voice sent a warm flush over her temples. He was talking about food . . . his career . . . and he was just agreeing with her. She picked at the seam of her latte cup, her gaze averted, afraid to look up and see herself in Luke's eyes.

"I used to feel that way about softball."

"I read your NCAA stats. Impressive."

"I had some good days on the field. What about you? Any Hell's Kitchen stats?"

"Sixteen fires, eight trips to the ER, five second-degree burns, a total of seventy-five stitches, one broken bone, thirty unique dish creations, and one year I clocked in three hundred and sixty-five days."

"My hat is off to you, chef. Very nice."

"They don't call it Hell's Kitchen for nothing." He eyed her over the rim of his coffee. "What about you? Any trips to the ER? Interesting burn or cut stories?"

His question cornered her. She shook her head slowly. "Actually, no." She peered at him, trying to be confident. "A cooking show isn't quite as hectic and dangerous as a Manhattan kitchen." Joy tucked her napkin around the cinnamon roll. She'd take it home to Annie-Rae. "Cooking on a show is rather beige most of the time."

"Beige?" He laughed. Good. He had been getting too serious. "The woman who invented Stupid Cooking Tricks? The host who brought deep-fried peanut butter and jelly sandwiches to culinary television?"

"All in an effort not to be beige. But enough about me." Joy reclined back, arms folded over her chest. "How did a rancher's son take up fine dining?"

"My mom died of an aneurism when I was sixteen, left Red and me."

"And who is Red?"

"My father. Earl Redmond, but everyone calls him Red." Luke cupped his hand around his coffee. "Mom left the two of us rattling around a big ranch house . . . felt like a sinkhole without her. She'd been gone about a year when I wandered into the kitchen and picked up her recipe box. I spent an entire weekend learning to make her lasagna. She made it with béchamel, and I used every bit of flour, which was probably over a year old, butter, and milk in the house. Red kept sending one of the hands after me, telling me to get my britches out to the corral and help with branding." Something changed in his expression as he reminisced.

"But you were falling in love with cooking."

"Guess I was, but that day I felt like I was keeping some part of Mom alive. She'd planned on teaching me to cook before she got sick . . ."

"Death is never timely." Joy twirled her stir stick between her fingers. "Daddy never planned to drop dead just when his show was gaining notoriety. So did you perfect her recipe?"

"After two trips to town for more ingredients, I produced something edible Sunday night. I invited my football buddies over, asked the hired hands to hang around, served the lasagna out on the back porch on paper plates. No salad or bread. Nothing to drink. Just Mom's lasagna."

"It was fabulous, wasn't it?"

"Best lasagna I ever ate." He lifted his chin, remembering. "The noodles were overcooked. The béchamel too thick. Too much cheese, if you can believe it, but that day, Red laughed for the first time since Mom died. And that's when I knew."

Joy leaned toward him. "Knew what?" A hushed curiosity bloomed between them.

"You know, Joy . . . the power of food."

"The power of food. Of course, right." Joy twisted around in her seat, arms on the table, folding a sweetener packet between her fingers. "So powerful . . . food."

"Food is an amazing force. It can bring people together, tear them apart. Provide comfort.

Entertain . . ." He smiled at her with a nod. "Give some folks purpose. On the other hand, food can overtake us, be a mask and a substitute."

"I never broke it down that way, but yeah, food is quite a force in our culture and lives." Joy retucked the ends of the napkin around the roll. Annie-Rae would be excited to wake up to such a treat.

"Thanks for coming out tonight. I just wanted to talk to you when we weren't trying to be chefs and hosts."

"Or racing down the riverwalk?"

He laughed. "Or that . . . I have no game tonight with these cockroach kickers I'm wearing." Luke kicked out his leg to show her his booted foot.

"No game, huh?" Joy jumped up, tucked the roll in her bag, and dashed out Common Ground's side door.

"Joy, hey, wait, girl—" His footsteps thumped after her, the heels of his boots resounding on the concrete.

Laughing, inhaling the river breeze, Joy dashed around the back of the building, cutting right toward the park lawn and riverwalk instead of left toward Bay Street and Luke's parked car.

Running. That'd keep him off balance, from peering too deep and seeing what she didn't want him to see.

# Eleven

The wind rushing over the Beaufort River Monday morning came from an offshore storm and threatened the outdoor *Food & Wine* photo shoot.

Yet Joy emerged from wardrobe and makeup in linen shorts and a light summer jacket, the blustery clouds threatening. Along the riverwalk, the photographer and his crew scurried around in some kind of organized chaos while another crew of men supervised the docking of two skiffs.

Slipping on her sunglasses, Joy spotted Luke by a concrete pylon. Instead of his plaid shirt and blue jeans, he wore a *Dining with Joy* chef's jacket and black trousers.

Since her coffee night and race with Luke last Thursday, Joy used the weekend to gain perspective. Luke wasn't trying to steal her show or peer into her soul and discover secrets. As far as she knew, he didn't suspect her of anything. He was just Allison's handsome addition to the show. A way to stir things up. Especially after a certain spontaneous kiss.

This morning Joy's thoughts were in check, focused on the day's task with her feet planted on lowcountry terra firma. Luke was a colleague.

And if she didn't remain guarded, he would be the dynamite to blow up her plan.

"It's like being at the circus." Luke gazed down at her when she came alongside. "You look nice."

"So do you. But I think I'm going to miss the pompadour." Allison had hired a new stylist for Luke.

A waifish man dressed in a black T-shirt and skinny jeans was speed-walking across the park lawn with his hands in the air and a chorus of black-clad assistants schooling around him.

"What is he doing? What are they doing?" Joy had worked with quite a few photographers, but Allison brought this one from New York because he considered himself an artist.

"Don't know, but he's hilarious to watch."

"Joy, great, you're ready." Allison approached wearing shorts, Birkenstocks, and a floppy hat. "The photographer was asking about you."

"Allison, why are we even out here?" Luke said. "We're a cooking show. Shouldn't we be in the studio kitchen?"

The photographer whisked past, eyes skyward, hands twirling.

"I wanted something fun for the cover of *Food & Wine*. We'll have plenty of kitchen shots. This is for the other part of our show, the fun, outside-the-studio, comedy side." Allison motioned to the photographer. "M, please come meet your subjects."

"Did she say M?" Luke's whisper warmed Joy's ear.

"I'm afraid so."

The photographer halted in front of them with a black-clad assistant. "This is the great M. I'm his first assistant, Raul. He's pleased to meet you."

"M." Joy offered her hand. "Do people call you Umm for short?"

Luke whirled around, his shoulders shaking. Joy concreted her expression as M cradled her chin in his hand and lifted her shades.

"M loves your bones. He thinks you have a beautiful aura," Raul said.

"I found the aura on sale at Overstock.com. But the bones . . ." She clicked her tongue. "Had to pay full price."

Luke snorted.

"Please," Raul tsked, waving his finger ticktock. "Sarcasm poisons M's atmosphere and stifles his creativity." Raul snatched at the air, pinching at the invisible. "I'm removing the negatives, M. Don't worry."

Yet M was on the move, strutting toward the river, swirling his arms. Raul interpreted. "People, gather around, M has something to say." Raul peered at M. "He says to climb into the boats. The river is our friend today. She possesses a positive light."

"Boats? Come on." Luke bent over the railing, eyeing the bobbing skiffs. "We're chefs, not sailors."

"You're looking a little green, chef." Joy angled over the railing next to him.

"Where I grew up, water came out of clouds and faucets. It was for drinking, cooking, and showering."

"Allison said M's photographs of Chef Jean Claude made him a household name."

"Chef Jean Claude is brilliant and his recipes made him a household name, not a photographer with a single-letter name." Luke scanned the park for a glimpse of Allison. "Jean Claude would never put his brand in a boat."

"How do you know?" Joy said.

Luke grinned. "He told me."

"He told you? Like you were visiting with the man and all of a sudden he said, 'By the way, never put your brand in a skiff and take a picture?' "

"Not in those specific words, no, but . . ."

Joy laughed, bumping her shoulder against him. He was too easy to be around.

"People . . ." Raul stepped between Joy and Luke. "Your negative vibes are disturbing M. Please get in the boats. Joy, glasses please." Raul mimed sunglasses removal.

"Please, Luke, get in the boat." Allison patted his back. "Trust me, time is money."

"I'm a chef. A New Yorker. A cowboy. Where does sailor fit in that description?"

"I'm adding it to your résumé."

Garth and Reba hovered with minicams as Joy and Luke made their way down to the dock.

"Are you afraid of water?" Joy asked, low.

"No." His lips pressed into a hard line. His jaw stiffened. Beneath his jacket, she could see his muscles tightening his broad body.

But once they were in the water, Joy saw the truth. A pale-faced Luke gripped the sides of his rocking boat with white knuckles while his brown bangs swept over his green gills.

Joy, meanwhile, rested easily with the motion of her boat. This was going to be fun. In the kitchen studio, Luke intimidated her. A lot. His cooking segments were delicious with details. He was so quick and agile, Ryan was starting to film Luke doing most of his own prep and cooking.

She, on the other hand, had to create more diversions and distractions because Luke hovered nearby. Ryan called "cut" a lot, took up time reframing Joy's cooking shot, then he'd claim they were running out of time and ask Sharon to bring out the already-prepared dishes.

Watching Luke struggle in the boat, Joy saw herself. That's how she felt with the show. Hanging on for dear life, facing fears, but unwilling to give up and give in.

Should she leave Luke on the outside of the secret? His stake in the show was growing day by day. If she brought him inside, he could be a real asset.

He could help her move the show in the direction that would free her from the prison of pretend. With him on her side, she could tell Allison the truth without risking everyone's careers.

Or he might be a tremendous risk. What did she really know of him? A man trying to rebuild his career and reputation in the foodie world after losing his up-and-coming establishment was an unknown threat. And knowledge was power.

"You're frowning." Luke's voice cut into her thought parade. "What's going on?"

How did he do that, break into her thoughts? "Nothing. Just relaxing my face before M demands I smile."

Luke stiffened as a second wave rocked the boat. "Could she have hired a flakier photographer?"

Above them on the walkway, M swept his hands in the air as if trying to rearrange light, his minions trailing after him, whispering his brilliance.

Raul stuck a megaphone to his lips. "Chefs, take up the oars and pretend to row." The assistant air-rowed as if Joy and Luke might be new to words like *oar* and *pretend*.

"This is the stupidest thing I have ever done," Luke growled, sitting forward, his legs spread, slowly dipping his oar in the air above the water.

Joy put a bit of pretend muscle into her stroke. "Comedy is part of our show too. Let loose. Have fun."

"This is not comedy. This is humiliation."

Garth and Reba drifted by in their own boat, with cameras rolling. Joy waved. Luke ducked behind his oar. "If my friends see this, I'll never be able to show my face in a Manhattan restaurant again."

M was shimmying and waving again. Raul megaphoned, "M wants you to stand and fight with the oars like they're swords."

"What? No." Luke jumped up too fast, holding his oar over his head, tipping his balance stern side. "Allison, come on."

"Stop, Luke." Joy skimmed the water with her oar and splashed him. "You're ruining M's aura."

M flailed his arms with abandon, and Raul interpreted through the megaphone. "What are you doing? You're poisoning the karma after M so graciously picked out all the negativity."

"I told you."

"If I had any karma, M would be suffocating on mine."

"Luke, Joy!" Allison had a megaphone? Joy wanted one. "Do as M says. We want to accent the two of you, your personalities, your conflict but common essence."

"And what about my personality is accented by a fake oar fight with Joy?"

M ducked behind the camera. "Hurry, M is losing the right light," Raul called.

"Just the light? Not his last marble? Can we at least get real swords?"

"Oar up, Redmond." Joy rode her boat like balancing on a seesaw. "Spar with me."

"I'd like to spar with someone. But not you." He winked, his first show of merriment.

Steady, girl. He's a friend. A colleague. And a potentially huge career risk. "Oar up." Wall up.

"I've done a lot of dumb things in my day," Luke muttered, swinging at Joy, struggling to stay balanced. "But this is just insane."

"Give yourselves to it," Raul beckoned. "Let the inner conflict and energy out, people."

"En garde." Joy thrust and parried.

The clack of wood vibrated across the water. Then another. Luke was swinging, fighting. His skiff swayed and dipped. Was he forgetting he stood on the water?

"Luke?"

His oar smashed hers with an air-splitting crack. Joy's oar broke from her hand and spiraled into the air. On instinct, she lunged for the paddle, banging her shin against the rim of the skiff, and plunged headfirst into the river, disappearing beneath the surface.

"Joy?" Luke hung over the side of his boat, parting the water with his hands until she surfaced. "Are you okay?" He offered her his hand.

"It's okay. Not the first time I've gone overboard." With a glint in her heart, Joy slipped her hand into his and with a quick, firm tug, propelled him over her head into the river. He parted the waters with a satisfying splash, surfacing after a long moment, sputtering, shaking the water from his hair.

"What's the matter with you?" he groused, shaking the water from his face as he reached up to cup his hands on Joy's head, propelling her under.

Gripping his wrists, she pulled herself to the surface, breaking into the warm midmorning air, gasping and laughing. "You think you can?"

His eyes locked with hers as his hands moved down her back. *Oh Luke, don't . . . don't kiss me.* She slipped her hands up his arms to his shoulders. Beneath the water she trembled.

"Joy?"

"Luke?" In an instant, she popped her hands onto his head and buried him under the water. When he surfaced—his head back, his mouth wide-open, gasping for air—a high and tight singsong, almost shrill voice filled the air. It was M speaking.

"Brilliant, yes. Finally, brilliant!"

"All right, folks, this is the first teaser for TruReality." Ryan called the set to order from his director's booth. "Joy, we're rolling, so start whenever you're ready."

"Hey, friends, I'm Joy Ballard, host of *Dining with Joy*. This fall, spend your Thursday nights with me beginning September twenty-fourth. We're going to have a blast entertaining you while making you yearn for smell-o-vision with our delectable recipes. Chef Luke Redmond joins me as cohost this season." He entered stage right, stopping just behind her right shoulder. "We'd love to hear from you. Visit us at DiningwithJoy.com. Find out all the ways you, our viewers and friends, can be a part of turning *Dining with Joy* into TruReality."

"Cut," Allison called over the intercom. "You forgot to say, 'It's true and it's reality.' "

"I said we're turning foodie television into TruReality." Joy searched for Allison beyond the spotlight. "What more do the folks need to hear?"

"Right, I'm with you, Joy, but TruReality's brand is for all hosts or commercial bites to say, 'It's true and it's reality.' "

Emphasis on *reality*.

"Okay, here we go . . ." *Chin up, shoulders back, breathe in, breathe out, gaze into the camera. Smile.* "It's true and it's reality." Joy punched the air with an ah-shucks fist.

"Cut. Perfect. That's my Joy."

"We love everything we've seen so far, Allison. Wild Woman Productions and *Dining with Joy* are exceeding our expectations."

"Glad to hear it, Dan." Allison reclined back in her desk chair, the bright July heat pressing against her window, warming the ends of her hair. "We're real pleased with what we've been able to accomplish."

"Kudos on *The Bette Hudson Show* too, Allison. She's five city blocks from us and we can't get half our hosts scheduled on her show."

"Then we need to talk, Dan. Bette and I go way back. I'll call in a few favors."

"I like how you roll." Dan Greene's laugh vibrated over the speakerphone. "We've decided sixteen shows is not enough. Joy's a real eye-pleaser—charming, engaging, and downright funny. We want to amend your contract for twenty shows. Can you do it?"

"Try and stop me."

"Allison, this is Mark Feinberg." She perked up. Head of sales. First time he'd been in on the call. "Our team has secured spots on *Dining with Joy* for all our key national accounts. Joy's winning everyone over with her strong fan base and previous sales numbers. People are catching the vision for breakout foodie television."

This was a good day. Better than good. Allison spun her chair around and glanced out the window. In a million years, she'd never imagined she'd find paradise in a small coastal town like Beaufort.

"We've set up test audiences in New York, Sacramento, Dallas, St. Louis, Seattle, Miami, and Atlanta. We want the first five shows in the can, ready for distribution by the end of August. Will you be ready?"

"I'm heading into the editing room as soon as we hang up to review the first three shows." Allison's confidence dimmed as she thought of her chore after this call. She'd rather stay focused on all the good news. But she had to face her biggest obstacle. Luke still came off a bit too stiff.

"We want you up for the screenings, then for a day of meetings about midseason replacements."

The word *midseason* buoyed her confidence. "I have a few shows in the works you might like, Dan. I'll have my assistant call your office." Allison doodled on a notepad. *Hire assistant.*

Allison exited her office, straining to gather her focus, put on her producer hat, and see what they had for the first three shows. But today's news called for a little bit of celebration.

So she crossed the studio, past the conference table, to Joy's office, entered without knocking, grabbed the girl's face, and kissed her forehead.

"You are pure magic."

"I take it the call went well." Joy rocked back in her chair, smiling, then sobered. "I want a raise."

"If this morning's call was any indication of the season we're going to have, you'll not only get a raise but a big one. And a bonus. The whole crew too." Allison folded into the seat next to Joy's desk. "TruReality loves us. Loves you."

"And Luke?"

"I've not shown them much. I'm about to review Ryan's edits of the first three shows." Allison rose to go. "The first five go to test-market in two weeks."

"Allison, did you read my e-mail? About bit ideas?"

She paused at the door. "Didn't I respond? I love your ideas, but let's get through the first half of taping. TruReality is talking about extending our season by four shows so we have plenty of time to introduce new segments." She twisted open the door. "I'm hiring an assistant and a staff writer too."

Joy stood, her expression pale. "But I do all the writing, Allison?"

"Once we hit the airways, you're not going to have time to do all the writing." Allison let the door close. "Joy, I like to do things my way. I'm a bit of a control freak. And hiring a staff writer is my way."

"I see." Joy came around her desk, her posture indicating she had something to say. "Then I'll speak my mind, let you know what I want." Allison regretted singing her praises too loud, too soon. Had she created a diva? "Luke should do more of the cooking segments, free me up to do more writing and producing, developing comedy and viewer segments. I want to get out more, among the people. The Joywalking segment could be as popular as Stupid Cooking Tricks. Send me out to ask people about cooking, spices, recipes, their favorite restaurant or family dinner."

"I love it." And she did. But not now. Not today. "But, Joy, I'm not replacing you for Luke. Don't worry."

"Worried?" She *pffbbtt*ed and flapped the air with her hand. "No, no, just started thinking how we could use Luke more, play to each other's strengths."

"You're the backbone of the show. Luke is still two-dimensional, and without you, I fear he'd be unbearable to watch. You make him funny. Real. You're not going to do less or turn segments of the show over to your cohost; you're going to do more." Allison regarded Joy, wondering for the first time if Joy truly understood what was about to happen. "Once *The Bette Hudson Show* airs, it'll be hair on fire, flying at Mach 10. That's why I'm hiring a writer. Shoot, I should hire two. Note to self."

"Mach 10?" Joy relaxed against her desk, arms and ankles folded, her laugh withering. "Let's pray I don't pass out."

"Good thing I know CPR." What caused the shadow on Joy's face? It seemed to cloud her excitement. Insecurity? Disbelief? Allison formed words to drill deeper, dig up the issue that troubled Joy, but she decided to leave it. Over the years, she'd learned show talent, and actors who struggled for their own answers lasted longer,

140

made better cast members. "I'll be in the editing room if you care to join me."

Allison grabbed a cup of coffee along the way and settled in the ten-by-ten editing room, reached for the clipboard, and pressed Play for the edited version of DWJ S4E1.

Joy came on screen and Allison instantly smiled, the warmth of success swirling around her heart, flowing over her mind. Poor Duncan. He had a gem like Joy and never polished her to shine her true potential. And Luke. Despite being cardboard now, he was the sexiest chef on television.

For the first two minutes and thirteen seconds, it was all Joy. Allison made no marks or comments on her clipboard. When Luke appeared, his cowboy smile sent a tingle to her toes.

Then he started talking and all the light faded from her heart.

# Twelve

"Tin man, what are we making today?" Joy hip-checked Luke as he walked onto the set.

"We are making Ami's lasagna." Under the lights, his perspiration production doubled. Someone shoot him, please. Put him out of his misery. His early days in Hell's Kitchen had been more successful. He hated watching himself fail. Like his last year of high school.

"This was your mother's recipe, right?" Joy emphasized every word, cuing him.

"Sure was, Joy."

She laughed a merry little laugh, angling toward the camera. "Sure was . . . don't you love him?" She wrapped him in a side hug, shaking him gently. "Once a cowboy, always a cowboy."

"Yeah, you can take the cowboy out of Oklahoma, but—" What was his line? Luke peeked at the teleprompter as he reached for the ground beef. Perspiration thickened along the base of his neck. Sometimes when he glanced up, the letters shimmied and transposed.

He'd come in determined to loosen up for the taping of show four, have fun. He knew the kitchen, he knew cooking. He'd been a top prankster in his Hell's Kitchen days.

Memorizing the script boosted his confidence,

some. He'd spent every evening this week reciting the script in front of the bathroom mirror, feigning laughs, mocking up spontaneous dialog. But the moment the camera light clicked on, words blurred, letters flip-flopped.

When he stood next to Joy, it was deep-freeze.

Then during the production meeting, Allison, loud and irritated, announced they were reshooting Luke's segments of shows one, two, and three today and tomorrow instead of moving on.

"We'll just have to eat the cost."

Every bit of good news she shared after that was lost on him. Something about national advertising accounts and additional shows. Sure, why not? Extend his humiliation.

"So, Luke, what are we going to do first?" Joy nudged his ribs with her elbow.

You're in your own kitchen, your own kitchen . . . "First, we sauté the onions and garlic." Luke put a fire under a skillet and added olive oil. "We don't need a lot of oil, because the onions will sweat and add moisture to the pan. But the oil adds a great flavor."

Today they worked without a re-shoot script. Allison believed if the cameras rolled, capturing Luke working without a script, he'd come across more relaxed. Instead, he felt out of sync, his instructions monotone in his ears. And how could he look natural when he had to keep checking with Joy for cues?

"This was the first recipe you ever made, isn't it?"

"Sure was."

"Sure was?" Joy dashed over to the heart chimes hanging over the sink and put them in motion with a wave of her fingers. The bright blue, red, and pink ceramic pieces rang through the kitchen station. "How about I ring the chimes every time Luke says 'sure was'?" The crew's cheer linked with her soft, merry laugh. Next to him again at the stove, Joy ran her hand gently down his back. *I'm with you here.*

"Now you make this with a béchamel sauce. Tell our friends at home why you want to do this."

"Béchamel is just a roux with milk. It makes a nice, thick base."

"'A roux with milk,' he says." Joy hip-butted him. "Luke, break it down for our frat bros. A *what* with milk?"

"Flour, butter, and milk." He set the saucepan on the back burner, feeling a bit more like himself. "I'm going to get the ground beef and add it to our onions and garlic. Our lovely onions are nice and clear." He motioned to the flour and butter. "Why don't you get started on the roux, Joy?"

"Why don't *you* get started on the roux?" She wore a funny expression. What was she doing?

"Yeah, why don't *you* get started on the roux?"

"I'd rather make the béchamel." Joy moved the

pan from the right back burner to the left. "I love that word, don't you? Béchamel, béchamel."

"Then you get the *béchamel* going, and I'll brown the meat." The aroma of onions and garlic coated his nerves like a warm balm.

"So for the frat boys at home, Luke, go over the béchamel recipe again. They might need to go shopping."

"I doubt it. Most guys, single or frat, have butter, milk, and flour lying around. Béchamel is simply five tablespoons of butter, four tablespoons of all-purpose flour, four cups of warm milk, two teaspoons of salt, and half a teaspoon of nutmeg."

"Nutmeg? How's that simple? Nutmeg is a once-a-year, Christmas spice. Show of hands, how many single men have nutmeg at home?" Joy strolled among the crew with her hand in the air. Reba followed with the remote camera on her shoulder.

"Fine, fine." Luke laughed, shaking his head. "Use cinnamon or ginger, whatever you have lying around that resembles nutmeg."

"Show of hands . . . cinnamon or ginger. Garth? You have . . . what . . . cinnamon? Cinnamon it is." Joy dashed back to the kitchen and moved the saucepan back to the right burner. "Know what we need? A béchamel song. Ryan?"

A blues beat hit Luke in his belly. A bass and drum rhythm. Joy slid up next to him, swaying, snapping her fingers.

"Five t'blespoons butter." Joy sang to the melody of "Bad to the Bone." The studio lights faded from bright white to cabaret gold.

"Ba-da-da-da-dump." The crew played the part of the chorus, snapping and swaying in time with Joy.

"Add your milk and your flour." Trombones and trumpets came in, boosting the melody.

"Ba-da-da-da-dump."

"And stir them together." Joy snap-stepped, jigged, and twirled her way around the studio.

"Ba-da-da-da-dump."

As an accent, the smell of browning meat rose from the skillet and mingled with the music and the lights. Luke stirred, smiling, freeing his thoughts from the tension of taping, grateful for Joy's showmanship. Over his head, one of the cameras eased down for a tight shot of his work.

"Cinnamon . . . ," Joy sang loud and strong, head back, arms wide.

"Ba-da-da-da-dump."

She promenaded toward Luke, hiding behind his back, snapping, tapping, then peeking around him on the downbeat.

"Cinn-a-mon."

"Ba-da-da-da-dump."

"Bé-cha-mel." She fluttered her hands out to her sides like the end of a jazz routine. What's that move called? Jazz hands? "Bé-cha-mel!"

"Cut." Ryan intercomed, his voice echoing in the silent chambers of the studio.

Then the crew burst out, Joy walked among them, slapping high-fives, reliving her song and snap-step move. Allison approached the stove as Luke stirred the meat. Sharon swooped in from the prep kitchen with a simmering pan of thick, white béchamel.

"Perfect, Luke. You're relaxing. Let the chemistry between you two do its thing, okay?"

"She makes it easy."

"And we're taking it to the bank. Now have fun."

"Luke, Joy, we're back in thirty seconds," Ryan directed. "Pick up with adding the béchamel to the meat and walk the viewers through the recipe. Sharon, is the baked lasagna camera-ready? Make sure the noodles are Vaselined well this time. Nice song, Joy."

Luke peered at her as she stood for a makeup retouch. She could've left him hanging, watched him timber flat on his face and by this time next week have her show back.

Luke would be at the Frogmore Café asking Andy for more hours. Or calling Red for a loan. As if he didn't owe the man enough already.

As of today, he knew what he had to do. Learn to love the camera. This show was his future, his way back to the world he loved. And he'd be darned if he'd ride there on Joy's coattails.

"Thank you," he said low, when she returned to the set, bubbling underneath from her routine.

"But you won't have to do that for me again. I'm going to get this down, Joy."

"Don't worry about it, cowboy." She hip-checked him and reached for a bit of beef. "Who knows, you might be able to do the same for me sometime."

Awake at midnight, Joy kicked off her covers. Her corner room was always hot around this time in August. No matter how low Mama ran the air.

Kicking free from her sheet, Joy crossed the creaking hardwood to the rolltop desk she'd inherited from her granny, pausing at the window. The moon's glow lit a path from the porch to the black edge of the creek, a pearly runner over Mama's textured lawn.

Since going to Common Ground with Luke, Joy struggled to define her passions. At twenty-nine, she didn't know what she wanted to be or how long she had before it was too late. *Oh, we're sorry, you've hit thirty . . . tick, tock, the game is locked . . . cooking show host the rest of your life.*

She'd be a cooking show host the rest of her life if she believed it was what she was really called to do.

What was the will of the One who sent her? Who created her. *God, show me Your will.*

Tugging open the bottom desk drawer, she peered at the deserted notebooks and journals. There could be worse fates than hosting *Dining with Joy.* She supposed she could just quit the show and be done with the charade, but the infernal question, "Then what?" rattled around her soul. Editing? Writing? How could she get those doors to swing open like the hosting door?

The truth was, she liked hosting. And last season she'd discovered her flair for producing. She liked being behind-the-scenes without the spotlight of the lie blaring down on her. Producing made an honest woman out of her.

Joy slipped one of the journals from the drawer and thumbed through the pages. It was from the year she took over the show.

Joy flipped through another journal. The entries were from the summer she attempted a novel, asking Heath McCord stealth questions at Luther's one night until he finally said, "What's going on, Joy?"

Eric McAllister wanted a wife. Yet between his friends, doting sisters, and a career in law, he didn't know he wanted a wife. Or even needed a wife in his rather full, complete days. That is, until he met Jane Darling, a striking woman with sapphire eyes and hair the color of honey.

Joy slammed the book shut. Drivel. A sad attempt at a Jane Austen knock-off. She reached for the next book, a journal with a thin leather tie. Joy fanned the pages, stopping near the end, where she'd written a verse and drawn copious circles around it.

"My food is to do the will of Him who sent Me."
John 4:34

"Aunt Joy?" Annie-Rae stood in the doorway, small and pale in the moon's light.

"What are you doing up?" Joy hugged the journal to her chest and crawled back in bed, patting the sheets as an invitation to Annie. "Bad dreams again?"

The girl burrowed under the covers. "Lyric yelled at me when I tried to sleep in her bed."

"Don't mind her. She's mad at the world right now." Joy tucked the covers around Annie-Rae's narrow shoulders and curled up next to her. "Hey, Annie, does Siri's brother like Lyric?"

"Parker. *Blech*. Lyric likes him."

"But does he like her?" Joy stretched her legs under the sheet, tucking her notebook under her pillow.

"Not if he's smart."

Joy laughed. "So, tell me, what was this dream of yours? Maybe it's not so scary."

"I can't remember." Annie-Rae yawned. "Dark stuff."

"Now that is a scary dream." Asleep or awake. "Want to sing a song?"

"Like what?" Annie-Rae snuggled her backside into Joy's hip. "I like 'Jesus Loves Me.'"

"Always a crowd-pleaser. You start."

Annie's sweet, high voice invoked instant peace.

Jesus loves me, this I know
for the Bible tells me so.

Joy drank in the words, sipped on the melody. Why did she keep forgetting this? Jesus loved her. At the end of it all, wasn't His love enough?

Saturday afternoon, as Luke seared a couple of steaks on the grill, Andy dropped a tub of fish on the prep counter and took up his filet knife.

"How's the show treating you? Customers are always asking after you round here."

"The show's good, I think. Still learning, feeling dull and stupid."

"Next to Joy, anyone would feel dull and stupid. The girl sure does shine, don't she?" Wrapped in a back brace, Andy tossed a cleaned catfish into a second tub. Luke had learned to fish along the shores of Brock and Lightning Creek with some of the best fishermen in central Oklahoma. But he'd never seen anyone clean and prep a fish as fast as Andy.

"Like the north star. Coming in here Saturday is my therapy. Reminds me I'm competent at something."

"The kitchen gets under your skin, don't it? Something always going on. Knowing we feed folks and make them smile with the dishes we cook up." Andy's baritone chuckle rumbled through his gallon-drum chest. "Well, Luke, ain't seen you in church since you started the show."

"I've been spending the last few Sundays preparing for Monday. Takes me awhile to get the script down. I work on my recipe, prep it in Miss Jeanne's kitchen. But I'll be back this week." Luke checked the order ticket for the temperature of the steak. Medium rare. "When I came down here, hired on with you, I promised myself I'd keep God first in my life. Why are good intentions so hard to keep?"

"Our spirits are willing but our flesh is weak, according to Jesus. We need to fight the good fight. Be vigilant. Become warriors. Listen to what the Spirit is saying." Andy tossed aside the tub, empty, a dozen filets cleaned and ready for his marinade.

"I'll be there Sunday, Andy." Luke pulled the steaks to let them rest. "I hear what you're telling me." For his first seven years in the city, Luke rode the long black train of ambition, living for himself, working to get ahead. But now that he had a chance to start over, he wanted to live differently. Change his priorities. "Tell you what, Andy." Luke grinned over his shoulder at his boss. "I'll be at church on Sunday, but when are you going to give me the secret to your marinade?"

Andy tossed another fish into the tub. "You're going to have to be in church a lot of Sundays before I give you my marinade secrets."

He soaked the filets in a dark, oily, aromatic sauce. Luke guessed he used teriyaki and

Worcestershire, ginger, and garlic, but there was a scent he didn't recognize. Yet.

"Well, now that you've been on the show a few weeks, Luke, have you figured her out yet?"

"Joy? Some." Beautiful and sexy, with a subtle vulnerability that made a man want to wrap her in his arms. But she was also self-assured, like she could knock that same man down a few pegs if need be. Luke stirred a handful of shiitake mushrooms in a skillet of melted butter and sizzling garlic.

"Mercy Bea said you fell for her in about sixty seconds."

"Mercy Bea likes to tell stories." Two more tickets came to the window. Luke turned to Russell, working prep. "Russ, two pot roast casseroles."

"But you don't know?" Andy rinsed his knife, then picked up another catfish. "About Joy?"

"Know what?" Luke pulled the steaks from the grill.

"Russell, he don't know." Andy sliced with the knife and added the fish to the tub.

"Know what?" Luke repeated siding the meat with fried green beans, mashed potatoes, and mushrooms.

"You *must* be in love," Andy said as he worked on another filet.

"Love? Come on, there's no love in this equation. My eyes are wide-open."

153

"Brother, look here at me." Andy motioned to his big brown eyes. "How long you been on the show? Three, four weeks?"

"Four."

"This show where you cook food?"

"Yeah, we cook food." What was his point?

"You're in love." Andy's declaration drifted through the kitchen. "No other reason. Looks like Mercy Bea's not the only storyteller round here. Russell, can you believe he don't know?"

"Serious?" Russell turned from the convection oven. "Luke, you really don't know?"

"Know what? And can I ask how you two know this secret?"

"Joy did a stint right here in this kitchen."

"She worked at the Frogmore? As a cook?" Luke set the steak plates under the heat lamps. "Table nine up."

"She worked here, yes." Andy tossed two more catfish in with the others. "But not as a cook." He glared over his shoulder at Luke.

"Okay, then what do I need to know?" Luke tossed the sauté pan into the sink. "She was married? She *is* married? She used to be a man?"

Andy's gorilla-size laugh consumed him. Russell burst through the screen door, snorting, gasping.

"Is that it? She used to be a man?" How did he get in on this joke? He'd kissed her . . . him. Her. Yes, definitely a her.

Mercy Bea appeared at the window. "Luke, sugar, someone's here to see you."

"Mercy, is there something about Joy I need to know?" He motioned toward the snickering Andy and Russell.

Mercy's expression soured. "Knock if off, you two boll weevils. Joy's our friend. Let Luke find out what he needs to on his own."

"Why do I feel like I have a big KICK ME sign stuck to my back?" Luke paused at the swinging doors.

"Because you're paranoid. Hush up, Andy and Russell." Mercy Bea escorted Luke through the doors. "Go on, you got company."

The café was quiet except for the hushed conversation of a few tanned tourists. Luke scanned the tables for his visitor, holding up when he spotted the visitor in the back booth. Red.

"What brings you here?" Luke slid into the booth across from his lean and wiry father, leathered from decades in the Oklahoma wind and sun.

"Don't you serve a man a cup of coffee in this place?"

"We do." Luke got Mercy's attention. "Coffee, please. Black and hot."

"Seems like a nice place."

"It is. Red, did you drive all the way here?" Red rarely traveled. Never been on a plane. Never driven west of Colorado, south of Texas, east of Arkansas.

"Well, I didn't walk." Red nodded at Mercy Bea when she set down his coffee with a bowl of creamers and a basket of Bubba's buttery biscuits.

"Who's tending the ranch?"

"Sam and Nick." Red scooted his coffee forward after one sip. He had something on his mind.

"I guess it's been awhile since we've seen each other?"

"Two years and three months." Red unsnapped his shirt pocket and pulled a paper across the table with his sun-dried hand. "Got this in the mail though. A few days ago."

"Red, I—" The check. For a thousand dollars. "I want to pay you back."

"So you send me a thousand dollars? How about a phone call? An e-mail. I got online because you told me it was the best way to keep in touch."

"Yeah, when I ran Ami's."

"So now what's your excuse?"

Luke eased against the leatherette booth, regarding his dad. "You drove all the way from Oklahoma to bust my chops about not e-mailing? To challenge a measly check?" He flicked the paper across the table. "Take this. I'll pay more as I can."

"So suddenly you've come into riches?" Red fiddled with the check like he might tear it in two.

"I'm cohosting a cooking show on TV. *Dining with Joy*. Just got my first paycheck. I'll add to it each time, but I'm saving up to pay off my friend Linus too."

"You're on television now? Well, which network? I'd like to watch. CBS, ABC, NBC?"

"None of the above." Luke smiled. He missed Red's simplicity. His *own* simplicity. "The show's on a cable network called TruReality."

"So it's not going to be on CBS, ABC, or NBC?" In the café's soft gold light, Red looked old and tired, as if he'd wrangled down every one of his seventy-five years. Born twenty years into his parents' marriage, Luke had always considered Red an old man.

"No, we're not going to be on the old favorite networks. Take that thousand I sent you, go into town with Sam, and tell him to help you pick out a high-definition television, then call the cable company. They'll set you up. With the payback money, you'll afford it just fine. *Dining with Joy* will be on Thursday nights this fall. Eight o'clock. Seven central."

Red tucked the check back into his pocket. "A thousand dollars on entertainment. I got hands to pay and livestock to feed." He snapped his pocket closed. "The money I lent you was from your mother's egg money. Did right nice just letting it sit in the account. She'd have wanted me to help you, so I did."

"I gave Ami's my best shot, Red. The restaurant business is—"

"Like ranching. Good years chasing bad, barely hanging on from day to day."

"I'm not savvy with the business end." Luke pressed his thumb over a recent burn spot and took a clean, deep breath. "Things got behind . . . I was overwhelmed."

"You're a good chef, Son. I bet a good businessman can't make a fancy French dish like you."

"Can I freshen up your coffee?" Mercy Bea started to pour in Red's cup, but he'd only taken a sip. "How about a nice ham plate with a side of scalloped potatoes?"

"Guess I could sit for a bite." Red slid his John Deere cap from the tabletop to the seat. He lifted his cup to his lips. "Got any pie?"

Mercy Bea smiled with a long, thick-lashed wink. "Now you're talking."

"My place is about two blocks from here, Red. I'll take you over after supper."

"Naw, naw, Luke, can't impose." Red held his coffee cup steady at chin level. "I just came to see how you fared." He patted the table with scarred, worked fingers. "I knew I didn't raise a quitter."

"You drove halfway across the country to see how I fared?" Luke hated the crater opening in his heart, the ambiguous hole that was his relationship with Red. "You could've called."

"Calling ain't seeing you."

"Then you'll stay."

"If you got room." Red nodded. Once. "Guess I should see the sights while I'm here. Never seen the ocean."

"You can see it out my window every night." Luke leaned across the table. "Red, is everything else okay?"

"Sure." Red stuck out his chin, peering out the window. "Just tired from the drive."

"All right." Luke regarded him a moment before sliding out of the booth, the soft edge of Red's emotions deflecting his bravado answer. "Have Mercy Bea bring you to the kitchen when you've finished supper. I'll take you on home."

# Thirteen

Sunday morning worship had just started when Joy slipped inside the sanctuary door, leading Lyric and Annie-Rae to seats in the back. The full room contained more than flesh and blood, more than beating human hearts.

Getting here with the girls about killed her last ounce of holiness. But the John verse she'd discovered the other night, the one that had been tacked up in her truck for months, maybe years, wedged its way into her soul.

What was the Father's will?

Glancing toward the front, Joy spotted Mama and her two best friends with their hands in the air, swaying in time with the music.

In Your presence, God, there is fullness of joy
I've got the joy, I've got the joy

Mama and her friends arrived early to teach Sunday school to the widows, divorcées, and never-marrieds. She'd given up urging Lyric and Annie-Rae out of bed in time to drive in with her. As long as Joy set the example of sleeping in, the battle was futile.

"Can we go?" Lyric crumpled forward in her chair.

"We just got here. Stand up. Sing." Joy hooked her hand under Lyric's elbow and pulled her to her feet.

"I don't know the song."

"Funny, you never say that when you're trying to follow along with Taylor Swift." Joy turned Lyric's face toward the screen behind the worship leader. "The words are up on the screen. This isn't about you, Lyric, it's about Jesus and what He deserves."

"And what do you know about Jesus?"

"Not as much as I should." Joy clapped to the rhythm, working on a resolve that didn't feel like she was negotiating with God. *If I pray three mornings a week, can You help me . . .*

Something, someone stood behind her. She peered around to see Luke, his gaze steady on her. She whipped back forward, closed her eyes, and tried to sing.

But she peeked around the thin veil of her hair to see if he was still there. He was, but he wasn't paying attention to her. His head was tipped back with his eyes closed, his hands raised in surrender. Tears swelled in her eyes. Luke seemed . . . captivated. Not just going through the motions like she did so often. And she envied him.

On her left, Annie-Rae's voice pierced the air with her clear song. Joy cupped her hand on the girl's shoulder and tried to find the river.

I've got the joy, I've got the joy

She reached down, fumbling for Lyric's hand, and intertwined their fingers. By the second verse,

Lyric curved in close and surrendered her cheek to Joy's shoulder.

In Your presence, God, there is fullness of joy

"My family is here." Mama hurried across Beaufort Community's green lawn as Joy exited the sanctuary with the girls. "What's wrong? Everything okay?" Mama clutched her old, peeling handbag to her chest. "It's Sawyer and Mindy, isn't it? Something happened to them."

Joy squeezed Annie-Rae's shoulders. "No, Mama, we came to worship."

"Well, good, good." Mama lowered her bag and shoved the wind from her curls.

Annie squirmed free to meet one of her friends. Lyric chatted with Siri and her brother, Parker, under the shade of a deep-rooted live oak.

"Beautiful day." Luke strolled toward Mama and Joy with an older, sun-kissed man. "This is my dad, Red Redmond. Red, this is Joy Ballard, my cohost. Boss, really. And her mother, Rosie."

"Nice to meet you." Red gripped his cowboy hat in his hand, thin wisps of his hair lifting in the breeze, revealing the same piercing blue eyes as his son.

"Same to you, Mr. Redmond." Joy took his rough and hardened palm in hers.

"Red, folks call me Red. Mr. Redmond was my father and, well, even at seventy-five, I ain't ready to tug on his boots." He settled his hat on his head.

162

His plaid shirt and stiff blue jeans looked new.

"No sir, you're your own man, I can see that." Mama slipped her arm through Red's. She had a way of just *knowing* folks. "Come to the house for lunch. I won't take no for an answer. Since our kids are hosting a show together, we're practically family."

"Mama," Joy called after her. "Don't force your will on Red and Luke. They might have other plans."

"No, no, we got no plans." Red lifted his hat as he glanced back at Luke. "Do we, Son? I'd love some home cooking."

"You okay with us coming over?" Luke asked Joy.

"Sure, why not?" So what if none of the Ballard women cooked? Joy called to Lyric and Annie-Rae, slowly following Mama and Red's trail.

"Think Annie-Rae could heat up some Chef Boyardee for us?" Luke laughed at his own suggestion.

Joy whirled around and stepped toward him. "What are you implying, Luke? Do you have something to say? Then say it."

"Whoa—" He backed up, hands surrendered. "I'm kidding, Joy. I figured after a hard week of work, you and Rosie wouldn't want to cook. I didn't mean anything by it."

Joy tucked her Bible under her arm, the noon sun hot on her skin. No, how could he? He didn't live inside her head, hear her thoughts, see her posing as someone she wasn't. She only imagined Luke saw right through her.

"Of course, I'm sorry, Luke." As she backed away, the air shifted the light behind Luke and the sights of the churchyard faded. The parade of summer dresses and shirts without ties blurred into the background, and the sea blue of Luke's eyes soaked her senses.

"Joy, did you hear me?" Luke snapped his fingers beside her ear.

"W–what?" She angled away and squinted down at her sandals. "Yeah, yeah, Chef Boyardee."

"No, I asked if you had a grill. I could run by Publix and—"

"A grill? Yes, charcoal, in the shed." Perfect. "Mama and I can haul out the picnic table, set it under the trees. It's nice with the breeze off the creek. When I was little, we were always picnicking. Weekend in and weekend out."

"Are you okay?" Luke brushed her hair away from her face. "You look pretty today."

"So do you."

His laugh was becoming one of her favorite sounds. "Steak or burgers?"

"Burgers. Hot dogs. Nothing fancy, Luke."

"Side dishes? Any preference?"

Red returned from escorting Mama to her truck and stood alongside Luke.

"Coleslaw, potato salad." Joy shrugged as she listed her favorites. "Cheetos."

"I'll pick up some peppers, onions, and mushrooms. We can cook them on the grill in tinfoil. And I have a great seasoning for wedge potatoes . . . Do you have chili powder at home?"

"Chili powder? Sure. I mean, who doesn't?" Joy lifted her wallet from her purse. "Luke, let me give you money. You're invited to our house for lunch."

"Forget it. Red practically invited himself. Meet you at your house in an hour or so."

Red tipped his hat at Joy.

Once the Spit Fire exited the parking lot, Red in the passenger seat holding on to his hat, Joy whistled and called for the girls and sprinted for the truck. Once they were in the cab and buckled up, she shot out of the church parking lot.

"Where are we going?" Lyric asked, hand jutting out to hang onto the dash.

"Bi-Lo." It was the opposite direction of Publix. "Lyric, get Granny on the phone. Annie-Rae, take the bulletin out of my Bible and start a list on the back. Write at the top 'tinfoil and chili powder.' "

Lunch under the canopy of swinging Spanish moss went in Luke's memory book as a perfect day, despite the fact that Red had insisted on manning the grill ("Give you young cook-show hosts a break."), firing the meat until it was cowhide tough.

Luke covered the well-done burgers with a blue cheese sauce stirred together in Rosie's kitchen. By the time Lyric begged off to be with her friends and Annie-Rae went inside to read, the table had been picked clean.

"Rosie, I've been looking at them trees along the creek." Red motioned toward the back of the yard, wielding a toothpick between his teeth. "You need to trim them back or they're going to take over."

"Now, Red, there is nothing wrong with those trees." Rosie led him away, pointing here, then there, with arching, sweeping gestures.

"If she listens to him, she'll have the whole yard torn up by nightfall." Luke slipped onto the table next to Joy, his feet flat on the wooden bench seat.

"I don't know . . . Mama's the yard queen around here." Joy peered up at him. "Your sauce saved the day. Thank you."

"I'd planned to make it anyway. Didn't know we'd need it so desperately."

"Thanks for letting Annie-Rae help. She loves the kitchen." Joy propped her arms on her thighs, the ends of her ponytail dusting her shoulders.

"So what's the deal with her parents being in Las Vegas?" While she stirred the sauce for him, Annie-Rae had chatted about her daddy and mama getting "good jobs" in Las Vegas and buying a house.

"My brother, Sawyer, and his wife, Mindy, married in college, had Lyric before they graduated, and by the time Annie-Rae came along five and a half years later, Mindy'd had enough. She was a trained dancer and tried to find an outlet with troupes in Charleston and Savannah, but last year she hung up motherhood and headed to Vegas. My brother followed her a few months later."

"Your nieces mean a lot to you, don't they?" Luke etched the moment in his mind when Joy didn't seem so guarded, and later, when all was quiet, he'd write the impression to his heart.

"We're all they have. They're family. My girls." Joy shifted back, propping her hands on the table behind her, crossing her legs and letting her flip-flop dangle from her toes. "Next to hosting the show, they are my life."

Oh boy. Luke exhaled as he gazed toward the creek, squinting toward the refracted light, trying to burn away the soft silhouette of her tanned, sculpted legs lingering in his mind. *Think of other things, like fishing, worms. Baseball. Burnt meat. His father, her mother talking twenty yards away. Cold, snowy winters. The cold walk-in at the Frogmore.*

". . . what's crazy is Mindy ended up getting a dancing gig in a show, which led to my brother being hired on as the customer service manager for the hotel."

"That's good, right?"

"For them. But, Luke, they don't write or call. They don't send money. And Lyric wears all the rejection right here." Joy patted her arm. "She's pretty bitter."

"And Annie?"

"She's the pleaser and peacemaker." Joy slid off the table and started collecting the ketchup and mustard, tucking the pickles and relish under her arm. "I think she gets what's going on somehow, in a deep, intangible way. She understands. It's a gift, I think."

"She's blessed. Say, I was thinking of a new recipe last night. An Italian sausage dish in a béchamel sauce. I think your frat boy fans would love it. Easy, rich, and tasty. You want to work it up and—"

"No, no," she tucked the pepper mill under her arm, "sounds like you have it under control. Go ahead. In fact, you can take one of my segments this week. You only had one—"

"It's really simple, Joy. We could do it together."

"I'm not a big Italian sausage fan." When she looked up at him, she smiled her television smile. "You can do a guys-to-guys recipe corner."

"Why don't you want to do it? The college men would much rather—"

"Because, Luke . . . what's the big deal? Your

idea. Your segment. I have plenty to do." She crammed a stack of napkins onto the load in her arms. "Do you want to cohost or not?"

"Sure, sure. I'll do it." What just happened here? The tone from the churchyard returned. Watching her, the breeze scented with rain, odd images and conversations from the past month started connecting.

The Water Festival cook-off . . . she'd left the work to him . . . her insistence about no competitions . . . a rider to her contract . . . Andy's baritone *Do you know about Joy?* . . . Ryan's quick, hard-edged "cut" fifteen seconds into Joy's cooking segments, then Sharon appearing with the finished sauce or cooked noodles or browned meat.

"The peppers and onions cooked up nice on the grill. That was a great idea." Joy started for the back porch. "You'd better get Red and head on out. It's late."

"Joy—"

The clap of the screen door reverberated across the yard and echoed over the creek.

 # Fourteen

On a Manhattan Tuesday morning, right in the heart of Broadway, Allison waited in Bette Hudson's office while her friend and mega talk show host greeted touring school children.

She relished the quiet moment to breathe out and assess the last ten days. They were a blur in her mind. Reshooting Luke's segments, then shooting the fourth show, editing with Ryan every evening and the weekend to get the shows ready for the test audience.

"Sorry, Allison." The dark-eyed, dark-skinned Bette breezed into her office and perched on the edge of her desk. "So, your girl is going to be on my show."

"And I'm grateful." Allison reached up to hug her old friend. "But don't think this makes us even. You still owe me a few."

"I don't know, Allison, I only book A-listers and a president or two, not up-and-coming cooking show hosts."

"And who convinced you to syndicate?" Allison enjoyed the camaraderie of the moment. Two old showbiz friends swapping stories.

"If that's the case, I'll owe you the rest of my life." Bette walked to the bookcase behind her desk and tugged on a red bound book. A refrigerator door opened. She took out two waters and handed one to Allison. "I saw the YouTube clip of your girl Joy kissing the chef. Thought my screen was going to combust. Can we have him on too? I'd love to have that chemistry on the show."

Allison twisted the cap off her water and took a long sip, considering the request. This was Bette Hudson asking, not some lowly talent coordinator or producer. "Luke's good, Bette, but he's not ready for your show. Joy can run with your A-listers and presidents, probably outshine half of them, but Luke's new to television. He's more chef than entertainer right now."

"So what? Any man who looks that good can come on the show and just sit by me." Bette patted the surface of her mahogany desk. "Maybe I'll fake a cook-off and see if he won't kiss me like he kissed Joy."

"She kissed him. That's what made it so sensational."

"Maybe she kissed him first, but he definitely kissed her back. I'm getting all hot and bothered just talking about it."

"He's not ready for prime time, Bette." Allison glared at her. *Hear what I'm saying to you.*

"Then we'll just play the YouTube clip." Bette swung around her desk and folded into the leather chair etched with a *B*. "Did I hear you're working a book deal too?"

"For a cookbook. This is my year. My twenty-five-year overnight success has arrived."

"Dan Greene giving you a hard time?"

"No, but he says you're giving him one. Won't put on any of his other reality hosts."

"Bring me more like Joy and I will."

Allison slipped a paper across the desk to Bette. "I'll fax one of these to your assistant, but I wanted you to see Joy's rider. Anything you see that doesn't work for you? She's hilarious and comedic, but skittish about a few things. Has a minor phobia."

"Only one? Allison, I have superstars on my show who think the world turns on their axis. We've booked superstitious athletes. The guests who want white walls with white furniture and white towels and white water, if you can believe it. A small request from your girl won't bother us a bit." Bette came around the desk to embrace her. "You know I'm glad to do this for you, friend. Your success means my success."

Allison kissed her fingertips. "From your lips to God's ears."

"See you in September."

Out of Bette's office, Allison hurried toward the elevators. She'd cut it close on her meeting with the publisher. But their office wasn't far and, depending on traffic, she'd arrive on time.

"Allison Wild."

She turned to see Wenda Divine catwalking

toward her. Allison pushed the Down elevator button.

"How are you? I'd forgotten your studio was in this building."

"How's it going on *Dining with Joy*?" Wenda glanced toward Bette's office.

"If it goes any better, I won't be able to stand it. We're on *The Bette Hudson Show* the afternoon before our premiere."

"Well, well, aren't you blessed?" Wenda tapped her foot in two-two time.

"I suppose we are." The elevator arrived with a *ping*. Allison stepped into the car. "Have a great season, Wenda."

"Allison." Wenda slammed her hand against the closing door. "I'm surprised you're carrying on the charade. Someone of your caliber usually demands more from their talent."

"What are you talking about?" Allison searched her eyes, scanned her expression. No wonder Joy refused to deal with her.

"Oh my gosh. Is she really that good?" Wenda folded her arms and had some kind of triumphant expression on her face. "Allison, Joy Ballard can't cook."

"Oh, now, Wenda, I would think someone of your caliber wouldn't stoop so low." The door closed and the elevator jerked, descending down, taking Allison away from Wenda's echoing cackle.

• • •

Monday morning Joy doodled with a number two pencil in the margin of her notepad as Allison recapped her trip to New York.

Across the table, Luke stirred, restless. During the week in the studio without Allison, they'd worked long hours to tape two more shows, keeping the air between them professional.

Ever since the picnic, Joy fought the urge to blurt out the truth. She'd even consulted Mama about it. She was tired of hiding, tired of turning cold every time Luke mentioned food, tired of suspecting him. Did he know? Was he trying to trap her?

If she had been reading about her predicament in a romance novel, she'd be tempted to scream at the heroine and toss the book across the room. *Just tell him, stupid girl!*

But her life wasn't a novel. Nor did her emotions comply with formulaic story structure. She had no author penning courage into her heart. No plot plan to show her it'd all work out in the end. If she told Luke, she'd be all but quitting. No, she had to play this out. Her way.

"Bette Hudson's excited to have you on the show, Joy. I sent your rider to her assistant and she was almost giddy. No live cooking competition? That's it? Some of their celebrity guests are pretty out-there with requests. Though I do think we should consider helping you work past that phobia. Luke, maybe you can work with Joy?"

"She can manage fine without me."

"I can." She shot him a fast glance. "And I'm not a celebrity with big demands, Allison. Give me a few more seasons and I'll celeb it up for y'all. Get a little dog, dress it in pink, carry it in a Louis Vuitton, and demand filet for dinner. For the dog, of course. For me, a lettuce salad, no dressing."

"Not our humble Joy," Sharon said, laughing.

Joy smiled at Sharon. The thirty-seven-year-old mother of two had been one of the voices of reason encouraging Joy to take her father's place when he died so suddenly. No one wanted the show to end.

Not even the dying Charles Ballard. *Do the show for me, Joy. Please.*

No, Joy couldn't tell Luke. She'd have to work this one day, one show, one segment at a time.

"But here's the biggest news." Allison held a small bundle of papers to her chest, looking proud and pleased. "This season gets better and better. We're publishing a cookbook." She held out two folders to Joy and Luke. "Your contracts."

"Luke?" Sharon surged forward, checking Allison's folder. "How'd he get in on this deal? He's only been on the show five weeks. The *Dining with Joy* recipes are mine . . . and . . . and Joy's . . . and her father's."

"Actually, they belong to the show," Allison said. "I know this is last minute, but the publisher and Wild Woman really want to take advantage of all the promo TruReality is launching for the show, so Joy, Luke, I need you to get to work right away on the cookbook. We go to press mid-October, to be in stores by Christmas."

Sharon sliced the air with a knifing glance toward Joy. *Hold it together, Sharon.* Joy cleared her throat. "This is great, Allison, but I really think Sharon should work on the cookbook with me. She's right, the show's recipes were developed before Luke joined the show. And we've only done four of his recipes."

So far, he'd not even picked up the contract Allison shuffled over to him. Ryan checked with him visually, Luke nodded, and Ryan picked up the contract.

"Luke, are you good with the extra time to work on a cookbook? Are you still working at the Frogmore on Saturdays? You might need the weekends to test recipes."

"I think Joy's right." He shifted in his chair and shoved his coffee mug to the center of the table. "The recipes need to come from previous shows. I'm too new. I'll contribute two of the four I've already done."

"What? And leave my backside open for litigation? No, no, you're part of the package, Luke. The publisher and TruReality want your name on the book. You'll have almost fifteen recipes by season's end. Go ahead and figure out what you want to do—shoot, even if we don't use them on the show, they'll be great for the book. Something new for the buyer. Joy, you can pull a few oldies from your dad. You can have Sharon help with that—"

"Oh goody. I get to help." Sharon angled over the table with an exaggerated posture, searched among the papers, coffee cups, and donut napkins. "Hmm, I don't see my contract."

"In my office, in the filing cabinet, in the folder that has your name on it, there's a contract that says you work for a salary plus bonus and that all recipes belong to the *Dining with Joy* show." Allison stood tall with her hands on her hips, the midmorning light wrapping around her shoulders. "Joy and Luke will be the names and faces of the show this fall, the ones who will sell the book." Allison bent to gather her notes and close her laptop. "The viewers don't know Sharon Jobe. We'll give you an inside byline if you want."

"Inside byline?" Sharon shot out of her chair, knocking it over. "I want a copyright." She fired a visual at Joy. "And a sixty-forty split on the royalties."

Allison's hazel eyes lit with her own firebreak. "I like confidence and boldness, Sharon, but you are out of line. This book deal is not on the table for negotiation. It's my show, my call. Joy is the show's star; Luke's the host and a noted Manhattan restaurateur."

"Noted? His place bombed. I'm the foodie around here, Allison." Sharon slapped her hand to her chest. "Me. I give us credibility."

"Is that right?" Allison picked up her phone, eyeing Sharon, challenging her. "So if I pick up my phone and call, oh, say, Wenda Divine, or the All Food Network, they'd know your name?"

"Those recipes are mine." Sharon trembled, shaking the hem of her bell sleeves.

"Let's just get to work, huh? Have a great show." Allison left the table, heading for her office.

Joy sat straight and stiff, her thoughts racing. *Don't do it, Sharon, don't do it.* She had to find a way around this before Sharon exploded the messy truth all over everyone.

Meanwhile, the rest of the crew slumped around the table, chins tucked to chests. Ryan scrolled through files on his phone. Garth stared at the waving summer leaves. And Reba collected the wadded napkins and scooped donut icing from the table.

"Traitors. All of you." Sharon headed for the studio door, crashed it open, and hammered down the stairs.

"Joy?" Ryan said, cutting a glance toward the stairs.

"I'll go get her. Give her a second to calm down." *And me time to think.* She could tell Allison she wouldn't do the cookbook without

Sharon, but grandstanding didn't win her any points with Allison. She'd just think Joy was caving to a temper tantrum.

Joy could cut a side deal with Sharon and give her half her royalties.

"Want to tell me what's going on here?" Allison came out of her office, glancing at the open studio door, and stopped beside Ryan's chair. "Sharon seems disproportionately upset."

"I think I'll go see how the food prep is coming along." Luke scooted away from the table, his heels resounding through the studio.

"She's had a long history with the show," Ryan said, his eyes on Joy. "We've not done a cookbook before, for various reasons, and finally talked about it last spring. Sharon expected to be a big part."

"She'll calm down." Joy tossed out her first pitch to include Sharon. "Allison, you need to include Sharon on this project."

"Why? Because she's upset? Joy, I need you to back me here. Maybe in the spring we can launch a second cookbook and include Sharon, but I'm not letting the show's first cookbook come off the press without my stars. The publisher expects big numbers." Allison shifted her stance. "Are we going to lose her? Is she going to steal our recipes?"

"I'll talk to her." Joy walked slow and methodical toward the door and stairs, her thoughts surfing possible solutions. "She loves the show, and even as mad as she is, stealing recipes would damage her own reputation more than hurt the show."

Joy half expected Sharon to be gone when she stepped out into the parking lot, but found her pacing beside her car, a cigarette dangling from her fingers. "Smoking? Really? It isn't worth it, Sharon."

"You listen to me." Sharon lunged at Joy. "For three years you and Duncan promised me a cookbook, that I'd get half the royalties, have my name and picture somewhere on the cover."

"Look around, Sharon, things have changed. Duncan isn't here, and he's the one who promised you, not me. You think I like this?"

"I have a contract. Those recipes are mine, Joy."

"Well, apparently Duncan didn't pass that one on to Allison. Just like he didn't tell her I can't cook. You know as well as I do, you can't copyright recipes."

Nose to nose. "Then tell her."

Joy stepped back. "Then we all lose. I have a plan . . . to move Luke into my cooking segments . . ."

"Just as I thought. Coward." Sharon flicked her cigarette to the pavement and ground it in with the ball of her foot. "Never thought you'd surrender your integrity to fame, Joy."

"Surrender my integrity? I stuck the white flag in my integrity a long time ago. For the show. For you, Ryan, and Duncan. For Daddy. Don't you see? This cookbook, *The Bette Hudson Show*, being on TruReality isn't about me. It's about all of us. Our show family. So what, I'm the face. If you take a minute to calm down, come back upstairs, Allison would probably talk to you about a spring book featuring you. I can ask her for a bonus for you. She'll feel a bit more generous if you're a team player." Joy paused, contemplating her offer. "I'll give you sixty-forty on my royalties."

"Oh my stars, how generous. I can't believe it." Sharon spun slowly, arms wide, facing the street. "Did you hear that, Beaufort? Our own Joy Ballard offered me, a poor show prep cook, forty percent of her cookbook money." Sharon shot Joy a steely glance. "No thanks. I don't want to be more indebted to you. And a team player? What a joke. A term invented by fat-cat CEOs to get their people to work harder for their own private wallets." Grit and pebbles crunched under Sharon's heels as she headed to her car. "Consider this my resignation."

"In the middle of taping?" A couple strolling past slowed, listening. Joy lowered her voice. "We have another two months of shows."

"Then it's a good thing you have Luke."

"Come on, don't do this, Sharon."

"Tell you what." Sharon paused before getting into her car. "I'll be in Monday to clear out my desk. If you get me on the cookbook deal by then, I'll stay, lips sealed. Otherwise, I'm gone. I have other options to consider."

"Other options? What other options?"

"See you Monday, Joy."

Joy crossed the dark studio toward the light burning under Allison's door and knocked softly.

"Come in." Allison glanced up as Joy entered and sat down. Her dark hair was pulled back in a messy, uneven ponytail as if she were ready for a long evening of work. "You're still worried about Sharon?"

Joy gripped her hands in her lap, sitting straight, feeling hollow. "Worried? No, but seeing more and more of her position."

"You understand why I'm doing it this way, right?" Allison rocked back in her chair and stuffed her pen in her hair.

"I do, but she doesn't." For a mountain of unexposed reasons. Joy exhaled, twisting her fingers together. It wasn't her integrity in the balance but her courage. "Allison, you need to include her as part of the cookbook project. She deserves it. Duncan promised her that when we published a *Dining with Joy* cookbook, it'd be hers."

"Hers? All of it? Aren't you generous? Now I see why Duncan never pursued the project. No one will buy a cookbook written by Sharon Jobe. It's marketing suicide."

"Yes, but the *Dining with Joy* cookbook by Joy Ballard and Sharon Jobe wouldn't be."

"There's no such thing as a Joy Ballard *and* Sharon Jobe as far as the viewers are concerned."

Joy rose from her chair. "But there is in here, in the studio. We all know it. Does everything have to be about marketing and the viewers?"

"That's odd coming from you, Joy. The one who pioneered this new way of involving viewers in the show's brand." Allison walked to the window and stood in the evening shadows. "Luke is who the viewers will connect with, and frankly, by the time the book comes out, everyone will be saying Joy Ballard *and Luke Redmond.* By the way, TruReality loved the retakes with Luke. You really brought him to life. Thank you."

"If you don't include Sharon, she'll resign, Allison."

"Then that's her call. I won't be threatened, Joy." Allison leaned against the windowsill. "Duncan may have had an agreement with her. You may promise her coauthorship, but I don't. I even checked her file, and there's nothing about a cookbook in there."

Joy headed for the door. "It doesn't seem fair."

"No, but she's the one shooting herself in the foot. I was open to doing another cookbook in the spring with her. But the first one? No."

Joy twisted open the door. She'd need to talk to Ryan before giving up the secret. He'd need to know his van payments were in jeopardy. "Thanks, Allison. But please, think about it. Will you?"

"I already have, Joy." Allison swung her chair aside to sit. "Joy, I just remembered. Guess who I ran into in New York?"

"If you tell me George Clooney—" Joy waited in the doorway.

"Don't I wish." Allison rocked back. "Your rival. Wenda Divine."

"Oh, please. Can we make her go away? Melt her with a bucket of water or something?"

"She had the gall to tell me you can't cook." Allison eyed Joy for long moment.

"Sh– she's—" Joy couldn't feel the knob beneath her hand.

"Crazy? No kidding. She'd better be careful or she's going to sabotage herself. I have a lot of friends in the industry. A few timely phone calls and she won't be able to pour Kool-Aid on a kiddie show."

Joy laughed, feigned and weak. "Ah, Wenda's all right, Allison. She's petty and competitive. Keeps it interesting for us. She's our Waldo. Never know where she's going to show up." Exhaling, Joy prepared for *the* question. *Come on, Allison, ask me. Follow up on Wenda's claim. Give me a reason to tell you.*

Instead, Allison laughed, swerving toward her laptop. "I like your attitude. I'm going to keep the

Waldo Wenda bit in mind. Maybe we can have fun with it next season."

Yeah, next season. " 'Night . . . Allison." Anything else?

" 'Night, Joy." She looked up, the bluish hue of the computer screen dancing across her cheek. "Don't worry about Sharon. Shake-ups always happen when a show changes hands. We can hire a new prep chef, Joy. There are hundreds of trained, qualified professionals waiting for a chance like this. She's not the only prep in the world."

No, but she is the only one with a secret. Crossing to her office, Joy fell against her door as she eased it closed.

Fifteen

When Joy arrived home at quarter after six, bone tired, the summer evening had just exhaled the heat of the day. Between Sharon, Allison, and putting up walls to keep Luke out, she felt beat up, emotionally suffocated.

She'd praised God today was Luke's day to demonstrate the recipe. Joy hid for a good portion of the afternoon in the prep kitchen, covering for Sharon with Reba's help. Even Ryan pitched in, helping to chop and stir.

Passing Mama's work truck, the doors painted boldly with BALLARD PAINT & BODY SHOP, Joy nearly collided with a mini mountain range of pine-scented mulch. "Mama?" She scanned the yard, the trees, and the porch, half expecting to see Mama come around the side of the house wearing camo and goggles, carrying a bazooka-size pesticide can. "Are you out here?"

Joy buried her big toe in the base of the mulch and stained it red. Up the front porch and through the unlocked door, Joy called, "Lyric? Annie-Rae?" She dumped her bags on the kitchen table and picked up the mail, glancing toward the ceiling, listening.

Silence. Even the house didn't settle and moan in greeting. Pizza boxes lay partway open on the counter.

"Yo, anyone home?" Joy swung open the pantry doors. But she wasn't hungry. Instead, she carried the burden of Sharon and Allison's response. And her guilt. Why didn't she tell her? Just . . . *blah* . . . there it is.

Joy dug in her bag for her phone and dialed Sharon, collapsing in a kitchen table chair, listening to voice mail.

"Sharon, hey, I talked to Allison. I'm so sorry, but she's doing this her way and since Duncan didn't pass along his—our—agreement with you, she's not going to budge. But she did say she wanted to do a book with you in the spring. So, please, stay. You're family. You know that we need you. I need you. This will work for good. I promise." She laughed, trying to sound casual, like she'd sounded a hundred times before while leaving voice mails. "See you Monday."

Joy ended the call with a stir of determination in her gut, knowing a foxhole confession wouldn't change the points of the book deal. Let Sharon air her beef with Duncan. He's the one who cut her out when he sold the show.

Joy jogged up the stairs, the moment of determination fading, wondering if she should just get in the truck and drive over to Sharon's and reason with her.

When she passed Annie's open door, she paused. "Well, there you are. Why didn't you answer when I called?" Joy dropped to the floor next to her niece and Annie's row of dolls. The fancy one in the middle was an American Girl collectible sent by Sawyer and Mindy a few months ago. "No friends over today?"

"Emma called, but I didn't feel like playing."

"Why not?" Joy brushed aside Annie-Rae's springy curls. She seemed sad. At nine, it was rare for her to play with dolls. She listened to music while reading or doing extra credit homework. "Which doll is this now?"

"Kirsten. She lived on the prairie. Like Laura Ingalls."

"She's very pretty." Joy peered toward the door. "Where's your sister?"

"Locked in her room, mad."

Fun, fun, fun, fun. "About?"

Annie-Rae shrugged.

"Did something happen at softball?"

"She didn't go to practice. She quit." Annie carried Kirsten to the closet and returned without her. When she sat back on the floor, she curled in the cradle of Joy's arm. "Can we rent a movie?"

"Sounds fun." Joy kissed her forehead. "Why don't you get online and pick one out while I see what's up with Lyric."

"It's your life." Annie-Rae hopped up and ran down the hall to Mama's room to use the "kids'" computer.

Joy stood in the shadowed hall and faced Lyric's door, feet apart, arms arching at her sides. She could take her. Lyric wasn't as clever as she imagined.

Joy knocked on the door, then pressed her back against the wall. Hadn't she been here before? Only she was on the other side of the door, with Mama outside hugging the wall, whispering to Jesus. Joy knocked again, feeling weary from the shackles of her debate with Sharon.

"Go away, Annie-Rae."

"It's not Annie." Joy clinched her hand at her side to keep from reaching for the knob. She preferred Lyric open the door freely.

"Aunt Joy?" Alarm boosted Lyric's pitched response.

"Yep, it's good ol' Aunt Joy. I wanted to be the tooth fairy, but—" A thud vibrated across the hardwood and under the door. She strained to listen. A heavy, tight whisper chased Lyric's frail one. "Lyric?" Joy rapped her knuckles against the door. "Open up."

The door careened open and Lyric stood in the low glow of evening light, out of breath. "What do you want?"

"Annie said you were mad. Why didn't you go to practice?" Joy crossed the threshold, scanned the room, and gasped. Except for the mound of covers in the corner, the room was bare.

"Lyric, where is your furniture?" Joy's chest expanded with the yell collecting in her lungs as she peered into the empty closet. All that remained of Lyric's clothes was a small pile on the floor. The girl had lost her mind.

"Didn't want it." Lyric tugged the thin strap of her top in place and tossed her loose hair over her shoulders.

"How can you not want your furniture and clothes? Granny moved out all of her furniture to make room for your things and set this up just like you wanted." Lyric's hair had the mussed look of being pressed against a pillow—or a mound of blankets on the floor.

"It's my stuff from *them*. I can do what I want with it." Lyric tumbled back onto the bedding and snatched one of her pillows into her arms.

"This is unbelievable. What did you do with your things?" Joy leaned out the window, expecting to see Lyric's clothes and dresser drawers strewn on the ground. But the only thing on the ground was Mama's manicured lawn soaking up the sunlight.

"I moved them to the garage."

"By yourself?" Joy stooped to meet her eye to eye, but Lyric concentrated on digging her toe into the carpet pile. "I heard whispering. Who was in here with you?" The branches of the hundred-year-old live oak made a perfect escape ladder.

"No one." Lyric buried her face in the bedding.

"Are you lying to me?"

Lyric looked up. "Do I look like I'm lying?"

Actually . . . "Lyric, just so we're clear, boys—specifically Parker Eaton—are never allowed in your room. In fact, he's not allowed on the second floor, ever. Do you hear me?"

"If Parker was here, don't you think Annie-Rae would be blabbing?" Lyric expired against her pillows as if the weight of the world exhausted her. "I should've known you wouldn't understand."

"I understand more than you know." Joy settled down on the edge of Lyric's pallet. "Not so long ago, I was fourteen going on fifteen, mad at my parents, especially my dad." Lyric's glassy eyes stared at the ceiling, her arms crossed over her chest. "Annie-Rae said you quit softball. Did something happen today?"

"See, I told you she's such a tattletale," Lyric shouted in the direction of Annie's room. "The girls on the team are snobs. They don't like me, and I don't like them."

"So you quit?"

"Sorry I'm not like you, some kind of softball freak." Lyric spit out the word *freak.*

Joy bit back her first response. She'd absorb Lyric's anger at her parents if it helped her process. "I didn't want to play softball in the first place. But Granny made me."

"Granny thought you'd enjoy it. Sports is a great way to gain confidence, make friends, open up opportunities."

"Well, I don't like softball." Firing off the bed,

Lyric searched around the blanket's edges. When she found her flip-flops, she slipped her toes through the thongs and started for the door.

"Lyric, where are you going?" Joy pushed up from the floor and trailed Lyric down the hall, catching the girl's arm before she rounded the banister for the stairs. "Don't ignore me."

"I'm going to Siri's." Lyric wrangled free, but the reflection in her eyes told Joy the whole story. She was hurting. More than Joy realized. But what could Joy say or do to change the damage inflicted by Sawyer and Mindy? "And don't worry, Parker's not there."

"Lyric, I want to trust you." Joy smiled, lifting her tone, lightening the moment. "Parker? Not so much."

From the porch, Joy watched Lyric trail the hem of the gravel drive to the road. Just before she started down the road, Joy cupped her hands around her mouth. "Be home by eight."

Lyric barely waved before she broke into an easy jog and disappeared around the bend.

A glint of light, like a silver flash, broke through the air just above Lyric's shoulder.

Joy leaned against the porch post, her eyes welling up. Perhaps it was the way the wind blew light through the ancient live oaks and pines, but the glint reflected with a holy memory, something Joy had witnessed once before as a girl—the soft southern tip of an angel's wing.

• • •

Saturday afternoon Luke carried Red's duffel bag from the third-floor loft out to the truck, cutting through the hazy drape of eastern light falling over Miss Jeanne's veranda.

"Going to be a scorcher." Red jumped from the top step to the grass, hitching up his jeans, scooping his hat onto his head.

"Red, why don't you wait and leave early Monday morning?" Luke opened the passenger door and set Red's bag on the floorboard.

"It'll be hot on Monday too. If not here, somewhere along the Georgia highway or Alabama. No offense, Son, but that room of yours ain't big enough for the both of us." Red shuddered. "Ain't that television show paying you good money?"

"Decent money. It's my first season. I'm saving to pay off debts." Luke leaned against the truck, the red paint faded and scarred from years on the ranch, and peered up at the nautical window just above the third-floor gable. The loft wasn't so bad. The room where he'd had some sweet talks with Jesus. "You going to be okay, Red? Mercy Bea insists you look peaked."

"Peaked? That woman is a fussbudget. I'm just a bit pale 'cause I ain't been in the sun for a few weeks. I'm fine."

"Live to be a hundred."

"Just to spite you." Red chuckled, hooked his thumbs through his belt loops, and kicked at the dirt. During Luke's life, he'd only known his dad to have two pairs of boots.

"This old truck running all right?" Luke patted the side panel.

"Better than any newfangled truck they got on the market today."

"Call if you need anything."

"Will you answer?"

Luke laughed. "I'll answer. Miss Jeanne's going to miss beating you at checkers."

"She cheats."

"So do you."

Red sighed and gazed toward the western horizon, squinting as if he could see his route home through the trees. "What's noodling *you,* boy?"

"Come again?" Luke tipped his head to see Red's face. "Noodling me?"

"You been quiet." Red shifted his gaze to Luke's face. "It's Joy, ain't it?"

"Joy?" Luke scoffed, walked around, tugged open the tailgate, and sat. The hinges coughed in protest. "Now why would she bother me? I've just been thinking about the show, reviewing the script for Monday."

"I haven't seen you pine for a girl in a long time. It's kind of nice." Red slipped onto the tailgate next to Luke. "I remember the gal from tenth grade. What was her name? She has a big real estate company now. 'Want to sell your home or business, come see . . .' ?"

"Cara Collins."

"Cara Collins." Red popped his hands together. "That's right. Let me tell you, the years have been good to her." His broad laugh shattered Luke's narrow, distant memory of the solemn man who raised him after Mom died. "Joy's a looker. Seems right sweet too."

"Red? Good, I caught you in time." Miss Jeanne stepped off the porch, a paper bag dangling from her hand. "You're leaving without the snacks I made for you."

Red's eyes pleaded with Luke. Miss Jeanne had many talents, including tap dancing, but cooking wasn't one of them.

"Stop grimacing, boys, it's just Oreos and Goldfish crackers." Miss Jeanne shoved the bag at Red's chest. "I'm going to miss you, you old coot. Something about you reminds me of my brother." Her blue eyes misted. "He was killed in '44 at Normandy."

"Then I'm right proud to remind you of him, Jeanne." Red patted the bag of goodies. "Thank you for these."

Luke stood on the veranda with Miss Jeanne, watching Red go, missing him and the years that used to be.

"Make sure he gets to the doctor, will you?" Miss Jeanne tapped Luke's arm as she turned for the door. "He looks peaked."

"That's what Mercy said." But no word from

Luke could make Red go to the doctor. He'd go when he was good and ready.

The screen door slammed behind Miss Jeanne as she went back inside. Luke eased down into one of the bentwood rockers and set it into motion, hearing Red's accusation of *pining*.

No use lying to himself sitting here in the quiet of the veranda. He liked Joy. Maybe, maybe, he loved her. And if Red saw it, Luke imagined others did too.

 # Sixteen

Luke weaved his way through the cars and trucks parked helter-skelter on Bodean Good's property. Shouts rose above the throng of voices melded in conversations. A beefy bass beat shook the ground and shimmied the veil of moonlight.

Red's absence left a bit of a gap in Luke's day. He'd cleaned his loft, did a load of laundry, then called the café to see if Andy needed him to work tonight after all. He didn't.

By the time the pink glow of twilight settled over a Beaufort evening, Luke roamed Miss Jeanne's, agitated and restless.

On impulse, he grabbed the Spit Fire keys, hollered "good night" to Miss Jeanne, and headed out, toying with the idea of wandering Joy's way when Heath called.

"Come out to Bodean's Mars versus Venus party."

So that's how Luke found himself at a field party where the women hung out on one side, Venus, and the men loitered on the other, Mars.

Luke slowed as he came to a Y in the tiki-lit path, glancing toward the Venus neon sign hanging from the trunk of a skinny pine. Strings of white lights swung from the lower tree branches, and he strained through the glare in hopes of spotting Joy.

The awkward ending to their Sunday barbecue spilled into the last two weeks of work. She avoided him except during taping, where she powered up her charm. Her ability to separate professional from personal was impressive.

Luke didn't want to separate professional from personal. He'd decided to plow ahead and confront her, find out what he'd said that was so offensive when Allison announced the cookbook deal. When Sharon quit, Joy huddled up with the crew, leaving Luke to watch from the outside.

"Cousin, you made it." Heath strolled toward Luke from the Mars side of the party and offered Luke a golden brown bottle. An icy root beer.

"Exactly where have I arrived? I've attended high school dances with more boy-girl interaction." The sweet soda soaked the parched patches of Luke's throat.

"In an hour the Martians will tire of playing their corn hole games and make their way toward Venus." Heath motioned to a circle of chairs under the canopy of twin live oaks. "The girls have all the food."

"Among other things." Luke grinned and took another cool swig. "You'd think women would figure it out. They have it. We want it. Men are completely at their mercy."

"Hush, man, you're breaking the male code of silence." Heath tipped back in his chair, balancing on the back legs, and raised his bottle at his passing wife. "Next dance is ours, Elle."

She gave Heath a quick, soft kiss as she passed, continuing on with her friends.

Would Joy be at the end of Elle's journey? Luke lost sight of her as she moved through the crowd and into the lights.

"Never thought I'd fall in love again after Ava died." Heath sat forward, the dew of his cold soda bottle dripping to the ground. "I just wanted to survive, take care of Tracey-Love and somehow get through the nights without Ava. Then the mornings, then the afternoons and the nights again."

"I'm still waiting for the first time." Actually, Luke had been in love once. *With Ami's.* With the adrenaline of owning a five-star restaurant, with the fantasy of being one of America's great chefs. But ambition was a cruel, stingy lover.

"Ah, come on, you've been in love." Heath tipped up his bottle. "What happened to the woman you introduced to Elle and me when we visited you in New York last year?"

"Tessa? The actress." She'd endured longer than his other three girlfriends. She put up with his obsessive work habits, indulged his love affair with the business, listened to his diatribes about vendors and lackluster profits. She even hired on at Ami's part-time just to be with him. "She bolted when the bankruptcy started, and I didn't blame her."

"What about that one over there?" Heath pointed to his left, drawing Luke's attention across the field and through a cluster of trees.

In the blue, red, and green hue of the plywood dance-floor lights, Luke spied Joy chatting to a walking-talking muscle in a deputy's uniform.

"Brrrr." Luke exaggerated a shiver.

"Really? I thought you two were hitting it off."

"We were. A couple of Sundays ago we had this great, spontaneous picnic at her place with Red, Rosie, and her nieces. We were talking, sharing, then I brought up a recipe idea for her to do on the show and *bam!* She slammed the door." Luke glanced at Heath. "It's been icy ever since."

The music wafting from the stage softened, and Elle appeared from the shadows to tug her husband to the dance floor.

Heath handed his empty bottle to Luke. "Duty calls."

Luke drained his soda in one guzzle, then returned both bottles to the crate. He moved across the mowed field toward the dance floor, the moon and music his wingmen. The heady scent of sunbaked grass escaped the ground where his feet broke over the grass.

About twenty yards away, Joy still engaged the deputy, laughing, flirting. Since when did deputies moonlight as comedians? Then the lawman gestured toward the dance floor.

Smiling, Joy backed up, shaking her head. That-a-girl. The deputy tried again. She refused and patted his arm, turning away. When the deputy cupped his hand around her waist, Joy spun free and glided away.

Luke moved into her path. "I thought I might have to step in to rescue you."

"From J.D.? He's harmless enough." She buried her hands in the folds of her skirt. "What are you doing here?"

"I heard there was a party." The fragrance of warm cotton permeated the air around her. Luke appreciated the way her pale yellow dress fit her curves and accented her auburn hair. "Red left today and Andy didn't need me at the café . . ."

He cleared his throat and reached for her elbow. "May I have this dance?"

Joy molded into his arms, resting her cheek against the plump of his chest. His hand warmed the small of her back. She found it difficult to remain professional toward him.

"I'm sorry, Luke, about the picnic." She tipped back her head to see his face. "I just . . ." What? What did she just . . . ?

"It's okay. I can be pushy."

She leaned against him again and followed his sway to the music as the band's lead singer crooned a George Strait cover, "You Look So Good in Love."

Luke pressed her closer. Joy softened her

posture when she inhaled the warm, woodsy scent slipping through the fibers of his shirt.

You look so good in love . . .

She should tell him. Just confess. Sharon had relented on her threat to quit and shown up for work this past week, her cheery old self. But Joy didn't trust the dark light in her eyes.

Stop thinking about the show. She was ruining the moment—dancing on a warm, starry night in the arms of a handsome man. Besides, really, if Luke hadn't figured out she can't cook yet, maybe he was too dumb to be on the show.

Luke ran his fingers along the hot texture of her neck, and Joy surrendered to the sensation of being wanted. When the song faded, she raised her face to his. *You can kiss me.*

"Can I ask you something?" He brushed her hair from her eyes with gentle strokes.

"A–a question?" She swallowed her desire. "While the breeze carries a George Strait tune? Even the stars are dancing."

The band moved into another slow, melodic song and the floor lights dimmed.

"Joy, if you can't . . ." He paused, letting the silence fill in the blank. "Will you let me teach you?"

She eased out of his arms. "Can't what? What are you asking me, Luke?" Her heart thumped at this moment of truth. Did she really want him to know? She'd not calculated his possible response.

"Ever since the picnic, something's been bugging me, but I didn't know what . . ." He looked at her, eyes narrowed, hands on his belt.

She could almost hear his thoughts cranking. "Luke, what's going on? You're making me nervous."

He grabbed her hand and led her off the dance floor to a secluded area behind the trees. "Can you cook, Joy? It's the only thing I can think of that makes sense. Even when Andy asked me—"

"Andy? W–what did he say?" After her first season, Joy worked her off-season at the Frogmore, and Andy took his turn at teaching her to cook.

"He asked me if 'I knew.' Then he and Russell had a good laugh about something."

"C–can I cook? What kind of question is that?" *Stop, just surrender. He's opening the door for you. He's asking.* But she'd protected the truth for so long she found it excruciating to confess. "You had me lip to lip, Luke." Her words trembled. "You could've kissed me and you asked me about cooking?"

"Am I right, Joy?" He regarded her, intense, demanding.

"The boys would banish you from Mars if they knew you asked me about cooking when you could've been kissing." Joy cut around him and maneuvered through the trees toward Venus. Toward safety.

"Answer the question, and I'll kiss the breath right out of you."

Luke's voice lassoed her and she whirled around to face him. "I'll keep the air I breathe, thank you very much." But she found it difficult to inhale deep and fill her lungs.

"Your cooking segments are always out of time." He walked slowly toward her, speaking as if more and more clues dawned. "Sharon does, or did, all of your cooking but only preps for me. I cook on set. You assemble, then she appears with the finished product. She went ballistic when Allison brought up the cookbook. Your pantry is full of microwavable food and Chef Boyardee."

She shivered as he neared, stopping in front of her to peer into her eyes. Confess, Joy. Be set free. *Yes, yes, it's true. I can't cook. I can't.* But the words crumbled back down to her soul once they reached the dry edge of her throat. It was as if her tongue didn't know how.

And oh, what would he think of her? How could she bear to see the reflection of her shame in his eyes?

"I don't need this." She spun around, but he moved in front of her and blocked her way.

"I can teach you." Calm. Undaunted. Sincere.

"Teach me what?" She faced him, arms crossed, shoulders squared. "You said yourself that cooking professionally kills the joy of cooking at home—thus my microwavable pantry."

"Okay, then do you cook professionally? On the set? At fairs and festivals? Did you fall off the Omaha stage to get away from Wenda?"

She laughed, bending back, patting her belly. Didn't know what else to do. "Oh, this is rich. Fall off a stage to get away from Wenda? Do you think I'm crazy too?"

"No, I don't. I think . . ." He sighed. "I can teach you." He spoke like a game show contestant, giving her clues, offering hints, waiting for her to spit out the answer.

But he didn't understand the real issue. No one could teach her. Not Daddy the summer of '96, not Sharon the fall of '07 or the winter of '08. Not Andy and Russell. "Thanks for the dance, Luke." She turned toward Venus with a long, leaving stride.

"We can start with the recipes for the cookbook. I bet you know more than you think—"

"Luke, stop. Just stop." She nosed herself under his expression. "You don't know what you're talking about."

"What are you afraid of, Joy?"

"What am I afraid of?" She angled away from him. "At the moment, you."

 # Seventeen

Sunday afternoon Joy drifted along the creek behind her house with her best friends since ninth grade, Elle and Caroline. The sun drifted westward leaving behind a burnished wake.

Anchored near the shady side of cypress and pine, Joy released the remnant of her argument last night with Luke with the gentle swell of the boat under the Atlantic's distant tide.

In the aft, Elle was pillowed against the extra life jackets and sketched, her pencil making a staccato scraping sound on the paper. Her golden hair was thick around her face, infused with the heat in the air and the moisture off the water.

Caroline lay in the middle, on the boat's bottom, with an etched smile on her face, her hands cradled around her belly like she'd just eaten the biggest steak at Outback.

"Joy, you've sighed three times. What's up?" Elle continued sketching, adjusting her sunglasses to keep her hair from her eyes.

"Just letting go of all the little nasties." She pinched the air over her body like M did that day by the dock.

"It's going to be all right, Joy. I feel it." Elle's sense could be trusted. She'd spent the last two years honing her spiritual ear in a seven a.m.

prayer meeting, six days a week. Touching heaven gifted Elle to bring a bit of its pure light to earth's dark souls.

"Luke knows."

Caroline lifted her head. Elle set aside her sketch pad. "What? How?"

"How? He's with me on the set, Elle. He's helped Annie-Rae nuke her SpaghettiOs. Peeked into my pantry. He's astute and clever. He asked me straight-out."

"Well, finally, you can confess. It's hard keeping this secret, Joy. The more famous you get, the harder it will be."

"I wanted to tell him, I opened my mouth, but the words never came." Joy propped her chin in her hands. Elle shared a stove with Joy in their tenth-grade cooking class. She'd been the first to witness her utter lack of skill and prowess in the kitchen. She'd been the first to see the smoke rising from the oven door.

"Joy, you've always said you'd confess if someone asked you straight-out. Why didn't you just admit it?"

"Because—" Joy stood so the boat dipped deep from starboard to port side. "Then what? I keep thinking if I have a little bit more time, I can execute my plan to gradually move the cooking to Luke. The truth won't need to come out."

"You should tell him." Elle, plain, simple. Right. "You said he asked outright."

Joy squinted at her. "He'll hate me." The boat had drifted to the edge of the shade and into the four o'clock sunlight.

"Why would Luke hate you, Joy?" Caroline spoke in a slow drawl, her eyes still closed, her words airy and soft.

"Gee, I don't know, Caroline. Because I've been faking a career as a foodie. Elle, how would you feel if a new artist getting a lot of press didn't do her own painting? Caroline, what if the latest country star was pulling a Milli Vanilli and outselling Mitch?"

"Angry."

"Cheated."

"Exactly." Joy sat back down and curled against the bow. "Look, we came out here to relax. Talking about this stirs me up. Caroline, are you looking forward to the fall tour with Mitch?"

"Hold on, Joy." Elle cut the air with her hand. "I just want to say you can trust Luke. He's not going to hate you or steal the show."

"He's not good enough on camera to *steal* the show." Joy pictured him on set, so tall and formal, but so smooth and proficient when preparing a dish. "Which makes the truth all the more ugly. He's trying to rebuild his career, get his life back on track, and who is he working with? A poser."

"Seems to me you need each other." Caroline smoothed her hand over Joy's foot. "If he knows, or thinks he knows, you're not going to be able to hide it much longer. He'll be watching you."

"So . . . I should just . . . tell him." It sounded so simple. Joy scooped her fingers through her hair and wished God would give her a do-over. A rewind back to the day Duncan told her the news. Besides, if Sharon decided this week the whole cookbook deal was indeed unfair and quit, the entire game changed.

"Give him a chance, Joy. Pray, ask the Lord to show you clearly what you need to do and say."

"Is it really that easy, Elle?" Joy absorbed her friend's wisdom, her heart reaching through the textured, warm day toward Jesus. "All right, enough about me. Someone else please share."

The breeze rippled the creek's surface and the boat slipped from sun back to shade.

"I'm pregnant," Caroline announced sweet and soft, her tenor colored with pastel emotions.

"Oh my gosh." Joy rose up. "Caroline."

"When? . . . How long? . . . I can't believe it." Elle lunged over the bench seat, her bracelets clattering, and collapsed on her friend. "You're going to be a mom."

"I'm know." Caroline's voice warbled. "And I'm terrified." She lay still, as if any movement might frighten her child.

Caroline sputtered, laughing, finally opening her eyes. "I want a girl." She gripped Elle's hand. "Like you." Then Joy's. "And you."

Joy rolled forward to brush Caroline's wind-tossed hair from her eyes. "No, sweetie, like you."

For a while they talked babies. Elle whispered she and Heath were prepared for Tracey-Love to be their only child.

"I want a baby, but not so bad that I force it, you know? That's me."

"What about you, Joy?" Caroline asked. "Marriage, babies? Are you over Tim?"

"Tim? Tim who? It's been seven years. Give me some credit." Joy smiled and squeezed Caroline's hand before letting go. "I want to get married, but how can I when I'm living this lie?"

"Trust Luke."

Joy laughed. "You make it sound like I want to marry him."

"Come on, Joy, don't tell me your heart doesn't go pitter-patter every time Luke walks on the set." Elle gently shoved Joy's shoulder.

Maybe, a little. "You're the reduction sauce of romance, Elle. Just put it out there."

"Reduction sauce? Do you even know what a reduction sauce is?"

"Please, I may be clumsy in the kitchen, perhaps started a few fires, but I can remember technical details." Joy dotted the air with her finger. "A reduction sauce is when you *reduce*."

Elle laughed. "I think six-year-old Tracey-Love could've figured out that one."

"It's when you boil all the . . . you know, stuff . . .

210

down to a thick . . ." She twirled her hand in the air. "Sauce."

"Boil what stuff?" Elle, little rat, just had to push.

"The ingredients."

"What ingredients?"

"Your smart-aleck questions, that's what ingredients."

"You know nothing about reduction sauces." Elle settled back in her seat, snickering. *"Nothing."*

"Sounds like it's time for five things," Caroline said, raising her hand, halting the banter.

She was right. It *was* time for five things. Caroline was pregnant. Elle was coming to terms with infertility, and Joy might be free from the lie. Maybe even open to love.

"Caroline, you go first. What five things are you thankful for today?" Joy gathered her soul and opened her heart to listen.

"The miracle of life." She patted her belly. "Mitch, his love and music. The feathery breeze. You two. This old Bluecloud skiff." She knocked the floor of the boat.

"Oh, me too," Elle said. "I love this old boat. Smells and all."

"I told you not to sit on those life jackets."

"I'm grateful for Caroline, who points out all my flaws," Elle said.

"What are friends for?"

"And for my Heath, who brought me the daughter of my heart, Tracey-Love. For this old sketch pad I found yesterday. For the gift of painting, and for Joy, the bravest person I know."

Brave? Oh, she was the opposite of brave. She personified coward.

"Joy, what are your five things?" Caroline said.

She shifted her position, reclining, propping her arms on the side of the skiff, watching the dolphin's fin break the surface of the water.

"My friends, Elle and Caroline, but that's a given. My job and what it's given to my family." She brushed away the broken bit of twig that landed on her leg. "I'm grateful for Mama, and the girls. Even in the busyness, they make the house a home. And I'm grateful for second chances. May there always be one waiting in the wings."

"That's only four." Elle motioned to Joy by waving her hand. "Come on. One more."

"Luke. I'm grateful for Luke."

During the Monday morning production meeting, Joy's gaze wandered between Luke and Sharon's empty chair. Where was she? Never late, she always sat at the head of the table with her tall latte and coffee cake.

"First order of the day." Allison set her laptop at the head of the table. "Sharon's resignation. She called me last night."

Joy rose to her feet. "What? Why? She was

212

happy last week. Didn't you promise her a spring cookbook, Allison? Or more money?"

"I'm not going to play her game, Joy. Frankly, if she feels that strongly, then I need to let her go. Is that okay with you?"

Joy settled down under Allison's laser stare. "She deserved more consideration is all." She let the truth beneath her chest simmer toward a boil. Ryan shifted and cleared his throat, and when Joy peered at him, he cut her a sharp glance.

I know, I know. I have to do something.

"Have you started on the cookbook?" Allison checked with Joy, then Luke. "The publisher set the deadline for October fifteenth. But they'd like a look-see as soon as possible so they can start conceptualizing cover and design. How's it going?"

"Slow."

"We're getting together tonight," Luke said as if it were true. "We'll be ready."

"Good, good. Also, I'm searching for a new food prep and recipe developer to replace Sharon. But, Luke, you're fine to take up some of the slack, right?"

"Fine with me."

"Excellent, I love a team player. Joy, why don't you write out a schedule for the cookbook so we can know what to expect. Shouldn't be too hard to collect the recipes since we already have them on the server." She paused. "And I checked last

Friday after Sharon left. Still there. So I suppose you two just need to make sure all the ingredients and instructions are correct. Don't be shy about bringing any botched recipes into the studio. I make a good guinea pig."

When the meeting ended, Joy headed for her office. Luke followed, shutting the door behind him.

"Guess this means you're going to have to speak to me."

"Guess it does. Love the way you jumped in and promised we'd work tonight." Joy dropped her phone and notepad on her desk. "My house? Seven o'clock?"

"Are we going to be friends through this, or are you going to have an attitude?"

"I won't have an attitude, no." *Joy, let go. Crash and burn already.*

"See you at seven?" Luke backed toward the door. "I'll bring the recipes I'm doing this fall. Want to do, rather. Subject to Allison's—"

"And my—"

"Approval. Of course, you too."

When he was gone, Joy collapsed into her chair, dropping her forehead to her desk. This had to end. At least with Luke. She had to tell him. Without Sharon around to cover for her, he'd confirm his solid suspicion. Sooner or later, the thing she possessed would possess her. If it didn't already.

Luke, you're right, I can't cook. Can't. But I never said I could, not really. I burn things, but cook, not so much. Good eye to pick up those nuances too.

"Joy?" Allison entered without knocking. Joy bolted upright. "Head on the desk? Are you okay?" She set a piece of paper in front of her.

"Didn't sleep well last night." Joy brushed her hand over the water on her cheeks. "What's this?" Smiling as much as her heart could muster, she scanned the paper Allison brought in.

"Schedule for Bette's show. I e-mailed it to you, but I like to pass out printed copies just in case e-mail goes haywire. In case you haven't noticed, I'm really excited about this show."

"Yeah, me too." Joy scanned the New York itinerary. "It's a great opportunity for us." She and Allison arrived in New York on Tuesday for a dinner meeting and photo op with TruReality execs. Wednesday, she'd guest on the seven o'clock hour of *The Morning Show*. Afterward, they would have lunch with the publisher followed by an afternoon with the media. Thursday, she'd tape *The Bette Hudson Show*.

"Strap in, Joy, we're going Mach 10 Premiere Week and not landing until spring." Allison exited Joy's office, then stepped back in, concern in her eyes. "I just happened to think. Sharon has a key to the studio, doesn't she?"

"We all do." Joy jiggled her mouse, waking up

215

her laptop. "But she wouldn't do anything that dastardly, Allison. She's hurt and mad, but not vengeful." With a couple of clicks, Joy maneuvered to the server where the recipes were stored.

But the folder was gone. What? Joy leaned closer to the screen. Was she in the wrong place? With a click on the drive, she started over, working through the files.

Finally opening the DWJ Recipes folder.

Empty. A chill swept over her. *They have to be here.* She clicked on Show Files. Maybe someone moved the files. But no documents appeared.

Joy tugged open the middle desk drawer, searching for the data stick. Gone. *Don't panic yet.* Ryan kept a backup in his office.

"Joy, is everything okay?" Allison asked.

"Yeah, I think so." In Ryan's office she shut the door. "They're gone, the recipes. I looked on the server and the folders are empty."

"I was afraid Sharon would do something stupid." After a few clicks Ryan confirmed it. No recipes. "Okay, then use the backups on the data stick."

"Mine's gone. I was hoping your backup of the backup was in your desk." Joy sighed a *thank you* to heaven when Ryan opened his middle desk drawer to reveal a silver thumb drive.

But when he checked it, the drive was blank, no backup recipes.

Well then, it'd come to this. "I'll go tell Allison."

Ryan followed, taking the lead when they entered the boss's office. "Sharon took the recipes, Allison. Or deleted them. But they're gone."

"Then we start over." So pragmatic and assured. Like it was so easy to develop years worth of recipes. "Joy, gather your recipes from home. Didn't your daddy have recipes and notes around the house?" She walked to her office door and called for Luke. When his broad form filled the doorway, she delivered the news. "Sharon took out her revenge on our recipes, Luke. We're building a cookbook from scratch." At the sound of her words, Allison smiled. "Seems kind of fitting. We're starting a cookbook from scratch. Maybe it was meant to be. I know it means more work, but I'd like to keep our deadline. Are we all in?"

"I'm going to talk to Sharon." Joy squeezed between Luke and Ryan.

"Joy, don't you dare. Don't call or e-mail her. If you see her on the street or in Publix, do not speak to her." Allison held up her phone. "Let me talk to my lawyer first. See what options we have. But I don't want her to come back accusing us of defamation or harassment."

The emotion of the week, the almost-confession with Luke, the sadness over Sharon's decision, the fruit her lie produced boiled in her chest until she thought she couldn't breathe. She had to get out of there.

Crossing the studio, Joy retrieved her handbag, her keys, and her phone from her office and headed for the stairs.

"Where're you going?" Ryan fell in step. "We have show notes to go over."

"I'm going to the park."

"The park? What for?"

"To run the bases."

Thick-bottomed clouds, laden with an August rain, hovered over the Basil Green Complex as Joy launched her shoes into the cab of the truck. Twisting her hair up with the rubber band she found in the glove box, she navigated the pebbles and crushed shells along the side of the street to the thick, warm grass.

The dirt along the diamond was scattered and mussed. Fallow ground waiting for Joy's footprint. Or the slide of her thigh.

The first time she ran the bases to clear her soul was the night of her third anniversary with Tim. Instead of bending on one knee and presenting her with the diamond solitaire they'd picked out at Hudson-Poole, he expressed doubt about their future plans and hinted at loving another.

In a single moment Joy's wholehearted devotion had been revealed as wholehearted foolishness.

Seven years later it became clear she'd repeated the pattern. Only this time not with a weak-willed man but with a television show. Wholehearted devotion turned to wholehearted foolishness. Why couldn't she learn to give up, give in, quit?

It started out as a promise to Daddy. A favor for Duncan. Then for the money, the small kiss of fame. It became a part of her, the center of her dreams. The girls moved in, and Mama opened Ballard Paint & Body. There just never seemed to be a right time to end her life as an acting cook.

Tagging up her bare foot to first base, Joy sprinted to second base. *Running* . . . She rounded second for third, the stiff, unused muscles of her legs aching, the rugged wind of her breathing howling in her ears.

Her foot smacked home plate and she crashed into the chain link backstop, buckling forward, working for air. Then she ran the bases again.

Kicking high and hard, she lengthened her stride, demanding her dormant form and college strength to awaken.

It's the bottom of the seventh with two outs. The Tide was down by one.

Joy tagged home, this time without crashing, without buckling, without the fainting spots of blue and purple.

Run it again. And again.

Sweat beaded over her skin, soaking into the thin cotton of her top and the waistband of her tiered skirt. Moisture dropped from the angles of her face and collected on the flyaway ends of her hair.

So what if Sharon quit. So what if Allison learns the truth. So what if Luke loses all respect for me and never speaks to me again. The *so whats* were muted by the crash of Joy's heartbeat.

She ran the bases again, heat of the midday sun rising. Joy launched from first, kicked second, and surged toward third. When she rounded for home, she pushed, breathing, running, defeating the chasing haunts. *Liar. Phony. Cheater. Hurry, touch home . . . before they tag you out.*

The breezeless diamond seemed to indulge her, watching in wonder. *Safe.* Joy ran over home plate and crashed into the backstop, releasing the tension in her legs and crumpling to the dirt.

She wiped the stinging sweat from her eyes with the hem of her top. Losing Luke? That would be the worst . . . That would be the worst. Stupid, stupid, when did she let him into her heart? Why did she let him in? She jumped up, pacing, shaking off the memory of his voice as he tried to talk to her.

I could teach you.

A rain-scented gust cooled her hot skin. *God, I quit, surrender, let go, whatever You want . . . If You want . . . My food is to do what You want. What else do I have? Nothing. I literally have nothing.*

"If you run, will they come?" Joy angled around to see Luke standing behind her, motioning to the empty stands.

"No, I guess not."

"Ryan said you went to run the bases."

"I'm out of shape." Joy brushed her red stained feet in the grass. Tugged her saturated top from her torso.

From the other side of the fence, Luke watched, his arms propped atop the chain link. "Why are you running bases?"

"Because . . ." She peered at him, their blue gazes meeting, holding steady. "Luke," big inhale, "I–I can't. Cook. I can't. Sharon quit because she developed most of the recipes, even Daddy's. Is that what you want to hear? Yes, ladies and gentlemen"—Joy jogged to the pitcher's mound, arms wide to her sides—"the host of *Dining with Joy*, coming to you soon on the *Tru*-Re-al-ity Network, can*not* cook."

"How's it feel?" Luke walked through the gate. "To confess?"

"You tell me, how's it feel to hear it?" Joy ran her hands over her arms, salty with sweat. "If you wait a day or two, I'm sure Allison will hand the show over to you. Better a cardboard host who can cook than a lively one who can't."

He shrugged. "I don't want the show without you, but I feel like I corralled a wild horse that's still itching to run free."

Joy brushed her hand over her eyes where the sweat trickled down. "Actually, you corralled a mule parading as a wild horse, hiding among the real mares and stallions. Corralling me is merciful."

"I guess it makes me mad, to be honest. Why'd you do it? Foodies are a close-knit, proud bunch, and they don't like being lied to. They take their culinary talent and passion seriously. And you're making fun of them. Couldn't you have been a show host with special guests? Hired a Luke Redmond from the get-go?" He stopped at the base of the mound.

"Except it wasn't my decision." Joy raised her eyes to meet his. "Duncan Tate called the shots like Allison Wild does now." She gestured in the direction of downtown and the studio. "Duncan had just built the studio and was up to his receding hairline in debt but expected the season to end in the black. Then his star dropped dead of a heart attack. So he grabbed the nearest Ballard he could find and shoved her in front of the camera."

"Like father, like daughter?"

"That's what Duncan believed." Joy sank slowly to the pitcher's mound, her legs shaking from the earlier exertion. "I rode to the hospital in the ambulance with Daddy. He was out of it most of the time, but just as they were unloading him, he squeezed my hand." She moved her fingers, remembering the feel of his cold, weak grip. "He asked me to do the show. It was as if he knew."

"And the world loved you."

"Well, some portions of the world. Fraternity men, career women on the go, and busy families."

Luke paced off the mound, running his hand over his hair. She watched his back, wondering if his anger would ebb or spike. When he turned to her, she gained no read from his fixed expression. "This impacts me too, now. I either go along with your lie or tell Allison. I don't like being in this position, Joy."

She scrambled to her feet. "I never invited you into this circle. You prodded your way in."

"I'm cohosting a cooking show with a woman who can't cook. Call me crazy, but I deserved to know from day one. You should've told me."

"I didn't even know you. I barely know you now."

"So you were just going to hoodwink me until—when? You found a way to get me fired? You're not the only one with dreams and goals."

"You think this was my dream, my big goal in life? 'Hi, America. I'm not a cook, but I play one on TV.'" She tipped her head back and balled her hands into fists. "Are you so obtuse? This is not what I wanted. This is what fell at my feet, Luke. If you don't like it, leave. Quit. Sharon did."

He narrowed his gaze. "Was that the plan? Wait for me to quit?"

"I didn't want you to quit. Because believe it or not, I saw you as my way out."

He crossed his arms, hands hooked around his elbows. "I'm listening."

"Forget it." She walked off, slicing into the stiff eastern wind, hungry and thirsty. The look on his face paralyzed her.

"Joy." Luke chased her, snatching hold of her arm. "Tell me."

She inhaled and let the plan escape. "To give more and more of the cooking segments to you while I worked on comedy and reality bits, traveled to fairs and festivals, conveniently doing less and less cooking."

"I see. But who would introduce deep-fried peanut butter and jelly sandwiches to the culinary world? Or the top ten new uses for garlic?"

"I see you've watched back episodes." She drew her arm free. "I tell you my heart and you make fun. You know what, I don't care. You want to tell Allison, go ahead. You want to quit, do it." Walking toward her truck, she pulled her keys from her pocket. "Don't let my secret trap you in my web."

"Let's just air it out, Joy." Luke followed on her heel, a slight adjustment in his tone. "What exactly do you mean by 'can't cook'? I have CIA-trained friends who absolutely must have a recipe. You'd never catch them in a cooking competition. I have other friends who couldn't follow a recipe to save their necks. One friend has to time everything. The number of seconds to sweat onions. The exact minutes to whip cream. One of my chef friends tends to overcook everything, so his sous chef has to watch his back."

"Luke, you're kidding, right?" Joy snapped her fingers in the air around his head. "Can't cook means *can't cook*. I could win *America's Worst Cook* show. Give me a recipe and watch me destroy it. More than likely, I'll destroy the kitchen along with it."

"How is that possible?" He regarded her with his focused blues, disbelief ringing in his question. "You're Charles Ballard's daughter."

"I inherited his flair for the camera but not for cooking. I'm telling you, I can't follow a boxed cake recipe without some kind of disaster." Joy made a strip motion across her eyebrows. "They're always the first to go. Ask Sharon."

"Where'd the deep-fried PB&J come from, then?"

"Okay, that was me, but I've always had a relationship with grease. As in fire. As in burns. Even for the fried PB&J show, Sharon had to mix up the batter and heat the oil." Joy jingled her keys against her palm. "I'm sorry—"

"It's okay." Luke backed toward his car. "At least I know."

He was leaving. That spoke louder than words. "Bye, Luke."

"See you, Joy." The Spit Fire rumbled and rattled toward Boundary Street, turned, and disappeared from view.

Joy exhaled, falling against the side of the truck, beige sand dusting over the red stains on her feet. Hard day. *Hard* day. But somewhere way deep down inside, she could finally hear the song of her soul.

 # Eighteen

When Joy pulled up at home, Mama was pushing a wheelbarrow of potted flowers toward Miss Dolly's backyard. Joy tucked her keys into her bag and sneaked up on her.

"What're you doing?"

"Joy." Mama slapped her hand over her heart, her cheeks flaming with heat. "You scared me to death. Now hush, or you'll blow my cover."

"You're putting flowers *in* Miss Dolly's yard?" Joy stooped to sniff one of the plant's petals. It was so perfect. So blue. "Did you inhale too many fumes at the shop today?"

"Back it up, Joy. Don't sniff the perfume from my blooms." Mama shoved Joy upright with the back of her hand. "My stars, what happened to you? You're all sweaty. And look at your feet. Do not walk into my house with those. Go down to the creek and wash them off. Where have you been?"

"Running the bases at Basil Green."

"Uh-oh." Mama folded her arms, a wry twist on her lips. She looked pretty in the afternoon's watermelon light, her blue eyes full of spunk, a kink in her brown coils. After Daddy died, she switched from blonde to her natural brown and exchanged her slacks and skirts for overalls and garden gloves. "Tell me what happened."

"Sharon quit."

"Aw, mercy, that girl is a loon." Mama ducked for a quick look through the hibiscus. "If I told Chick once I told him a hundred times, Sharon is only out for herself."

"Out for herself? Mama, she hung around the show for three years, helping me—graciously, I might add. She never said a disagreeable word until the cookbook deal."

"Which is the deal she always had with your daddy. She'd share the book rights and royalties, have her name on the cover."

"Can you blame her? She's developed some great recipes. Duncan promised her the same thing. Enter Allison and—"

"And the hound bit you in the butt, didn't she? I told you to be careful. She did the same thing to Chick. If Sharon suggested basil instead of bay in a recipe, she wanted her name on it. I told you to get ahold of those recipes, get copies or something."

"We had copies." Joy traced her finger lightly over the tiger lily's thick, creamy bloom. "Sharon took them."

"In some places, folks call that stealing." Mama swatted at her hand. "You're getting your oily fingerprint all over my lily. Stop."

Joy stuffed her hands in her pockets. "I need Daddy's recipe books. Allison wants me and Luke to start from scratch, use our own recipes. Then on my way home, she texted me about writing stories or anecdotes to add to the cookbook."

"Well, you'll finally get to use your creative writing degree and make up little stories about how you and your daddy baked banana bread in the kitchen while singing 'Mockingbird.' "

"Next time you bust my chops for sarcasm, I'm throwing this moment back at you. Maybe I won't write stories about my life with Daddy, just his life with the food." Joy eyed her mama. "I'm going to need to ask you a lot of questions."

"He used to keep his recipe notebooks in the attic, underneath a floorboard. If they're not there, I have no idea where he kept them. He might have taken them to the studio." Mama hoisted up her wheelbarrow and wedged her way through the bushes. "You want pizza for dinner? Dave over at Upper Crust owes me a free large veggie."

"No, he doesn't. I told you—"

"I'm telling you those peppers were really anchovies." The hibiscus leaves wrapped around Mama as she disappeared through the hedge. "Now, if she'd just get going to bridge club. Ah, there she goes. Have fun at bridge, Dolly. Don't drink too much julep."

Joy poked her head into the bush blind. "Dare I ask why you're planting flowers in Miss Dolly's garden?"

Mama shoved forward, breaking through to Dolly's yard. "Remember how you told me not to spray pesticides?"

• • •

At five minutes until seven, Luke swung into the Ballards' driveway, cut the engine, and climbed out with his personal cookbook and a trunkload of groceries.

The front door swung open and Annie-Rae came out with a slice of pizza in her hand. "I thought you were Lyric." She giggled, hunching up her shoulders. "But you're prettier."

"No, you're prettier." He stooped to her eye level. "Is your Aunt Joy here?"

"Yep."

"Is she in a good mood or a bad mood?"

"I don't know." Annie-Rae shrugged. "Good, I guess. Unless you're Lyric, then she's in a bad mood."

"What if you're Luke?"

"Don't tell him, Annie-Rae, he's just using you to get information."

Luke raised his gaze to see Joy standing in the door, swinging a dish towel. "You looking to pop someone with that thing?"

"Anyone whose name starts with L."

"Then I'll be going." He took the steps up, passing Joy his cookbook. "Start picking out what you think should go in the book. I have groceries in the car."

"What are you doing here?"

"Um, working on a cookbook. Seven o'clock, right?" He jumped the steps, motioning for Annie to follow him. "Let's unload."

"Wow, groceries." She dove in, headfirst, loading up her thin arms, drawing her lips back as she carried her load to the house. "Looky, Aunt Joy, groceries."

"Yeah, baby, shh, let me help you." Their voices faded as they disappeared into the house. "Why are you acting like we've never bought groceries before?"

"I can't remember . . ."

Luke carried the last bags in, closing the door with his foot, striding for the kitchen. He'd been ticked for a while, but then he put himself in her place and, well, he'd have done the same thing. "I bought everything I thought we'd need for tonight."

Annie brought a tall stool around the counter, set it in the middle of the kitchen, and climbed on, her hazel eyes thirsty sponges, absorbing the scene.

"Can I see you on the porch?" Joy led Luke through the sliding glass door. "What are you doing? We have no *Dining with Joy* recipes. Ryan called to say he's e-mailing the dish names from the show's database, but a title isn't going to get us very far. I can't cook. Your reputation is on the line. Just call Allison and get it over with."

"And then what?" He captured her with a pointed glance. "You go to work with your mom at Ballard Paint & Body? Try to find a writing or editing job? I think you're more experienced at fake cooking than editing and writing."

231

She stepped back. "You're enjoying this? Mocking me?"

"I'm not mocking you. I've thought about this. I've prayed about it, and I'm in, Joy. Let's execute your plan. I'll take over more and more of the cooking while you entertain, make us laugh, do the spontaneous stuff that's so genuine. Think about it. No other cooking show is like *Dining with Joy*. It's why TruReality loves you. Besides, what good is a show called *Dining with Joy* without the Joy?"

"What about all the purist foodies?"

"They can sit in their white chocolate towers and sneer. We'll be boots on the ground having fun, bringing good food to people who'd never turn on the food channels."

"Then tell Allison." She remained with her arms crossed and shoulders stiff, her tone flatly demanding.

"Yeah, about that . . ." He exhaled, scuffing his boot over the porch boards. "I tried."

"Oh my gosh." She slapped her hands on her head. "You tried? You tried." Joy slapped out the screen door.

"I was mad, Joy. I was nervous. I wasn't sure I wanted to cohost, knowing it was a sham. Give me a break, I had to take a second to consider my own career."

"What'd she say?" Joy stopped by the side of the house, reached for the shovel leaning there, and rammed the edge into the ground.

"When you didn't come back this afternoon, she came to my cubicle and started talking. I probed her thoughts on me doing more cooking, which she's open to, but, Joy, you're her golden goose. No way is she backing you away from any part of the show. Then I said," Luke yanked the shovel from her, " 'wouldn't it be a fun show if the host couldn't cook?' Allison turned white and she looked like she'd seen a black widow. She said, 'Not in my world. A cooking show with a host who couldn't cook would be the death knell of any production company.' So, no, she didn't think it was funny."

"Oh my gosh, oh my gosh." Joy spun toward the wooded half of the yard, hands over her head, then slicking down her ponytail. "Here I am again. It's Duncan all over. The balance and weight of the show is on me. If I quit, Allison loses everything she's invested. Her reputation with TruReality is shot. The crew is out. You're back at the Frogmore."

"What do you want?" Luke eased the shovel against the side of the house. "For once, Joy, decide for yourself. If you want to go on with the show, I'm with you. But if you want a way out, Joy, this is it. I'll tell Allison with you."

"You'd do that?" Her shoulders rounded forward as the fire in her heart flickered low.

"Yeah, I'd do that for you." He lowered his hands before he lost his senses and swept her into his arms. She had a way of burrowing under his skin and into his heart. With every passing second, she burrowed deeper, leaving him marked by her presence.

Without a word, she stepped into him, crushed her forehead into his chest, and wept.

The intimate friendship, got-your-back moment from the yard that swelled in Joy's heart with a sense of well-being and hope vanished within the hour.

"What is hard about an omelet, Joy?" Luke took the skillet from her. "It's eggs folded over. I've turned ex-cons and recovering alcoholics into top Manhattan sous and line chefs. But I can't teach an ex-softball player how to make a simple omelet?"

"I told you. I told you. I can't do it. I don't get it." Joy backed into the counter, crossing, uncrossing her arms, treading to stay above a meltdown.

"It's eggs in a pan. What's not to get?"

"She's just no good." Annie-Rae, still perched in the center of the kitchen, shook her head with exasperation in her eyes. "Never has been."

"Thank you, mini-Granny." Joy bent toward her. "Gee, isn't it past your bedtime?"

Annie popped up straight and softened her expression. "Lyric's not home yet."

The girl was too smart for her own good. Joy peered at the stove clock. Nine thirty. Lyric was late. Again. Her infatuation with Parker was turning to obsession. "Run upstairs and call her. Siri's number is by the phone in Granny's room. Tell her to get home. Now."

Annie hopped off the stool and scurried up the stairs. Luke dumped the burned omelet into the trash. It was her fifth one. The first three were raw and runny. The last two, burnt.

"I told you not to turn up the heat," he said.

"You know what?" Joy pulled off her apron, the one he'd tied for her, his nearness driving her to decide he could kiss her tonight. "I don't need this. It's like being in here with Daddy."

"What's that supposed to mean?" Luke turned on the faucet and rammed the skillet under the stream.

How did she know? She wasn't monitoring her words well tonight. Those little beauts popped off her lips before checking with her brain. "Daddy, I don't know . . . he possessed this kitchen like some men possess the garage or a workshop."

"And it had to be his way or no way? Perfect? If you moved a utensil or pan he'd know it? If you used his vinegar or sherry, he'd demand to know why?"

She eyed him. "I can promise you we never touched his vinegar or sherry, but we were guilty of using a slotted spoon or spatula from time to time."

"I worked for a chef who was a control freak." Luke set the skillet on the stove and started cleaning up. "I don't want to do that to you, Joy. I'd convinced myself your issues were just a matter of confidence. That it was all psychosomatic. Most bad cooks just need to relax, have fun, enjoy the process."

"Then we're doomed." Joy sat on Annie's stool. "I don't enjoy the kitchen. I don't get the big deal about cooking. How in the world can it be relaxing? All the chopping and dicing, the mess, the cleanup, the time standing in front of a hot stove. Slap together a PB&J and I'm off to a movie or softball game or floating on the creek with my friends."

"So what do you want to do?" Luke tucked his cookbook under his arm. "Tell Allison and see what happens. I still want to teach you to cook."

"Well," she shrugged, interrupted by Mama coming through the sliding door.

"What's burning? Luke, you didn't let her cook, did you?"

"I tried."

"Next time, if there is a next time, let me show you where the fire extinguisher is first."

"All right, Mama, one small kitchen fire—"

"One?"

"Okay, good night, take a shower, go read your book, here are your Cheetos." Joy hopped off the stool, slid open the pantry, and tossed Mama her nightly snack.

"Giving me the old brush-off."

"Yes. Did you plant the flowers?"

"Oh yeah, I planted the flowers." Snickering, Mama headed for the stairs.

"What was that about?" Luke leaned to see out the dark window.

"Yard wars. Long story." Joy sat on the stool again. If she was going to commit to the show, she needed to commit to Luke, the cookbook, the process, and maybe seeing the kitchen from another man's perspective.

"I acted just like him, didn't I? Your dad."

He did it again. Peered into her soul and listened to her thoughts. "Pretty much." She slouched, gripping her hands against her legs. "Don't think I realized it until the fifth omelet."

"I'm sorry." Luke inched closer to her. "I kept thinking any NCAA All-American who pitches eighteen no-hitters on the ride to the national championship could take some coaching, fold over a few eggs."

"Surprise."

The front door slammed, shaking the house. "I'm home. Happy?"

"I'm glad." Joy met Lyric in the living room. "But you're late."

"Do you know how embarrassing it is to have your little sister call and tell you it's time to come home?"

"The only person to blame is yourself, Lyric. You broke curfew."

"It's almost the end of summer vacation." She collapsed on the sofa. "All my friends are out having fun, going to the drive-in or the beach, having parties, and I have to be home by nine. I'm not a baby."

"Current temper tantrum aside—"

"What's that smell?" Lyric curled her lip. "You haven't been cooking, have you?"

"That was me." Luke stood at the other end of the living room. "I was trying something." He glanced at Joy. "Didn't work out."

"You'll have to try again," Joy said. "Maybe take it slower, relax."

"Easy for you to say."

"What in the world are you two talking about?" Lyric pulled herself off the sofa and thumped upstairs.

"Tomorrow night? I'll do the cooking, you do the testing?"

"Sounds like a plan." Joy propped against the wall.

"By the way, I think Lyric had a date with a vampire tonight." He tugged his keys from his pocket and motioned to his neck, nodding toward the stairs. "On her neck, under her ear."

"Nice, can't wait to have that conversation."

"See you tomorrow?"

"If I survive the night." Joy walked him out to the porch, then leaned against the post as he cranked up the Spit Fire.

As he eased down the drive, he glanced at her through the rearview mirror. She may be caught in the memories of Charles Ballard, but by the end of this season, he'd see that she was free, gazing forward, discovering the Joy inside.

Nineteen

The following Saturday evening Luke staffed on at the Frogmore, settling into the solitude of the kitchen, the ting of the spatula on the grill, the clatter of dishes, the sizzle of a good sear, an old-home melody.

Luke plated the day's special, barbecue chicken, his thoughts drifting over the past week of cooking with Joy. Man, she could be exasperating. Then the next moment his heart would be beating, his arms aching to grab hold of her.

She couldn't cook, but she'd taken the lead in dictating which recipes—from his own collection—went in the cookbook. Thursday night he argued with her for fifteen minutes about corned beef.

"Mercy." Luke slid the plate through the window. "Bebecue chicken is up."

"Got a visitor, Luke." Mercy peered through the window as she picked up her order.

"Me? Who is it?" He angled to see the deep part of the dining room. He hoped to see Joy at the counter or a back booth.

"Some dude with a Yankee accent."

Yankee accent? Didn't narrow it down much. Wandering through the kitchen doors, he scanned the room. A familiar face watched him from the back corner booth.

"Linus Cariboni." Luke squinted at his Manhattan friend as he slid into the booth. "Slumming in the lowcountry. What's up?"

Linus slapped him a side-five. "Did I hear right? You cohosting an avant-garde cooking comedy show, *Dining with Joy*?"

"Seems the rumor mills are getting it right these days." Luke shifted forward, arms on the table. "We're in the middle of taping the season."

Linus clicked his tongue and added a low whistle. "Looked her up on the Internet. She's hot. Funny too."

"You drove all the way down from New York to tell me Joy Ballard is *hot*?"

"I've done more for less." In his early forties Linus was a gambler. Not in the tradition of Atlantic City, Reno, or Vegas, but in restaurants, bistros, and all things food. Handsome in a stock-Italian kind of way, he used his charm and wealth to hedge his bets for restaurants, chefs, food writers, foodies, and their patrons.

"Still losing your hair, I see." Luke grinned.

"And are you still poorer than a church mouse?" Linus knocked his diamond-studded platinum ring on the polyurethane-coated tabletop.

"As a matter of fact, I'm saving up to pay you back." Luke motioned for Paris to bring around a couple of teas and hoped God might lend him some wisdom here. Linus didn't just *happen* by Beaufort. No one happened by the coastal city. Linus was on a mission. As an original investor in Ami's—with a handshake and an envelope of cash—he'd lost out in bankruptcy proceedings. Luke's pledge to repay him was his only collateral. But that's how Linus did business. Payback came in the form of favors. Imbedded, serious favors.

"You think I'd show up in this dive for a couple of measly grand?" Linus sat back, regarding Luke down his Michelangelo-sculpted nose. "I want more than money."

"A pound of flesh. And I owe you more than a couple of measly grand." More like twenty-five.

"Forget the money. And the pound of flesh. I want the whole bag of bones. All six-one, hundred and eighty pounds of you. Give or take a few. Have you been hitting the weights?" Linus winked at Paris as she set down the teas. "Thank you, beautiful."

"What's going on, Linus?"

"Ami's was a top-notch restaurant with unique recipes. Good Midwest food with French panache. You were on the cusp of culinary greatness." He smiled and nodded at the couple at the next booth like he knew them. "How're you folks doing? Listen, Luke"—he tapped his ring against his glass—"I came to save you. And eventually, get some of my money back. My partners and I are opening a place in Portland, Maine. We'll run the business side, but we want you to be our executive chef."

"Maine? At the top of the world Maine?" Maine without Joy Maine? "Way too cold."

"It's a fantastic place, Luke. Portland is the fastest-growing culinary hot spot in the country." Linus reached for a napkin, then took the pen from Luke's chest pocket. "We need to get in there before the chains and tourist hounds turn the city into Broadway and 42nd. Loading up the town with run-of-the-mill, you-can-find-this-stuff-anywhere places. In the ten years I've known you, Luke, you've never turned down an opportunity for a new kitchen. At least not until you opened Ami's."

"I have no reason to go, Linus. I'm doing well here, finally on my feet again. I've got the show. Working here on Saturdays keeps me in the kitchen. My cousin is here. I'm making friends—"

"I bet you are, and she has long flaming hair and a great face. I'd say more but you look like you're going to punch me." Linus slid the napkin across the table.

"Maine is too far from Red and Oklahoma. I'm all he's got, and he's not getting any younger." Luke refused to look at the napkin, knowing the number would bug out his eyes and shove his heart into his ribs.

"Take your time. We don't need an answer

tomorrow." Linus tapped his manicured finger on the napkin. "This is your salary, but we can negotiate and I'll be generous on vacations. Once you get a crew in place, of course."

"Of course. And what constitutes the crew being in place? A mini-me as exec when I'm not there? A clone? I know you, Linus, you'll build the restaurant's rep around the skills of your exec. I'll never be able to leave because someone or something will always be on the horizon. If we're losing money or making money, the executive chef must be in-house."

"My partners and I want you. We're willing to be flexible." He shoved the napkin to the edge of the table, under Luke's line of vision. "To a point. But that's your first year's salary plus bonus. We stay in the black, that number goes up by ten percent. Eventually, you buy in. I'm not sure if I can match the pay of a *classy* culinary show like *Dining with Joy*, but this is the bucking bronc you've been dying to ride, Luke. Designing the menu and kitchen the way you want, but without any of the financial responsibility. We'll control the business, and everything else is yours."

The figure was ridiculous. Too much for a startup place. But Linus loved the ridiculous. He loved shooting the whole wad on a chance the next card gave him twenty-one.

"When?" Luke folded the napkin and tucked it into his pocket.

"Couple of months. Still working out details. Should we buy or lease . . . you know the hassle. But we'd like to be open by December. For the holidays."

"I'm contracted to the show for a year."

"When are you through taping? October? November? Send me your contract. I'll have my lawyer look into it."

"The show debuts in September and the season is twenty shows. We've done eight." The leatherette creaked under Luke as he shifted forward, then back, letting his emotions settle. Six weeks ago this offer would've been a no-brainer. Even in the early weeks of the show, he'd have leapt at this offer. The white paper napkin exposed his heart. Money wasn't it for him. Luke was attached to Joy. "I'll have to think about it. Pray."

"I figured as much." Linus held him with a long, hard gaze. "We can get you where you want to be, Luke. You know it. We have contacts all over the food world. You won't have to play second fiddle to a home-trained show host. I don't care how gorgeous she is, am I right? Or play sous chef to whoever runs this dive."

"See, Linus, there you go, assuming, talking without authority."

"Maybe, but I know you." Linus exited the booth. "The first day you opened Ami's, I saw your hunger. The yearning for success. But you didn't make it." He picked up his tea for a final swig, letting his words gum up the air and stick to Luke. "And I'm betting that doesn't sit well with you. I'll be in touch."

The bells clattered as Linus left the café. Luke yanked the napkin from his pocket, tore it in two, and stuffed it in the remains of Linus's tea. The thin paper swirled and dissolved as it drifted to the bottom.

Dan Greene's command and presence consumed the air in Allison's office. He perched across from her with his vice-president-of-programming-glare fixed on her as she skimmed the focus group survey results.

No reading required. Dan bullhorned the news. *Not good.* Okay, attitude up, creative solutions in motion, this need not be the end of the world as she knew it.

"We'll reshoot." Smiling, shaking her hair a bit as she tossed the survey to her desk.

"Are you going to reshoot every Luke segment?" Dan remained steady, unmoved, his brow arched. "That's nine shows. You have that kind of money stocked, Allison?"

Her sigh slipped out. "The crew is committed . . . But, Dan, let's think outside the box." She snatched up the survey and walked around to the front of her desk. "Why not let Luke be a bit bland? He's real. It's the true part of the show. He's the everyday man. What was it the women consistently said—" She flipped the pages. " 'Monotone but great to look at' . . . 'He can come to my kitchen any day of the week' . . . 'Luke is the best-looking chef on television' . . . 'I'll watch if he's on, even if he's kind of boring.' This is real, Dan. We can use this to our advantage. Joy *is* the show, the star, then in walks this man who could've come from anybody's living room or frat house. Besides, honestly, can we really stomach two shining hosts? No."

"You're right, you're right." Dan sat back, resting his arms casually over his crossed legs, his conciliatory tone not comforting. "And none of that would matter if there was chemistry. It's all gone, Allison. Where's the spark I saw on YouTube? We loved the show with Joy, but when you wanted to add Luke, it was for sex appeal, spice, getting the audience to wonder what those two are doing offscreen. With what you've given us, I get visions of Scrabble and crossword puzzles. No one is tuning in to watch two beautiful people figure out a double word score."

"Then I'll reshoot. There's good feedback on those first few shows we reshot. I'll do it again. We'll get Joy to spice it up. She's the one who kissed him at the cook-off."

"I want more from Joy too. She's too safe, too in command. Predictable in her zaniness." Allison felt Dan's puppeteer strings tightening, manipulating, moving her the way he and

TruReality wanted. "What can you do to spur on the competition between Joy and Wenda Divine? I hear Wenda thinks Joy is a hack. And where are we on the cookbook?"

"Joy and Luke are working on the cookbook. And Wenda is a first-class witch, if you know what I mean."

"If you mean she's great entertainment for our side, I do. If you're avoiding her, then you disappoint me, Allison. Don't make me sorry I took a chance with you. We go back a ways, but I'll kick you to the curb along with my own mama if you don't deliver. We're not airing a cooking show. We're airing a reality show. We want drama and conflict and tension. We want the viewers wondering from week to week if Joy's life matches what they see on the set. And it's our job to make sure the show is as real as we can make it."

"Joy doesn't want anything to do with Wenda. She faced her this summer down here and beat her. End of story for our star."

"Doesn't mean it's end of story for our purposes." Dan cocked his eyebrow as he lowered his chin.

Allison's door shoved open and Joy entered. "Allison, we need to talk about the fall bookings. I'm not sure we can manage . . . Dan, I didn't know you were here."

Allison eyed Joy as she turned back to her desk. "He brought the focus group results."

"If the tension between you two is any indication of the results, I take it they didn't quite love us."

Dan laughed. Too exuberant, and it annoyed Allison. "Have a seat, Joy." Dan patted the chair next to him. "The viewers love you and the show's format. But we're just struggling with your cohost. He's still too bland and boring for our viewers' taste. Next to you, he's a sundried jellyfish."

"He's an amazing chef. We've been working on the cookbook for the past two weeks and I think I've gained five pounds."

"I'm thinking of reshooting," Allison said, her tone firm, trying to communicate to Dan she'd produce her show her way and make him like it. She trusted her instincts, her gut reaction for good programming and great chemistry. Bringing Luke to the show had not been a mistake.

"By the way, did you find your father's recipes yet?"

"Not yet . . . but, Allison, Luke is a different chef when he cooks in my kitchen. Relaxed, funny, makes everything look easy. Why not send Garth and Reba over, let them capture him in the moment, unscripted? See what you get." So, Joy donned her producer hat and sounded savvy, chic, and confident. "My youngest niece likes to watch and help. Luke loves teaching her, showing her how cooking is done. In the studio, I think he feels like he has to perform. At the house, he's himself."

"Great idea." Allison went with the suggestion. "Set up hidden cameras—"

"No, that's not fair. He has to know. Send Garth and Reba, but my guess is it won't bother Luke in a home setting."

"No, I say we hide—"

"Joy's right." Dan smacked his palms together. "Shoot at her place. We'll see a different Luke. Good thinking. I like you, and it'll be my pleasure to see you a household name, darling."

Allison snatched up her pen and clicked the button, on, off, on, off. "Is tonight a good time, Joy? And find your father's cookbook. Adding his recipes with vignettes about him written by you, an at-my-father's-stove angle, will tug at heartstrings. The publisher wants to add it as part of our marketing plan."

Joy agreed to keep looking, then excused herself, and Allison boiled over.

"Don't undermine me again, Dan. This is my show."

"On my network." He scooted to the end of his seat, balancing his girth on the thin metal frame. "Now that we've created a little swirl for Luke, cooking at home with Joy and her little niece, showcasing He-Man sex appeal . . . no woman can resist a masculine man in the kitchen. Our college men will identify with him. Now I want a swirl for

Joy. I want Wenda. Get her in another cook-off with Wenda."

"What for? Wenda is trailer trash. We don't need her."

"Oh, but we do. Put Joy in conflict. Give her trouble. Let the viewers side with her, root for her. Heck, send Luke in on a white horse to rescue her." Dan stood, smoothing the tuck of his starched blue shirt into his waistband, pressing his fingers against the soft leather of his belt. "There's always *The Bette Hudson Show*. Figure something out. Anyway, I'll see you for dinner." He paused at the door. "I'm counting on you. Get this show right."

When his footsteps echoed down the stairs and the roar of a rental car motor vibrated against her office window, Allison pitched her pen at the door and swore, low, dark, and venomous.

# Twenty

"Forget they're here." Standing in the hall, between the front door and the kitchen, Joy gripped Luke's shoulders. "Just do what you've been doing in this kitchen."

Falling in love with you? "It's killing my ego here, you know. I'm still *that* boring?" Luke glanced at the lens Garth aimed at him.

"No, but I think Dan Greene is really busting Allison for a bigger, better show than she sold him."

"Don't lie to me." Luke paced halfway down the front hall. "I saw the focus group survey. Hunky but snoresville. I was the class clown in seventh grade. Got sent to the principal's office weekly for cutting up, making the girls laugh."

"You don't have to be entertaining, Luke. That's my job. Just loosen up. You're getting better with each shoot."

He exhaled. Each shoot. Half the season was in the can already. "Let's do it." *Forget the cameras, forget the cameras.*

In the kitchen, Annie-Rae perched on her stool, her elbows back on the counter, a homemade something on her lap. "How's my Annie?" Luke squished her curls like he did every night.

"I'm going to be on TV too."

"Luke, are you ready?" Garth prompted him to get started.

He scanned the counter. Today's focus was ricotta cheese pancakes *and* cookies. He loved this recipe, developed it for Ami's opening. Prepping the ingredients this afternoon reminded him of why he loved the gastronome life, and for one short breath, he contemplated Linus's invitation. It would be good to be back in the kitchen.

"Let's do this."

Joy faced the camera. He loved watching her, so easy and natural, as if she believed a million of her best friends were on the other end of that lens, stopping by for the evening. Without Ryan or a script, she soared higher. Ad lib was her element. Garth and Reba just let the cameras roll, moving around to find the best angles and shots.

"Tonight we're cooking in a real home kitchen—yes, mine. There, are you happy? I can hear it now: 'Stan, where do you think she is? Is that her home . . . oh, I bet they rented a big fancy kitchen for this one.'" Joy stepped aside. "As you can see, no, we did not rent a big fancy kitchen for this show. It's my small, boring one, and please do not send me decorating ideas or offers. Tonight's segment? Luke Redmond's raspberry ricotta pancakes and cookies. I cannot wait to try these. Luke, are you ready? Wait, Annie, how could I forget you? This is my niece,

Annie-Rae, everyone. Sweetie, introduce Luke for us."

Annie giggled and scrunched up her shoulders. Something about her presence enabled Luke to forget the cameras circling the kitchen. Or that at the moment, pixie Reba stood on the counter with her remote aimed at his head.

"I can't." Annie hid her smile behind her hand.

"Sure you can."

Reba moved slowly, stepping over the sink, her foot landing right between the flour and the cheese.

Annie-Rae inhaled, sucked in her gut, closed her eyes, and tipped back her head. "Hey, good lookin', whatcha got cookin'?"

Luke buckled forward, shimmying, trying not to discourage Annie with his laugh. A couple of dishes clattered behind him. Garth's chest rumbled.

"All right, Luke." Joy motioned to him, straight-faced, eyes alight. "Whatcha got cookin'?"

"Okay, tonight we're working with one of my favorite ingredients. Ricotta cheese." He reached for the tub on the counter by Reba's foot. "But when most of us think of ricotta, we think—"

"Italiano." Joy kissed her fingertips and thumb.

"Exactly." Luke shoved the prep bowls around. "Stuffed shells, lasagna. All great dishes. But you've not tasted ricotta until you've tasted it the Luke Redmond way, in cookies and pancakes."

"Then teach us, oh great chef." Joy tied on her apron.

A random thought hit him. No. He couldn't. But Dan wanted him to liven up . . . "The rest of the ingredients are standard. Eggs, baking soda, flour, salt, cinnamon, and nutmeg." Even with Garth's warm breath practically breezing through his hair, this kitchen felt like home. "So, Joy, I'm going to need you to warm up the eggs before adding them to the room temperature butter." He dropped two eggs in her hand.

"You're kidding. I know if you add eggs to heated butter, the eggs can cook, but cold eggs mess with room temp butter? Help us out here, oh great one, and tell us why."

"Because I said so. No, Joy, cup your hands like this," he demonstrated, making a bowl with his hands, "to warm the eggs. Like a nest."

She made a face at the camera. "New York Yankee chefs . . . Down here we just toss it all together and let the recipe come out like it's supposed to."

"First, we're going to cut the flour with baking soda and salt." Luke set the empty bowls aside. Joy stood watching, cradling her eggs.

She looked so cute he almost hated to pull his prank. But . . . In one quicksilver move, Luke clapped his hands around hers. The shells crunched. Raw whites and yolks slithered from the bottom of her hands, between her fingers.

"Oh my . . . what the . . ." Joy gaped at him, blue eyes snapping. "You've got to be kidding me."

Garth and Reba circled, hungry vultures descending on a wounded prey.

"Oh, Aunt Joy, Luke, *two whole eggs?*" Annie-Rae whined at the travesty of wasting good food.

"Luke, my, my, seems you forgot to do your hair for the show." Joy spread her hands, yolk going all over, and smashed them down on Luke's head, smearing the slimy eggs through his hair. He could feel her molding it to a point on top. "There now." She angled back for a good look. "Don't you look dapper—I've been missing your pompadour. Eggs work better than the finest hair gel."

Her eyes urged him, *Come on, this is the stuff.* But he didn't care about the stuff. He cared about her. His pulse muddied. His lungs expelled the last ounce of breathable air. The kitchen walls expanded, leaving him alone with Joy on a kitchen island. The lights morphed to glassy stars. The voices became the rush of fluttering wings against his ears. Garth and Reba were tall coconut palms.

He wrapped his arms around Joy and tipped his head, covering her lips with his, unsure, tentative, until she laced her arms around his neck, molded against him, and joined the kiss.

Luke drew her tighter, tasting her skin, inhaling her fragrance, fanning the embers of his heart, sensing somehow if the kiss ended too soon, his hunger would never cease.

When she broke away, Luke's lips lingered on hers. He brushed her cheek with the back of his hand.

"For the cameras?" she whispered.

"Cameras?" He kissed her again, breathing in deep. "What cameras?"

"What do you think?" Joy crouched on the kitchen floor over the last page of the mock-up cookbook. "Pretty clever, huh?" She nudged Luke with her elbow.

"I think it's noon on Saturday," he ran his hands over his face, then stretched his fingers, "and you've had me kneeling on a hard tile floor for three hours, cutting food out of magazines with kiddie scissors."

"But we have a mock-up of the cookbook." Joy jigged around the kitchen, tugging Annie-Rae to her feet and spinning her around. "We have recipe names based off Ryan's list. Now all we need are the ingredients and the how-to." Sigh.

"Leave the simple part to last." Luke hobbled to the counter and perched on the stool, hand pressed against the small of his back. "My knees and back . . . I can't believe you called me at six a.m."

"Ryan's list inspired me. Got to strike while the iron's hot. Mock up a cookbook, get a visual. Feels real to me now."

"Even Red never woke me up at six for branding days." His clear blue eyes laughed at his own fabrication. He looked funny with his tired expression and shocks of Spit Fire-dried hair going every which way.

"Right, he probably woke you up at five. Or four. Come on, cowboy." Joy jigged over to him. "Can't let a little paste and paper defeat you." She roped her arm around his shoulders, the bend of her elbow fitting the nape of his neck. His shoulder felt solid and warm beneath her hand. "What happened to the bubba who survived Hell's Kitchen?"

"Did I mention I failed kindergarten?"

"Poor baby." On instinct, without thinking, she kissed his cheek. Affectionate. More intimate than yesterday's moment in front of the camera. She could feel his pulse surge with his quick and short breaths. When he gazed up at her, his blue eyes ignited a wildfire in her belly.

"Luke." She tucked her hair behind her ears as she backed away, then motioned to the mock-up. "We have a cookbook. Look." She straightened the last page with her toe. "I say we glue that sucker together and turn it in to Allison. Here's the cookbook. Go make millions."

"I don't know. Annie-Rae and I were having fun cooking, testing the recipes." Luke flowed with the moment and she appreciated it.

She didn't quite know what to do with the sudden

passion that kept exploding between them. In the middle of the night, she'd woken up with heart palpitations. Was the only spark between them going to be on the show? The embers of sexual tension fueled by a spontaneous kiss? Allison and Dan Greene may love it, but Joy didn't. Did Luke?

"How's the project?" Mama tugged open the pantry door and took out her bag of Cheetos. "You know what they say, everything you need to know in life you learn in kindergarten."

Luke slipped off his stool to join Joy. "We've broken up the book into sections. We have soups. Oyster?"

"Chick made a lovely oyster soup." Mama leaned over the magazine picture of a can of Campbell's soup.

"It'd be great if we could find his recipes, Rosie. Otherwise, I'll have to develop one. And there's no story or history about it."

Joy sat on the kitchen tile, listening to Mama and Luke. When had Luke become one of them? The perfect spice to the house female blend?

"We included sandwiches because Chick loved sandwiches, right?" Luke stooped to straighten the pages pasted with McDonald's, Subway, and Panera products. "I've got a recipe for homemade potato chips that people seem to love." He tapped a picture of Lays.

"Chick used to make homemade ketchup. Remember, Joy?"

"When did Daddy make homemade ketchup?"

"When you were kids. Early on in his cooking days. You don't remember?" Mama continued listening to Luke, hunched over, as he talked about the meat dishes with optional sides, then the casseroles and party dishes.

"Chick was always up for a party." Mama approved, pinching her chin with her fingers.

"Now *that* I remember," Joy said. "Sawyer and I used to sneak downstairs, grab a handful of tortilla chips, scoop Daddy's famous Mexican hat dip into a cup, and skedaddle before anyone saw us."

"We saw you every time, Joy." Mama tore open the Cheetos bag. "You two giggled like hyenas thinking you got away with something."

"So if you didn't bury Chick with his recipes," Luke glanced between Joy and Mama, "and they aren't in the studio, they must be here, right?"

"We've looked." Mama munched on Cheetos. "After Chick died, Sharon and I scoured the attic."

"You don't think she—"

"No, I never let her out of my sight. I didn't trust her like you and Duncan did."

"Then we'll just have to get busy and develop his recipes ourselves. Rosie, you can help us taste test." Luke scooted to the next section of construction paper and paste. Desserts. Annie-Rae's schoolgirl handwriting adorned the pages pasted with instant pudding and Pop-Tart cutouts.

A dormant guilt stirred around Joy's heart. She'd grown up with a father who loved to cook good food. Annie-Rae was growing up with an aunt who couldn't turn eggs into an omelet.

Joy had grown up chasing cousins around Granny and Granddaddy's yard, playing tag in the sweltering sun, the heady aroma of grilling meat spicing the air. When the dinner bell rang, she clambered to picnic tables laden with southern richness—homemade salads and desserts, warm breads and jams, and soul-stirring sweet tea.

What did Annie-Rae get when the dinner bell rang? Meals of solitude with a commercially pressed pastry. Standing in the kitchen, eating pizza from a box. Best of all, she got to dump her SpaghettiOs into a microwaveable bowl and watch it spin.

"Did Chick bake much?" Luke regarded Mama.

"Some. He liked to make French bread and yeast rolls." Cheeto dust fell on the cookbook's pages. "But his specialty was banana bread. Sweet Georgia Brown, it was to die for."

"Really, I'm sorry I won't get a taste of that." Luke shuffled the pages around. "My mom had a chiffon cake I can add. I've wanted to do more baking, so it'll be a fun challenge to work up some recipes."

"Stop." Joy sliced the air with her hands. "Just stop. Luke, you don't have to keep adding your own recipes." She sighed at the reflection of her image on the mock pages. "In fact, you *shouldn't* add any of your recipes."

"Joy, come on, I don't mind. It's for the show. Besides, I'll add dishes I'm doing for the season. Allison—"

"Luke." Joy rose off the floor. "You've been on the show for what . . . six weeks? And now you're helping me with a cookbook. I've hosted the show for three years, and I can't remember one recipe. Not one."

Mama slipped away, the din of munching hanging in the air. Annie-Rae peered up at Joy from her spot next to Luke.

"It's not a big deal." He shuffled pages absently.

"But it *is* a big deal." She spun, facing the window outside. "I grew up with Charles Ballard and I can't boil water. What kind of woman doesn't learn to roast meat and steam veggies? What kind of television host doesn't learn her craft?"

"Remember the summer of '08?" Mama said from the living room, the low hum of the television riding her words. "You tried to learn, Joy."

"Don't make excuses for me, Mama."

"I'm adding my recipes, Joy." Defiance fortified Luke's tone. "We're going to compile the best recipe book in the foodie kingdom."

"Stop. You're too nice to me. I don't deserve this."

Annie-Rae launched off the floor and ran for the stairs.

"Annie, honey, where are you going? We're not arguing, just discussing."

Mama came around, eyes on the stairs, setting the Cheetos bag on the counter, her stained fingers splayed. "I'll go check on her. I need to call Lyric home anyway. Her room, what's left of it, is a mess. I'll be so glad when school starts next week."

But as Mama arrived at the stairs, Annie-Rae raced back down, launching off the bottom step, a white laminated card in her hand. "Can we make this?" Annie shook the card under Luke's nose, then Joy's. "I found this. It says banana bread. Papaw made banana bread."

"I'll be darned . . ." Mama gripped Annie's hand, holding it steady. "This is Chick's recipe. In his own hand. Maybe the original. See here, the date, October '85."

"Annie, where did you find this?" Joy peered at the card, the hard ground of her soul softening at the sight of Daddy's neat, angled handwriting.

"In the attic." She looked up at Mama. "You didn't say we couldn't go up there."

Joy broke from the huddle, taking the stairs two at a time. At the end of the hall, the narrow attic door stood ajar. Up the curved narrow staircase, Joy burst into Daddy's office.

A square of sunlight hit the sun-baked hardwood from the skylight. Under the pitched roof, the room, hot and fragrant with the scent of warm wood and molding books, was everything Joy hated about Daddy.

His devotion to food, not to her, Mama, or Sawyer. Hours and hours he spent at the rolltop desk pushed against the wall, reading and writing until he came down to test his masterpieces, turning the family kitchen into his private laboratory where children were not seen or heard.

When Granny and Granddaddy died, Daddy's brothers scattered and the light of love seemed to fade from the family. No more picnics with the cousins playing tag. No more meat-scented air. No more hot buttered rolls with black raspberry jam.

"Do you want me to go?" Luke's voice rescued her from the emotional swirl.

Joy motioned to the bookshelves. "Mama said Sharon shook every cookbook trying to dislodge Daddy's notes and recipes, but nothing slipped from the pages."

"Annie said she found the card behind the desk, on the floor."

Joy glanced at the rolltop. "She probably did. I've only been up here once since he died. And I didn't look for recipes. But I remember he always had a leather book . . . like a journal."

She'd been so mad at him when he died. Why didn't he take care of himself? Give up salt, cream and sugar, fatty foods? He'd be with them today if he'd just . . .

"Joy, talk to me." Luke's hands caressed her shoulders, his fingers brushing her neck so that intoxicating tingles tightened her skin.

"He loved food more than us." She stared at the recipe. *Three ripened bananas . . .*

"Men can get lost in their careers and passions, but he'd have been a fool to love food more than his family."

"He was here physically, but emotionally—" Joy shook her head. "He missed ball games and award ceremonies. He barely made it to my graduation." She swept the tears from under her eyes with her fingers, inhaled, and heeled her racing emotions. "Will you help me look for the cookbook?"

"Tell me where to start." Luke glanced around the room. "Any secret hiding places in here?"

"Not that I know of."

"All right, Lord." Luke closed his eyes and tipped back his head. "Where would Charles Ballard stash his secrets?"

God, where do we look? Joy gripped the arm of the Barcalounger, the seat and back permanently molded with Daddy's form, and lifted, glancing underneath.

Luke pressed along the wall, stomping his foot. Joy snorted.

"What?"

"We're insane, that's what." Joy stomped on the boards under her feet. "Daddy's looking down from heaven right now going, 'Cold, cold, brrr, you're getting colder, oh my, you're in polar bear country now.'"

"It's got to be here somewhere."

Joy dug through the desk and checked for secret panels while Luke shook the cookbooks and knocked on the shelves.

The heat of the room soaked Joy's skin as she rifled through the old blue chest in the corner. "Come on, room. Give up Daddy's cookbook." The quest became about more than recipes for the show.

On her hands and knees, she knocked on the floorboards along the wall, waiting for the hollow echo reply.

"Luke, do you hide your recipes?" Joy sat back on her heels, wiped the moisture from her brow. "Of course not, you're giving them to the show."

"Well, not all of them." Luke stooped over into the alcove. "I'm keeping some to myself, waiting for a special show or my own cookbook. Don't nominate me for sainthood yet. Restaurant chefs can be very proprietary, especially in big cities. Since we can't copyright the work we slave over to perfect, we just don't share. What's behind this little door?"

Joy angled to see. "Asbestos and trusses."

"And boxes. Labeled 'taxes.'" Luke retrieved a file box with a glance back at Joy. "If I were going to hide my recipes . . . I'd hide them to look like boring old tax papers."

In the third box she examined, on the bottom, under a manila folder, Joy retrieved a soft, well-worn leather journal, thick with notes and pressed spices, bound together with rubber bands.

"Daddy's recipe book."

Twenty-one

On the porch, Joy rocked, listening to the night's song, the wind in the trees, the chorus of the creek. She'd found Daddy's book. In a box of tax papers.

Daddy had sketches and notes on every page, thoughts jotted along every edge. It was a map into his heart and mind.

Mama came to the door. "It's eleven."

"I'll be in."

"Don't mull too long, Joy. It ain't worth it. The past is the past." Mama stepped onto the porch, the screen door squeaking closed.

"Was I as horrible as I remember? Did I yell and scream a lot?"

"You were a handful, downright ugly at times, but not *so* horrible. You wanted Chick's attention, but he didn't get it. He was kind of obtuse at times. He didn't see you for you. He only saw what he thought you needed from him."

"Luke asked to take the book home to study and pull out recipes, but I wanted to keep it tonight." As she fanned through the pages in the porch light, she couldn't see much, but the cacophony of notes and jots, sketches and pressed herbs somehow comforted her. "I came home from that year in London to get to know Daddy. Joined the show. Then he died."

"We went on two different journeys, you and me. When your daddy died, I went on a quest to find myself, do what I wanted to do. You, on the other hand, went on a journey to find him." Mama's rough palm caught on Joy's hair, sending a soft tingle running over her scalp. "Maybe in part that's what you did tonight with the book."

"It was Luke. He said to look in the tax boxes."

"He's a good man, that Luke."

"He's all right."

Mama tugged Joy's hair, her soft laugh raining over her. "Good night, my dear Joy who lives so much of her life in denial."

"Please, I'm not in denial."

"He's a good man, Joy. In case you haven't noticed, good men are quite hard to find."

"In case you haven't noticed," Joy flipped the corner of the notebook with her thumb, "I'm busy keeping a show afloat and helping you raise your son's daughters."

"Oh, I noticed. But just don't keep too busy, hear me? And miss out on love." For a moment Mama stood against the side of the house, breathing deeply. "You know, I'm looking forward to tasting Chick's banana bread again."

The door closed softly.

Resting her head against the back of the rocker, Joy replayed Mama's words. Luke was a good man. And his kisses ignited a part of her heart she'd not put before a flame in a long time, not since Tim, but—

Joy lifted her head. A bump resounded from the other side of the porch. Around the side of the house. She listened, shivers running over her skin. There. Another thump. And a . . . giggle followed by a low hush. Then a muffled response.

Joy slid off the rocker and inched along the porch, her heart thumping as she walked into the billow of whispers. Reaching down, she nabbed one of her flip-flops. Properly thrown, it could inflict pain to the face. Sure. Why not.

"Hey, who's here? Anyone? Come out into the light."

Joy lunged back as a thick frame scrambled from the porch floor and into the thin shadows. Parker Eaton? His unbuttoned shirt hung open and loose around his lean chest.

"Aunt Joy. What are you doing?" Lyric, breathless, sat up, twisting and tugging, gathering herself. "You were going to hit us with a flip-flop?"

"Get inside, Lyric." Joy dropped her shoe to the porch and slipped it on. "Parker, get on home."

He jumped over the rail without a word or backward glance, stumbling over a root or one of Mama's potted plants and crawling a good twenty yards before launching to his feet.

"There, you happy? You scared him off." Lyric

passed Joy with the defiance of an angry fourteen-year-old.

"You're darn right I scared him off."

"Now he'll never come back."

"Good. If he only wants you because you're making out with him, then you don't need him."

"He's the coolest boy in school, Aunt Joy." Lyric flared, her long waves wild and free, her spirit a gathering storm. "And he loves me. Lyric Ballard. Me."

"Is that what he said? He loves you?"

"Why do you ruin everything?"

"I'm trying to keep *you* from getting ruined. Please, go inside and don't say another word. I'm so angry with you right now, and I don't want to say things I don't mean."

Lyric jerked the screen so hard the handle slapped the side of the house. Through the house and up the stairs, her heels thudded.

Joy picked up Daddy's recipe book from the floor and collapsed against the porch post, her emotions churning in her chest. It was painful to get a glimpse of her former self in fiery Lyric.

Sawyer and Mindy had better come home. Soon.

Twenty-two

Luke idled the Spit Fire in front of the Ballards' and dialed Joy. "Come outside . . . because . . . Joy, the cookbook can wait. It's Friday night. We've been working all week."

The front door flew open and Joy stood on the porch, the sexiest sight he'd ever seen, haloed in the light of home.

She still held her phone to her ear. "No, come inside. I picked up fresh shrimp from Gay's. We need to remake the scampi."

"We?" He stepped toward her, slow, casual, trying to detach from being her colleague. At least for tonight.

She gazed down at his feet and ended the call, lowering her hand by her side. "You're wearing flip-flops. The cowboy has toes." Joy angled for a better look.

"What's this about the scampi?" He stepped up onto the bottom step.

"I didn't write it down." She moved back an inch, her eyes latching with his. "I was too busy eating . . ." Joy smoothed her hand over her shorts. "I think I've gained another five pounds this week."

"If you did, it's in all the right places." He moved closer, her fragrance like walking into a cottony wall.

"Luke, what are you up to?"

"We're not cooking tonight." He reached for her hand but decided she looked leery enough. Odd to have the barrier be handholding instead of something as intimate as kissing. He ached to travel that familiar path, but promised that tonight, heaven help him, was all about Joy. And the treasure of her father's recipe book. He'd been reading and studying it since Joy gave it to him the day after she found it. "We've been reshooting every day and taping new shows, then cooking every night. I'm exhausted. How much smiling can an introverted chef do in five days?"

"But I bought shrimp."

"It'll keep."

"It'll keep?" Joy made a face. "What's going on, Luke?"

"Get in the car and find out."

Her eyes widened. "No, I'm wearing old shorts. My hair is in a ponytail—"

"For crying out loud." Luke swooped Joy into his arms, cradling her against his chest as he carried her off the porch. "I've branded calves more cooperative than you."

Driving down Hwy 170 under the last of the August sky, Joy settled in the passenger seat. Luke blessed the wild idea of taking Joy on a date. "I think we both need a night off."

"I didn't know I was so tired. I just kept gearing up for the next thing."

Luke braked and cut off the highway, taking a dirt road through the pines and palmettos. Rube said the turnoff would come up fast . . .

"How do I know you're not driving me into the swamp to kill me?"

"You don't."

"Should I turn on my phone's GPS?"

"If it makes you feel better."

She reached back, tugging her iPhone from her hip pocket. "Does anything rattle you?"

"Sure. Burnt meat. Overcooked pasta. People who refrigerate tomatoes. Mispronouncing *béchamel.*"

"Then you must be a nervous wreck around me." She rode with her feet on the dash, the setting sun glinting off smooth, sculptured legs.

"I am. But not for those reasons." Maybe it wasn't a good idea to be alone with her in the meadow on a sultry summer night.

Rube Butler appeared on the horizon atop his horse, standing guard over the fire pit and picnic spread.

When Luke stopped the car, he glanced at Joy. "Wait."

She nodded. And in her eyes he saw what he hoped for—Joy the woman, not a colleague. Stepping out, Luke tossed his keys to Rube. "Give us a couple of hours?"

"See you then." Rube dropped the horse's reins to the ground.

"Joy, this is Rube." Luke held her door open. "And he's letting me borrow a square of his land for the night."

Rube nodded, tipping his hat. "I seen you on TV." He gunned the Spit Fire and fishtailed through the grass, grinding the gears as he sped away.

"How do you know him?"

"Café. He comes in every week." Luke slipped his arm around her. "Hungry?"

"What are you doing?" Stiffening, Joy regarded him, but didn't pull away.

He shrugged. "Just wanted to spend time with you when cameras weren't watching. Or Annie-Rae." Luke released her, the soft scent of her skin challenging his resolve. "I–I made a picnic." He cleared his throat and dropped to the blanket. "We have homemade bread and store-bought cheese. I haven't mastered dairy yet. Sliced apples with caramel chocolate sauce. Beef tips on the spit over the pit. And my own special lemon raspberry iced tea."

"Luke, when did you put all of this together?" She curled her legs under her as she sat on the blanket, reaching for the glass of tea he offered.

"It didn't take long. Just started the bread last night." He broke a piece off the loaf. "Open your mouth and close your eyes."

She stared at him. "Why? It makes me feel weird."

"Please." Luke cradled the bread in his palm, taking up a slice of cheese. "I want to show you something."

"With my eyes closed?" She laughed, loud and nervous.

"Joy." He grasped her arm and she shivered. "Open your mouth and close your eyes."

She surrendered to Luke as he settled the bread and cheese in her mouth. His pulse charged through his veins. But tonight was about the sensation of food and nothing more.

"What do you taste?"

"Warm and crunchy but with a tangy cream." She covered her mouth as she chewed and kept her eyes closed.

"Breathe deep. Do you taste the layers of the bread and cheese?"

"Mmm, so good."

"What kind of cheese?"

"Swiss."

"Try again." Luke prepared a portion for himself.

"Brie?"

"Very good, chef. Now, what kind of bread?"

"French." Joy laughed, swallowing. "Who came up with this game, Luke? Name That Food."

"Cyrano used words. I use food."

Joy's eyes fluttered open. "Use food for what?"

"Hey, no peeking. Close your eyes and taste. Don't think or fret. Just taste, Joy." Luke settled a new bite on her tongue. "What are you tasting?"

"Apples with chocolate."

"And?"

"Caramel."

"Good, but those are surface flavors. What else are you tasting or feeling?"

"Sweet and tart. The thickness of caramel, the smooth flavor of chocolate. It's going good, isn't it, Luke? You cooking and me tasting?"

"I think it's the most amazing time of my life." He touched his finger to her eyelids. "Keep them closed. Here's another bite. Forget the apples, the chocolate and caramel, what are you *tasting?*"

"I taste . . ." She pressed her hand over her middle, then a thin veil of moisture touched her lashes. "Memories." Her chin quivered.

"Yeah? Like what? What do you remember when you taste bread or apples or chocolate and caramel?"

She brushed the water from under her eyes. "Well, the bread makes me think of holidays at Granny Ballard's. She always had a big spread with homemade rolls, jams, desserts. The whole family was together. I mean, everyone. No one missed a Thanksgiving or Christmas. In-laws of in-laws came to Granny's. When she and Granddaddy died, it was as if death took the whole family. It was seven years before everyone came together again. For Daddy's funeral."

"Food is powerful with families. What else?"

"The apples remind me of Daddy in the fall. At

Halloween. He'd make caramel apples outside by a fire pit. All the kids in the neighborhood came over and we'd run around in costumes. Daddy showed us how to dip apples and cool them on wax paper. Then drizzle them with warm chocolate. He went all out. He . . ." Joy hesitated, a pool of water collecting under her eyes. "He made it fun."

"You're tasting his recipe. I found it in the book." Luke lightly touched the smudge of chocolate on the corner of her lip. His finger sizzled and he felt weakened by the music of the fire and smoky hues of twilight.

"We should . . . add it . . ." Her breathing inflated each word. ". . . to the book."

He cleared his throat, drawing his hand back to the food. "Think Annie will lend us more construction paper for our mocked-up book?"

She laughed. "We might need to make a Walmart run."

"Joy, did you read through the book at all before you gave it to me to take home?"

"I flipped through the pages, but I didn't really read it." She sighed in a way that made him feel like he never wanted to leave home. She gathered her legs in her arms, eyes still closed. "I was afraid reading all those ingredients and notes would remind me of the bad times. And how he loved food more than us." Joy peered at Luke through a watery sheen. "I just wanted to hug the book. Hug him."

The wind snapped low and stirred the fire. Luke's heart caressed her words. "Eyes closed again." He reached for the skewer sizzling with meat, luscious juices dripping into the fire. "Now what do you taste?" Luke cooled the meat, then offered it to Joy's tongue.

She laughed, fanning her parted mouth. "Hot, but mmm, so good. Savory, with a hint of sweet. Is that brown sugar?"

"Joy Ballard, you are your father's daughter. It's his brown sugar and honey barbecue sauce."

"This . . ." Joy chewed, the expression on her face more than a thousand words. "Is definitely going into the book."

In the background, the mare stomped and whinnied. "Easy, girl." Luke looked around as the mare tossed her head. She wanted to run. *In a minute.* Turning back to Joy, he lifted Chick's recipe book out of the basket. "You know that verse in the Bible where Jesus says, 'My food is to do the will of Him who sent Me?' "

Joy snapped up straight, eyes open. "It's the verse in my truck. I've been trying to memorize it for . . . ever." She anchored her chin against her knees. "I don't think I understand it."

"I think it has to be something like this. Feeding on God's Word, the bread," he motioned to the broken French bread, "it's like when I feed people with my creations. Like your dad. When Jesus said, 'My food is to do the will of Him who sent

Me,' was He saying God feeds me? He's my satisfaction? So, is the Father our spiritual chef? For lack of a better phrase." Luke thumbed the book's pages. "I don't make a very good preacher, but—"

"You sound passionate." Joy lightly swept her fingers over his arm. "It's good to be passionate."

"What do you think the Father sent you to do, Joy? I know I'm to serve food. What about you?"

She cradled her face against her arms. "I have no idea. And I'm too terrified to ask. What if the answer is 'nothing'?" She raised her head. "No *food* for you, Joy."

"Impossible." Luke brushed her hair from her eyes and Joy leaned into his touch. "He loves you too much. Why would He leave you, or any of us, out?"

"Don't you ever doubt, Luke?"

"I do, less today than I did yesterday. Faith in God is a journey, a marathon. We want it to be a sprint." He held up the book. "I want to read to you. Is that okay?" If he didn't move on to the purpose of this picnic, he'd scoop her in his arms and ease her down on the blanket.

"I don't know. If you're going to read 'brine the meat in a container of water and sea salt for at least twenty-four hours,' I'm going to be snoring in six seconds or less."

Luke laughed, flipping through the pages. "When you repeat recipes, you use your TV voice."

"I don't have a TV voice."

"Yeah, you do." Luke squared his shoulders, raised his chin, and tried to mimic the voice he heard in his head. "Brine the meat in a container of water and sea salt."

"Oh my gosh. Is that how I sound? Like Mrs. Doubtfire ate Julia Child?" Joy flung her arms wide with dramatic flair.

"Something like that, only younger. And funnier." Luke propped on his elbow to read Chick's pages by the firelight. This was a good night. "Here we go. Date: February first. 'Joy's birthday. Ordering softball cake from Magnolia Bakery. My baking skills inadequate for such a feat.'"

Joy angled to lean against Luke, the press of her shoulder soft against his back. "What are you reading?" She sat next to him, tucking her hair behind her ears, pressing the book lower to see the pages in the firelight.

"Your dad's recipe book." Face-to-face with her, he felt himself sinking. "It's full of personal notes. Like a journal."

"I remember the softball cake. I was fourteen going on fifteen. Same as Lyric. The beginning of the turbulence. The emergence of me as a smart-mouthed teen. He was still writing a food column for the paper and doing morning talk shows."

Luke turned to the next marked page. "July sixteenth. 'Perfected my banana bread recipe by adjusting the flour and baking soda measurements. Made it for Joy. She loves banana bread. Rosie called from the field saying Joy pitched a no-hitter. Guess I forgot her game again.'"

Silence. Then, "He missed my game to adjust flour and baking soda measurements. See what I was up against?"

Luke closed the book, marking his place with his thumb. "Don't you see, Joy? Your dad wasn't measuring just flour and baking soda. He was crafting a gift for you. I see my mom on these pages. Myself too, I guess."

"If he wanted to do something for me, why didn't he come to my games?"

"Why'd you join the show? Come on, years of turbulence with Chick, and you come home from a year in London and suddenly join the show?"

"Because." Joy balled up, knees to her chest. She stared at the flames. "When I lived in London, I was waiting tables, trying to write freelance, and getting no work. What started out as adventure quickly turned to drudgery. Then Daddy had his first heart episode and I realized how fragile life could be. What if he'd died? What if my last words to my father were, 'Whatever, Daddy . . .' as I walked out of the house? I can't even remember the argument. I quit my fine job sloshing warm beer to Englishmen with accents I couldn't understand, told my roommate good-bye, and flew home. Somehow I knew my season of getting to know him had arrived." She regarded him. "Why are you doing this, Luke?"

If Jesus can't resist loving you, how can I? "Because," he raised the book, "I'm trying to get to know my own father too. Helping you helps me. But instead of a book of his private thoughts to read, I have a living, breathing, stubborn man to dig into." *Call Red tomorrow after church.* "You don't have Chick, but you have his private thoughts." Luke opened the book again, smoothing his hands over the pages. " 'Sawyer dating a nice girl in college. Mindy. Coming this weekend. Making his favorite, pecan sweet potatoes. Note: Joy's grown an inch or two. She's very pretty. Reminds me of my first mama.' "

"He wrote I was very pretty?" Joy pushed against Luke's arm to see the words.

"Well, I didn't make it up." He showed her the words. "What does he mean by 'first mama'?"

"Daddy was adopted. His biological mother wanted to be an actress, so she left him at a bus station with a note and a sack lunch, and boarded a bus for New York. He was four years old."

"And he spent his life trying to nurture your family."

"I see what you're doing. Trying to get me to understand that Daddy's love affair with food came from his deep love to nurture us."

"Got any better ideas?"

Luke left Joy alone with her thoughts for a few

moments. Then turned to his next marked page. "Here's another entry. Chick wrote, 'Joy barred in her room. Feel I'm failing her. She's so impatient with me. Thinks I spend too much time in the kitchen. But I do it for her, Sawyer, and Rosie. Note: I'm quite satisfied with banana bread recipe.'"

Joy wiped her cheeks with the back of her hand. "The banana bread love letter . . ."

"Now there's a book title for you." Luke read the next entry. "'Joy turns sixteen. Fear my inadequacies hinder her.'" Luke tapped her foot with his. "He fears his inadequacies a lot. 'I say a word and she flies at me. So much potential in that girl lest anger gets her. Rosie suggests I change. The notion overwhelms. Success with gumbo and biscuits on Charleston morning show. Recipe note: reduce béchamel extra minute.'" Luke flipped through the pages to another entry he'd marked. "'August. Went to Joy's game. Stayed in car so not to cause a stir and break her concentration. Her team won. Banana bread is in order! And pizza. Joy likes my pizza. Thin crust. Calling it Pitcher's Choice Pizza. I suppose it was worth losing all the bark on Rosie's prized palmetto for Joy to learn to pitch so well.'"

Joy laughed. "Poor tree never saw me coming."

Luke placed the book on the blanket beside him. "When I first started going through the book looking for recipes, his notes on the side were

284

annoying. Then I realized Chick was working out his own thoughts and emotions through food, through his recipes. Whenever things heated up with you, instead of changing himself, it seems he'd adjust a recipe. My guess is the attic has more of these books."

Joy reached for the book and examined the pages. "I never knew any of this."

"Let's add your memories to the book we're putting together, Joy. Of Ballard family picnics. Of working with your dad on the show. Coming home from London. Allison will love it."

"Luke, who's going to make Daddy's barbecue ribs recipe if I write, 'I hated my daddy when he spent eight hours in the kitchen working on his barbecue sauces. But here it is for y'all. Hope your family loves it.' "

"No, Joy, write how it makes you feel *now*. Write how it made you feel when you ate the ribs. Pleasant memories are buried in your heart, Joy. I know it. Like the apples with chocolate and caramel. Sweet and tart. You remembered Halloween, dunking apples, a yard full of friends." He brushed her jaw with his fingertips.

"Luke?" Joy angled toward him.

He jumped up so fast Joy tumbled forward. No kissing. Not on a sultry August night, alone with Joy on the meadow. "Let's give this horse some exercise while there's the last bit of light." Luke grabbed her hand, jerked her to her feet, and led her to the old mare. "Ever ridden?" Luke mounted the mare, then leaned down, offering Joy his hand.

"Does a Shetland pony at the fair count?"

She landed in the saddle behind him with a yelp, then a laugh, slipping her arms about his waist. The mare stirred, ready to gallop. Joy nestled her face against Luke's back. His heart beat in a staccato rhythm.

"Joy, you know, back there—" Luke urged the horse forward, holding her to a slow gait.

"You wanted to kiss me?"

He felt the breath of her smile. "More than you know." Luke chirruped to the mare, loosened the reins, and let her run.

Twenty-three

Hooked it. Again. Luke watched his golf ball honing for the trees like a round, featherless pigeon.

"It's the heat. Too darn hot to play decent golf."

"I hate to see a man play bad golf." Heath shielded his eyes as the ball crashed through limbs and leaves.

"I hate to hear a man make sad excuses for his bad golf." On Luke's right, Mitch leaned on his club. "The heat? You mean your hot picnic with Joy?"

"Looking for song material, O'Neal? Don't come knockin' here, the kitchen is closed." Luke started for the tree line. What was wrong with his swing?

"That's not what I heard." Mitch teased him from the green.

"A horse ride?" Heath added his two cents. "Picnic with bread and cheese? Apples and dipping sauce? You're a chef, man."

Yeah, yeah, whatever . . . He beat the scrub brush with his club. Nothing could rain on his memory of Joy. And bread, cheese, apples, and sweet tea. The combo breathed romance. "You're just jealous you didn't think of it."

Finding the ball on the edge of the trees, Luke

waited, watching Mitch's nearly perfect swing send his ball on an under-par trajectory. It landed on the green with a thump, kept rolling, and slipped off the green into the rough.

"Tough break, O'Neal," Luke shouted through the trees. Served him right.

Heath's ball landed safely on the green because Heath always landed safely. Luke lined up for an easy chip shot. The ball plopped onto the green three feet from the cup.

Luke and Mitch applauded and bowed irreverently.

"Thank you for your support."

Mitch's turn. He was determined to make a stellar shot. He walked the green, crouching to check the cut and curve of the grass, running his palm over the blades, checking the wind.

"Just shoot already, O'Neal. I'm aging while we wait."

"He gets lost in all the faux adoration, aiming for perfection. Until Caroline gets ahold of him." Heath knocked a bit of mud from his shoe. "So, you and Joy . . ."

"Friends, Heath."

"A starlight picnic with a horseback ride and you're 'just friends'?" Heath air quoted *just friends*.

Heath's challenge made Luke wonder if he wasn't completely upside down, turned around, and inside out. "We are friends, Heath. But every once in a while we get caught in this weird vortex and next thing I know, we're lip-locked, sinking into this great, heart-numbing kiss." The memory stirred eager feelings. "I've been in a lot of relationships, but Joy is special, and I want to do things differently. This is my first attempt to walk with God in a relationship. Suddenly all the red-blooded American boy urges are more annoying than exciting. To top it off, she's my boss." He leaned on his club. "O'Neal, shoot. I can feel my beard growing."

She was his boss. His friend. His student. The first face he saw in the morning when he woke up and the last name on his mind as he drifted to sleep. Joy made Luke feel at home. As if he could exhale and tip face-first into a mountain of sun-dried pillows and linens.

In the reflection of her friendship, Luke could see how selfish he'd been since leaving home for New York. It saddened him. What was it . . . the other day . . . he woke up and had a sentimental feeling for those Christmas dinners he'd eaten with Red at the VFW, watching a bunch of old men gum their turkey.

"What's up with the restaurant job in Portland?"

"Linus still wants me to come up. His lawyer thinks I can get out of my contract with Wild Woman, but if the show goes well, he thinks he can work a deal with Allison for me to still be on the show. That is if I can become less boring on camera."

"And what do you want?"

Joy. "I'd like to run my own kitchen without the headache of running a business. But the show is fun and—"

"You work with a gorgeous show host." Heath cupped his hand beside his mouth. "Mitch, you're not out here with Phil Mickelson."

As Heath's words caught on the wind, the country crooner tapped his ball.

"Right on track for a hole in one. Can you believe it?" Luke tipped his head to one side, squinting at the green. Unbelievable. "We'll never be able to hurry Mitch again." Luke's cell buzzed from his pocket. "Hey, Red, what's up?"

"Not much, not much. How're things your way?"

"Busy, but good. Playing a bit of golf today." What was it Luke heard in his dad's voice? "You all right, Red?"

"Well." Red cleared his throat. "If it ain't no bother, I was wondering if you could come home for a bit. The doc wants to cut me open and clean out my heart wires. I told him I'd have to check with you. Can you come sit with me? If I die, I'd like not to be alone."

At her computer, Joy typed in the final Snow on the Mountain recipe she and Luke duplicated from Daddy's book. The aroma of succulent chicken hung in the air, drawing out all the delicious aromas of the past and thickening the warmth of the kitchen.

Joy exhaled, propping her cheek against her hand, and stared out the porch door. The slant of the late August sun glinted off the glass. She'd lost track of the evening and weekend hours she'd worked with Luke cooking, testing, and writing.

She still couldn't cook, but she no longer hated the kitchen. Especially when Luke worked at the stove. Confident and decisive, he added new life to Daddy's old recipes.

Through cryptic conversation, they'd hinted about their working friendship and how good it was to be "just friends," but later that night, when Luke burned his hand, Joy smoothed ointment on the red-hot spot and nearly ignited her own passion's fire.

His warm breath had brushed her face in quick succession. The pulse in his wrist throbbed. When she released him with a weak, "All better," his gaze stayed on her lips until she nearly swooned against the counter. But he didn't sweep her in his arms to taste her kiss. He merely tapped his finger on the burn and whispered, "It's not cooling off yet."

Well, enough daydreaming. Back to the recipe. Luke would be here soon to go over the final pages. Allison would be pleased they were on track for the October deadline.

The house was so quiet Joy could hardly

concentrate. Lyric holed away in her room, working on homework. School started last week and the grounded Lyric was liberated. After the incident with Parker on the porch, an icy, silent tension moved into the Ballard house, sat at the table for dinner, curled on the couch to watch TV, even picked out a towel and took a nightly shower.

Joy pushed away from her computer, stretching, rubbing the tension out of her neck. In the past few days, Lyric had returned to her normal teenager self. Her room was still empty of anything but clothes and bedding, but she'd kept a lamp Mama had snuck in to help with her studies. And now, her schoolbooks were piled in a corner. Joy called Sawyer with an update to his voice mail about his blossoming daughter, but he'd yet to return her call.

Annie-Rae, on last look, read a book and listened to music, propped against her bed pillows. Mama was . . . Where was Mama? Rising, Joy walked to the sliding doors and stepped onto the porch. Wasn't she planning on working in the yard?

The warm evening air swirled around her, peaceful, quiet.

"Get back here, Rosie!"

Mama broke into Joy's plane of sight with Miss Dolly puffing and huffing after her. Mama ran toward her work shed, a brown-haired streak of heels and elbows, her moppy hair bouncing.

"What now, Mama?" Joy stepped off the back porch and squinted toward the action, curling her toes around the thick blades of grass.

"Joy Ballard, you do something with your mama, and I mean now." Miss Dolly shuffled toward Joy, the hem of her silky blouse bulging at her waist, a wilted, so-sad looking flower slumping over her hand. "Look what that . . . that . . . woman did to my garden." She tried to wave the flower, but the stem just sank lower. "Plastic. And how do I find out? When the garden club comes to supper. Regina Whetstone nearly suffocated when she snorted up a nose full of wax. Every garden club in Beaufort and Jasper County has heard by now." Miss Dolly threw the wilting bloom to the ground and faced Mama, who was propped securely against the work shed's door. "I'll get you for this, Rosie, if it's the last thing I do."

"Oh, Dolly, get over yourself." Mama eased across the yard, hand in her shorts pocket. "Regina Whetstone would've spread some rumor about you no matter what, and you know I'm telling the truth. Might as well give her something good to tell. But as long as you know, I'll confess. I sprayed pesticide to kill those worms of yours feasting on my hibiscus and your weak little blooms choked to death. So I replaced them."

"You replaced my prize black-eyed Susans with wax?" Miss Dolly wobbled, her eyes rolling back in her head, red cheeks jiggling.

293

"I don't know what went wrong," Mama said with a singsong. "They were guaranteed up to a hundred and ten degrees."

Steam shot from Miss Dolly's ears, and Joy could've sworn she heard the faintest sound of hissing. Miss Dolly tore through the hedge to her yard, peppering the air with a string of wax-melting phrases.

"And she calls herself a lady." Mama sauntered around Joy toward the porch door. "Is Luke cooking dinner tonight? I'm getting spoiled."

"No, we're having pizza. He's cooked enough." Joy followed Mama to the porch. "Speaking of ladies, you really put wax flowers in Miss Dolly's garden?"

"I did, and I'd do it again." Mama collapsed into a wrought iron chair, crossing her legs with exaggerated energy. "Did you see her face? I need to get one of those phones with a camera."

"Mama, what are you going to do to make this up to her?" Joy perched on the edge of the rocker. "She's pretty upset."

"She should've thought about that when she was moving all her bugs and worms into my lawn *and* telling the garden club she saw me out on the dock smoking a pipe like a hick granny from the hills. A pipe. I never. Not even a cigarette. These lungs are tobacco virgins."

"So you ruined her garden. You'd have tanned my hide and fed me soap for a lesser crime. And since when do you care about the garden club?"

"It's the principle." Mama shot Joy a narrowed glance. "Simmer down. I'll talk to her tomorrow. Offer to pay for a new, *real* garden. Just let me have fun for tonight, will you?"

"How will you be able to sleep?"

"Right fine. Unless I get to picturing her face. Then I'll start laughing all over again." Mama moved to the chair next to Joy, stretched out her tanned legs, and locked her hands behind her head. "Only thing better would've been to see Regina Whetstone with blue wax dripping from the end of her cosmetically enhanced nose."

"I've a good mind to send you to bed without supper."

"Go ahead. I have MoonPies tucked away in the closet."

"Aunt Joy, Granny?" Lyric peered through the door, her hair swinging over her shoulder. "I did my homework."

Mama angled around to see her. "And? You want to do something, don't you?"

Lyric twisted her hair around her hand. "Can Parker come for pizza? Please?"

"On a Friday night? Doesn't he have a football game?"

"It's tomorrow night. Out of town. He can come for pizza. Please, Aunt Joy."

Joy peeked at Mama, who voted yes with a glance. Lyric had humbled up some since the porch debacle. Softened. And in the last few days she had bloomed into a bright-eyed freshman.

When did Joy become old? At twenty-nine?

"Okay, but he goes home by eight."

"Thank you." Lyric fired onto the porch, reaching over the chairs to hug their necks. "Oh, Aunt Joy, your man is here."

"He's not my—"

Lyric disappeared in a golden blonde dash. Mama laughed. Joy flicked the top of her hair as she headed to greet her friend, her *colleague*. Her cohost. Nothing more.

Twenty-four

Entertainment News

Quirky cooking show host Joy Ballard of *Dining with Joy* will guest on *The Bette Hudson Show* Thursday, September 24, promoting her debut on the supernetwork TruReality. Ballard first gained notoriety for her Letterman-like show format and popularity among college students after taking over *Dining with Charles* when her father, Charles Ballard, died of a heart attack at the age of fifty-six.

Owner of Wild Woman Productions, Allison Wild, said, "We are thrilled to be a part of the TruReality team. This is big for Wild Woman, for *Dining with Joy*, and for TruReality. Joy is the face of their fall lineup."

Ballard and her cohost, Luke Redmond, acclaimed chef and former Manhattan restaurateur, release their first cookbook together this fall, the eponymous *Dining with Joy*.

"We have a really great guest with us today . . ."

In the green room, Joy waited perfectly still on the edge of the sofa. However, jitters rumbled over her heart, knocking terror into her excitement.

Eyes closed, she listened to Bette introduce the show. Joy hadn't seen the set, nor Bette, today. She liked to enter fresh, unpolished, as if she were a first-time guest in someone's home. She wanted all her reactions to be genuine.

Luke quizzed her for two days before the show. Then she flew to New York, and he hopped a plane to Oklahoma for Red's surgery.

"What's your favorite spice?"

"Posh. No, Sporty."

"What are you talking about?"

"The Spice Girls. Please tell me you're not that square?"

"Like your great-grandma at a rock concert. How about cinnamon as your favorite spice? Is there a cinnamon Spice Girl? Because cinnamon is a great favorite spice. Why? Because it goes with everything. Joy? Joy. Attention. You were seeing yourself as Cinnamon Spice, weren't you?"

"You think I'd need a tan to pull it off? Hey, how about vanilla? It could be my favorite spice."

She'd pinched the pale skin under her forearm, and when she let go, a red dot marked the spot. He laughed, a resonating tenor she'd tucked away in her heart and labeled Favorite Melody.

A knock fired Allison out of her chair.

"Five minutes, Miss Ballard."

"Thank you." Allison cupped her hands around her mouth, yelling as if the door were steel, the walls poured concrete. But there was no need. The walls didn't even go all the way up to the ceiling.

Joy's phone pinged from her handbag. Luke. She cradled her phone in her palm.

Praying 4 u. Own the show, Joy.

Praying 4 u, 2. How's Red?

Resting. He looks old.

He just came out of surgery, cowboy! Sheesh, give him a break.

Ok, ok. Down girl . . . Call me when ur off set.

K

"That Luke?" Allison beamed from the other side of the room where she checked e-mail on her BlackBerry. "Tell him the publisher's test kitchen is loving the recipes we've sent so far. And I forgot to tell you, but I pitched the idea of you writing anecdotes. They were all over it. I asked for an extra week since we're still in show production." Allison rattled off her words without a breath.

Joy messaged Luke.

Allison said, wahwah, wahwah, wah.

Huh?

LOL. Test kitchen, loves recipes. Publisher likes anecdote idea.

Was there ever a question?

"Dan is thrilled with the retakes too. Your mojo

with Luke is finally coming through. Please tell me you two are romantically involved." Allison arched her brow, asking the personal question.

"No, no, we're friends. Period."

"Really? 'Cause the chemistry on the set is changing." Allison gasped, sitting back, mouth parted. "So you two are keeping it *professional?*" She laughed. "Perfect. The sexual tension is simply perfect. You still scare him a bit. I like it."

Allison says ur a wimp. I scare u.

Ha, u don't scare me, u terrify me.

"What's he saying?"

"That his dad is recovering from surgery."

"Oh right, yes." Allison's thumbs flew over her phone's miniscule keypad. "Give him my best."

Allison wishes Red well.

Thx. How long b4 u go on?

"Two minutes, Miss Ballard." The floor manager peeked through the door this time, checking for Joy's acknowledgment.

2 mins.

"I'll be right there."

Go get em.

Joy checked her hair and makeup in the lighted mirror as she passed to the door. Bette's stylist gave her the just-walked-into-a-wind-machine look. Hand on the knob, Joy pulled back, tipped her head forward, and shook the stiffness from her hair, combing her fingers through the spray. Better. The just-ran-off-the-softball-field look.

"Just be yourself, Joy." Allison quick-grabbed Joy's arm.

"Do I have a choice?" An uneasiness shimmied through Joy. "Unless something's going on. Alli, is there something I should know?"

"Just that this is it. Our big moment. *The Bette Hudson Show.* I've worked my whole life for this and here it is . . . in your hands." She slowly opened her palms to Joy. "After twenty-five years in the business, my own production company is moving to the center stage." Her eyes glistened. "Thank you."

"You're . . . welcome." Joy fell stiff into Allison's tight hug. The revelation of Allison's heart was unexpected. Troublesome. Her hopes and dreams, the validation of her life's work rested on Joy?

"Allison." Joy inhaled all the air between them. If Allison was dishing out burdens, Joy might as well reciprocate. *I can't cook.* What better time? Right before the ballyhooed debut on *The Bette Hudson Show.* At least Allison couldn't, wouldn't, kill her. "This is probably the worst possible time, or perhaps the best possible time, depends on whose perspective you're coming from, but I need to tell you—"

"No, don't." Allison backed up, palms pushing against the invisible. "Don't jinx this. Nothing negative. Or positive. Don't stir the cosmos. Whatever you have to say can wait. Right? It can wait."

"Miss Ballard, thirty seconds."

"Yeah, Allison, it can wait." So much for the coward's road to truth. Drop the bomb, then exit stage left. Joy owed Allison the right to have a proper conniption.

"Break a leg, Joy." Allison smoothed her hand down Joy's arm. "Be funny, witty, all the things you are on the show."

And a fraud. Sure, no problem. Joy paused at the door with a quick smile. "I'll try." Allison gave her thumbs-up with an excited scrunch of her shoulders.

The long walk down the dimly lit hall to the main stage echoed with Joy's footsteps.

On Bette Hudson's elevated, in-the-round stage, Joy waved to the applauding audience, letting the *love* sink in. She might be able to get used to this.

"Joy, it is so good to see you." Bette hugged and welcomed Joy as if she belonged on her opulent stage designed to seat A-listers and presidents.

"It's great to be here. Thank you for having me." Joy smoothed her skirt before sitting in the white leather club chair. She reached for the glass of water and took a long drink, cooling her hot nerves. "I love your necklace, Bette. It's gorgeous." Joy angled within the acceptable personal space for a closer look at the turquoise and silver piece. If she knew one thing in her years of faux cooking show hosting, it was always, always compliment the host.

"You like it? I wasn't sure when my husband bought it for me last year in New Mexico, but my New Year's resolution was to try new things, go outside of my comfort zone, especially when it comes to fashion. When Stan showed it to me I was like, 'Turquoise? What? Am I in seventh grade?' "

"It's fabulous. You were smart to wear it. I might have to go to New Mexico to get one for myself."

"Girl, you do not." Bette reached up behind her neck. "I'd love to give you this one. A gift from me to you."

The audience ohhed, then applauded. Through the years, Bette solidified her fan base with lavish gift shows. The producer had briefed Joy before the show to *"accept a gift no matter what Bette should offer. But she's only given a gift to new guests twice in the last five years, so you're probably safe. She has to really like you."*

"Bette, I'm honored." Joy shrugged and grinned at the audience as she lifted her hair for Bette to clasp the piece around her neck. She was just one of them—unknown and undeserving. "I hope this doesn't mean I'm somehow engaged to Stan."

The audience rumbled with a swelling laugh. Bette joined in with a louder-than-necessary cackle, hugging Joy's shoulders. "I don't know . . . something could be arranged."

"I'm afraid of what just happened here." Joy fingered the heavy silver piece, eyeing Bette, gauging when the bit was over.

Bette collapsed back in her seat. "I'm mad Allison didn't introduce you to me earlier. We are going to be friends, Joy Ballard. So tell me about your new show. It sounds exciting. And girl, I've seen that cohost of yours." Bette cocked her eyebrows and puckered her lips. "I'll trade you two Stans for him."

"Luke Redmond is a great guy and a fabulous chef. He's been a fun addition this year." She liked talking about him. "*Dining with Joy* is about food and fun. Not always in that order. We do a lot of comedy and give our viewers a chance to participate in the show. I'm not a trained chef. I'm like every other cooking woman out there, so we wanted to open up the show, let the outside in, tell the world what you're cooking. Most cooking shows have a closed, canned feel. We wanted something open, inviting."

"Just like you." Bette squeezed Joy's arm. "I love this path you're paving for cooking shows. You're real and accessible. Like we're neighbors, running across the yard to each other's kitchens. Being innovative is how I got to where I am. You're going to be a star, Joy. I can tell these things."

Okay, from your lips to God's ears. All obstacles aside.

304

"Now listen, I have to ask you this." Bette read her teleprompter. "Is this true? Did you say everything should taste like Froot Loops?"

"What?" Joy squinted at the teleprompter. "Bette, please. I never said everything should taste like Froot Loops. I hate Froot Loops. I said everything should taste like Cocoa Pebbles. Or Honeycomb. Cap'n Crunch, if you're out of the other two."

Joy settled back, arms stretched along the sides of the chair, her torso filled with the joy of laughter.

"A star, I tell you. Don't y'all agree? Let's take a look at Joy in action. Here we go. A preview of *Dining with Joy*." Bette introduced the clip as the house lights dimmed. Joy watched the floor monitor, wincing, smiling as she deep-fried a peanut butter and jelly sandwich, then the flip-flop. The beginning of the zaniness. The image morphed to a Stupid Cooking Trick, to a guest appearance by an Atlanta Falcons football player, to the kiss with Luke. Joy tensed and tingled.

The audience, mostly women, sighed and moaned.

She'd avoided the YouTube version of the kiss, only viewing the fading image in her mind from time to time. The kiss that started it all. One impulsive, surreal moment. But seeing it now, vivid with all the colors restored, Joy's heart knocked on its own door. *Hey, crazy girl, let him in.*

Sinking, sinking, she'd blissfully submerged

into his kiss and embrace, the muffled din of the audience, the paling lights, the swelling aroma of sweet and savory peach sauced pork were merely ambrosia.

Joy dug her fingers into the arms of the chair. This wasn't Allison's moment to broadcast to the world. It was Joy's. Luke's. A yearning for him twisted around her heart.

Then the monitor faded to black and the lights burned bright, exposing the mesmerized audience.

"Joy, look what you've done." Bette fanned herself, then the audience. "You've stunned us. I'm on fire here. Who cares about food when you have Luke Redmond in the house?"

The audience stirred with a spattering of applause.

"Joy, the show looks fantastic. And that kiss?"

"Well, there's more than one way to beat Wenda Divine." Uncomfortable laugh. Shifting in her seat, exposed by the audience peeking into her heart.

"So that was the kiss that defeated Wenda? Goodness. I'm about to puddle on the floor. Aren't you all?" Bette arched her brow with wonder. "So, you and Luke are—" She crossed her fingers. "Like this?"

"I'm not sure what that means." Joy motioned to Bette's fingers. "But we're just friends."

"Oh, I see." Bette tapped Joy's leg and winked. "We'll talk later."

"We can talk now. There's nothing between

Luke and me. Friends. Cohosts." Joy resituated in her chair, her emotions awakening from the swoon of reliving the kiss with Luke, and flirted with the audience. "He has bigger things ahead of him than me."

"Not if he's in his right mind. Sheesh, you're gorgeous. Now you used to play softball in college. I can see you're still in great shape."

"Well, as you can see from the clip, cooking is aerobic for me."

Nice applause. Nice laughter.

"Joy, you should know I love surprises. And by that kiss you gave Luke, I can tell you love surprises too." The sound of Bette's voice cast a gray shadow over Joy's blue peace. "A friend of yours came by my office and wanted to come out and say hi."

Friend? In this building? Joy didn't have a friend in this building. The studio lights changed to a rolling, flashing blue, yellow, green, and red. *Dining with Joy* theme music played as the dais rolled backward.

A kitchen set appeared. Joy rose slowly, her legs nearly betraying her. Her lungs scrambled for air. Wenda.

"Ladies and gents, please welcome Wenda Divine from *Cook-Off!*" Bette linked her arm with Joy's and walked across the stage to Wenda and a waiting *Cook-Off!* setup. "It's all about food today on *The Bette Hudson Show*."

Twenty-five

The show faded to commercial. Bette walked off with the floor manager. Wenda snarled. Joy dashed behind the kitchen set, fell against the wall, and fumbled for her phone. Why she carried it on stage was beyond her, but now she praised heaven.

"Allison . . . get out here and save me."

"Joy, now calm down."

"Calm down? Did you know about this?"

"Just do the segment, Joy. Our premiere ratings will be through the roof, it'll give Bette a good show, and—"

"Get out here now. Stop this."

"I can't. I'm down at the local Starbucks."

"Oh my gosh, Allison, and I thought *I* was a coward." Joy ended the call. No wonder the woman acted so strange in the Green Room. She knew about this. Luke . . . must call Luke. The phone slipped from Joy's icy fingers. She snatched it from the floor. Got to call . . . Luke . . . phone . . . number. She couldn't get a decent breath.

Dropping her mocha suede jacket to the floor, Joy billowed her blouse. Perspiration trickled across her brow and down her neck, seeping through the silk arms of her top. *Luke, pick up.*

Up. Why was it so cold in here? Her thoughts were like mini icebergs.

"Hi, you're done already? How'd it—"

"Weeeendddaaaaa . . ." Joy's teeth clattered the moment her lips moved. "Here. On the show. Cook-off! Sixty seconds . . ." She crouched forward with a hiss. *"Sixty seconds!"*

"Wenda? What are you talking about? Sixty seconds?"

"Luke! W*eennnn*daaa!" A TNT-proportion panic attack, no, a nuclear panic attack exploded in her chest. Joy gulped air.

"Wenda's there? On *The Bette Hudson Show*?"

"No, I'm at Coney Island and she just stole my hot dog. *Yessssss,* she's on the show."

"Easy, girl. Calm down. You can do this. Easy-peasy."

"Easy-peasy. Luke, it's me, Joy. You know that, right? I tell you, she's out to get me. Oh, I should've seen this coming." Joy gritted her teeth. Balled her hand into a fist. "I let my guard down and *bam!* Right between the eyes. Happens every time."

"Joy, steady. Breathe. Listen to me. You. Can. Do. This. Tell me the setup."

"The setup? *I'm* the setup. Luke, get on an airplane and fly here, right now. I'll stall. I once juggled five hours straight for charity. I can do it again."

"Joy, I'm in Oklahoma, not Kansas or Oz. And

unless there's a magical pair of ruby red shoes in size twelve men's, I'm not going to make it to *The Bette Hudson Show* today. And you juggled for five hours?"

"Focus, Luke. What am I going to *doooo?* Help. Me."

"Where's Allison? Isn't this outside your rider? Refuse."

"She's down at the corner Starbucks, hiding. She set me up, then hightailed it out of here." Joy paced, chewing the tip of her thumbnail. "To think, I almost told her, Luke, before I came out here. That I can't cook. But she looked so desperate for me to do well. I chickened out. *Bak-bak-bak.*"

"Did you bring any flip-flops to fry?"

"Luke—"

"What kind of shoes are you wearing now?"

"No, no way, these are brand-new Christian Louboutins." Purchased on a Manhattan shopping spree with that Benedict Arnold, Allison. "This may be my last chance to own a pair of Louboutins." Joy conked her fist to her forehead. "Why didn't I pay attention all the nights you cooked at the house?"

"Or the years you've been cooking on a show?"

"Sure, bring that up. Okay, Jesus, right now, I just repent of all my sins. Please, forgive me. I know I haven't been spending much time with You lately, kind of doing my own thing, but I'm sorry about that and can you please, please, deliver me from this evil."

"Joy?"

"Yes, Jesus? You're taking me home to heaven?"

"Joy, focus. He's not coming for you this minute, but I'm pretty sure He'd tell you to go out there and cook up a storm. Have fun. Be confident. He's with you."

"Luke, please . . ."

"I know, babe."

The tender, mellow resonance of his voice sank through her. "I wish you were here."

"Me too."

"But you're not, and I have a job to do." Joy snapped to attention, surging with confidence. "I'm an award-winning athlete. SEC and NCAA Player of the Year. I can do this. Just go out there and cook. Win this thing. I'm a champion."

"There's the spirit."

"Okay, it's the top of the seventh inning and the team is up by one. I just have to strike out the next three hitters."

"Joy, listen to me. Just fry everything. Don't overheat the pans, but make sure the oil is at the right temperature before cooking. Pick a meat, batter and fry it. Batter is eggs, milk, flour, salt. If it's a vegetable, batter and fry it, add a spice of some kind. Garlic. Take your time. Think. You know more than you realize. Make the caramel and chocolate for apples as a dessert. Easy. You're there."

"Miss Ballard, Miss Ballard, twenty seconds." The floor manager careened around the side of the set. "There you are. Twenty seconds, Miss Ballard."

"Luke, it was nice knowing you. And I just want to say I really wish you had kissed me at the Mars versus Venus party. And the night in the meadow. And then when you burned your hand. There, I've said it."

"Yeah, I guess you did." His tenor anchored her and flooded her heart with confidence. "Maybe I'll kiss you when I see you again."

"If I survive." Stage lights flooded the kitchen set. Bette's intro music played. "I feel like a gladiator. The coliseum awaits."

"Die with dignity."

"Not screaming and wailing obscenities at Wenda? Shoot, you're no fun."

"Hey, Joy, seriously, I'm praying for you."

"Please welcome Joy Ballard and Wenda Divine."

The cook-off wasn't centered on a secret ingredient but a recipe. A Joy Ballard recipe dug from show archives.

How did they get a show archive? Joy fussed with pots, clamoring about her kitchen station. The recipe they were making was her own chili.

This was beyond horrible. Horrible would be a summer prairie right now. *Think, think, think, remember the Tailgate Chili.* But all Joy remembered was it tasted really good.

She eyed the exit. What if she just walked? Laid claim to her rider and exited stage left? Next segment, she'd quit. Leave. And then what? How would she recover, explain it to Allison and TruReality? The notions nailed her feet to the stage floor.

"Our staff made the chili from Joy's show archives." Bette stomped her foot playfully at Joy. "You've got to get recipes up on your site, girl. What are y'all thinking?" Her faux accent was getting annoying. "I guess you will with your new cookbook. We're going to tell you all about that later in the show. Anyway, Wenda tasted the recipe and will attempt, in a daring feat, to duplicate Joy's recipe, including a secret ingredient."

"Oooo," said the crowd. Joy went numb.

"Are we good to go?" Bette rested one hand on Joy's back. The other on Wenda's. "This should be a breeze for you, Joy."

Like a solar gust from hell, sure. *Seriously, Jesus, how do I get out of this?*

Joy shot Wenda a dagger-glance. She caught it with a glance of glee and mouthed, *You're going down.*

"You have twenty minutes to make the chili and

313

the corresponding dessert with the Ballard Tailgate package. Peanut Butter Football Pie or Overtime Chocolate Cookies." Bette laughed. "Don't you just love these names? Then our judges, Gina Laredo, Vic Dean, and Nancy Partridge from the Food Channel, will judge our winner. Ready, ladies?" Bette dashed off the set. "And we're cooking off!"

Luke flipped through channels from the chaise-like chair next to Red's bed. It'd been six hours since Joy called. What was she doing?

Red slept with steady, even breathing. The surgery to unclog two arteries had gone well. Dr. Hester was pleased.

Luke pulled his phone out of his pocket, flipped it open, then set it aside. In a moment of panic, she confessed some stupid desire to be kissed. *Don't go thinking she's in love with you, man.*

Luke surfed through the channels, looking but not seeing.

She's probably out on the town, down in Tribeca, celebrating her success with Allison and Bette, maybe Dan and some handsome producer with Hugh Jackman eyes.

Out Red's hospital window, the plains of Oklahoma stretched toward an end-of-day horizon, east meeting west, a pinkish-gold sky touching the dark arc of earth.

In Beaufort, he missed the prairie, the stretch of

treeless land to nowhere. But now he missed the steam of the lowcountry and the scent of pine and palmetto.

He missed Joy.

He should stop whining about bankruptcy, third-floor lofts, and lack of a future. He should seize the day. Tell her they belonged together. Lyric and Annie-Rae needed a man to look after them. He could do it, step up to the plate, lose himself in the tight and turbulent cocoon of their home.

Luke exhaled in time with Red. When he glanced back, it blessed him to see his father sleeping peacefully. He was glad he came. Red needed him. The door shoved open and two nurses entered, chatting, then flirting with Luke when they caught him looking.

". . . I've watched it on YouTube a dozen times already, but it never gets better. I mean, how embarrassing." Stephanie, the petite one with cat eyes, checked Red's vitals.

"I thought she was funny, playing around at first, then, oh my gosh, did you see the judge's face?" Zoe, the tall one with a braid halfway down her butt, shot something into Red's IV.

"What did that judge from the Food Channel say? 'I think I threw up in my mouth.'" Stephanie laughed, batting her lashes at Luke. "Looks like your dad is doing good."

"Yeah, he's sleeping well." He sat forward,

muting the television. "What were you two talking about?"

"Some video on YouTube. Zoe, tuck in that side of Mr. Redmond's sheet. Do you know that TV show host, Joy Ballard? I'd never heard of her before, but she was on *The Bette Hudson Show* today, and oh my gosh—"

"The woman could not even make her own chili recipe." Zoe untucked, then tucked Red's sheet corner in a square. "Blood shot right out of Bette's eyes."

Her own recipe? Wenda trapped Joy with her own recipe? An evil notion wrapped in brilliance. A secret ingredient could be botched by the best chef. But Joy's own recipe left her without excuse. Outing Joy would take more than sticky pasta or undercooked chicken. And Wenda knew it.

"Stephanie, I need to see this video."

"We're not supposed to let anyone on our computers, but I suppose if you're just looking over my shoulder."

Luke jerked open the door. Stephanie scurried after him.

"Do you know this chick or something?"

"Yeah, she's a good friend."

Half a million hits already. Did they put out a press release? Come watch a cooking show host crash and burn.

The funniest part wasn't Joy but Bette yelling, boxing the air, striding from one side of the set to the other, the crew scattering. This particular footage was taken by someone in the audience.

In the right-hand margin, several more videos had been posted. Joy's expression told the whole story. Her apron was stained. Strands of hair clung to her face. Mascara bled around the edges of her eyes. Her blouse sat cockeyed across her shoulders.

"It's on television news now." Zoe returned to the nurse's station. "Just saw it on Fox News. Your daddy is doing much better, Luke. Bet you're glad."

Glad? Yes. For Red. But his heart was breaking. While he sat with his recovering, now-healthy father, his best friend was fourteen hundred miles away, dying.

Twenty-six

Beyond her window, New York City bloomed in a sea of lights. If Joy had a way to dive into that ocean, she'd be gone. She wanted to get lost in the city that never sleeps, become one with the lights, the music, the rhythm of heels crunching against pavement, the demand of a cab's horn along Broadway.

Instead, she was trapped inside. In her humiliation. It'd been six, seven hours since Bette gaped at her with a menagerie of horror and disgust, spitting out her large slurp of Joy's chili.

For the tenth time in as many minutes, Joy's phone rang, its light breaking the room's darkness.

But she didn't move. The ringtone ended. Joy collapsed forward, burying her forehead between her knees. The edges of her nose burned from the hotel's rough tissues. Every blink scraped her eyelids against her swollen eyes.

The darkness deepened and Joy relived the disaster over and over without pause. Bricks of shame stacked up, enclosing her emotions.

In twenty minutes Wenda had created Joy's chili the way Daddy used to and revealed the secret ingredient. Cinnamon.

Foiled by cinnamon.

When Joy said, "Cinnamon? Really?" her mike

communicated every nuance of her surprise. She caught herself and attempted to play it off and putty the crack. "I make so many recipes. It's easy to forget a secret ingredient."

But the putty was no match for the dynamite Joy mixed together in her chili pot. So anxious and nervous, working with a fantasy confidence that she could actually beat Wenda, she didn't brown the meat before adding tomatoes and beans. No, Joy just dumped them all together, boiled, and stirred.

She mistook sugar for salt. Well, they look the same. Especially when sitting next to each other in small, open dishes.

Then she added garlic in an effort to nail her own secret flavor. And cumin? Not a dot or dash. Half a palm full. Sugar, cumin, and garlic. All swimming in a greasy pool of boiled ground sirloin.

The one judge, a cheeky man with a curl on his lip, said . . . what did he say? "I think I threw up in my mouth."

Wenda boomed in with a cackle and shouted. *Shouted.* "I knew it, I knew it, I knew it. Joy Ballard is a hack and a fraud. She can*not* cook." Wenda danced a jig. "She can't even make her own chili. Joy, my eight-year-old knows to brown the meat before adding the tomatoes and beans."

As the judges spit out their bites of Joy's chili,

319

choking, reaching for their water, the studio audience watched in syrupy silence.

The light of friendship in Bette's eyes flamed red. The director called cut. The floor manager snapped to and ordered the audience evacuated. Bette exploded, swearing like a jilted lover, tearing into her producer and crew for not vetting her guests, declaring they were all working overtime, yes, weekends, to prep a new show to take this *bleeping* one's slot.

Allison chose that particular time to return from Starbucks and stand in the wings. Bette tore into her.

"You set me up with this fraud? Allison, we are *not* friends anymore. How could you do this to me? All the favors I owe you? Paid. In. Full." Her words flew, cut in two. "And you, Wenda Divine. Friendly rivalry? You lying cretin. You've humiliated me. Tell your agent to never call me. For you or any of his clients. You disgust me."

"You're overreacting. Bette, this is great TV."

Joy slapped her hands to the sides of her head as if to stop the continual play of voices and images. So tired . . . so tired. She wanted to sleep, but when she closed her eyes she saw her defeated form standing in Bette's studio as folks shuffled past her. No one spoke or glimpsed her way. It was worse than being cussed out. She was invisible.

Joy leapt out of her chair. Her knees buckled, her legs shimmied. Pacing the room, she tried to find her logical bearings, the North for her emotional compass. Where was Jesus? If He was with her, how could she crash and burn so vividly?

His name rose in her spirit and slipped through her lips. *Jesus*. In her darkness and distance, He was still her only Light. Standing at the foot of her bed, Joy gathered herself, shouting His name into her soul to awaken her hope.

After she'd been abandoned and left alone by Bette's staff and crew, Joy exited the studio into the nippy fall air and hailed a cab. The limo that had picked her up with chilled mimosas and warm bagels had long since left. But as she reached for the cab's door, a staffer from the show appeared out of nowhere, lifted Joy's hair, and removed the turquoise necklace. Her humiliation was complete.

When she got to the hotel, she wasn't even sure she'd have a reservation for the night. Or if she did, whether she'd have to pay the bill. But she did. And Joy never felt so grateful.

In the cascading light of the Chrysler Building, Joy resigned herself to her fate. It was over. The world would know, if they didn't already. She should be relieved. Grateful for the charade to be ended.

But she was sad. She'd ruined the show, tarnished the last of Daddy's name, and killed any chance for Luke's talent to shine. The money would be missed. The potential money even more. She'd wanted to do something fun with the girls for Christmas this year.

She'd miss getting up in the morning with a purpose. Even in her early, unsure days on the show, Joy loved going to work, earning her way.

Falling back onto the bed, Joy reached for her phone and scanned the call list. Allison. Allison. Allison. Mama. Mama. Mama. But none from Luke. Joy tossed the phone toward the pillows.

He'd never talk to her again.

Why didn't I walk off? Refuse? A diva display would've been better than humiliation. Why didn't I break a leg? But, no, I couldn't quit.

Jesus, what do I do now? What is the food of the One who sent me?

Red was awake and eating his green Jell-O when Luke returned to the room. "Look at you, Son. Who died?" Red chuckled. "I can ask that now that I know it's not going to be me."

"Joy."

"Joy?" Red's Jell-O cube wiggled off his spoon and dropped to his lap.

"She didn't die physically, Red. She was on *The Bette Hudson Show*. Blew a cook-off, and it's all over YouTube."

"Blew a cook-off? That ain't nothin'." Red popped the cube into his mouth and wiped the green stain from his hospital gown with the heel of his hand. "Any chef can have a bad day. And she's just a home cook, ain't she?"

"Red, she didn't have a bad day; she crashed and burned. Her career is over. My career is over." *Dang it, Joy, you couldn't even brown meat?*

Red shoved his tray to the side. "Is that what's bothering you, Luke? Joy blowing your career?"

"I've been on the phone for an hour with friends from my restaurant days. They're up in arms about her, calling her a fraud, a poser. Asking me if I knew and how I could've protected her." He huffed against the rain-stained windowpane. Beyond the sparse parking lot lights on the edge of the blacktop, there was nothing but darkness. "Even have entertainment news shows calling, wanting to know what's going on."

Luke's leg twitched with the urge to ride. Saddle up Trixie and gallop across the prairie night with only the moon as comfort and put this whole summer behind him.

"Can't be that bad. What's the big deal?"

"To foodies, it is a big deal. They feel defrauded, cheated. I helped Joy pull off the masquerade, so I'm just as guilty."

"Well then, you got a problem, don't you, boy?"

"Yeah, I do." *Lord, really, this was Your big plan for me?*

"Your problem is you're in love with her. Just like I told you when I was in Beaufort." Red settled back, head dug into his pillow, eyes closed.

"In love?" What he felt at the moment wasn't love. "No. Definitely no." Because he was going to leave Beaufort for Portland. He'd decided it during his third viewing of the YouTube clip.

"Simmer down. You're mad now, but you'll realize. You love her."

"Got yourself a couple of new heart parts and you think you know everything about love."

Red chuckled. "It's good to have you here, but you best get on home. See if you can comfort that gal."

"She doesn't need my comfort." Luke peered down at his phone vibrating in his hand. Linus.

"Got your message, Luke. Checked out YouTube. So, when can I expect you in Portland?"

"Joy, I know you're in there." The heavy hotel room door vibrated with fist pounding.

Joy flopped her arm over the side of the bed. She'd just drifted off. Sitting up, she shoved her hair from her eyes and stared at the twinkling Chrysler building lights until her vision blurred.

The pounding didn't stop. "Joy, open up!"

"She died and went to heaven." Joy's words stumbled over her parched lips.

"Joy! Open. Up." Allison added kicking to the pounding. "I can do this all night."

Rolling off the bed, Joy crawled toward the door, pushing to her feet before gripping the door handle's cold, hard surface. "You're drunk."

"You bet I am." Allison teetered and wobbled as she entered the room. "Because if I were sober, I'd want to punch the living daylights out of you."

Joy raised her arms, leaving her torso exposed and unprotected. "Come on, take your best shot."

"You know what you are, Joy?" Allison stumbled backward into a chair, a bottle of caramel-colored liquid dangling from her grip. Dark wisps of her hair danced and shimmied above her head and outlined her face. "A dream killer. Dream. Killer." She tipped the bottle to her lips. A splash of bourbon ran down her chin.

"I'm ordering coffee." At the bedside table, Joy clicked on the lamp and reached for the phone. Her weak fingers trembled, barely gripping the receiver, and her exhausted eyes refused to focus on the phone's small-print directory. She mashed zero and asked the operator for room service.

"What the heck, Joy? Chili. It was chili. You couldn't even make your own chili recipe? Ground beef and beans." Allison fell back against the chair. "Unbelievable." Another swig of bourbon. "Don't order me coffee. I got my comfort right here." She patted the side of the bottle, her words sloppy and slurring.

Ordering coffee drained Joy's last ounce of energy and she nestled among the pillows, her eyes on Allison, her own thin, taut emotions suffocating her heart. Her belly rumbled. The clock beamed 11:32. She couldn't remember when or what she'd last eaten.

"How can you not cook? You host a cooking show, Joy." Allison guzzled this time. "Unbelievable. And I don't want to even ask how you got a show hosting cooking when you can't cook. Downright un-be-lieve-able."

"After Daddy's second heart attack, when he was in the ER, barely breathing, he asked me to help Duncan do the show. Then Duncan begged me to step in as host since he'd invested so much in the new studio." The story sounded old and sour to Joy now. "I couldn't say no."

"I'm going to kill Duncan. First you, then Duncan. Hollywood career, my hide. Tried to tell me you had some kind of phobia. Ha. I'll phobia him. He'll be lucky to get a job painting sets on a local morning news show after my smear campaign."

"I know this isn't going to change anything, Allison, but I'm sor—"

"Dan Greene's called me a dozen times. But I'm not answering . . . No, siree. TruReality will sue me." She tapped her fingernails against the bottle. "The universe will not, *will not,* cut me a break." She raised the bottle to Joy. "Nail in the coffin. Thank you, Joy Ballard. Never thought my own star would bury me. Twenty-five years, and all I have to show for it is a boatload of humiliation. Bette won't speak to me. What good is a producer if she can't promote her own shows? No good, that's what. No. Good."

"This could've been avoided if you'd honored my rider. Why do you think Duncan and I had such a stupid clause?"

"No, no, Joy, a phobia is not the same as I-can't-cook. Besides, Bette wasn't going to honor a lowly cooking show host rider. *Psssht.* Nobodys like you get a shot at a show like hers, and riders go out the window. I wanted you to beat Wenda on Bette's show. Dan Greene would've kicked my hide if I turned down such a rich opportunity. But look now, Wenda and her ilk are laughing all the way to the bank. Though Bette is spitting nails at her too."

The odor of bourbon began to permeate the room.

"So, Allison, nothing about the way Ryan shot my food segments tipped you off? Or when Sharon quit in such a huff?"

"No, I've seen that kind of stuff on cooking shows before." Allison dropped her head against the back of the chair and stared at the ceiling. "Poor Luke. He'll be lucky to get a job at McDonald's."

"You're exaggerating."

"Oh no, no, the foodie community is small and close-knit. They don't like being mocked. You mocked them *and* made Luke your accomplice. You made *me* your accomplice. Do you know how many lives you've ruined? When I said I wanted to make you a household name, this is not what I had in mind, Joy, not what I had in mind."

"I'm sorry, Allison." Joy brushed the fresh remorse from her chapped cheeks. "Truly sorry."

Allison slid out of the chair and teetered toward the door. "My lawyer will be in touch."

 # Twenty-seven

Joy woke to the sound of rain. The thick drops drummed on the roof, slipped down the windowpane, and soaked her soul.

Shivering, she burrowed deeper under her blankets. From the low gray light beyond the shading oak by her window, Joy couldn't tell if the world slipped toward morning or turned toward evening.

"Aunt Joy?" Annie-Rae's whisper chased the echo of the creaking hinges.

Don't breathe.

"Are you awake?" The mattress gave as Annie leaned against the side. Joy could smell her hair and skin. "I want to make this, Papaw's banana bread. Granny said it used to make you happy."

"Go away, Annie, please."

The door slammed and Joy squeezed her eyes to keep from weeping. She'd never yelled at Annie-Rae like that before, and the boomerang of her tone added to her sorrow. The door's hinges creaked again. "Annie-Rae, I told you—"

"It's me, Lyric."

Joy sighed. Mama mentioned something when Joy slithered home about Parker standing up Lyric. "What is it?"

The girl inched into the room. "Can I talk to you?"

Joy sat up, twisting her top in place, squaring away her jeans. She'd fallen into bed last night—no, the night before—not bothering to change. "What's up?" In the glimmer of a second, it felt good to talk about something beside herself.

Lyric dropped to the bed so the mattress shook and sighed. Joy plumped a pillow behind her back. Lyric picked at the frayed hem of her shorts. Joy closed her eyes.

"Lyric, is he ignoring you? You think he likes someone else?"

She shrugged. "I don't know . . ."

"What's going on?"

"At school, he walks past me like he doesn't know me. Then when I go see Siri, he comes in to watch TV with me and holds my hand. Then he kisses me when Siri's not looking."

"How does that make you feel?" The rain thickened against the window. "Does he try more than kissing?"

Lyric let her hair slip over her shoulder and cover her face.

"Teenage boys are these weird monsters, Lyric. They like a girl because she's pretty and fun, or easy to talk to, then it becomes all about what's under her clothes. And you've shown Parker a bit of the goods and whetted his appetite."

"It's not true. He likes me. He really, really likes me."

"Then ask him why he ignores you in school."

"He's with his friends, the team, and they don't talk to any girls." Lyric lifted her head, shifting the wavy river of her hair over her shoulder, piercing Joy with a fiery glance. "Why do you hate him?"

"I don't hate him, but I don't like him taking advantage of you. You deserve better, Lyric." *Sawyer, oh my brother, your neglect is destroying your girl.*

"He says I'm his girlfriend."

"When he's kissing you, running his fingers along the top of your shirt, or wiggling them underneath?" Joy kicked out of the covers, her skin warm, her passion for Lyric flaring. "Baby, he's not into you for you, only what he can get from you for his own gratification. If you let him have his way, he wins and you lose. There's no win for you here. You're daydreaming of happily ever after while he's boasting of his conquest in the locker room."

Horror lit her eyes, tainted her cheeks. "No, he is not. That's mean, Aunt Joy."

"You think he's in love with you?" Joy slipped her hand down Lyric's arm. "That he wants to marry you the day after you graduate? Well, he doesn't. If you let him, he'll go as far as he can, and when you either give in and go all the way, or push back and end his sexual pursuits, he'll be gone. He's already started ignoring you in school. Does he talk to other girls?"

"It's because I'm a freshman. His friends will tease him because I'm so young." Lyric puffed out her chest. "But I'll be fifteen in a month."

"Lyric, listen to me, he's out for one thing."

"No, no, he's not." She fired off the bed. "Gosh, just because you can't get Luke to love you—"

"Luke? Love me? Who said anything about love and Luke?" He'd tried to call, finally, but by then she'd had enough fortitude not to answer. Had he called in the hotel the night Allison visited, she'd have answered, weeping and blubbering in his ear. Time and sleep saved her that additional humiliation.

"Parker loves me. I know it."

"Then why are you in here complaining about him?"

Lyric opened her mouth, stuttered, then exited Joy's room without a word.

"You're in love with her. Poor soul." Rosie nodded toward the tinfoil-covered plate in Luke's hand. "What'd you make her? She hasn't eaten since she got home. Probably hasn't eaten in days."

"It's risotto. I made it on the show a few weeks ago and she liked it. Why'd you call me a 'poor soul'?"

"Joy is one tough bird when it comes to love. She'll give her whole heart without condition *if* she lets go. Then she falls hard and deep. There was a ballplayer in college, Tim, who chased her from sophomore to junior year. Finally, in their senior year Joy gave in, committed, fell in love, came home talking about a wedding, and then when she expected a proposal, he dumped her for her roommate two months before graduating."

"So she ran off to Europe." Light broke over his thoughts as a low rumbling thunder rolled over the house.

"That'd be the end of the romance tale, yes." Rosie motioned toward the stairs. "End of the hall, first door on the right."

"So, what about since then? Who has she loved?"

"No one. I told you she's tough. But if you're a hearty man, she's worth it."

Luke started upstairs, slow, thinking. His anger after the YouTube fiasco subsided into sorrow for Joy, then a veiled brand of pity. Back to anger again when he continued to field challenges from his foodie friends. Linus continued to be a beacon in this storm.

The day after the show, Luke drove Red home, set him up with a nurse, and headed to the airport, drumming the steering wheel, pressing the speed limit, praying to catch an earlier flight.

He prayed during the flight to Charleston and the trip home to Beaufort. Conversations with God about his future, about Joy, about the man God called him to be. Luke listened, waiting, sensing the breath of God.

As he crept up the stairs, all he knew was he had to see Joy. "Hello, there's a man upstairs. Everyone decent?"

Rosie had told him Lyric had left. And Luke had patted Annie-Rae's curly head when he crossed the living room. Crimping the tinfoil around the plate, Luke approached Joy's door. It stood ajar. He knocked once. "Joy, hey, it's me."

Beyond the wall, the sheets didn't rustle.

"Joy?" He peered around the door to see her sitting with her back against the headboard, staring toward the rain-washed window.

"When I was sixteen, I decided to pitch. I was tired of standing between third and second base, playing shortstop, frustrated with our pitcher who wanted to 'give the batter a chance.' She shouldn't have been playing softball. Most pitchers started in their early teens, so I had a lot of work to do. But I wanted it, to pitch, to command the game. To this day, I throw a wicked fastball. I found Coach, showed her what I could do, and she said, 'Let's get to work.' That's always what I've done, gotten to work, made it happen. But this time, I failed." She looked at him. "How's Red?"

"Off to move cattle to a different pasture." He entered the room and set the plate on the bed next to her. From his right pocket he pulled a fork wrapped in a linen napkin. From his left, a bottle of water. Losing Ami's didn't take away his love of fine dining. "Risotto."

"From the show?" She peeled away the tinfoil, unleashing the fragrance of rice, cheese, and sauce. The garlic hint was subtle, but alluring. "Thank you." She brushed her cheek with the back of her hand.

Luke sat in the rocker across the room and watched her eat. She ate tentatively at first, then hungrily, scooping the rice with vigor. Her countenance began to change. She was beat up but oh, so beautiful.

Yeah, she'd come out of this all right. Made the delivery of his news easier. Less like he was abandoning her in her hour of need. Leaving Beaufort and the beautiful Ballard women rent his heart in a way closing Ami's never did, but he had to get his feet in a level place. He couldn't make Bubba's buttery biscuits at the Frogmore Café the rest of his life.

Joy set the cleaned plate on her nightstand and twisted open the water. "Do you hate me?"

"Hate you?" Her tentative question twisted around his heart, and he rocked back. Disappointed? Yes. Hate? "Impossible."

"It's all a blur." She drank deep from the bottle, drawing her knees to her chest, wiggling her toes against the bunched-up sheets.

"That's probably a blessing." The air in the room was hot and stale but Luke rested in the midst of it, unwilling to disturb the atmosphere of Joy's open heart.

"Probably." She collapsed against her pillows, cradling the water against her chest. "I can't bring myself to watch the news, read e-mail, answer calls."

"The YouTube clips already have close to two million hits. You're more popular than ever."

"For all the wrong reasons. Bunch of rubberneckers." The sheen in her eyes was unmistakable in the rainy gray shadows.

"Ah, there's your infamous wit. I was worried you'd go completely to the dark side." Luke leaned forward, drawn by her vulnerability, wanting to crawl onto the bed and wrap her in his arms and whisper everything would be all right. But it wasn't his privilege or place.

"The dark side, huh? I was tempted, but the clothes are hideous." She peered at him with clear, blue eyes. "I'm sorry, Luke."

"Hey, you tried. You can't brown hamburger, but I can't pitch a fastball to a palm tree."

"Yeah, those two things are exactly alike." She covered her face with her hands. "I just quit replaying the show in my head, and now there it is again." She bolted upright and her jerky motion caused Luke to sway back in the rocker. "And oh, Luke, what I said, about kissing and all?" She shook her head and hands with a wild-eyed, silent scream. "I was cuckoo for Cocoa Puffs."

"I see. Well." He'd been dead serious about kissing her the next time he saw her, but now that he was leaving, it didn't seem right. "So, what's next? Any plan?"

What . . . what if she moved to Portland with him? *No, no, come on, man. And then what?*

"Sleep." Joy got out of bed and paced to the dresser under the slanted dormer ceiling. She absently moved a jewelry box from one side to the other. "Find courage. Go on somehow. Folks have survived worse, right?"

"Sure, much worse."

"What about you?" She shrugged. "Allison said you wouldn't be able to get a job at McDonald's."

"Did she now?" Luke ran his palms against his jeans. How could he tell her? *I'm leaving.* The chips were down and he was bailing. "I–I have an offer . . ."

"An offer?" Joy sat lightly on the edge of the bed in front of him.

"A friend of mine is opening a new place in Portland."

"Oregon?"

"Maine. He wants me as his new exec. Portland is a hot little place these days and the restaurant will be a teaching kitchen . . . which I love. I'd like to give back . . ." Her eyes glistened. "Help out new chefs."

"Maine. It's a long way from Oklahoma." Joy scooted off the edge of the bed and landed on the floor. When she gazed up at him, his feelings for her crashed through his heart's thin lattice barrier.

"It's a long way from here." He dropped to one knee, facing her.

"But Beaufort isn't home." The tips of her fingers touched his. "You have Heath and Elle, but—"

"I have Rosie, Lyric, and Annie-Rae." He entwined his fingers with hers. "You."

Her lips trembled as she checked her tears. "I can't, Luke."

"You can't or you won't?"

"Can't. Can't."

"Choose me, Joy. Choose us. Come with me to Portland."

"Then what? Carry on in a pity relationship? We don't even know how we'd be together. We only know each other around the kitchen, on the set, in front of cameras. Besides, I can't leave Mama and the girls."

"Let's find out how we are beyond the show. Move to Portland. Write articles, freelance edit or whatever literary people do. Rosie is very self-sufficient. The girls have parents, Joy. Stop doing their job. Stop doing your dad's job. Stop clinging to your past and all the mistakes." He caressed her cheek and the tender skin melted against his palm. This wasn't going at all like he'd planned, but he rowed with the flow of his heart. "You've paid any debt you owed to your dad, and now it's time to live for you, to find your destiny."

"In Portland? What could I possibly find for

myself in Portland, Luke?" She jumped up, turning her back to him, scooping her hair away from her face.

"Me. Be my wife, Joy." Luke jumped at the sound of his voice. The unplanned proposal ignited him. "Come with me and—"

"Be your wife?" She whirled around, hands on her hips. "How is that different than what I've been doing? You just accused me of not living my own life. That I am doing Daddy's will, raising Sawyer and Mindy's kids."

"There's no replacement Mrs. Luke Redmond, Joy." Luke's courage careened against his chest as he argued his case. "You're not standing in for another woman."

"I can't believe this. No, I'm not going to Portland. I was the daughter of a chef, and I'll be darned if I'm going to be the wife of one. I watched Mama and decided it was a pretty rotten existence."

"I'm not Charles Ballard."

"You're not. But I have no idea who you'll be when the honeymoon is over."

"You have to trust me."

"Trust you? How about love you? Does love factor into your recipe for solving my problems? Do you even love me? No, don't answer. I don't want to know. Because my answer is no, Luke. I'm not going to Portland with you."

"Seems you have it all figured out." He needed

to leave. Now. His footsteps hammered the hardwood. But he paused at the top of the stairs. "Your mom told me about Tim, the guy who broke your heart. I hate him for what he did to you."

"This has nothing to do with Tim." She faced Luke in the hall, brash and uncompromised. "This has to do with you offering marriage because you pity me. Who does that, Luke?"

"Pity? Is that what you think this is?"

"Hey, go to Portland. Get on with your life. Forget you knew me. Hopefully the rest of the world will too."

He lingered on the top step, regarding her, torn with each beat of his heart.

"Go. I said, go." She stomped her foot and gestured to the stairs.

"You can't boss me, Joy." Luke reversed his steps and walked back to Joy in long strides, swept her into his arms, and kissed her, loving the taste of his risotto on her lips.

When he lifted his head, he held her face in his hands. "My offer still stands."

"So does my answer."

 # Twenty-eight

The next morning Joy barreled into Miss Jeanne's driveway, braking, cutting the ignition, and hopping out of the driver's side door before the engine finished its sigh.

Up the veranda steps in a single bound, Joy mashed the doorbell over and over. "Be here, Luke." She'd passed the Frogmore Café on her way to see if his car sat in the shade of the century-old live oaks, but the ragtop was absent from the lot.

After he left last night, she'd cried herself to sleep. How could he do that to her? A spontaneous proposal on the heels of national humiliation. But when she woke up with the morning sun breaking through her window, her soul refreshed, she ached to see him.

"Miss Jeanne, hey, are you home?" Joy eased open the screen door and cupped her hands around her eyes to peer inside the front door. "Miss Jeanne? Luke?"

Miss Jeanne waved, inching down the hall, her hand pressed against the skirt of her housedress.

"How do, Joy." The foyer smelled of vanilla and lemon with a hint of Pine-Sol. "To what do I owe the honor?"

"It's good to see you, Miss Jeanne." Joy cupped

the woman's cheeks and kissed her forehead. "But I'm a woman on a mission." Bounding up the stairs two at time, Joy could barely breathe. At the end of this journey, she'd see Luke. There would be time for air later.

She knocked on his door, her adrenaline rising, her legs trembling. When he opened the door, she planned to fall into him and express her heart, lip to lip. "I love you, Luke Redmond."

"Luke, hey"—she rattled his door—"don't tell me you're still in bed, lazybones. It's noon o'clock. Fall is in the air."

Silence. In the warm hall, perspiration dotted Joy's brow and the back of her neck. The midday sun baked the attic eaves and scented the air with warm wood.

"Luke?" Joy knocked and rattled, then peered out the nautical window at the end of the hall. Miss Jeanne's 1950s Plymouth was parked under a tree outside the open garage door, Mama's orange-and-red-flame design streaking along the blue side panels.

Where Luke's car had been parked, tire tracks matted the grass. "Luke?" Joy tapped on his door again, then turned the knob.

On the bed, the thick mattress was naked and exposed. Without linens. The closet door stood ajar, and the only item on the nightstand was an old Tiffany lamp.

Hello, my way out, where did you go?

"He left last night." Joy spun around to see Miss Jeanne in the doorway, her arms folded, a look of mercy on her heart-shaped face. "I tried to get him to wait a day, but he seemed upset, all fired up and in a hurry. Mumbled a few things about you, but in the end he had to go."

"Miss Jeanne, what did he say?"

"Something about falling in love and being stupid to trust a woman who lied her way through a cooking show, but oh, she just got under his skin until he couldn't figure out his own thoughts. He was slapping his clothes into the suitcase." Miss Jeanne demonstrated, tossing imaginary clothes into an imaginary suitcase with imaginary force.

"He's right. I'm a liar. And a coward." Joy eased down into the rocker by the window and folded her torso over her legs, cradling her face in her hands. "Everything I touch falls apart."

"Come on." Miss Jeanne disappeared through the door. "What you need is some lemonade."

"Miss Jeanne, really, if this is about life handing you lemons so you can make lemonade, I'm up to my eyeballs with that kind of fluffy advice." Joy lifted herself from the chair and followed Miss Jeanne downstairs. Best not let her heart sink any further and get lost in a wallow of emotions and failures.

Expecting to find herself in Miss Jeanne's Westinghouse kitchen, Joy was surprised when the older woman slipped her pocketbook over her arm and whistled to the dog. "Come on, Ebony, we're going for a ride."

"Miss Jeanne." Weariness mantled Joy's shoulders. It was okay not to wallow for the moment, but the prospect of rattling around town made her feel exhausted. "I think I'll just go on home. Crawl into bed, wait for the New Year, new decade, new millennium."

"Pish-posh nonsense. You're going with me."

"Are you kidnapping me?" Ebony, a black-and-white Border collie with wisdom in his brown eyes, watched Joy from the top porch step.

"I'm rescuing you. Hurry up, now."

Joy fumbled down the steps, Ebony herding at her heels, escorting her to the big, boxy car. "Where is this lemonade of which you speak?" She buckled the lap belt around her waist and gripped the door handle.

"Hang on." Miss Jeanne cranked the engine, powered down the windows, and fired backward out the driveway. The car swayed from side to side, the suspension squeaking. Ebony settled against Joy, his pink tongue dripping drool, and panted with the heat.

Joy buried one hand in his onyx fur and surfed her other out the window.

Heavy on the gas, light on the brake, Miss Jeanne rumbled down Port Royal like a tanker on a mission, riding up on folks' bumpers, honking her horn, motioning for drivers to "get out of the way."

By the second red light, Joy's toes cramped against the floorboard. But really, all things considered, perishing at this stage of the game wouldn't be so bad, would it?

"So you're in love with Luke?" Miss Jeanne mashed the gas, pushing Joy against the seat. The wind rushing through the windows teased her hair.

"I don't know, maybe. I'd like to see." *Car, Miss Jeanne, car.* Joy tensed for impact.

"I saw the YouTube clip of *The Bette Hudson Show.*" Miss Jeanne wrangled the beastmobile to a roaring stop, just shy of the lead car's bumper.

Joy pressed her hand to her chest, holding her raging heart inside. "You watch YouTube, Miss Jeanne?" Now she knew the whole world had seen her monumental failure.

Ebony nudged Joy's hand, and when she gazed down at him, he was watching her. As if he knew, as if he could see through her. *Peace. It'll be all right.* Then he sighed, rested his chin on her knee, and closed his eyes with a contented exhale. *Trust.*

"Life is a series of choices, Joy," Miss Jeanne said. "When I came of age I went to law school. The only woman in my class."

"Got any courage to spare, Miss Jeanne?" Joy held on to Ebony as Miss Jeanne mashed the brake and jerked the boxy Plymouth across two lanes of oncoming traffic for a wide, wild left turn. A billow of dust and gravel spewed from under the skidding tires as Miss Jeanne parked at a petite hotdog stand, Silly Dog.

"I come here every day for lunch." She looped her arm through her pocketbook and stepped out of the car. "My treat today."

Two tall lemonades and foot-long hotdogs later, Joy sat across the picnic table from Miss Jeanne.

"So, Silly Dog is a favorite. Have any others?" Joy bit into the soft bun and warm meat, the tingle of mustard and onion on her tongue.

"Well, I take my dinner at the Frogmore Café every day." Miss Jeanne slurped her lemonade.

"I take it you never learned to cook either?"

"All girls in my day learned to cook. Even the ones who wanted to be lawyers. But I never did enjoy it much. When my father passed, I put away my pots and pans. I'll fix toast or a sandwich, but that's about all."

"How come you never married, Miss Jeanne?"

"I had a beau in law school. Franklin Wolfe, a very lovely, traditional man. He was to join his father's law firm, and had I agreed to marry him, I would've been relegated to the wives' club. I didn't go to law school to watch the men work while I served tea and crumpets."

"Did you love him?"

"Most certainly. I'd never waste my time on a man I didn't love." Miss Jeanne's bold tone contrasted with her dainty, almost fragile appearance.

"But not enough to marry him."

"Not enough to give up my dream, my education. If he didn't want me to practice law, why'd he ask me on a date? There were plenty of girls hanging around who didn't care a whit about the law."

"See, Miss Jeanne, that's what I love about you. Courage. You stuck to your principles instead of letting Franklin Wolfe force you into a mold."

"I didn't see it as courage, Joy. It was a sad day when I walked away from Franklin, but I couldn't see myself being the woman he needed." Her voice faded. "He's gone now. Seems so strange to think the young, handsome man with the stiff white collar and perfectly tied tie no longer walks on God's green earth." Miss Jeanne broke off the end of her hotdog and handed it to Ebony.

"I still can't believe Daddy is gone some days." Joy took another hearty bite of her hotdog. Nothing had tasted so good to her in months. She would have to add this place to her personal favorites list.

"Joy, your problem isn't lack of courage. Your problem is that you don't recognize the courage you do possess. A coward wouldn't take over *Dining with Joy* like you did. A coward wouldn't take in her young nieces and raise them as her own." Miss Jeanne thumped the table. "Courage is running up to Luke's room to tell him you love him. Just what is it you think you need, missy? You have everything you need right inside."

"What would that be?"

"Jesus. My darling girl, Jesus. He is good, and He is love."

"Miss Jeanne, God can have whatever He wants from me, of me, about me. I have nothing. Nada. Zip. I'm almost thirty, with no career, no husband, no children, no passion. If God has need of someone like that to stand with her finger in the hole in the dike, there's no one more available than me."

My food is to do the will of Him who sent Me.

"Complete surrender is the sweetest place to be. I know you have a few obstacles to face. The fallout from the show must be pert-near overwhelming, but you'll face it and overcome. The Lord will move you on, dear. Listen to ol' Miss Jeanne." Ebony raised his nose and offered a textured bark. "Even Ebony agrees with me."

"Really? Ebony understands complex English sentences?"

"He understands a lot of things." Miss Jeanne wiggled her eyebrows and began to gather her trash. "And it wouldn't be the first time he understood the heart of God. Now let's go. I need an ice-cream cone. Then we can run to Walmart."

"Ice cream? Where?" Joy shoved the last of the hotdog into her mouth. Protesting the ice cream and Walmart seemed futile. "A chocolate dip cone would be good."

"There's a place just down the road. Joy, what about law school?"

"For me? *Nooo,* three more years of school? My heart can't take it."

"Coaching?" Miss Jeanne slipped in behind the wheel. "Give back to young athletes."

"I'd like to write again, but I'm so far removed from written words and stories." Joy climbed into the passenger seat with a sigh and snapped on her seat belt. "I am a blank slate. Whatever God wants."

"Remember the gifts I gave you in the summer?" Miss Jeanne gunned the Plymouth's gas then turned to Joy, cupping her hands to her chest. "Two gold coins. God is love. God is good."

Joy studied her open palms. "I remember."

"So what are you going to do with that purchase power?" The tires scored the dirt as Miss Jeanne fired the old girl out of the parking lot into the lane.

"Believe." Joy stretched her hand out the window as Miss Jeanne cruised down the highway, cutting through the thick air, collecting the sunbeams. She was rich. Rich.

God is good. God is love.

 # Twenty-nine

The last place Allison Wild thought she'd be a week after Joy Ballard blew up her career on *The Bette Hudson Show* was Dan Greene's office. But he'd called. And here she stood, about to rap on his walnut-stained office door.

"Allison, good to see you." Dan stepped back, allowing her to enter. She'd gone shopping for today's meeting. The new slacks and jacket bolstered her with faux power in place of her frail confidence.

"Dan, thank you for calling. I've been thinking a lot."

"Allison, please have a seat."

When she turned toward the board table, she stopped short. Wenda Divine. "What's going on?" Allison took a single step forward, her guard rising. The last person she ever wanted to see again was Joy Ballard. The second to last? Wenda Divine.

"Now that we've all had a few days to calm down and gain some perspective . . . Allison, please have a seat. I assure you, this is going to go well." Dan patted the suede chair next to his.

"Wenda? Go well? She ruined my career."

"I told you Joy couldn't cook."

"So you outed her, and me, and TruReality on

The Bette Hudson Show?" Allison tossed her attaché to the table. "Dan, I can't believe you're entertaining any idea with this she-devil."

"Dan Greene is a businessman." Wenda took her seat. "And a brilliant program director."

"Listen to her." Allison snapped her fingers at Dan. "Wake up. She's charming you into her she-devil den."

"Sit down, Allison. Listen. You're going to love this idea."

"And if I don't?" Allison pulled out her chair and sat with her eyes on Wenda.

Dan smiled. "Trust me. You will."

A frosty, blue-gray dawn broke over Portland as Luke unlocked the kitchen door of Roth House. Flipping on the lights, he paused for a moment, still in awe of the kitchen Linus built.

If he intended to impress Luke with state-of-the-art equipment, mission accomplished. Every appliance and device was pristine, out-of-the-box, right down to the fixtures and floor mats. Linus also hired two excellent sous and line chefs from Manhattan. Longtime friends of Luke's.

In his office, Luke tugged the chain dangling from the desk lamp and powered up the computer. He planned to work on the house menu before meeting with Linus to talk about his choice for vendors and accounts.

Since Portland sat by the sea, Luke's palate

tasted seafood, hearty soups, and thick, warm breads. He had an Irish stew recipe he loved. And an Amsterdam potato soup with bacon and chives recipe.

Luke launched his document, but then opened up the web and surfed over to *Dining with Joy*'s website, glad to find it was still up. Her face made him smile, and twitterpation swirled in his belly.

He missed her.

But TruReality had moved on. Joy's brilliant smile no longer splashed on his screen when he navigated to their site. But they had yet to find a face to replace Joy for their Thursday night lineup. Good luck, Dan Greene.

Luke clicked off the page and went back to his menu. But writing about food, planning menus, his passion, pained him. He felt like he'd left his right arm in Miss Jeanne's third-floor apartment when he drove away. He missed Joy.

He missed the creaking eaves of the Ballard home. The crinkle of Rosie's Cheetos bag and the rhythm of her crunching. The curl of Annie-Rae in the Alabama beanbag chair reading a book and listening to music.

He missed Joy.

He missed his warm loft apartment in historic downtown Beaufort. Miss Jeanne's morning soprano song, "My Redeemer Lives." His skin tingled for the balmy breeze off the river, his ears strained for the swish of Spanish moss dangling from the trees. He missed the Frogmore Café, big Andy, and crusty Mercy Bea. He missed Heath and Elle.

He missed Joy. So bad he ached.

Rocking back, Luke rubbed his fingers over his closed eyes and doubted his decision. He'd popped *the* question in the shadow of Joy's tragedy, then hardened over her refusal. Did he give her a moment, a chance? No. He took her at face value, packed up, and drove north. Eighteen mind-numbing hours.

By the time he'd arrived in Portland, the chill of his heart matched the temperature. He was tired, grumpy, and once again starting over. Alone. And he hated it.

God, all I need is You. And Joy. Right? Joy? And, okay, Red. I need Red too.

For the past three nights Luke had slept about eight hours total. Maybe ten. The oceanfront Braxton Road apartment Linus rented for him would be a waste. Luke's waking hours would be at the restaurant. The apartment would be for sleeping and showers and storing leftovers from the restaurant to reheat for breakfast.

"Seafood vendor meeting in an hour." Linus popped his head into the office. "How's the menu?"

Luke glanced toward the door. So far, he'd only managed to type one word: Menu. "A work in progress." But in the clarity of the moment, Linus's presence was a hand up out of the swirl. Luke remembered a dessert item. He typed "Charles Ballard's Banana Bread" on the page.

Linus angled to see the screen. "Banana bread? That's dessert?"

"For starters, yes. We're going to need a good produce vendor. I'm also going to add sweet tea, with and without flavors, to the drink list."

"I like it, Luke. You know you can do what you want with the menu." Linus fell against the desk, arms folded. "You look like your horse and your dog died. How long are you going to pine for her, Luke? Or is this the final stage?"

"Pining? I'm exhausted, Linus. Drove eighteen hours from Beaufort, showered, napped, then for the past two days I've been in this kitchen." Who Luke pined for was not Linus's business.

"Call her. Tell her to come on up." Linus had all the answers, didn't he?

"I tried." Luke shoved back from the desk. "She said no."

"Did you try hard enough?"

"I proposed marriage. I'd say that was my best shot."

Linus whistled and patted Luke's shoulder. "Sorry, man." The slip of his Italian loafers echoed off the kitchen tile.

Maybe Luke should call it a day at a quarter to six in the morning and go home, crawl in bed, sleep until his head cleared. Kneel and pray. Get his heart in line with God's, with his new life.

The Italian loafers echoed again. "Here." Linus smacked two shot glasses on the desk and splashed them with bourbon. "To Joy, the beautiful one that got away."

"To Joy." Luke raised his glass, then set it back on the desk without tossing down the shot, refusing to toast *the one that got away*. Besides, he'd given up medicating his emotions with a shot of alcohol, no matter how small. Feeling was healing.

"Speaking of Joy . . ." Linus downed the liquid in Luke's glass.

"Were we speaking of Joy?"

"We have a spot on *Good Morning America* next week. Be ready to answer questions about Joy."

"I'm not going to talk about Joy on *Good Morning America* or any other show." Luke braced for Linus's challenge, keeping his gaze steady on his friend's Old World features.

"She played with fire, Luke." Linus dashed another shot of bourbon in his glass. "And got burned. The foodies are demanding answers. You need to ingratiate yourself back into your community."

"Ingratiate, nothing. Don't tell me there's not a one of them who wouldn't have done the same thing. Shoot, half of them would've sold their soul to stand in Joy's shadow."

"Oh man, you are gone. So gone. *Choo, choo . . .*" Linus tugged an imaginary whistle cord. "All aboard the love train."

"Are you through?" Luke went back to his Menu page. "I have work to do. Isn't it a little early in the day to be doing shots?"

"Luke, go on the show." Linus stacked the shot glasses in his hand. "Do a little yada, yada about Joy, then I'll plug the restaurant. We'll be eating breakfast at Eatery's before most of the country is awake."

"Linus, Joy is off limits to *Good Morning America*."

"But you'll do the show?" Linus peered down at Luke.

Luke sighed. "You're exhausting. I'll do the show. They bring up Joy, I'll walk off the set."

Joy never thought spending time with Miss Jeanne would be a divine setup, but God knew exactly what she needed. The wisdom and spiritual insight of an eighty-something. For the third day in a row, Joy joined Miss Jeanne for lunch at Silly Dog.

What was it she said today? *"You can't get your faith from your feeling or your truth from your experience."*

The pain of losing the show still smarted when Joy drew in a quick breath, and she missed Luke. How many times a day did she reach for her phone to call him, but resisted? He was gone. Let him go.

Pulling the truck alongside the house, Joy glanced at the faded memory verse. *My food is to do the will of Him who sent Me.* God, what is Your *food* for me?

A mustard slathered hotdog in a soft bun was a good start, washed back with a sweet, tart lemonade and topped off with a chocolate dip cone. But as she moved away from the Bette Hudson disaster and losing her career, Joy began to hunger for more.

Tucking her keys into her pocket, she let the truck door shut, eyeing an abandoned pallet of flowers in the backyard, Mama's spade, and gloves scattered haphazardly on the grass as if she'd removed them on the run.

But since there was no sign of blood, Joy headed on into the house, dropping her handbag on the table. "Hey, who's home? Lyric? Annie?" School let out at noon today. The girls should be home by now.

Wandering into the kitchen, Joy halted. Bananas, flour, and sugar had exploded all over the counter. Batter dotted the granite surface in sporadic clumps until it finally spilled over the side and collected on the floor tile. A bag of semisweet chocolate chips sat open, half empty.

Joy spotted a laminated recipe card peeking out from under a dish towel.

"Annie-Rae?" Lifting the spoon from the mixing bowl, Joy stirred the thin, runny batter.

"Mercy, girl, you were trying to make the banana bread." Brown dust circled the bowl. Cinnamon and brown sugar.

Joy checked to make sure the stove was off, then walked to the stairs and leaned against the banister. "Annie-Rae, were you making banana bread?"

The silence of the house disturbed Joy's peace. She jogged halfway up the steps and peered through the banister rungs. A veil of evening light warmed the worn hallway runner and exposed the dust dancing and twirling in the air.

Mama's bedroom light was off, the door ajar. Lyric's door stood wide, as did Annie's. Joy patted her pockets for her cell, realizing she'd left it in her truck, tucked in the glove box, banned from disturbing her day.

As she reached for the house phone to give Mama a call, it rang beneath her palm.

"Where have you been? We've been calling all over for you." J. D. Rand? Why was the Beaufort County Sheriff calling her?

"J.D., this is scaring me."

"I'm sorry, Joy. But it's Lyric. She's been in a bad accident."

Joy found Mama in the Beaufort Memorial waiting room. "Is she all right?"

Mama released into Joy's arms. "She's in surgery, oh Joy, shug, she's all broken and cut up."

Mama's Ballard Paint & Body shirt was splattered with paint and her brown-gray curls were wrapped in a do-rag. "If anything happened to that girl on my watch, I won't be able to live with myself."

"Our watch, Mama, it's our watch." Joy cradled her hand against Mama's shoulder and spied J.D. across the room with Annie. "Mama, go sit with Annie, and I'll talk to J.D."

J.D. rose, ruffled Annie-Rae's hair, and gave his seat to Mama. Joy led him to the other side of the waiting area. "What happened?"

"She was riding in the back of a truck." J.D.'s reflective sunglasses rode on top of his short-clipped hair. Thick biceps choked his uniform sleeves, and his cologne tinted the air around him.

"Whose truck, J.D.? Why was she in the back?"

"Promise me you won't go off half-cocked, swinging ball bats."

"Parker Eaton. She was riding in the back of Parker's truck, wasn't she?" Joy wrapped her hand around J.D.'s wrist, squeezing out the truth.

"I guess you know it was a half day at school today. Parker and some of the boys were going down to the beach before football practice. A car pulled out in front of them and he overcorrected, hit a tree. The boys are corroborating the story."

"The boys?"

J.D. switched the grip so he held on to Joy's wrist. "Some of the guys from the team."

"And they were taking Lyric out to the beach?"

"Yeah . . . I don't know what that was about, Joy." His fingers pressed into her skin. "But let's assume the best."

"She's barely fifteen, J.D. I will not assume the best." Joy twisted her hand free. "How bad is it?"

"Broken femur, broken arm and collar bone. From what I saw, her face was pretty cut up too. But it's hard to tell with the blood."

"Oh my gosh." Joy pressed her hand to her forehead. "My beautiful Lyric." *Everything I touch falls apart.* "What about the boys? Are they all right?"

"Bruised and banged up, but home. Nothing serious."

"And Parker?"

"His truck is totaled, and his wrist is sprained so he won't be catching footballs this weekend, but he's fine."

"Fine? He's fine while beautiful, innocent Lyric is in surgery?"

"Joy, settle down. He didn't do this on purpose."

"He most certainly did do this on purpose. Maybe not crash the truck, but he led Lyric on, played with her emotions. The back of the truck, J.D.? Even in your dog-days you wouldn't have put the girl in the back of the truck."

She whirled toward the door, a boiling scream in her chest, and sprinted toward the exit.

"Joy, where are you going?" J.D. thudded after

her, his fingertip grazing her skin. "Stop, right there."

"I'm going to his house, going to call him out, and, and . . . that no-good, football-playing, arrogant, son of—"

First step into the parking lot, J.D. grabbed hold and clamped a cool metal ring around her wrist.

"Handcuffs? Are you kidding me?" The cuff bit into her arm when she tried to twist free. "Okay, J.D., take it off."

"You're not going to Parker's. Don't make this worse than it is." J.D. pulled Joy to his chest. "When you calm down, I'll go with you. But you have to promise to behave."

"Did Parker behave? Not since the day he met Lyric. Why should I?"

"Then you're cuffed to me."

"J.D., please, let me go. I'll absolve you of all foreknowledge. I'll make sure his body is never found."

"Inside." He pressed his hand into her back and walked her to the ER. "And stop jerking your wrist around. You're going to hurt both of us."

"Then let me go." When Annie-Rae saw Joy, she jumped to her feet, her eyes wide and scared. "Aunt Joy, are you arrested?"

"No, just shackled to this lummox." She plopped into a chair.

"What'd she do, J.D?" Mama asked with a sigh.

"Nothing. It was what she wanted to do."

"I told you she'd try to go to Parker's." Mama patted Joy's leg. "Not our week around here, is it? Beating up Parker isn't going to fix Lyric. Or get your job back. Or Luke."

"This is not about me or the show. Certainly not about Luke."

Joy leaned forward when echoes and whispers rounded into the waiting room from the hall. J.D. removed the cuff. "Go see if you can find out what's going on."

The nurse at the desk knew only that Lyric remained in surgery. Joy returned to her seat between Annie-Rae and J.D.

"Do we know why she went with those boys in the first place?"

"Hanging out after school, I reckon." Mama slipped off her do-rag and ran her fingers through her hair. Her curls remained flat and asleep. "She's so into that boy she'd go anywhere or do anything to keep his attention. Been moping around the house for days waiting for him to call. She visits Siri, hoping he'll be there. Then just when I think she'll hear me if I tell her to move on, he calls. Five minutes on the phone with him and my little wilted sunflower blooms under the power of his rain."

"Want me to talk to him?" J.D. said, sounding tender and sweet.

"With a Louisville slugger?" Joy answered, sounding angry and vengeful.

J.D. rattled his cuffs.

Joy rocked forward and buried her face in her hands. "The waiting is making me crazy." The peaceful lunch with Miss Jeanne seemed like a dream.

"Aunt Joy, can I play a game on your phone?" Annie-Rae propped against her knee.

"Was that you trying to make banana bread in the kitchen?" Joy surrendered her phone, brushing her hand over Annie's hair, catching her finger on a clump of batter.

"Mercy, yes." Mama's low chuckle withered away. "She was hard at work when I came in to . . . Well, here we are."

"I wanted to make the bread for Mama and Daddy. And Aunt Joy." Annie-Rae moved to the neighboring chair. "Granddaddy said it used to make her happy."

"Someone's been reading the old recipe book."

"Someone shouldn't leave it lying around." Annie-Rae mimicked Joy, sitting back, tapping the face of Joy's phone.

Mama motioned for Joy to lean toward her across the aisle. "I haven't called Sawyer and Mindy yet. I thought I'd wait until Lyric came out of surgery."

Maybe this time Sawyer would answer. "Go ahead and call, Mama. Give them time to get here. Wouldn't it be great for Lyric to see them first thing in the morning?"

"Oh, Joy, baby, they can't move that fast."

"Let's give them a chance." Joy lightly brushed J.D.'s shoulder. Her sense of reason returned. Her peace. Rising from her seat, she paced to the window, propped her forehead against the glass, and prayed.

For Lyric's sake, she needed to confront Parker. "J.D.," Joy asked, turning from the window, "can you take me to the Eatons'? Please?"

Thirty

Luke's phone buzzed from the rented dresser across the bedroom. Afternoon light framed his drawn shades, and his intention to sleep until he woke up kept being interrupted by Linus, the restaurant gambler, working his odds.

None of it was earth-shattering, have-to-do-it-now. "Sorry to disturb you, buddy, but just one more thing. If we have one less seafood dish, we can marginalize our costs . . ."

When the buzzing stopped, Luke drifted back to sleep. Later, on his way to work, he'd lob his phone into the Atlantic. He didn't need it anyway.

Only one who ever called was Linus. A house phone would suffice for calls from the restaurant, Red, and Heath. Should he send Joy his landline number if and when he switched over? She had yet to call. But to be fair, he'd not called her since the day he left her standing in the upstairs hall.

Did she think of him? He couldn't get her out of his head. He dreamed of her, turned his fare at the phantom scent of her skin, grinned at the memory of her voice teasing him about talking in "recipe."

On the last show they taped, she made up a whole bit about him.

"We're going to take a one fourth commercial break and earn some luscious green money. Don't

you just love that color? We'll be back for the last two thirds of our show after this level tablespoon of a commercial break. Don't forget to set your timers. Back in one sixtieth of an hour."

Luke buried his head under his pillow, groaning. He'd never survive up here if she dominated his thoughts. With his nose against the sheets, he tried to fall back asleep, but his mind was awake. His stomach rumbled. Might as well get up and shower. And maybe . . . he stared at his phone . . . call Joy. Then his phone pinged. Not a call or voice mail notice, but a text.

Crossing the room, Luke opened the window shade and reached for his phone.

Mr. Luke?

Joy's name displayed on the screen, but she'd never called him Mr. Luke. He texted back, *Hello?*

Its Annie-Rae.

Annie? *How r u?*

Lyric is hurt.

Lyric? Texting took too long for this. Luke hit Call. "Annie, what happened?"

"She was riding in Parker's truck. She broke her leg and stuff. Granny and I are waiting for her to get out of an operation."

"Are you okay?"

"Yeah . . . I'm scared."

"I know, I know, but everything will be all right. Is Granny with you? And Aunt Joy? Is she there?"

"She went with Mr. J.D. to beat Parker up with a baseball bat."

He grinned. *I bet.*

"But Mr. J.D. handcuffed her." She snickered. "She looked funny."

"Can I talk to Granny?"

"Okay, oh, she's sleeping . . . Granny?" The girl's whisper awakened every dormant cell in Luke's body. Why was he here? In cold, dark Portland?

"Annie-Rae? Don't wake your granny."

"Okay."

"But don't leave the waiting room. Stay put until Aunt Joy or Mr. J.D. comes back. Hear me?"

"I tried to make Papaw's banana bread." Annie-Rae sighed with a settled-in kind of resolve.

"You did? By yourself?" Luke scooted onto the bed, stuffing pillows behind his back. "I'm impressed."

"Yeah, there was no one to help me. But I can do it. It's just fractions." Her small but bold voice was fast becoming his favorite sound.

"Well, fractions are a start. So, tell me how you worked the recipe. From the beginning."

"First, see, I mashed up the bananas in the bowl." The pitch of her voice arched. "Is that right? I can barely read Papaw's handwriting. How'd you do it, Mr. Luke?"

"A lot of squinting."

She giggled. "I can try that too."

367

Was he ever more enchanted by a banana bread recipe? Luke's smile sank all the way to his soul and silenced the whispers of loneliness.

Flanked by Elle and Caroline outside room 321, Joy talked with Dr. Shapiro. She was commanding, intense about caring for her patients.

"She's been sleeping well, but we've had her sedated. A broken femur is painful and slow healing. The break was above her knee, barely missing the growth plate. She's a lucky girl. We're going to keep her for a few more days to keep an eye on her. "

"She has a guardian angel. Can I see her?"

"She's been awake this afternoon and asking for you. Go on in." Dr. Shapiro finally smiled.

Elle ran her hand along Joy's back. "Caroline and I will be in the waiting room. If you want, we can grab a bite at the Frogmore afterward and talk."

Lyric's eyes were closed as Joy set her bag and sweater on the chair. She picked up the chair to move it closer to the bed when Lyric spoke.

"I'm sorry, Aunt Joy." Her weak words struggled to be heard.

"It's okay, baby." Joy smoothed Lyric's hair and kissed the spot on her forehead not gathered in stitches. Lyric struggled to open her swollen eyes. Her lips were cut and bruised. A cast encased her arm and damaged leg. "You look like Franken-stein's bride."

She winced, trying to smile. "It was an accident."

"Lyric, you could've been killed. Our hearts would've been broken. You are blessed to only have broken bones and cuts."

"Parker . . . wanted me to . . . go . . ." She worked for every word.

"To the beach? With his friends? And do what, Lyric?"

"No, Aunt Joy." Tears soaked her eyelashes. "Parker and me . . . but then the others . . . got in . . . no room in cab . . ."

"So he put you in the bed?"

"Me, no, me." Lyric moaned. Even in her pain, she clung to him.

"I paid a visit to Parker, Lyric, and he said he didn't know you were in the back."

Her eyes fluttered open. Joy could see her heartbeat spike on the monitor. "Whaa—Yeah, he, he did."

"Hey, you know what, this is not important right now." Joy kissed her wounded cheek. "Let's forget about it, okay? You focus on getting better."

"Is Mama, Daddy—" Lyric exhaled with great exertion through her dry, pale lips.

"They are frantic, baby." Joy stretched for Lyric's water and set the straw to her mouth. "So worried." As of this morning, no word. Mama was fit to be tied. "They're getting here as soon as they can." Joy would see to it.

"Is Parker coming? And Luke?"

"Mama's coming later today. She had to stop by the shop. You know how Pyle and Bean can get." Joy laughed for Lyric's sake. "Won't get anything done if Mama's not there."

"Call Parker . . ."

"Lyric, we don't need Parker around here."

"Please . . . and, and Luke."

"Baby, Luke's gone. He's working for a new restaurant in Maine." Joy reached for a tissue on the bedside table and patted Lyric's eyes. "He'd be here otherwise."

"Maine? Doesn't he . . . love . . . ?"

"Love you? Yes."

"You love . . . him?" Oh, Lyric. Such a lover and a dreamer.

"I love you and Annie-Rae. That's who I love."

"Pfffbbttt." The sound carved the edge from Joy's concern. The real Lyric surfaced. "Luke . . . you love . . . Luke."

"Okay, you just need to go sleep. The drugs are making you crazy."

"I'm sorry—"

"No, Lyric, I'm sorry. I'm not letting you go, remember." Joy stood holding out her palms. "I learned a lesson from Miss Jeanne." Joy smoothed her palms over Lyric's. "God is love.

And God is good. Now you have the gold coins too."

"Am I rich?"

"Very."

Lyric's energy ebbed and Joy sat in the chair by her bed, praying and polishing her own gold coins until Lyric's breathing deepened.

Standing by the elevator with Elle and Caroline, Joy punched the Down button. "Sawyer and Mindy have twenty-four hours to get here. Then I'm flying to Vegas and dragging them home." The elevator arrived and Joy stepped inside the car. "What is wrong with those two?"

But Elle and Caroline remained in the hallway. "Joy, get off the elevator."

"Why? Did something happen?" Her heart thudded as she exited the elevator. "Is it Mama? Annie? What? Elle, you're scaring me."

Caroline held the door open. "You have a visitor in the waiting room."

"Visitor?" Joy angled backward. "Who? The chairs are empty."

"Keep looking." Elle pointed around the wall. "We'll see you later." She entered the elevator car with Caroline and mashed the button.

"See me later? Wait. Who's here? You're leaving me? Order me a tea." Joy smacked the steel doors with her palm. "Did you hear me? Order me a tea."

She'd been looking forward to Bubba's buttery

biscuits and a bowl of seafood chowder. Her mouth watered at the idea of the warm, creamy soup.

Joy peeked into the waiting area, scanning the row of empty chairs under the window. What if it was Parker wanting to see Lyric? Joy tucked back by the elevators. What would she say to him? The other night Mr. Eaton spoke for his son, stepping onto the porch, delivering an explanation and apology in one smooth soliloquy.

Perhaps J.D. waited on the other side. He'd been more than attentive the night of the accident, going above and beyond the call of deputy duty. But for Parker or J.D., Elle and Caroline could've waited.

Did Sawyer and Mindy finally arrive? They must have. That was the only explanation. Inhaling, Joy rounded the corner, stepping into the waiting area, braced for emotional impact.

But it wasn't her brother and sister-in-law waiting to see her. "Luke." Her eyes embraced him.

"Hey." He stepped into the light falling though the window. "I hope this isn't a bad time. I came as soon as I could."

"Oh my gosh. You're here." Joy dropped her purse and the sweater she carried over her arm. She flew over the particleboard coffee table and launched into his arms.

He swooped her up, lifting her off the ground,

and turned in a slow circle, his face buried against her neck. "I've missed you."

"Luke . . ." She released her burdens onto his broad shoulders. "You came, you came."

God is good. God is love.

Thirty-one

The evening October air was warm but thin, scented with the fragrance of fall. Luke sat at the picnic table with Rosie, Joy, and Annie-Rae, sipping sweet tea, watching the sun's rays traipse across the horizon in a reddish-gold brigade.

The melody of the fading, rattling leaves captured Luke in a memory of picnics as a kid on his aunt's lawn, the croquet mallets popping the air and his uncle muttering at the wadded and twisted badminton net.

"Got a badminton game?" he asked without really thinking. If they said yes, he'd have to get up to play, and he'd eaten one scoop of dumplings too many.

"We used to, but it got damaged one spring when the creek overflowed to the shed," Rosie said, chin in her hand, staring toward Miss Dolly's.

"We should get another one. Run over to Walmart," Joy said without moving.

Luke smiled and sipped his tea, the conversation so much like home he struggled to think of leaving.

Joy's perfume caught a ride on the breeze, and when he glanced over at her, she was watching him over the rim of her sweating mason jar. Luke's heart did a free fall.

In the past, he'd be halfway out the door by now. Too busy with his career for romance. But Joy, with all her weird baggage and career fiasco, had embedded herself into his heart. In Portland, he'd convinced himself he'd be over her in a month or so. But Annie-Rae's call undid it all. Within an hour, he found himself speeding south with a giant mug full of coffee.

She was complicated. A paradox of fears and love, strengths weighted by weakness. But at the end of it all, she was Joy. Simply Joy.

"What's funny, Mr. Luke?" Across from him, Annie-Rae chewed on a Cheeto. The heel of her hand squished her cheek up to her eye. A swath of sunlight barely touched the tip-top of her coarse curls.

"Just enjoying the evening, Annie."

"Don't you want to stay here with us? Portland is too far away." *Munch, munch, munch.*

"It is far. But I need a job so I can earn money."

"You can stay here with us."

Rosie wrapped her arm around Annie's shoulders and touched her fingers to the girl's orange-dusted lips. "Luke, those were the best chicken and dumplings I've had in a while. Sure appreciate you cooking."

"It was your husband's recipe."

"I recognized it." Rosie smiled as she collected wadded-up napkins and dirty plastic plates. "For thirty years I ate everything that man made. After a while, I knew his recipes the same way a woman knows a man's touch or the rhythm of his footsteps over the hardwood."

"Interesting observation. Never thought of it like that, but I imagine food defines us as much as anything."

"Every time I see an Orangina bottle, I think of Joy. Frying bacon and brewing coffee takes me back to my childhood, on the farm with my granny. You bet—food and its aroma defines us."

Luke peered at Joy. "Orangina, huh?"

"Orangina." She tipped her face to the breeze, her hair flowing away from her long neck.

Checking his urge to kiss her right here, right now, Luke turned back to Rosie. "If you two don't mind, I'd like to use Chick's oyster stew recipe and his crab biscuits for the restaurant."

"Fine by me." Rosie gave Joy a wry glance, holding open a black garbage bag for her trash. "They won't be used any other way. Take the whole book."

"Mama—" Joy stuffed her plate and napkin in the bag.

"Chili. It was chili, Joy. You saw your daddy make it a hundred times."

"I *never* saw Daddy make it. Not up close anyway."

Rosie patted Joy's hair. "Annie-Rae, help me cart this stuff inside, then run up for your bath."

"But I want to go to the hospital to see Lyric. I drew her a picture."

"You went this afternoon. I want you in bed early tonight. I can see in your eyes how tired you are. Get in your pajamas and I'll watch a video with you, how's that? Joy, are you spending the night with Lyric tonight or am I?"

"No, I'll go."

Rosie and Annie-Rae walked off chatting, then the clap of the screen door echoed over the water.

"When do you have to go back?" Joy reached for the pitcher and refilled her glass with tea.

"Tomorrow. Linus agreed to let me come, but he's panicked. You saw how many times he called this afternoon."

Luke and Joy had shopped for dumpling fixings after leaving the hospital, the conversation stilted as they ignored their confrontation before Luke left for Portland. Then, just as the awkwardness faded, Linus would call. Every time Luke hung up, he'd have to start all over with Joy.

But somewhere between simmering the chicken and measuring flour for dumplings, the tension vanished.

"I'm scared for Lyric, cowboy," Joy said, as if in midthought. She stared toward a coupling of redbirds fluttering in the trees. "She's angry, wounded, stubborn. Can't see Parker is bad for her. When I was in that stage, Daddy was around. I hated him at times, but deep down I knew he was the brick wall I could run to, hide behind. Where's Sawyer for Lyric and Annie-Rae?"

"You can't bear the burden, Joy. All you can do is love them and pray for them. And for your brother and his wife."

Joy slipped her legs out from under the table. "Come on, let's sit on the dock and tease the fish with our toes."

Luke followed, carrying their glasses of tea. She brushed dried leaves from the dock's dirty planks, sat and stretched her foot to stir the face of the water.

"You left without saying anything."

"You told me good-bye."

"And you listened to me?" A low growl strutted along with her laugh.

"You were kidding around?"

"No, guess I wasn't." She peered at him through wisps of her reddish hair. "I'm sorry, Luke, about everything. The day in my room, *The Bette Hudson Show*. I'm glad you're in Portland, moving on with your life. I'm such a coward."

"You're the bravest woman I know." Luke turned her to look at him. "You say you don't have courage, but you do. Even on *The Bette Hudson Show*, especially on *The Bette Hudson Show*. You called for help. You stayed in the game when the odds were against you. The word *quit* isn't in your vocabulary. You made the chili."

"Oh no you don't. I *tried* to make the chili. I *made* something that tasted like barf."

"But you stayed. I'd have been off that set so fast . . . *You* sink with the ship. I cry *abandon* if there's a leak in the bathroom."

"Come on. You do not." Joy laughed and bumped her shoulder against his. "You hung in with Ami's, right? Tried to keep her afloat."

"Only as the foolish captain of the vessel. I quit commanding long before she sank." He squinted at her. "Any reason we're talking nautical?"

"Metaphor. Go with it. And please, what have you ever quit?"

"High school. I dropped out at seventeen."

"He said so casually." She turned completely to face him, crossing her legs. "Why did you drop out?"

"I'm dyslexic. When I was young, my mom made it her mission to teach me to read. But I never liked school, sitting at a desk, staring at a blackboard. When Mom died, Red didn't know how to help me . . . we were both pretty lost and unsure. I flunked English Lit and got booted from the football team." He inhaled deep and slow to contain the swell in his chest. "So I dropped out and didn't tell Red for three months—which was *not* a good idea."

"But look, you became this great chef. You overcame your problem and found your passion. That's courage, Luke."

The screen door banged and Luke looked back to see Annie-Rae sprinting across the lawn, her legs beating against the hem of her nightgown. When she got to the dock, she jumped against him, squeezing her arms around his neck.

"You smell good," he said, with a big, exaggerated sniff.

"Granny put her powder on me." Annie-Rae angled back to see his face. " 'Night, Luke." Then she curled up in Joy's arms for a big hug. " 'Night, Aunt Joy."

" 'Night, baby."

"Can I sleep in your bed, please?" Annie-Rae pinched Joy's cheeks with her hands.

"Okay, but if you snore, I'm kicking you to the curb."

Luke plunged deeper. Portland, Linus, Roth House . . . figments of his imagination. Days he'd lived in a dream. How could he climb in the Spit Fire with the intent of leaving Beaufort in the morning?

"Come with me," Luke said as Annie ran toward the house. "Come to Portland."

Joy shook her head, picking at the leaves scooting over the dock. "I have the girls, Luke. I can't just go to Portland."

"Bring them with you."

"And leave Mama, the paint-and-body-shop, yard-war queen to her own devices?"

"You want to be courageous? Take a chance. Sail away with me." Luke exhaled, his jaw tight. "Sawyer and Mindy could walk through the front door, miraculously healed of whatever took them to Vegas, and take the girls. Then what?"

"No." She shivered, wagging her finger at him. "You're not doing this to me. This is what Duncan did when he wanted me to take over the show. Reasoned me into it. My college boyfriend chased me for two years, wore me down, talked me into a relationship, then broke my heart. All the while, I hung on for dear life. Going down with the ship."

"Okay, then don't do what I want. Do what you want." He gripped her hands. "Do you know what you want, Joy?" The way she landed in his arms when she saw him in the hospital waiting room, he'd hoped she wanted him. But he could tell her mind won over her heart.

Her back stiffened and she refused to look at him. "I'm not sure." She tore at the leaf in her fingers. "Except to make sure those girls have a good life."

Luke held out his hand and Joy dropped the tattered pieces into his palm. "Then you do that, Joy." He kissed the top of her hair. "You know I'd prefer to be here, figuring out a way to knock you off your feet, but I have to go back to Portland, Joy. I can't quit on Linus."

"Luke, you are one of the best things to come into my life since Jesus and softball, but I don't know if you can knock me off my feet. But God is good. God is love. Maybe I just need to wait. Enjoy this crazy journey."

He touched his nose to hers, then kissed her, light at first, then with the power of his heart, getting lost in the taste of her sweetness and the fresh saltiness of her tears.

Thirty-two

Center field of Basil Green, Joy sat face-to-face, knees touching, with Luke on her worn Alabama blanket. Luke's picnic basket sat between them.

Last night they'd sat on the dock, talking and kissing, until he called Linus to tell him he'd be in Beaufort one more day, and then she had gone to the hospital to be with Lyric.

"Can I just say it's so sexy to know a man who travels with his own picnic basket." Joy laughed as she peeled away the crisp golden skin of batter-fried chicken.

"You are talking my language today." Luke stretched across the basket to steal a kiss.

"Thank you for coming for Lyric. For staying one more day." She brushed her hand over his face. Her confident chef with his broad build and bold posture, the man who rescued her three months ago from Wenda Divine's ambush, had sneaked his way into her heart.

"Yeah, but it's making leaving harder." Luke tugged a bottle of water from the cooler. "Joy, have you been to TruReality's website?"

"Are you kidding?" She wiped the chicken juice from her fingers. "Why torture myself?"

"When I got home last night, Heath said he saw

a spot for TruReality's Thursday night lineup while surfing channels. I checked the website."

She stared at him. "Do I want to know?"

"Probably not."

"Then don't tell me. Wait, tell me. Better you than someone else, right? No, don't tell me. Yes." She nodded, thinking, testing her emotions. "Tell me."

"It's Wenda. She has a new show. *Dining with Divine*."

The chicken dropped from Joy's fingers. "My show? They gave my show to Wenda?" The chipper colors of the fall day faded. "Why? Why would they do that? She's evil."

"It's a Wild Woman production."

Joy slumped, her heart souring. "I guess I'm not surprised." She reached for a napkin to wipe her fingers. Now her humiliation was complete.

"Did I make a bad judgment call by telling you?"

"I'm surprised Wenda hasn't called to rub it in." Joy wiped the water pooling in the corners of her eyes, then lifted her chin and squared her shoulders. "It's the past. Time to move on."

"Your destiny is right there, Joy, on the horizon. Your future is full of opportunities."

"Then why doesn't it feel like it?" Joy rose to her knees and held Luke's face in her hands. "Maybe I'll write a tell-all book about the gorgeous chef who rescued me and became my friend." She touched his lips with hers.

"He sounds like a smart man." Luke slipped his arms around her waist.

"He's an amazing man." When she leaned into him, he brought her down on the blanket next to him. When she looked up at him, her heart was wide-open. "You are going to be the best chef in Portland, Luke. I know it."

"What if I fail again? Failed high school. Failed Ami's. Failed Red." He brushed his fingers around her jaw and down her neck. "You."

"Me?" Joy breathed in his confession as the glide of his fingers spread a soaking heat into her skin. "You saved me, Luke. If anyone's failed, it's—"

"Joy, marr—"

"Luke"—she sprang upright and pressed her finger to his lips—"don't ask me, please. I can't say yes and I don't want to tell you no. But how can I agree to marry you just because I don't know what else to do?"

The passion and pull of his kiss challenged her resolve, stirred and awakened her desires. Why didn't she just say yes? Tell him. *I love you.*

When the kiss ended, Luke moved away and pointed to Joy's side of the blanket. "Better sit over there. Being out in the open is no barrier for me."

"Right, right . . ." Her knees caved as she moved back to her spot and picked up her chicken again, carrying the twinkle of Luke's blue eyes. He had a way of making her forget all about Wenda Divine and national humiliation.

"Tell me about this Roth House you're opening with your friend Linus."

"It's part of an old warehouse . . . high ceilings, brick walls, thick walnut trim, original windows." She loved the tenor of his voice. "But Linus does not do cheap. He's set up a spectacular place. The kitchen is all new, state-of-the-art. Imported crystal and linens."

Under the autumn sky, they talked about Portland and restaurant life, about Lyric and Annie, growing up with Sawyer, and what went wrong with his decisions. About Red and ranching, winning rodeos and football games. From accepting NCAA Player of the Year, to life in the world's finest kitchens, to raising kids.

"I have a question." Luke wadded up his napkin, reached for the jug of iced tea, grinning. "Could I hit your fastball? Be honest now."

Joy sputtered, choked, and spewed the crust of her Chocolate Pluff Mud Pie. "Please?"

"Come on, I used to be a jock in my former life. Rode rodeo, played football, a little baseball."

"Little league?" Joy covered her mouth to keep from losing her pie. Luke. Hit her fastball? It was just too funny to imagine.

"No, I played a season in high school." Luke shook his head. "I batted four hundred. Tell you what, Ballard, I think I could swing with you."

"Each man is entitled to his own fantasy, I guess. But there is no way you could get a hit off me."

He considered his answer. "Yeah, I could." Oh, foolish man.

Joy set her pie down, wiped her mouth, then hopped up. "Let's go, cowboy."

"Go? Where?"

"See if you can hit my fastball. My gear's in the truck."

"You have softball gear in your truck?" He jogged next to her, laughing.

"Asked the man with a picnic basket."

"Can I just say it's so sexy to know a woman who travels with her own softball gear."

"Luke, you're talking my language."

At the truck, she tugged on her Bama cap and kicked off her flip-flops in exchange for cleats.

"Cleats? Seriously. You're wearing cleats." Luke drew a bat from the bag and took a test swing, his button-down flowing about his waist, his baggy shorts pulling taut just above his knees.

"Getting scared, Redmond?"

"Yeah, maybe a little." He tested another bat with a sharp test swing.

Joy raised her brow. "O-okay." She chose a ball. It'd been a long time since she'd gripped a softball, and it felt good and right in her hand. A loose emotional wire grounded.

"O-okay? What does that mean. *Ooooo*-kay." Luke cut the air with another swing.

"I'm just saying, cowboy, I'll still respect you if you want to back out."

"Forget it." He chose another bat, swung, and headed for the field. "You just be sure to give me your best shot. I don't want any pity pitches."

"Trust me, no pity here."

Joy fired practice pitches into the backstop. Her arm balked against the motion, but pitch after pitch, her muscle memory returned. When she finally called "batter up," Luke looked ashen. "It's not too late."

"Just pitch. But right when I'm about to swing, close your eyes."

"What? And get beamed in the head? No, no, I'm looking and I'm laughing." This was going to be a blast. She'd been longing for a good, soul-boosting laugh.

On the mound, Joy picked up her old routine. Wipe dirt between the lines, stand in the center of the mound, and face the scoreboard. She imagined a winning score before scanning the outfield, checking in with her imaginary teammates. When she faced the batter, she tossed the ball in her glove three times, closed her eyes, and mentally rehearsed her first pitch.

The wind twisted the ends of her hair and the hem of her top. With a deep breath, she let everything of the past weeks go—the show, Wenda, Lyric, the balance of her future.

When she opened her eyes, Luke waited at the plate.

This was a good day.

"Right here, Ballard." Luke tapped his bat on the outside edge of the plate. "Then say good-bye."

She wound up without a word and let the ball fly. The same stinking fastball that burned the bark off Mama's tree and cinched her first National Championship. The ball crashed into the backstop. Luke didn't swing, move, or even blink.

"I'm ready . . . whenever you are . . . just let it go." Then he broke, laughing, and tossed the ball back. "That was just to throw you off guard. I'm ready now that I've seen your pitch. I'm onto you. Just had to get my rhythm."

"You have no idea what I'm doing. I'm the Road Runner and you are Wile E. Coyote."

"Watch out, Joy." Luke gave a couple of practice swings. "It's going over the fence this time."

"Which fence?" Joy pointed to the outfield. "That fence?" She fired her drop ball at the plate. Luke stepped into the motion, cutting hard, twisting all the way around until he stumbled to the dirt.

"Which fence did you mean? That fence, Luke?" Joy pointed behind her. "There?"

"Shaddup." Crawling off the ground, his back plastered with dirt, he bent for the ball and lobbed it to Joy. "I'm just warming up."

"Yeah? Me too."

She pitched, pitched, pitched, pitched, pitched. Luke whiffed, whiffed, whiffed, whiffed, whiffed.

"Come on, cowboy, give me something. A foul tip. A first-baser." Joy bent forward, holding the ball behind her back, her fingers on the seams. "A bunt. Something."

"At least I can cook."

Joy stood up, laughing. "You're rescuing your pride with cooking?"

"It's all I got." He wiped his brow with the edge of his sleeve, then raised the bat, bent-kneed, waiting for the pitch. Joy threw another fastball. Luke cut hard, but whiffed.

A work truck rumbled up to the field and Pete Jordan leaned out the window. "Need a catcher?"

"Help me," Luke begged in a deep-blue hush.

The BellSouth worker jogged onto the field, popping his fist in his glove, and knelt behind Luke. Joy pitched. He got a piece of it, tipping the ball foul. Pete scrambled for the catch.

A little compact car slowed as it passed the field, then turned sharp and pulled off in the grass.

"Joy's on the field." A couple of girls from Lyric's former Dixie Belle league took to the field with their gloves, calling strategy and popping open cell phones to call for backup.

A Beaufort County Sheriff cruiser rolled past with blue lights flashing. Bodean and J.D. and two other deputies—one male, one female—climbed out, already dressed for PT.

"Looks like we got enough for a game." Bodean strode toward home plate, taking command. "Boys against girls? Joy's worth two men. Who bats first?" Bodean tossed a bat to Joy. She watched it spin as it plummeted to the dirt, then snatched the bat at the base of the neck just before it hit the ground.

Bodean grinned. "Should've known better. Men, we're in the field. Girls are at bat."

"Wait for me." Marley, Bodean's wife, ran onto the field, kicking off her heels, drawing her hair back into a ponytail. She kissed her husband and started testing bats. "What's at stake?"

Joy looked at Bo, who looked at J.D., who looked at Marley. "Bragging rights? Get to pick the music at the next Mars versus Venus party?"

"Okay, pretty good, but let's just up the ante. Bragging rights, pick the music, and . . ." Marley hooked her arm around Joy's shoulder with an ornery and deviant sigh. "J.D.'s corn hole game."

"Corn hole?" J.D. snapped to attention. "You can't barter my game. It's a Mars versus Venus party legend."

Bo flashed his palm at J.D.'s nose. "What about the game?"

Marley jutted out her hip and clucked her tongue against her cheek. "You win, we never complain about the stupid game again. We'll embrace it.

You can toss beanbags into plywood holes until the coyotes howl. But if we win? It burns."

Joy gasped. J.D. sputtered, then stomped his foot to the rhythm of his fake laugh, patting Bodean on the back. "Funny, Marley, funny. Nice try, but we're not—"

"Deal." Bo stepped forward and shook his wife's hand.

"Deal? Bo, hold on, you can't barter my game." J.D. appealed to Marley. "You're not burning my game."

"Stop worrying, J.D. Contain Joy and we can win this thing. Men, to the outfield." Bo ran to the pitcher's mound, calling out positions and strategy.

As they set up, another friend from high school, Wild Wally, and his suntanned, grass-stained lawn crew careened into the parking lot. "We got a cooler of water and sodas." They filed into the bleachers, set a giant cooler on the bottom seat, and cracked open sodas, sitting back to watch the game.

"Luke, let's go. You're on first." Bodean motioned him out to the field.

Luke slipped his hand around Joy's waist and leaned into her ear. "J.D. is sure going to miss that corn hole game."

"Oh, it'll burn tonight. It'll burn bright."

"Joy, batter up." Marley beckoned to the plate. "Swing for the fence. The boys are too tired and too lazy to run."

Luke backed down the faded white line toward first, then jogged back to Joy. "Next time you doubt yourself, Joy, and wonder what God has for you, I want you to remember this, right here, right now." He gestured to the field and the players.

"A softball game?"

"A game. Friends. The power of you. These people ran onto the field because of you. See how you impact the world around you? The influence you exert? People connect with you." He turned and ran to first base, waving to the fielders. "Back up, boys, Joy's swinging for the fence."

Luke couldn't sleep. In Elle and Heath's kitchen he brewed a cup of coffee, doctored it with cream, then folded into one of the wrought iron chairs on the porch to watch the sunrise.

A strip of twilight knitted the dawn to a remnant shadows of night. A crane lifted from the bulrushes by silent Coffin Creek. Luke followed its flight until its white body became a dark silhouette.

Sipping his coffee, he complained to God that it didn't seem fair he had to return to Portland. Alone. How could he and Joy nurture and feed their newfound affection if he was a thousand miles away?

The moment he stepped back into Roth's House kitchen, he'd be embedded, working eighteen hours a day. Any less risked failure. And he couldn't fail, couldn't let Linus down. Himself. Joy. And in a year, if they were solvent, he'd take a day to sleep. Maybe have Red come for a visit. He liked the idea of Red traveling, seeing more of this great country.

When he heard about Lyric, he drove down to be with his friend, the woman he might love. But yesterday, he'd fallen in love. Between the dawn and the twilight.

"You're up early." The porch boards creaked as Heath moved the Adirondack chair next to Luke. He sat with a sigh, setting his coffee on the wrought iron table. "Did you sleep?"

"Five minutes."

"You fooled around and fell in love, didn't you?" Heath stretched his legs long and whistled to the dog roaming across the yard.

"Maybe."

"Want my opinion?"

"If I say no?"

"She's worth it." Heath reached for his coffee as he angled sideways to see Luke. "But give her time."

"That's what her mom said."

"Good coffee, man. Are you sure you have to leave?"

Luke laughed low. "Don't tempt me."

"If it's meant to be—"

"It'll be."

"I heard the softball game was pretty wild."

"I feared for my life at one point." The competitive Joy was not the charmer he knew on the show. She was intense, fierce, and beyond confident.

Heath's chuckle echoed with familiarity. "Bodean and Joy go toe-to-toe?"

"Like crazed, hungry wolves. She kicked dirt on his shoes and he accused her of throwing a spitball."

"She probably did." Heath got up to open the door for a brindle bulldog named Toby. He dropped to the porch, panting. "What was the outcome?"

"Let's just say you won't be playing corn hole at Bo's parties anymore."

"The corn hole game? J.D. must be in mourning. I'll have to call him later."

"He's already planning a bigger, better game." Luke stretched as he stood. "I'm loaded up. Guess I should head out." He clapped his hand with his cousin's.

"Door's always open."

"Tell Elle and Tracey-Love good-bye. And ask Elle, if she could, to do a bit of espionage on Joy."

"Don't worry, cuz, she's got your back."

Behind the wheel of the Spit Fire, with the engine rumbling, Luke texted Joy. *You awake?*

Never slept. On ur way?

Ditto. Yes, on my way.

· · ·

Joy rolled onto her side, cradling her phone against her chest. Luke was on his way. As it should be. Portland waited. His text awakened her heart and she regretted answering because she ached, missing him.

Last night Marley's ceremonious burning of the beanbag game turned into a bonfire. Settled on the blanket with the flames warming her skin, Luke's chest against her back, Joy tossed her own logs and twigs on the fire. Fears and doubts, debris from the past. Her broken relationship with Daddy. The college boyfriend. Ruining *Dining with Joy*.

As the day's first light slipped around her blinds and cut a white box onto the bedroom floor, she felt reset. Renewed to get back to her game, to figure out what was next.

Jesus, what do You need me to do today?

The aroma of brewing coffee wafted up from the kitchen. Wonder how far Luke had driven. And if he missed her. Last night was the best night. Though a sad night. Joy curled into a ball remembering how they lingered on the porch, kissing.

"Aunt Joy?" Annie-Rae jumped under the covers and pressed her palms to Joy's cheeks. "It'll be all right. You're just sad."

"A little." Joy kissed the girl's sweet pudgy hands.

"Lyric comes home today." Annie popped her eyes wide with excitement. "Granny said she gets to have crutches."

"She'll be in a bit of pain still, so we'll have to be extra patient with her." Joy brushed her hand over Annie's hair. She'd make an appointment for her at Julianne's. Get her hair conditioned and trimmed.

"Extra patient." Annie-Rae curled her lip and sighed. "I don't got none to spare."

Joy laughed low. "I imagine life is hard for a nine-year-old."

"If Lyric is your sister, sure is." Annie sighed away the weight of the world. "Can we make banana bread? For Lyric?"

"I don't know, Annie." Not everything made it to the fire last night. "We'll see."

"But you don't have to do the show. Or go to work or school. You have all day."

"Annie, go, get ready for school."

"Okay." She rolled out of bed, dragging the covers with her, a slump rounding her shoulders.

And the winner of the rotten aunt award? Joy Ballard.

Wrestling with her attitude toward Annie, Joy rolled onto her side. They couldn't make banana bread. There were no bananas in the house. An image of the brown-spotted yellow bananas on the kitchen counter flashed into Joy's mind. Right. There were bananas. Joy squeezed her eyes shut.

Bake banana bread.

She sat up, eyes wide. The resonance of the statement swirled in her chest, sinking. *Lord, are You telling me to bake banana bread?* What an odd thing for the Creator of the universe to ask.

But the words coated her heart. Joy kicked off her covers. Bake banana bread? For what? Surely it wasn't something God would ask of her. All that sugar and flour and chocolate chips.

What she needed to do was clean out her e-mail Inbox. She'd peeked at it last night and there were over a thousand unread messages. Most of them were about Joy's Bette Hudson fiasco, but one from a former teammate asking her if she was interested in coaching caught her eye. And another, from an agent, inquiring if she wanted to a write a memoir about her journey with Charles Ballard and the show.

Carrying her laptop back to bed, Joy tried to envision the opening pages of her story, but the words "banana bread" wouldn't stop whispering across her mind. She could taste it. Smell it.

Twenty minutes later she started down the stairs, fresh from a shower, unable to free herself from the idea. Bake banana bread. What Annie-Rae started, God was finishing.

Mama sat at the table reading the paper, her coveralls clean but stained with paint. Joy slid the pantry doors open.

"Do we have any chocolate chips?"

"Don't think so."

See, God, too bad. Can't make the banana bread without chocolate chips. Or peanut butter chips.

"Annie-Rae, get a move on. We need to get going." Mama folded the paper and shoved away from the table. "You're on Lyric detail, right?"

"Picking her up at noon." Joy poured a cup of coffee but let it sit without tasting it, then wandered down the hall to open the front door. The cool fall air slipped through the screen.

It was a beautiful morning . . . Joy shoved through the screen door. "What? I thought you left." In the driveway, Luke leaned against his car, arms folded. Joy ran off the porch and into his arms. "I was missing you."

"I had to see you one more time." He nuzzled her neck, warming her skin.

"How long were you going to wait?"

"Until you came out." He kissed her ear. "And if it was too late to leave today, then—"

"Don't move. I'll go back inside, come out in a few hours."

He laughed, grabbing her hand. "I really do need to go, but I need a kiss for the road." His warm lips captured hers.

"Now, I'm not sure about this." Luke reached into the car and pulled out two Publix grocery bags. "But I couldn't shake this urge in my spirit to buy fixings for banana bread."

Joy peeked into the bag. Chocolate and peanut

butter chips. Brown sugar. Cinnamon. Flour. Sugar. Eggs. Vanilla. Buttermilk. "Everything but the bananas," she whispered.

Luke stretched inside the Spit Fire and brought out a final bag. "Several bunches of just-brown-enough. In case the first batch doesn't go well."

"Oh, Luke." She collapsed against him, the bags swinging from her hands. His hands felt good tracing the long line of her spine. When she finally glanced up, he held her face in his hands.

"I love you. You need to know that. I love you."

A trail of tears ran down her cheek. "I don't deserve you."

"Too bad. You're stuck with me."

Mama and Annie-Rae came out as Luke bent for a final kiss and their last good-bye was full of commotion and conversation. A bright place to be.

As Luke motored away, Joy stood in the driveway with bags in hand, the ardor of his love filling up her heart.

# Thirty-three

Making banana bread was easy. It had to be. Annie-Rae had the ingredients mixed in a bowl all by herself the other day. Surely Joy could conquer bananas, sugar, flour, and eggs. Mash, mash, swirl, swirl. Pour in bowl. Bake at three-seventy-five. Easy.

Lining up the banana bread fixings, Joy eyed them from the center of the kitchen, hands on her hips, approaching the task as if she faced the opposing team's big hitter.

This was just unsanctified fear. "Daddy," Joy pressed her palms together. "I know you loved me. You didn't mean to ignore me." Her heart fluttered under the power of truth.

Flipping to the marked page in Daddy's recipe book, Joy wedged the top corners under the flour and sugar canisters, smoothed her hand over the paper, and squinted at Daddy's handwriting.

Banana Bread. For my Joy.

For a long moment she read the words over and over. *For my Joy.* Truth sank into the cracks created by the lie. Shifting her stance, Joy drew a long, strong breath, clearing her soul of all guilt. She'd been the other player in her relationship with Daddy, not really wanting to know him, see the truth about him.

Never did she have to wonder where he was at night. She knew. Always knew. In the kitchen or in his attic office. Only she chose to see him as absent.

"Daddy, I'm sorry." No tears or painful sorrow. Just an honest, cleansing confession. She startled when her phone pinged from the kitchen table. Luke's message appeared on the screen.

U can do it.

How do u know?

B cause u whipped me with ur fastball 15x.

Please tell me ur still here.

Getting gas. At hiwy. I still love u.

Still don't deserve u.

Joy waited to see if he would respond, then on impulse, ran to the living room window, imagining him turning into the driveway and parking in the dappled sunlight cascading through the trees.

But he didn't. With a sigh, she returned to the kitchen, yanking her worn Bama ball cap from the hook by the sliding door. It was time. Game on.

Tugging the hat onto her head with the bill in the back, Joy jigged around the kitchen. Might as well have fun with this. She smiled her TV smile and faced a pretend camera.

"Hi everyone, Joy Ballard here, and today I am making my father's fabulous banana bread. All by myself. Yes, all by myself. I'm going to make Charles Ballard proud." Joy snatched up the first banana and started to peel. "Cooking, baking, seemed like impossible tasks to me, but now I know my heart beats with the same blood of a truly devoted foodie gastronome. Don't you love that word, *gastronome?* It's like Old World sophisticated meets third-grade snickering. Can't you see a couple of kids on the school playground going, 'She said gastronome. Hehe.'" Joy plopped the banana into the bowl with a rising sense of peace and pleasure. "First, we're going to mash up three ripe bananas. Then stir in the eggs and vanilla . . ."

I DID IT! 4 tries.
So proud. Knew u had it in u.
Wish u were here for the 1st bite.

Luke,
   I saw on the news it's sleeting in Portland. Ha! I'd send you some long undies but Walmart is still selling beach gear here. Want a float ring? I hope you're warm. How's Roth House?
   After two weeks at home, Lyric is back in school. Thank goodness. The family is saved. Either she went back to school or the rest of us were moving into a hotel.
   Otherwise, she's doing well, hobbling around on her crutches, dealing with the pain, which has eased up. The accident has made

her a mini celebrity. The boys felt so guilty for shoving her out of the cab to the bed of the truck, they dote on her a bit.

Even Parker humbled and apologized to me and Mama, brought Lyric flowers. So he's graduated from scum of the earth to just dirtbag.

Haven't made any decisions about what's next for me. Kind of enjoying not knowing, leaping out, aiming for the hand of God. Such an odd sensation. But thrilling.

God is good. God is love.

Missing you,

Joy

P.S. Made so much banana bread, Mama banned it until Thanksgiving. Sheesh, first she wants me to cook, and now . . .

Joy, short note to say I'm thinking of you daily. Roth House is swamped. We are going nonstop from the time we open until we close. I won't see the end of eighteen-hour days for a while.

Still loving you,

Luke

"Any word from Sawyer and Mindy?" Joy asked, entering Mama's room and curling up next to her on the bed, dipping into the Cheetos bag.

"He did call, Joy. Talked to Lyric last night when you went to Elle's."

Joy sat up. "Why didn't you tell me?"

"Didn't want to get you all stirred up. It wasn't a big deal."

"Mama, it's a huge deal." Joy rolled off the bed. "What did he say? What did they talk about?"

"See, this is why I didn't tell you. You're getting all worked up."

"You bet I am." Joy paced along the width of the footboard. "He doesn't call, doesn't e-mail or make contact, then finally, after she's out of the hospital for two weeks." She came back to Mama's side of the bed. "I'm thinking of suing for custody."

"Oh, Joy." Mama closed her novel and tossed it to the nightstand. "No, you're not. Those kids belong with Sawyer and Mindy. He sounded good when I talked to him. Settled, confident. I think maybe they're getting their act together."

"*Act* is right."

"You know those girls belong with their parents. It's what they want. It's the reason for the sadness in Annie-Rae's eyes. Do you realize she never mentions them, Joy? Does that seem right to you? She and Lyric love Saw and Mindy. And they love the girls." Mama popped her palm in front of Joy. "I know what you're going to say, so just button it."

Joy lowered Mama's hand. "Loving them is not

the problem. Sending them off to Saw and Mindy's Viva Las Vegas world is the problem. You want the girls living in Sin City? Look at the trouble Lyric found right here in Beaufort, with you and me watching, plus half the town. What will happen to her and Annie-Rae if they go to Vegas? No," Joy waved her hands, "they are better here with us. I just learned how to bake banana bread. I can teach Annie-Rae, pass on Daddy's recipe. We're their family, Mama. We're home."

"Speaking of family." Mama plumped a pillow behind her back. "I have something to tell you. But first, there will be no suing. If Sawyer and Mindy want the girls, they'll have them. You can still teach them to make banana bread."

Joy reclined on the second pillow, stretching out, staring at the ceiling. "I'm worried for nothing, right? Why would they show up now when Lyric needs so much care? That would cramp their style." Disaster avoided.

"I want you to know . . ." Mama hesitated. Joy glanced over at her, thinking she looked so young and pretty.

"Are you blushing?"

"Am I?" Mama pressed her hands to her cheeks. "I'm going on . . . well, I've been asked . . . mercy." Mama fanned her face with her fingers. "I feel like I'm the daughter and you're the mother."

"Really." Joy sat up. "Is this where I get to tell you how I walked to school uphill both ways and never had a TV or record player until I was married?"

"A date." Mama rushed Joy with her words. "I'm going on a date. There, I said it."

"A date?" Joy sat up, squared her shoulders. "Really? With who?"

"Baxter McMullens. And I don't want to hear another word." Mama reached for her book and started turning pages.

"*The* Baxter McMullens? The one who owns half the lowcountry?"

"Is there another?"

"Holy shamoly, Mama. How'd you meet him?" Baxter McMullens was the great grandson of Irish immigrants with a compulsion for hard work and a keen ability to make money.

"The shop." Mama lowered her book to her lap, her countenance changing with the glow of a girlish blush. "He'd heard of me. Can you believe that, Joy? So he called about his vintage Jag. We got to talking on the phone, hit it off, so when he came in, it was like seeing an old friend. Today he asked me to dinner."

"Like dinner-dinner. Or *dinn*-er."

"The kind with linen tablecloths and candlelight." Mama ducked behind a shy smile. "He's handsome, makes me feel young, and I like him."

"Mama, fifty-six is young. It's prime time, baby." Joy flopped onto her back again and drummed her belly with her hands. "Look at the Ballard women now. Growing up, going on dates, making banana bread."

"Speaking of growing up . . . Joy, give that Luke a chance. He's a fine man, Joy. Don't think you'll do better."

"He can cook. We know that much." And kiss. Mm, he was a fine kisser. Not that she had many to compare him to, but the way he made her feel was proof enough.

"Listen, I know you." Mama popped Joy's arm with her book. "You get all stubborn and cling to an idea until you've wrung the life out of it. Or it's wrung the life out of you. But don't make him wait long, Joy. If you love him, go to Portland."

"It's cold in Portland."

"It won't be if you marry Luke." Mama pinched back her smile as she returned to the pages of her book.

"Mama!" Heat crept from Joy's cheeks all the way to her toes. "Luke and I are talking . . . he understands the girls need me. You need—"

"Nothing. I don't need you that much, Joy. We love you and you're good company, but don't you dare hide behind me and the girls."

"I'm not hiding. If I cling to things until I can't cling anymore, then I'm more likely to do whatever is in front of me. I'm not doing that this time. I like Luke a lot, but I don't know if I love him enough to hightail it up to Portland." Joy crawled off the bed. "I have a rare opportunity to wait on God. I literally have nothing. It's good, Mama. It feels really good."

"I'm happy for you then," Mama said. "And are you happy for me? Going out with Baxter?"

"More than happy." Joy angled down and kissed her mama's flushed cheeks. "Daddy wasn't always easy, was he?"

"Oh no, but he was a good man and I loved him." Mama's grip tightened around Joy's hand. "He really loved you, Joy. I never doubted his devotion to me or you kids."

"I think I'm finally figuring that out, learning to speak his language. Food."

"In which he was quite fluent. And don't worry about Saw and Mindy, Joy. It's going to be fine."

"As long as they stay in Vegas, all will be well."

Thirty-four

Joy, Lyric, and Annie-Rae stared out over the backyard, through the screen porch.

"I think she's gone crazy." Lyric leaned on her crutches, scanning the landscape.

"Poor Granny." Annie-Rae pressed her face to the screen.

The entire backyard was gone, tilled up, with its red dirt bottom facing heavenward. Having gone down to Savannah for the afternoon with the girls, shopping, easing Lyric's weekend restlessness, Joy came home to this.

"Maybe Granny didn't do this." It was the only logical explanation. Mama didn't do it. Joy tugged her phone from her pocket and snapped a picture for Luke.

Pray. Backyard. Red dirt. Yard war escalates. We may be refugees soon.

In the past few days, texting became the rhythm of their relationship. Luke answered when he had a break in the kitchen. Two days ago a conversation lasted all day. Then yesterday he'd sent her a picture of his newest dish, something-or-other with fish. She pictured back her dinner. A bowl of Cocoa Pebbles.

Fish and cereal, a match made in heaven.

Joy dialed Mama, but when she didn't answer, she

left a message. "Just to warn you, someone stole our backyard. Could be Miss Dolly retaliating."

"Miss Dolly." Annie gasped. "Could she be this mean?"

"Granny planted wax flowers in her yard, Annie-Rae." Lyric hobbled toward the sliding glass. "I'm going inside. My leg is starting to hurt."

"I'll help you, Lyric." Annie-Rae lent Lyric her small, steady shoulder.

As she held the door, Joy noticed a mason jar on the table with dark, wriggly *things* in it. Lifting the jar, she peered inside. Oh . . . she dropped the jar to the table. It was full of mean-looking worms slithering together.

A motor whined from the side of the house. Joy cocked her head to listen. The sound came closer. When Joy stepped off the porch, Mama, freewheeling a backhoe, grinding the gears, halting and starting, nearly ran her over.

"What are you doing?" Joy's flip-flops sank into the moist soil as she scurried after the yellow and black machine. "Did you do this to our beautiful yard?"

When Mama inched to a stop, Joy glared at her, leaning with one hand against the machine. "Explain, please, or I'm calling the authorities. Was this you or Dolly?"

Mama lifted her goggles. Joy rolled her eyes. "Armyworms. Eating up the whole yard. Can't have it. Next spring, the garden club is having a contest for the most beautiful lawn." Mama leaned toward Joy, whispering. "And I'm going to win. Putting in golf course grass."

"So you backhoed the yard? What happened to the wonder of pesticides?" Realizing she stood in the armyworm-infested dirt, Joy lifted her right foot, then her left.

"Oh, I'm spraying and fertilizing, putting in a sprinkler system. Then I'm carpeting the whole yard with zoysia." Mama hopped off the backhoe and swept her hands across the plane of the yard. "You'll be able to putt a golf ball on our grass."

"I'm in a Bill Murray movie." The clap of a car door echoed over the house. Joy quizzed Mama with a glance. "Your date's not tonight, is it?"

"Noooo." Mama tugged off her gloves and started around the side of the house. "Tomorrow night. Saturday."

At the end of her sentence, the breeze carried high-pitched, excited voices. Squeals. *Mama. Daddy.* Joy hurried with Mama to the front yard, slowing, her heart sinking when she glimpsed the girls return their parents' embrace. So they finally came. Sawyer and Mindy.

Mama hurried forward, arms wide. "Well, look at you two. All the way from Las Vegas."

Luke sat in the parking lot with his collar flipped up around his neck, the engine of his Spit Fire idling, chilly air seeping through the weak spots in his convertible top.

He glanced at the name and number on the card in his gloved hand. *Emily Carmen, Andover College. Culinary Arts.*

Luke pressed the clutch and shifted into drive, tossing the card onto the seat. Whatever made him think he could teach? Like he had time to teach. Even if he was qualified. He was a high school dropout. Dyslexic. His own system of reading and understanding didn't translate into everyday life.

How could he inspire young men and women to achieve when he was a quitter? He'd only offered to help Joy learn to cook because she needed him. Or rather, he needed her.

His phone pinged as he eased the car to a stop.

R u in the building?

Not yet.

Don't make me come up there.

Then I'm never going in.

Luuuukkeee, go in!!

All right already.

Y r u being such a chicken?

Asked the banana bread queen?

Whatever. Hey, Sawyer and Mindy showed up.

Wow, that's good right?

I guess. U should see the buy-off gifts.

I bet. Wanna talk?

No! Go in. Become a great chef teacher person.

LOL. I'll put that down on the official application.

Luke shifted into reverse, fired into a parking spot, and cut the engine. Walking backward toward the building, he snapped his picture and forwarded it to Joy.

I'm going in.

Yay! Bout time. Praying 4 u.

She'd waited long enough. With the girls tucked in bed and the evening rolling toward midnight, Joy paced the back porch, listening to Mama's easy chatter.

The entire evening, with Upper Crust Pizza and ice cream, was all so casual, as if Sawyer and Mindy were long-lost cousins home from an exotic world tour.

Actually, they looked the same. Sawyer still wore his hair short and tight. His jeans were the kind he'd worn every year since high school.

Mindy had lost a few pounds, but otherwise she looked the same. The ends of her dark hair brushed her jawline, and her ocean-green eyes, nestled deep under perfect eyebrows, observed the world from her smooth, fresh face.

"Rosie, you should see our house." Mindy reached for Sawyer's hand. "It's fabulous. Four bedrooms, three baths, pool, game room, fenced yard. A mother-in-law suite. The girls are going to love it."

"Love it? Mindy, how do you know?" Joy whirled around to confront her brother and sister-in-law. She'd had enough of playing nice. "I can't believe what I'm hearing. You've been absent for over a year. And silent. Until you called Lyric the other night, Sawyer, when was the last time you called your daughters? You didn't even call Lyric on her birthday. How do you know what they're going to love?"

Mindy's countenance darkened as she glanced at Sawyer.

"Joy," he started, "we've both been working eighty hours a week, saving money for the house, getting out of debt, figuring out our relationship. With the time difference, it was almost impossible to call."

"You could e-mail. Send a letter."

"Our computer died. And I suppose we could've sent letters, but we just never got around to it. Same reason we didn't get out to buy a new computer."

"Time differences? Dead computer? Too lazy to write letters? What's next, the dog wet on your bedclothes and the washing machine broke down? These excuses are *inexcusable*. What kind of parents—"

"Bad parents." Mindy was on her feet. "Is that what you want to hear, Joy? Yes, we've been neglectful, bad parents, but we're here now, and we're taking our girls."

"This isn't a contest, Mindy. They aren't prizes to be taken home only when it's convenient. You think buying them all those gifts will make up for your absence? Who's going to take care of them when you're working all the time?" Joy stopped in front of Sawyer. "I left you messages about what was going on with Lyric and Parker Eaton and what did you do? Nothing. She needed you, Saw."

"We can do a mighty better job of taking care of our girls than you, Joy." Mindy's tone carried like a sack of stones. "We left Lyric in your hands, and she was almost killed."

Joy filled her sling. "It was an accident. If you two had been on the job, she wouldn't have been around a truckload of boys, hungering for attention. Who knows what would've happened to her on the beach? How can I expect you'll watch out for her in Vegas?"

"Listen to me, Miss High and Mighty, we are—"

"Mindy." Sawyer pressed his hand on her leg. She sank slowly to the rocker. "Joy, I got a new position, working days. I'll be home with the girls at night. Mindy will be around in the mornings. We left the girls with you and Mama because we knew they'd be safe and cared for. Yeah, we didn't do a bang-up job of keeping in touch, but we talked about them every day. We worked like crazy so we could have them with us."

Joy stared toward the creek, wrestling against

the true sincerity in her brother's voice. It made it hard to be mad. "When do you leave?"

"Tomorrow or day after. We need to get back before our vacation ends so we can register the girls for school."

"You can't take them in the middle of the term. At least wait until Christmas. Or better yet, the summer."

"Joy, it's time. We've been apart long enough. It's still early in the school year. They'll be fine."

"Please don't take them." Joy waved for Mama to chime in. "We're a family. We have a routine." *What will I do without them?*

"We appreciate what you and Rosie have done, but we're their parents, Joy." Mindy linked her arm through Sawyer's. "When Lyric got hurt, we realized we couldn't wait any longer. Even if Saw doesn't get the promotion, we've decided to bring the girls to Vegas."

Then what could Joy say? Nothing. Mindy was right and it pained her. Joy slid the sliding glass door open and stepped into the quiet, stale house. Mama came in behind her.

"You're mad because they're right," she said.

"I'm mad because they don't deserve those girls, Mama." Joy shoved an askew kitchen chair under the table and started to gather the used pizza plates.

"I'm going to miss them like my own limbs." Mama held Joy's chin with her fingers. "But it's

417

time and you know it. Time for Lyric and Annie-Rae to be with their parents. Time for me to move on. And oh, my darling Joy, time for you."

"Look at them, three kids and Annie-Rae." Joy leaned against the porch post, watching Sawyer and Mindy attempt to stuff Lyric into the back of their SUV.

Mindy coached Sawyer to "be careful" after he banged Lyric's cast against the side of the vehicle. Lyric simply beamed, the pleasure of being with her parents numbing her pain. Annie-Rae the Wise tenderly lifted Lyric's foot to keep it from crashing against the bumper.

"Let's just see what good things God has for us, Joy." Mama rested her head against Joy's shoulder. "And them."

Joy nodded, chocking back the rise of emotion. If she spoke, she feared she'd break into pieces and bleed the life of her soul into the soil. First Luke. Now her girls.

Last night Lyric's friends came to say good-bye and Joy manned the spontaneous party with chips, dip, and cokes, keeping her mounting sorrow at bay by being in constant motion.

Annie-Rae's friend Emma stopped by with her parents to say good-bye. Joy marveled at Annie, who seemed so accepting of the situation, her tender heart able to see the future while holding on to the past.

"When I grow up," Joy glanced down at Mama, breathing deep to clear the tears from her words, "I want to be like Annie. Selfless and wise. Comfortable in my own skin."

"Where do you think she gets those traits?" Mama wrapped her arm around Joy's waist. "From you."

"Mama." Sawyer approached the porch. "Thank you." His contrite tone revealed a man Joy didn't see last night on the porch. A father. "Come to Vegas." He wrapped Mama in a son's embrace. "We have the room. Joy?" He offered his hand. "Thank you. For everything. Even the chewing out."

Her eyes welled up as she bypassed his hand for a hug. "Take care of my girls."

"We will, Mama Bear." He patted her back as emotion thinned his voice.

"Thank y'all so much." Mindy stepped up to the porch, hugging Mama, then Joy. "Come see us. Please. Joy, lots of good-looking, fun men in Vegas."

"I'll keep that in mind." Vegas could keep its good-looking, fun men. There was a cowboy in Portland who watched her back, wooed her heart.

Mama walked with Sawyer and Mindy to the car, exclaiming over how snuggly Lyric looked in the back. When Joy shifted her gaze, her eyes caught Annie-Rae standing in the yard, her marble eyes swimming, her jutted lip quivering.

Joy lunged off the porch the same moment Annie-Rae rushed toward her and leapt into her arms.

"Aunt Joy, Aunt Joy—"

"Oh, baby girl, I'm going to miss you." Joy clutched the stout, quivering body as Annie sobbed against her hair.

"Don't be lonely, Aunt Joy. You can come see us."

"Hey now, don't you worry about me." Joy squeezed tighter. "I'm going to be just fine. You have fun and enjoy being a kid, promise?"

"Promise."

"Next time we see each other, we'll make a whole bunch of banana bread." Joy set Annie to the ground. "You have the recipe card, right?"

"In my suitcase. Mr. Luke said I could call him anytime for help."

Joy brushed Annie's curls from her eyes. "He's one of the good ones, isn't he?"

"Yeah, I think he is."

Joy laughed. "Well, my little counselor, let's get you buckled up."

The crunch of the SUV's tires lingered in Joy's soul for a good while after Sawyer exited the driveway. Mama leaned with her arms on the porch rail as if waiting to see if they'd turn around. Then she scanned the yard, murmured something about trimming the front hedges before she dug up the dirt for the sprinkler system, then patted Joy's arm.

"I need to go into the shop. Are you going to be all right?"

"Yeah, Mama, I am. I really am." The quiet around her settled into her spirit, and for the rest of the morning, Joy sat on the porch praying, watching the wind in the trees.

Thirty-five

Saturday evening Baxter McMullen picked up Mama for their date in his vintage Jag. Joy observed from the window, suspecting Mama fell in love between the porch and the passenger door. Her laugh muffled against the window with a young, airy sound as Baxter opened her door and whispered something in her ear. *You go, Mama.*

Turning back to the living room, Joy wandered to the kitchen, stirring herself to get something going tonight. She didn't need to sit home, listening to the echo of an empty house, casing Mama's bag of Cheetos until she succumbed to temptation.

Sawyer and Mindy had called earlier from the road, said they were having a blast. By now, they should be pulling into their Vegas driveway. Annie would be in the pool the moment the luggage was put away.

All right, get something going. Joy snatched up her phone. She had friends. Good friends. Why spend her Saturday night staining her fingers orange and watching sappy black-and-white movies? That was for another time.

Dialing Elle, Joy opened the sliding glass door and stepped onto the porch, listening to the voice mail kick on and tell Joy to leave a message. "It's me. Saturday night. Call if you can."

Joy pressed End. She'd call Caroline, but she was on tour with Mitch. Gazing toward the creek, Joy welcomed a phantom sensation of Annie-Rae's clinging good-bye hug, deciding she'd give the girls a call tomorrow afternoon.

Back in the house, Joy wandered into the kitchen. Maybe she should just go into town, pop into Luther's for a burger. Sooner or later she'd have to face the townspeople.

She might run into Wild Wally, maybe J.D., or Bodean and Marley. She peered down at her phone, the thought of Luke gentling across her mind. He'd been quiet the last few days, but the Roth House official grand opening was this weekend. Linus moved the opening up two weeks early. Luke said he wanted to catch October's fall festivities before November rolled around with grey clouds and icy winds.

Setting her phone on the counter, Joy noticed Daddy's recipe book. The tender leather gave way under her hand when she picked it up. She could make dinner. For herself. Joy flipped through the pages, Daddy's familiar handwriting making her homesick for him.

Chick's Country Fried Rice

Joy had *loved* country fried rice when she was a girl. Her finger traced Daddy's comments. *One of Joy's favorites.* He knew. When she believed him to be a clueless ogre, he knew.

The recipe called for brown rice, shortening, chicken, bread crumbs, chopped-up broccoli florets. She didn't have to open the fridge or pantry to know none of those ingredients were in the house.

Her mouth tingled at the idea of the crisp hot rice, and a burger seemed like a cheap substitute. She *needed* to make this country fried rice and chicken. She needed to feed herself.

Hunting down a scrap of paper, Joy scribbled a shopping list, grabbed her keys, and headed for the door. This was crazy, exciting. For the first time in her twenty-nine years, besides nuking a frozen pizza or box macaroni, Joy was going to cook for herself.

Out the front door into the twilight, Joy sank to the porch steps and pulled out her phone.

Guess what I'm doing?

She waited for Luke to respond. The cool night air wrapped around her legs. Shorts season would end soon. When he didn't answer, she continued her message.

Cooking dinner. By myself, for myself. Country fried rice and chicken. Aren't you proud?

Still no response. Joy exhaled, aching for him, but subtly aware that tonight wasn't about Luke, or Daddy, or what was, or what would come. But about discovering something of herself.

Her food was to do the will of *the* Father. And for some bizarre reason, the step involved country fried rice and chicken.

Aiming her key fob at the truck and pushing the Unlock button, Joy took the yard in long strides and climbed behind the wheel, excited, nervous, anticipating the taste of God's goodness feeding her heart.

Sunday night around eight, the air quieted in the Roth House kitchen and Luke stepped out the back door into the cold night air.

His stomach rumbled. His eyes burned from lack of sleep. Three hours a night for the last five. The grand opening on Thursday met with a full house from dinner until closing. And by the goofy grin on Linus's face this afternoon, the weekend would end in the black.

"Chef?" The maître d' popped out the door. "Someone left something for you on the counter."

"What kind of something?" Luke tipped his head against the bricks, fighting irritation. The crew was still so needy. He could fall asleep right here, right now.

"Chef?" A server appeared beside the maître d'. "Table thirteen is still unhappy. They want to speak to you."

"What's the problem?" Some clients of high-end restaurants complain until the chef appears and then everything is wonderful. They know they'll get a complimentary entrée or dessert. Perhaps a round from the bar.

"They say the food is cold."

"I pulled it from the grill and plated it myself." Luke pushed up from the wall, his legs weak, and followed the server into the kitchen. The maître d' closed the door behind him. "I'll be out in a second." Luke stopped at the sink to wash his face. "But ask what you can do for them and agree to everything. Wine, got it. Dessert? Done." Luke eyed the server to make sure she understood. "Kill them with kindness."

"Yes, sir, Chef." She spun off for the battleground of table thirteen.

Back behind the window, Luke checked the tickets waiting to be completed, scanning the dining room for table thirteen. The server was smiling and nodding, the guests were shaking their heads and frowning. He'd have to go out. Just as he started for the kitchen door, Luke spotted a plate of banana bread on the counter.

"Who put this here? With a toothpick flag?" He lifted the plate to examine the bread. Where did this come from? The bread was overcooked, dry and thick. It'd been served without the icing. "Let's not get sloppy, people." Luke dumped the bread into the trash and dropped the plate into a tub of dirty dishes. "We're just getting started."

In a corner booth with a view of the ocean, Joy shivered, pressing her hands together. It'd been at least ten minutes. The elegant dining room with linen covered tables, candlelight, and live stringed music was wasted on her.

"Excuse me." She reached for the maître d' who seated her.

"Yes, ma'am."

"Did you give the bread, with the flag"—*last-minute idea*—"to Luke Redmond?"

"Yes, ma'am, I did. Can I get you anything?"

Yes, the chef. "No thank you." Joy fell against the plush booth, her heart suspended between panic and peace. But she'd let go, jumped off the cliff, winging toward Portland in faith, and now found herself landing on a monumentally bad idea.

She was bleary-eyed and lacked the energy to reason through her options. But . . .

One, stay and wait. Two, leave before she was discovered and never mention this to *anyone*. Or three, march into the kitchen, grab Luke by the ears, and kiss him till he couldn't breathe.

She'd driven all the way up the Eastern seaboard with a foil-wrapped loaf of banana bread in the passenger seat, finally embracing her true reality. *I love Luke Redmond.*

He'd waited. Treated her kind. Watched her from the ground while she languished in her tower, refusing to let down her hair. Luke deserved a grand gesture of love, didn't he?

A two-day drive with her homemade banana bread seemed perfect. Until now. She'd not heard from him in days. Maybe he'd change his mind about her. Doubt bloomed in the fallow soil of her heart.

As Joy watched for him to come from the kitchen, her legs twitched, eager to run. Just go, duck out before it's too late. Gathering her purse, she slid to the edge of the booth, with one eye on the door. But just as she was about to stand, Luke Redmond burst into the dining room.

"Good evening." Luke stopped at table thirteen. The patrons sat up tall.

"Chef, the food is wonderful."

"It's not too cold?" The foursome looked to be from old New England money. The men wore vests under their suit jackets and the wives, diamonds. They liked to be on the inside with artists and chefs. They were bored and demanded attention by complaining.

"The food is perfect. Simply wonderful."

Just as he thought. "Please enjoy dessert on me tonight." Luke backed away with a nod. "I know you'll take care of the server."

"Yes, yes, of course. How generous, Chef, thank you."

"I recommend the banana bread." Luke moved to the next table, but one of the servers, Ron, tapped his arm. "The woman at table five has been waiting awhile."

"For her food? Who's her server?" Luke angled to see the corner booth.

"No, she's been waiting for you."

Luke's heart stopped. Joy's luminous baby blues gazed at him. What was she doing here? Luke cut through the center tables to her booth. Her frail smile trembled.

"Surprise."

Without a word, Luke slid in next to her and gathered her in his arms, his heart drumming, and he kissed her. Again and again.

The warmth of Luke's kisses sank through Joy like an incandescent pearl.

"What are you doing here?" He rested his forehead against hers.

"I wanted to tell you something." Joy ran her fingers along the buttons of his chef's whites.

"You drove a thousand miles just to tell me something?"

"It seemed like a good idea at the time." Joy laughed, still weak from his kiss. "Did you get my banana bread?"

"The banana bread? Oh, *the* banana bread. With the flag?"

"I had the server give it to you."

"Right, right, yeah, he did. But we serve banana bread here." Luke motioned for a passing server to hand him a menu. "I thought the bread was from the house."

In the candlelight, Joy scanned the desserts. *Chick's Banana Bread. Courtesy of Charles*

Ballard and his daughter, Joy. She covered her lips with her fingers. "You thought my banana bread was the restaurant's?" Laughter bubbled in her chest.

"Actually, I wasn't sure, but—"

"What'd you do with it—"

"Tossed it."

Now she laughed, a guttural melody disturbing the synchronized harmonies of the stringed-quartet. "I can just picture your face. 'What is this?' "

"You know me too well." Luke tugged Joy close to him and bent in for another deep kiss. "Please tell me you didn't drive all this way to bring me banana bread."

"No, I didn't." Courage. "I drove all this way to tell you . . . Luke . . ." Her feelings for Luke surfaced, producing tears in her eyes, "I love you. I drove a thousand miles to look into your eyes and tell you I love you."

He shrunk back, watching her for a moment. Her heartbeat spiked at his unexpected reaction. She envisioned cheering and kissing, a response of "I love you too."

Instead, Luke slid out of the booth and disappeared around the dining room corner. She exhaled, batting the sting of tears from her eyes. *Luke?*

Her server set a single glass of wine in front of her. "Compliments of the house, ma'am."

"Thank you." Joy glanced back for Luke again. She drove a thousand miles for this? She pushed the wine aside, gathered her jacket and handbag, and slid out of the booth. So much for faith and courage and taking chances.

Luke emerged in a blue button-down, creased jeans, and a shiny pair of boots. "Were you leaving?" He grabbed her hand, leading her to the front door. "Put on your jacket. It's cold outside."

Outside, down the walk, he covered the sidewalk in long, heel-thumping strides until he came to a park bench under a bare-branch tree.

"Luke?"

"Sit, please."

Joy obeyed.

The evening was a misty wash of sea spray, starlight, and amber street lamps. Joy cupped her hands in her lap, gathering the silky material of her skirt with her fingers. Luke knelt in front of her, the soft Atlantic waves crashing against the ocean wall behind him.

"Luke?"

"Joy Ballard, now that you're here, I'm not letting you go. I love you. Very much. Please, do me the honor of marrying me." Luke offered her a small velvet box. "It was my mother's and before that my great-great grandmother's. It's a coal miner's cut. I had it reset for you in a platinum band." His fingers fumbled as he tried to release the ring from the velvet slit.

431

"You already had it set for me?" The stone caught the amber light and reflected the colors of the rainbow on her hand. "Luke, it's beautiful."

"I fell in love with you the first night we met in the café." He still held out the ring, offering. "But I didn't have it set until you made the banana bread."

"Banana bread." Joy laughed through her tears, brushing her hand along his jaw. "Who knew, huh? I don't know when I fell in love with you, but when I cooked dinner for myself for the very first time, I realized I could feed myself. I could choose love."

"You cooked dinner?"

"Didn't you get my text?"

"I haven't looked at my phone in a week, babe. I'm sorry."

"Well, I did. I sat down to country fried rice and chicken, took half a dozen bites, and I knew. It's like I've lived under this mist and I never knew it. Once it cleared away, I realized . . . I love you, Luke. I. Love. You."

"I'm putting country fried rice on the Roth House menu tomorrow." Luke jerked her into his arms, lifted her off her feet, and whirled her around. "I love this woman and she loves me."

Head back, arms around his neck, Joy joined in the song. "I love Luke Redmond." So this was the sensation of freedom.

Their voices echoed over the water, resounding,

enlarging, bouncing back over them. When Luke set her feet on the ground, kissing her, he offered her the ring box again. "So, are you going to be my wife?"

"Yes, Luke, I'll be your wife." Her skin tingled as he slipped the ring on her finger.

"Come on. Let's celebrate." Luke ran with her back inside the restaurant, taking her to the center of the room. Joy gazed around, breathless, folding her ring hand against her side. "Ladies and gentlemen, please indulge me. This amazing woman has agreed to be my wife tonight." Luke cradled her against him. "The beautiful and talented Joy Ballard. She can't cook."

An affectionate laughter rose from the tables.

"I'm not sure she can sing or sew. But she's brilliant, clever, and funny. She pitches the meanest fastball I've ever seen, and she's taught me a thousand lessons on loving others. She's the most courageous woman I know, and I am the luckiest man on Earth."

The servers quickly moved among the tables, setting down tall flutes of golden bubbly.

"I'm the lucky one." This was Joy's season for tears. "This man displayed more kindness and patience than I deserved. He coaxed and prodded and exhorted me out of my fears and off my couch of comfort." She peered into his eyes. "He's seen me at my absolute worst, and when I tried to hide, he found me."

His hungry kiss met her heart. The air never stirred. The hush of the room rested, listening. Whispers, the clinking glasses faded. Joy and Luke were the only two in the room.

This kiss was for real. Not for show. Not inspired by the heat of the moment, but by love and trust. It was better than the kiss that inspired Allison Wild and stunned Bette Hudson and her audience. Finer than the kiss viewed by millions on YouTube.

It was the first kiss of forever. Meant only for two. Joy and Luke.

Luke captured Joy in his arms again and swung her around. The Roth House patrons applauded as if they enjoyed being a part of this moment.

God was good. God was love.

"So, Chef, when are you getting married?" The maître d' prompted the patrons to raise their glasses in toast.

"Tomorrow if she's willing, or the day after." His fiery gaze meshed with Joy's heart. "One thing I know, I'm spending the rest of my life dining with Joy."

 Epilogue

Portland, Maine. Former cooking show host Joy Ballard, who was exposed two years ago during a disastrous cook-off on *The Bette Hudson Show*, announced the release of her first book this fall, a memoire entitled *The Banana Bread Diaries: My Life and Food*.

Ballard, now Joy Ballard Redmond, also a former NCAA All-Star, married Portland executive chef and instructor Luke Redmond last spring in Beaufort, South Carolina.

The two make their home in Portland and are expecting their first child.

New York, New York. TruReality announced its fall cancellations. Among them, the promising but disappointing *Dining with Divine*.

Recipes

Charles Ballard's Banana Bread

From Connie Spangler

1¾ cups flour
1 cup sugar
½ cup brown sugar
1t. baking soda
½ t. salt
½ t. cinnamon
2 eggs
3 mashed ripe bananas
½ cup oil (I use canola)
¼ cup plus 1 T. buttermilk
1 t. vanilla
½ cup chocolate chips
½ cup peanut butter chips

In a large bowl, stir together flour, sugars, baking soda, salt, and cinnamon. In another bowl, combine eggs, bananas, oil, buttermilk, and vanilla. Add to flour mixture, stirring just until moistened. Fold in chips. Pour into a greased 9-in. x 3-in. loaf pan. Bake at 325 degrees for 1 hour and 20 minutes or until it tests done. Cool on a rack 10 minutes before removing from pan.

Tips for baking banana bread:

DON'T over mix the batter, just until moistened. Banana bread is always best if it is wrapped up after it has cooled and is served the next day.

Snow on the Mountain

Provided by Debbie Macomber

Line up the eleven dishes in the order below. Pile the ingredients on your plate, starting with step one, and build a mountain.

6–8 cups cooked rice

Chicken in gravy. (Stew whole chicken, take the meat off the bone, and use the broth for making the gravy.)

4 sliced tomatoes

2 cups chopped raw onions

11 oz. crispy Chow Mein noodles

1 cup sliced celery

7 oz. sliced green olives (or black if preferred)

12 oz. shredded cheddar cheese

1 lb. can crushed pineapple

1 cup sliced almonds

1 small package coconut

Rachel's Béchamel Sausage

1 large garlic clove, chopped
1 large onion, chopped
1 large green bell pepper, chopped
4 medium Italian turkey sausages
1 can Italian-spiced diced tomatoes

Béchamel

5 tablespoons butter
4 tablespoons all-purpose flour
4 cups milk
2 teaspoons salt
½ teaspoon freshly grated nutmeg

In a medium saucepan, heat the butter over medium-low heat until melted. Add the flour and stir until smooth. Over medium heat, cook until the mixture turns a light, golden sandy color, about 6 to 7 minutes.

Meanwhile, heat the milk in a separate pan until just about to boil. Add the hot milk to the butter mixture 1 cup at a time, whisking continuously until very smooth. Bring to a boil. Cook 10 minutes, stirring constantly, then remove from heat. Season with salt and nutmeg, and set aside until ready to use.

In a warmed, large skillet, sauté onions and garlic. When caramelized, add chopped green pepper.

Crumble sausage into the skillet and brown. Drain off excess oil. Add béchamel and cook to bubbling. Add can of Italian-spiced diced tomatoes.

Cook on medium heat for 15 minutes or to taste.

 # Acknowledgments

I read an article once where the author panned and criticized the Acknowledgments at the end of a book. He claimed they weren't necessary. Obviously, he had never written a novel. In the course of penning a story, my heart becomes overwhelmed with gratitude toward everyone who's helped me along the way, prayed, offered encouragement, listened to recaps of my struggles and why "this book is driving me crazy."

So, it's to them I write this page; to those who paused out of their busy lives to give a piece of themselves to me and this story.

Thank you to Thomas Nelson and the incredible team there for enduring with me: publisher Allen Arnold, marketing director Jennifer Deshler, publicist Katie Bond, senior editor Natalie Hanemann, and art director Kristen Vasgaard. Thank you for your work on my behalf.

Ami McConnell, senior acquisitions editor and friend for championing me and this book. What would I do without you? You are an amazing woman and a true lover of story and fiction. Your keen eye and heart for this story made it shine.

Ellen Tarver, friend and editor, who gave up a weekend for me, last minute, to edit the manuscript. Thank you so very much!

Jennifer Stair, editor and encourager. Thank you for your time and effort on this book.

Susan May Warren, brainstorm partner and dear friend, for helping me craft ideas for Joy and Luke, then enduring my phone calls when I explained how those first thoughts *just weren't going to work.* Your never-ceasing patience and encouragement are treasures. Thank you from the bottom of my heart.

My church family at Church on the Rock Melbourne. I value and covet your prayers.

Debbie Macomber for being a friend and encourager, and for giving me one of your recipes to share with the readers.

My fabulous agent, Chip MacGregor, who works unselfishly for me. Thank you for the phone calls, prayers, and witty lines that make me laugh.

My husband who never fails to keep me on track, sane, and laughing. Thank you so much, babe. I think there's a memoir in this for you: *A Survival Guide to Living with a Writer.*

Jesus, You are with me more than I know and more than I deserve. I'm so blessed by Your love and how You daily invite me to dine with joy in Your presence. What must eternity be if I have this much of Your heart now?

To those who gave me knowledge about cooking, television production, and softball:

Dan Portnoy, of Portnoy Media Group, for

validating my idea and giving me advice and scenarios.

Neal Kinard of hankproductions.com for cooking show and production advice.

Torry Martin for cooking and story ideas and the laughs.

Chef Caleb Zickefoose for his advice and help and for giving me the subtle insight I needed to make the opening cooking scene work!

Cheryl Hyatt Smith of Culture Smith Consulting for introducing me to Dan and Caleb. And for being such a friend on Twitter. I've enjoyed our talks.

Emily Dellas at First Class Cooking for helping me understand the mind-set of a cooking teacher and of those who know even less than I do about cooking.

Connie Spangler for the banana bread recipe. It's fantastic!

Kristy Kelnhofer for the Beaufort, South Carolina, softball information. Thank you.

Connie Hipp, my feet and eyes on the ground in Beaufort. I appreciate you.

Dr. Julie Gelman, my doctor and friend, who gave me many great ideas about food.

To all the gastronomes who wrote about their life in food, thank you! I enjoyed reading about passion.

Last but not least, to the lovely and talented Kelsi Dunne, star softball pitcher for the Alabama

Crimson Tide. I appreciate your time and advice. I love watching how you exemplify excellence. Some of Joy is modeled after you.

Note to readers: but it's still ALL fiction! Looking forward to all the good things God has planned for your life!

 # Reading Group Guide

1. Joy's life is not one she planned but one she inherited. Are you in a job or situation because of another person's actions? How does this impact your life? Is your situation suitable to you? If not, how can you change it?

2. Joy's "lie" about her career seems to be justified. Her producer and family support her in this role. She's made the situation work. But is this the best way to pursue a life? Is there ever a time to hide the truth for the good of others?

3. Luke moved to the lowcountry to regroup after losing his restaurant. But not all of us have the luxury of picking up and moving at will. What are ways to regain our center after a loss like a relationship or business? List ways you deal with disappointment or stress.

4. The verse Joy has on her dashboard carries a lot of meaning. Jesus said, "My food is to do the will of Him who sent Me." What do you make of this verse? How does it apply to your life? Do you know God's "food" for your life?

5. One of the reason's Joy took over the show

was to honor her father with whom she had a stormy relationship. Discuss things you've done or said in order to bridge a broken relationship. Was the action successful?

6. Love is an amazing emotion. Meeting someone special comes with all kinds of highs and lows. Reminisce about how you met your spouse or someone special. What were those awkward moments you now laugh about? Since not everyone is in a romantic relationship, talk about how you met your best friend.

7. Show of hands, does anyone have a Wenda Divine character in their life? Discuss ways to love this person.

8. What character did you relate to the most and why?

9. If you could learn something you never took the time to learn, what would it be? Why can't you take the time to learn now?

10. How many like to cook? Share a favorite cooking moment. If you don't like to cook, share how you prepare food for yourself or your family. Why do you like to cook? Why do you not like to cook?

11. Discuss family food traditions. How many still eat a traditional evening meal? If not, what eating traditions have your family or friends developed?

12. Luke discovered the power of food when

his father smiled for the first time after his mother's death. Have any of you experienced the power of food in your life or observed it in others?

13. When the spontaneous softball game takes off, Luke tells Joy, "This is the power of you." We all have some kind of "power" or charm that wins over others. Go around the room and tell the person next to you what you see in them, the same way Luke encouraged Joy.

14. What is the symbolic message of Joy finally cooking for herself? In what ways do you need to "cook" for yourself?

15. Discuss any final thoughts or ideas you had about the story.

 # About the Author

RITA-finalist Rachel Hauck lives in Florida with her husband, Tony. She is the author of *Dining with Joy*; *Sweet Caroline*; *Love Starts with Elle*; and *The Sweet By and By*, co-authored with Sara Evans.

Center Point Publishing
600 Brooks Road ● PO Box 1
Thorndike ME 04986-0001 USA

(207) 568-3717

US & Canada:
1 800 929-9108
www.centerpointlargeprint.com